CARTHAGE

NOVELS BY JOYCE CAROL OATES

CARTHAGE

JOYCE CAROL OATES

ecco

An Imprint of HarperCollins*Publishers*

Title page image by andreiuc88/Shutterstock, Inc.

HarperCollins books may be purchased for educational, business, or sales promotional use. For information please e-mail the Special Markets Department at SPsales@harpercollins.com.

FIRST EDITION

Designed by Suet Yee Chong

Library of Congress Cataloging-in-Publication Data has been applied for.

ISBN 978-0-06-220812-5

14 15 16 17 18   OV/RRD   10 9 8 7 6 5 4 3 2 1

To Charlie Gross
my husband and first reader

ACKNOWLEDGMENTS

A shortened version of chapter two appeared in *Fighting Words,* edited by Roddy Doyle, 2011.

Thanks to former Marine Mariette Kalinowski, Sergeant, USMC (ret.), and to Martin Quinn for reading this manuscript with special care as Hertog Research Fellows at Hunter College, and thanks to Greg Johnson for his continued friendship, sharp eye and ear, and impeccable literary judgment.

"Go at once, this very minute, stand at the cross-roads, bow down, first kiss the earth which you have defiled and then bow down to all the world and say to all men, 'I am a murderer!' Then God will send you life again."

—SONIA TO RASKOLNIKOV, IN *CRIME AND PUNISHMENT*,
FYODOR DOSTOYEVSKY

I don't feel young now. I think I am old in my heart.

—AMERICAN IRAQ WAR VETERAN, 2005

CARTHAGE

July 2005

*D*IDN'T LOVE ME ENOUGH.

 Why I vanished. Nineteen years old. Tossed my life like dice!

 In this vast place—wilderness—pine trees repeated to infinity, steep slopes of the Adirondacks like a brain jammed full to bursting.

 The Nautauga State Forest Preserve is three hundred thousand acres of mountainous, boulder-strewn and densely wooded wilderness bounded at its northern edge by the St. Lawrence River and the Canadian border and at its southern edge by the Nautauga River, Beechum County. It was believed that I was "lost" here—wandering on foot—confused, or injured—or more likely, my body had been "dumped." Much of the Preserve is remote, uninhabitable and unreachable except by the most intrepid hikers and mountain climbers. For most of three days in midsummer heat rescue workers and volunteers were searching in ever-widening concentric circles spiraling out from the dead end of an unpaved road that followed the northern bank of the Nautauga River three miles north of Wolf's Head Lake, in the southern part of the Preserve. This was an area approximately eleven miles from my parents' house in Carthage, New York.

 This was an area contiguous with Wolf's Head Lake where at one of the old lakeside inns I'd been last seen by "witnesses" at midnight of the previous night in the company of the suspected agent of my vanishing.

It was very hot. Insect-swarming heat following torrential rains in late June. Searchers were plagued by mosquitoes, biting flies, gnats. The most persistent were the gnats. That special panic of gnats in your eyelashes, gnats in your eyes, gnats in your mouth. That panic of having to breathe inside a swarm of gnats.

Yet, you can't cease breathing. If you try, your lungs will breathe for you. Despite you.

Among experienced rescue workers there was qualified expectation of finding the missing girl alive after the first full day of the search, when rescue dogs had failed to pick up the girl's scent. Law enforcement officers had even less expectation. But the younger park rangers and those volunteer searchers who knew the Mayfields were determined to find her alive. For the Mayfields were a well-known family in Carthage. For Zeno Mayfield was a man with a public reputation in Carthage and many of his friends, acquaintances and associates turned out to search for his missing daughter scarcely known to most of them by name.

None of the searchers making their way through the underbrush of the Preserve, into ravines and gullies, scrambling up rocky hillsides and climbing, at times crawling across the mottled faces of enormous boulders brushing gnats from their faces, wanted to think that in the Adirondack heat which registered in the upper 90s Fahrenheit after sunset a girl's lifeless body, possibly an unclothed body on or in the ground, sticky with blood, would begin to decompose quickly after death.

None of the searchers would have wished to utter the crude thought (second nature to seasoned rescue workers) that they might smell the girl before they discovered her.

Such a remark would be uttered grimly. Out of earshot of the frantic Zeno Mayfield.

Shouting himself hoarse, sweat-soaked and exhausted—"Cressida! Honey! Can you hear me? Where are you?"

He'd been a hiker, once. He'd been a man who'd needed to get away into *the solitude of the mountains that had seemed to him once a place of refuge, consolation. But not for a long time now. And not now.*

In this hot humid insect-breeding midsummer of 2005 in which Zeno Mayfield's younger daughter vanished into the Nautauga State Forest Preserve with the seeming ease of a snake writhing out of its desiccated and torn outer skin.

PART I

✦ ⬦ ✦

Lost Girl

ONE

The Search

July 10, 2005

*T*HAT GIRL THAT GOT lost *in the Nautauga Preserve. Or, that girl that was killed somehow, and her body hid.*

Where Zeno Mayfield's daughter had disappeared to, and whether there was much likelihood of her being found alive, or in any reasonable state between alive and dead, was a question to confound everyone in Beechum County.

Everyone who knew the Mayfields, or even knew of them.

And for those who knew the Kincaid boy—the *war hero*—the question was yet more confounding.

Already by late morning of Sunday, July 10, news of the quickly organized search for *the missing girl* had been released into the rippling media-sea—"breaking news" on local Carthage radio and TV news programs, shortly then state-wide and AP syndicated news.

Dozens of rescue workers, professional and volunteer, are searching for 19-year-old Cressida Mayfield of Carthage, N.Y., believed to be missing in the Nautauga State Forest Preserve since the previous night July 9.

Corporal Brett Kincaid, 26, also of Carthage, identified by witnesses as having been in the company of the missing girl on the night of July 9, has been taken into custody by the Beechum County Sheriff's Department for questioning.

No arrest has been made. No official statement regarding Corporal Kincaid has been released by the Sheriff's Department.

Anyone with information regarding the whereabouts of Cressida Mayfield please contact . . .

HE KNEW: she was alive.

He knew: if he persevered, if he did not despair, he would find her.

She was his younger child. She was the difficult child. She was the one to break his heart.

There was a reason for that, he supposed.

If she hated him. If she'd let herself be hurt, to hurt *him*.

BUT HE HAD no doubt, she was alive.

"I would know. I would feel it. If my daughter was gone from this earth—there would be an emptiness, unmistakably. I would feel it."

HE HATED THAT she was identified as *missing*.

He'd insisted that she was *lost*.

That is, *probably lost.*

She'd wandered off, or run off. Somehow, she'd *gotten lost* in the Nautauga Preserve. The young man she'd been with—(this, the father didn't understand: for the daughter had told her parents that she was going to spend the evening with other friends)—had insisted he didn't know where she was, she'd left *him*.

In the front seat of the young man's Jeep Wrangler there were said to be bloodstains. A smear of blood on the inside of the windshield on the passenger's side, as if a bleeding face, or head, had been struck against it with some force.

Stray hairs, and a single clump of hair, dark in color as the hair of the *missing girl,* had been collected from the passenger's seat and from the young man's shirt.

Outside the vehicle there were no footprints—the shoulder of

Sandhill Road was grassy, and then rocky, declining steeply to the fast-rushing Nautauga River.

The father didn't (yet) know details. He knew that the young corporal had been taken into police custody having been found in a semiconscious alcoholic state inside his vehicle, haphazardly parked on a narrow unpaved road just inside the Nautauga Preserve, at about 8 A.M. of Sunday, July 10, 2005.

Allegedly, the young corporal, Brett Kincaid, was the last person to have seen Cressida Mayfield before her "disappearance."

Kincaid was a friend of the Mayfield family, or had been. Until the previous week he'd been engaged to the *missing girl's* older sister.

The father had tried to see him: just to speak to him!

To look the young corporal in the eye. To see how the young corporal looked at *him*.

The father had been refused. For the time being.

The young corporal was *in custody*. As news reports took care to note *No arrests have yet been made.*

How disorienting all this was!—the father who'd long prided himself on being smart, shrewd, just a little quicker and a little more informed than anyone else was likely to be in his vicinity, could not comprehend what seemed to be set out before him like cards dealt by a sinister dealer.

His life—his life of routine complex as the workings of an expensive watch, yet unfailingly in his control—had been so abruptly altered. Not just the surprise—the shock—of his daughter's "disappearance" but the circumstances of the "disappearance."

It was not possible that Cressida had lied to him and to her mother—and yet, obviously, it seemed that Cressida had lied.

At any rate, she'd told them less than the truth about where she'd planned to go the previous night.

How out of character this was! Cressida had always scorned lying as moral weakness. It was cowardice to care so much of others' opinions, one would stoop to *lie*.

And that she'd met up with her sister's ex-fiancé, at a lakeside inn—that was even more astonishing.

The Mayfields had to tell police officers—they'd had to tell them all that they knew. It wasn't police procedure to search for an adult who has been missing for such a relatively short period of time unless "foul play" is suspected.

The father had to insist that he was concerned that his daughter was "lost" in the Nautauga Preserve even as he couldn't bring himself to acknowledge the possibility that she'd been "hurt."

Or, if "hurt"—"seriously hurt."

Not wanting to think *sexually abused, raped.*

Not wanting to think *And worse . . .*

Cressida was nineteen but a very young nineteen. Small-boned, childlike in her demeanor, with the body of a young boy—lithe, narrow-hipped, flat-chested. The father had seen men—(not boys: men)—staring at Cressida, especially in summer when she wore baggy T-shirts, jeans or cutoffs, her striking face pale without makeup; staring at Cressida in a kind of baffled yearning as if trying to determine if she was a young girl or a young boy; and why, though they stared so avidly at her, she remained oblivious of *them.*

So far as her parents knew, Cressida was inexperienced with boys or men.

She had the puritan ferocity of one who scorns not so much sexual experience as any sort of shared and intimate physical experience.

As her sister Juliet had said *Oh I am sure that Cressida has never been—you know—with anyone . . . I mean . . . I'm sure that she's a . . .*

Too sensitive of her sister's feelings to say *virgin.*

THE FATHER WAS VERY EXCITED. Adrenaline ran in his veins, his heart beat with an unnatural urgency. Telling himself *This is the excitement of the search. Knowing that Cressida is near.*

He felt this, his daughter's nearness. This man who never listened with any sort of sympathy to talk of such "mystical crap" as extrasensory perception had a conviction now, tramping through the

Nautauga Preserve, that he could sense his daughter somewhere nearby. He could sense her thinking of *him*.

Even as with a part of his mind he understood that, if she'd been anywhere near the entrance to the Preserve, anywhere near Sandhill Road and Sandhill Point, someone would have found her by now.

For he was trained in the law, and he had by nature the lawyer's temperament—doubt, questioning, more questioning.

For he was trained to respond *Yes, but—?*

The father thought how ironic, the daughter had never liked camping or hiking. Wilderness was boring to her, she'd said.

Meaning wilderness frightened her. Wilderness did not care for *her*.

He'd known other people like that, and all of them, perhaps by chance, women. The female is most secure in a confined space, a clearly designated space in which one's identity is mirrored in others' eyes: in such a place, one cannot become easily *lost*.

The rapacity of nature, Zeno thought. You never think of it when you're in control. And when you're no longer in control, it's too late.

The father glanced upward, anxiously. High overhead, just visible through the dense pine boughs, a hawk—two hawks—red-shouldered hawks hunting together in long swooping arcs.

Vivid against the sky then suddenly plummeting, gone.

He'd seen owls swoop to the kill. An owl is a feathery killing machine and silent at such times when the only outcry is the cry of the prey.

Underfoot as he pushed through briars were scuttling things—rabbits, pack rats—a family of skunks—snakes. From somewhere close by the liquidy-gobbling cries of wild turkeys.

Wilderness too vast for the girl, the younger daughter. Zeno had not liked that in her: giving up too easily. Claiming she was bored, wanted to go home to her books and "art."

Needing to squeeze all that she could into her brain. And you can't squeeze three hundred thousand acres into a brain.

Cressida don't do this to us! If you are somewhere close by let us know.

The father had grown hoarse calling the daughter's name. It was a foolish waste of energy, he knew—none of the other volunteer searchers was calling the girl's name.

From remarks made to him, and within his hearing, the father gathered that other, younger searchers were impressed with him, so far: a man of his age, much older than they, apparently an experienced hiker, in reasonably good physical condition.

At the start of the search this seemed so, at least.

"Mr. Mayfield? Here."

He'd drunk his water too quickly. Breathing through his mouth which isn't recommended for a serious hiker.

"Thanks, I'm OK. You'll need it for yourself."

"Mr. Mayfield, take it. I've got another bottle."

The young man, sleek-muscled, lean, like a greyhound or a whippet—one of the Beechum County deputies, in T-shirt, shorts, hiking boots. The father wondered if the deputy was someone who knew his daughter—either of his daughters. He wondered if the deputy knew more about what might have happened to Cressida than he, the father, had yet been allowed to know.

The father was the kind of man more comfortable overseeing others, pressing favors upon others, than accepting favors himself. The father was a man who prided himself on being *strong, protective*.

Still, it isn't a good idea to become dehydrated. Light-headed. Random rushes of adrenaline leave you depleted, exhausted.

He took the water bottle. He drank.

Initially this morning they'd searched along the banks of the Nautauga River in the area in which the young corporal's Jeep Wrangler had been parked. This was a stretch of river where fishermen came often, both marshy and rock-strewn; there were numerous footprints amid the rocks, overlaid upon one another, filled with water since a recent rain. Rescue dogs leapt forward barking excitedly having been given articles of the girl's clothing to smell but soon lost the trail, if there was a trail, whimpered and drifted about clueless. Miles along the river curving and twisting through the rock-strewn land and then they'd decided to alter their strategy fanning out in more or less concentric circles from the Point. Some had searched for lost hikers and children previously in the Preserve and had their particular way of searching but Beechum County law enforcement strategy was to keep close together, only a few yards apart, though it was difficult where there was underbrush and masses of trees, yet the point was not to overlook what might have fallen to the ground, torn clothing in briars, scraped against a tree, any sign that the lost girl had passed this way, a crucial sign that might save her life.

The father listened to what was told to him, explained to him, with an air of calm. In any public gathering Zeno Mayfield presented himself as the most reasonable of men: a man you could trust.

He'd had a career as a man who addressed others, with unfailing intelligence, enthusiasm. But now, there was no opportunity for him to give orders to others. He felt a clutch of helplessness, in the Preserve. Tramping on foot, dependent upon his physical strength, not his more customary cunning.

But O God if his daughter was hurt. If his daughter had been hurt.

Not wanting to think if she'd fallen somewhere, if she'd broken a leg, if she lay unconscious, unable to hear them calling her, unable to respond. Trying not to think if she was nowhere within earshot, borne away in the fast-flowing river that was elevated after heavy rainstorms the previous week, thirty miles downstream to the west where the Nautauga River emptied into Lake Ontario.

Through the morning there were false alarms, false sightings. A female camper wearing a red shirt, staring at them as they approached her campsite. And her partner, another young woman, emerging from a tent, for a moment frightened, hostile.

Excuse us have you seen?

. . . girl of nineteen, looks younger. We think she is somewhere in the vicinity . . .

IN THE SEVENTH HOUR of the first-day's search, early Sunday afternoon the father sighted his daughter ahead, less than one hundred yards away.

Jolted awake, shouting—"Cressida!"

A desperate run, a heedless run, down a steep incline as other searchers stopped in their tracks to stare.

Several saw what the father was seeing: on the farther bank of a narrow mountain stream where the girl had fallen or lain down exhausted to sleep.

Rivulets of sweat ran into the father's eyes burning like acid. He was running clumsily downhill, sharp pains between his shoulder blades and in his legs. A great ungainly beast on its hind legs, staggering.

"Cressida!"

The daughter lay motionless on the farther side of the stream, part-hidden by underbrush. One of her limbs—a leg, or an arm—lay trailing into the stream. The father was shouting hoarsely—"Cressida!" He could not believe that his daughter was injured or broken but only just sleeping, waiting for him.

Others were approaching now, on the run. The father paid no heed to them, he was determined to reach his daughter first, to waken her, and lift her in his arms.

"Cressida! Honey! It's me . . ."

Zeno Mayfield was fifty-three years old. He had not run like this for years. Once he'd been an athlete—in high school a very long time ago. Now his heart was a massive fist in his chest. A sharp pain, a sequence of small sharp pains, struck between his shoulder blades. He ran on reckless, desperate, as if hoping to escape the sharp-darting pains. He was a tall deep-chested man with a broad muscled back; his hair was still thick, licorice-colored except where threaded with gray; his face that had been flushed from the exertion of hours in the Adirondack heat was now draining of blood, mottled and sickly; his heart was pounding so laboriously, it seemed to be drawing oxygen from his brain; at such a pace, he could not breathe; he could not think coherently: his thick clumsy legs could hardly keep him from falling. He was thinking *She is all right. Of course, Cressida is all right.* But when he reached the mountain stream he saw that the thing on

the farther bank wasn't his daughter but the carcass of a partly de-
composed deer, a young doe, the still-beautiful head lacking antlers
and a jagged bloody section of her chest torn away by scavengers.

The father cried out, in horror.

A choked animal-cry, as if he'd been kicked in the chest.

The father fell to his knees. All strength drained from his limbs.

He'd been searching for the daughter since ten o'clock that morning. And now he'd found his daughter asleep beside a little mountain
stream like a girl in a child's storybook and in front of his eyes his
daughter had been transformed into a hideous decaying carcass.

Zeno Mayfield hadn't wept since his mother's death twelve years
before. And then, he hadn't wept like this. His body shook with sobs.
A terrible pity for the killed and part-devoured doe overcame him.

His name was being called. Hands beneath his armpits, lifting.

Wanting to hide from them the obvious fact that he was having
difficulty breathing. Pains between his shoulder blades had coalesced
into a single piercing pain like cartoon zigzag lightning.

He'd insisted early that morning, he would join the search team
in the Preserve. Of course, the father of the *missing girl* must search
for her.

They had him on his feet now. The wounded beast swaying.

It is a terrible thing how swiftly a man's strength can drain from
him, like his pride.

These were young volunteers, Zeno didn't know their names. But
they knew his name: "Mr. Mayfield . . . "

He pushed their hands from him. He was upright, and he was
breathing normally again, or—almost.

Would've insisted upon returning to the search after a few minutes' rest, lukewarm water out of the Evian bottle and a nervous
splattering urination behind a lichen-pocked boulder but blackness
rose inside his skull another time, to his shame he sighed and sank
into it.

GOD TAKE ME *instead of her. If you take anyone—take me.*

Bride-to-Be

July 4, 2005

Y ES YOU KNOW. Know that I do. Of course—you know me.
How could you doubt *me*.

IT IS A SHOCK—of course. We are all—we are all very—sad . . .

No! *Sad* is what I said. We are all—everyone who loves you—and
me—especially. We are *sad*.

NO, WAIT. We are *very happy* that you are alive, Brett, and returned
to us of course.

We are *not sad* about that, we are *very happy* about that.

All those months we prayed. Prayed and *prayed*.

And now, you are returned home to us.

And now, you are returned to us.

I KNEW YOU would return of course—I never doubted.

Even when we were out of contact—when you were *in combat*—I
did not doubt.

In that terrible place—how do you pronounce it—"Diyala" . . .

PLEASE BELIEVE ME, darling: I love you like always.

That is why I wanted us to be engaged before you left—in case there was something that happened . . . over there.

But you know me, I am . . . I am your girl.

I am your *fiancée*. Your *bride-to-be*.

That will not change.

EXCEPT NOW: there is so much for us to plan!

Makes my head swim so much to plan . . .

Your mother promised to help but now . . .

. . . (should not have said *promised*. I did not mean *promised*.)

But, before this, before—this . . . The surgeries, and the recovery and rehab. Before this, your mother was excited about planning the wedding, with my mother, and grandmother, and we were planning the wedding to take place as soon as you were . . .

Well yes: there is a *before*, and there is *now*.

OH IS IT WRONG to say *before*? And—*now*?

Brett why do you look at me like that . . .

Why are you angry at *me* . . .

Why do you seem to hate *me* . . .

. . . look at me like I am a stranger. And you are a stranger to me and I—I am frightened of you at such times.

BECAUSE I LOVE YOU, Brett. I love *you*.

I *love you* and so sometimes this other—it's like *this other*—is staring at me out of your eyes . . .

It is very frightening to me. For I don't know what I can do, to placate *this other*.

I PLEDGE TO YOU to be *your loving wife forever & ever Amen*.

I pledge to you as to Jesus our Savior *forever & ever Amen*.

I am not ashamed of loving you. Of being with you as we did . . .

I would not have been ashamed if I had been pregnant (as I had worried I might be, as you know) and I think now (almost) that I am sorry that I was not.

(Are you sorry?)

(It would be so different now!)

I feel that I am already your wife. But I feel sometimes that you are not my husband—exactly.

I feel that there is Brett my darling, and there is—*this other*.

Sometimes.

HERE IS THE *bridal gown* design.

It's so lovely—isn't it? Do you like it?

Please tell me *yes*. I am so eager to hear *yes*.

I know it doesn't interest you—much. Of course . . .

Some dresses are very expensive. This is a bargain, we found online—"Bonnie Bell Designs."

And so beautiful, I think.

Ivory silk. Ivory lace. One-shoulder neckline with a sheer lace back. The pleated bodice is "fitted" and the skirt "flared."

The veil is gossamer chiffon. The train is three feet long.

And these are the shoes: ivory satin pumps.

Let me hold the picture to the light, maybe you can see better . . .

Do you think that I will look . . . pretty . . . in this?

You'd said I was your *beautiful girl*. Many times you'd said that, Brett. I believed you then, and I want to believe you now.

Please say *yes*.

YOU WILL WEAR your U.S. Army dress uniform. So handsome in your dress uniform with "decorations."

You will wear the dark glasses. You will wear white gloves. The dress cap, so *elegant*.

Corporal Brett Kincaid. My husband.

We will practice. We have months to practice.

(YOU'D HAD A "stateside" promotion—you'd said.)

(All things have a meaning in the military—you'd said. And so *stateside* had a meaning but what is that meaning?—we did not know.)

(We know only that we are so proud of our *Corporal Brett Kincaid*.)

YOU ARE MISTAKEN—YOU *do not look wounded.*

You *do not look "battered."*

You *do not look "like shit"*!

You are my handsome fiancé, you are not truly changed. There will be more surgeries. There must be time to heal, the surgeon has explained. There will be a "natural healing"—in time.

You can't expect a miracle to be perfect!

The ears, the scalp, the forehead, the lids of the eyes. The throat beneath the jaw, on your right side. Except in bright light you would think it was an ordinary burn—burns.

Oh please don't flinch, Brett—when I kiss you. Please.

It's like a sliver of glass in the heart—when you push me from you.

IF PEOPLE ARE *looking at you* in Carthage it is only because they know of you—your medals, your honors. They are admiring of you, for you are a *war hero* but they would not want to intrude.

Like Daddy. He is so admiring of you, Brett!—but Daddy has a funny way about him when he's emotional—gets very quiet—people wouldn't believe that Zeno Mayfield is a shy man really.

Well I mean—*essentially.*

It's hard for men to talk about—certain things. Daddy had not ever had a son, only daughters. To us, Daddy *talks*. We *listen.*

And Mom talks about you all the time. When you were in Iraq, in combat, she prayed for you all the time. *She* worried more when we didn't hear from you than I did, almost . . .

All of my family, Brett. All of the Mayfields.

Try to believe—*we love you.*

I WISH YOU would come back to church with me, Brett.

Everyone is missing you there.

We have a new minister—he's very nice.

And his wife, she's very nice.

They ask after you every Sunday. They know about you of course.

I mean—they know that you are returned to us safely.

There are other veterans in the congregation, I think. They don't come every week. But I think you know two of them at least—Denny Bisher and Brandon Kranach. Maybe they'd been in Iraq, or maybe Afghanistan.

Denny is in a wheelchair. Denny's younger brother wheels him in. Or his mother. *How's Brett* Denny is always asking me and I tell him you'll contact him soon . . .

How's Corporal Kincaid. How's that cool dude.

No, please! Don't be angry with me, I am sorry.

. . . I will not bring Denny up again.

. . . I will not bring church up again.

Don't be angry at me, please *I am sorry.*

JUST FIREWORKS, BRETT! Over at Palisade Park.

The windows are shut. Air conditioner is on.

I can turn the music higher so you won't hear.

I said honey—just *fireworks.* You know—*Fourth of July in the park.*

Yes better not to go this year.

I told them not to expect us—Mom and Dad. We have other things to do.

WHICH TABLETS?—the white ones, or . . .

I can bring you a glass of water.

OK, a glass of beer. But the doctor said . . .

. . . not a good idea to mix "alcohol" and "meds" . . .

Don't—please.

WE WILL PRACTICE, in the church. Before the wedding rehearsal, we will practice.

You *do not limp*. Only just—sometimes—you seem to lose your balance—you make that sudden jerking movement with your legs like in a dream.

I think it *is not real*. It is just *something in your head*.

HAND-EYE COORDINATION. THEY have promised.

In the video, you can see how that boy improved.

There are many miracles. The great miracle God has provided is, *you are alive and we are together*.

The doctor—neurologist—says it is a matter of *neuron-recircuiting*.

It is a matter of *new brain cells learning to take over from the damaged brain cells*. It is *neurogenesis*.

Like not-sleeping. The brain "forgets" how to sleep. Like—sometimes—the brain forgets how to control "elimination." *It is no one's fault*.

These reflexes will come back in time, the doctor said.

WHEN THE GRENADE exploded, and the wall collapsed.

It was combat. It was *in action*. Which is why you have been awarded a Purple Heart.

And the Infantry Combat Badge which is a special badge beautiful gold-braided in the shape of a U with a miniature facsimile of a long-barreled rifle against a blue background. A badge to hold in the hand and contemplate like a gem.

Like a gem that is a riddle, or a riddle that is a gem.

How brave you were, from the start.

Which is why you must not feel shame, that you are returned to us.

You are not *a traitor* or *a coward*. You did not *let your platoon down*. You were injured, and you are convalescing. And you are in rehab.

And you will be married.

WE WILL HAVE CHILDREN, I vow. A son.

I know this. This is possible!

We will do it. We will surprise them. In rehab they have promised—the older doctor said, to me—*If you love your future husband and will not give up but persevere a pregnancy is not impossible.*

Lots of disabled vets have fathered children. This is well known.

The MRI did not detect any growth. The MRI did not detect any blood-clots. The MRI did not detect any "irregularities."

Whatever you see in your head like in dreams is *not real*. You know this!

CORPORAL BRETT GRAHAM KINCAID.

On the maps, we tried to follow you.

Baghdad—that was the first.

Diyala Province. Sadah.

Where you were hurt—Kirkuk.

Where the maps gave out—faded.

So far from Carthage.

OPERATION IRAQI FREEDOM.

Very few people in Carthage know the difference—if there is a difference—between "Iraq" and "Afghanistan."

I know: for I am your fiancée and it is necessary for me to know.

But still I am confused, and there is no one to ask.

For I dare not ask *you*.

The look in your eyes, at such times!—I feel such cold, a shudder comes over me.

He does not love me. He does not even know me.

Reverend Doig was explaining last Sunday there is no end, there can be no end, never an end to war for there is a "seed of harm" in the human soul that can never be wholly eradicated until Jesus returns to save mankind.

But when will this be?—Jesus returning to *us*?

Like Corporal Kincaid returning.

Yes I believe this! I want to believe this.

Must believe that there is a way of believing it—for both of us. When Reverend Doig marries us.

WHAT DID I tell them, I told them the truth—it was an accident.

I slipped and fell and struck the door—so silly.

At the ER they took an X-ray. My jaw is not dislocated.

It's sore, it's hard to swallow but the bruises will fade.

I know, you did not mean it.

I am sorry to upset you.

I am not crying, truly!

We will look back on this time of trial and we will say—*It was a test of our love. We did not weaken.*

THIS MORNING in my bed which is so lonely. Oh Brett I miss our special times together before you went away when I could come to you in your apartment and we could be alone together . . .

When that happens again, we will be happy as we were. This is not a normal way for us to be, living as we are. It's no wonder there is strain between us. But this time will pass, this time of trial.

I wish your mother did not dislike me. When I am trying so hard to love her.

She said to me *You don't have to pretend. You can stop pretending. Any day now, you can stop pretending.* And I didn't know how to answer her—there was such dislike in her eyes . . . And finally I said *But I am not pretending anything, Mrs. Kincaid! I love Brett and want only to marry him and be his wife and take care of him as he might need me, this is all I dream of.*

This morning when I could not sleep after I'd wakened early—(there is a rooster somewhere behind where we live, up the hill behind the cemetery on the Post Road, I like to hear the rooster crowing but it means that the night is over and I will probably not get back to sleep)—I was remembering when we said good-bye, that last time.

In the Albany airport. And there were other soldiers arriving at the security check and some of them younger than you even. And that older officer—a lieutenant. And everyone—civilians—looking at you with respect.

So sad to kiss you good-bye! And everybody wanting to hug you and kiss you at the last minute and you were laughing saying *But Julie is my fiancée not you guys*.

There are so many of us who love you, Brett. I wish you would know this.

You gave me your "special letter" then. I knew what it meant—I think I knew—I felt that I might faint—but hid it away quickly of course and never spoke of it to anyone.

I will never open it now. Now you are safely returned to us.

Yes, I still have it of course. Hidden in my room.

My sister knows of the letter—I mean, she saw it in my hand. She has no idea what is inside it. She will not ever know.

She has told me I am not worthy of you—I am "too happy"—"too shallow"—to comprehend you.

In fact Cressida knows nothing of what there is between us. No one knows, except us.

Those special times between us, Brett. We will have those special times again . . .

Cressida is a good person in her heart!—but this is not always evident.

It's hurtful to her to observe happiness in others. Even people she loves. I think it has made a difference to her, to see you as you are now—she has been deeply affected though she would not say so.

But if you speak to her of anything personal she will stare at you coldly. *Excuse me. You are utterly mistaken.*

She has refused to be my maid of honor, she was scornful saying she hasn't worn anything like a dress or a skirt since she'd been a baby and wasn't going to start now. She laughed saying *weddings are rituals in an extinct religion in which I don't believe.*

I said to Cressida *What is the religion in which you do believe?*

This question I put to her seriously and not sarcastically as Cressida herself speaks. For truly I wanted to know.

But Cressida had no reply. Turned away from me as if she was ashamed and did not speak.

I wish—I am praying for this!—that Cressida will come to church with us sometime. Or just with me, if you don't want to come. I know that she has been wounded in some way, she has been hurt by someone or something, she would never confide in me. I feel that her heart is empty and yearning to be filled—to *cross over*.

NO, BRETT! Not ever.

You must not say such things.

We could not feel more pride for you, truly. It is a feeling beyond pride—such as you would feel for any true hero, who has acted in a way few others could act, in a time of great danger.

What you said at the going-away party, such simple words you said made everyone cry—*I just want to serve my country, I want to be the very best soldier I know how to be.*

This is what you have done. Please, Brett! Have faith.

The war in Iraq was the most exciting time in your life, I know. Those months you were gone from us—"deployed." It was a dangerous time and an exciting time and (I understand) a secret time for you, we could know nothing of in Carthage.

Operation Iraqi Freedom. Those words!

We tried to follow in the news. On the Internet. We prayed for you.

Daddy would remove from the newspaper things he didn't want me to see. Particularly the *New York Times,* he gets on Sundays mostly.

Photos of soldiers who have died in the war—the wars. Since 2001.

I have seen some of them of course. Couldn't help but look for women among the rows of men looking young as boys.

There are not many female soldiers. But it is shocking to see them, their pictures with all the men.

And always smiling. Like high school girls.

In Carthage, there are some people who do not "support" the war—the wars. But they support our troops, they make that clear.

Daddy has always made that clear.

Daddy respects *you*. Daddy is just awkward now, he doesn't know how to talk to you but that's how some men are. He was never a soldier himself and has strong feelings about the Vietnam War which was the war when he was growing up. But Daddy does not mean anything personal.

You have said *It's a toss of the dice*. You have said *Who gives a shit who lives, who dies. A toss of the dice.*

I know you don't mean this. This is not Brett speaking but *the other.*

You must not despair. Life is a gift. Our lives are gifts. Our love for each other.

It was surprising, my mother is not very religious but while you were gone—she came to church with me, almost every Sunday. She prayed.

All of the congregation prayed for you. For you and the others in the war—the wars.

So many have died in the wars, it is hard for me to remember the numbers—more than one thousand?

Most of them soldiers like you, not officers. And all beloved of God, you'd wish to think.

For all are *beloved of God*. Even the enemy.

Just so, we must defend ourselves. A Christian must defend himself against the enemies of Christ.

This war against terror. It is a war against the enemies of Christ.

I know you did not want to kill anyone. I know you, my darling Brett, and I know this—you did not want to kill the enemy, or—anyone. But you were a soldier, this was your duty.

You were promoted because you were a good soldier. We were so proud of you then.

Your mother is proud of you, I wish she could show it better.

I wish she did not seem to blame *me*.

I am not sure why she would wish to blame *me*.

Maybe she thought I was—pregnant. Maybe she thought that was why we wanted to get married. And maybe she thought that was why you enlisted in the army—to get away.

I wish that I could speak with your mother but I—I have tried . . . I have tried and failed. Your mother does not like me.

My mother says *We'll keep trying! Mrs. Kincaid is fearful of losing her son.*

I know that you don't like me to talk about your mother—I am sorry, I will try not to. Only just sometimes, I feel so *hurt*.

I know, the war is a terrible thing for you to remember. When you start classes at Plattsburgh in September, or maybe—maybe it will be January—you will have other things to think about . . . By then, we will be married and things will be easier, in just one place.

I will take courses at Plattsburgh, too. I think I will. Part-time graduate school, in the M.A. in education program.

With a master's degree I could teach high school English. I would be qualified for "administration"—Daddy thinks I should be a principal, one day.

Daddy has such plans for us! Both of us.

I WISH YOU would speak of it to me, dear Brett.

I've seen documentaries on TV. I think I know what it was like—in a way.

I know it was a "high" for you—I've heard you say to your friends. Search missions in the Iraqi homes when you didn't know what would happen to you, or what you would do.

What you'd never say to me or to your mother you would say to Rod Halifax and "Stump"—or maybe you would say it to a stranger you met in a bar.

Another vet, you would speak with. Someone who didn't know Corporal Brett Kincaid as he'd used to be.

There is no "high" like that in Carthage. Tossing your life like dice.

Our lives since high school—it's like looking through the wrong end of a telescope, I guess—so small.

Those sad little cardboard houses beneath a Christmas tree, houses and a church and fake snow like frosting. *Small.*

EVEN OUR WOUNDS here are *small.*

IN CARTHAGE, your life is waiting for you. It is not a thrilling life like the other. It is not a life to serve Democracy like the other. You said such a strange thing when you saw us waiting for you by the baggage claim, we were thrilled you were walking unassisted and this look came in your face I had not ever seen before and it was like you were afraid of us for just a moment you said *Oh Christ are you all still alive? I was thinking you were all dead. I'd been to the other place, and I saw you all there.*

THREE

The Father

O H DADDY WHY'D YOU *call me such a name*—Cressida.
Because it's an unusual name, honey. And it's a beautiful name.

FIRE SHONE INTO the father's face. His eyes were sockets of fire.

He hadn't the strength to open his eyes. Or the courage.

The doe's torso had been torn open, its bloody interior crawling with flies, maggots. Yet the eyes were still beautiful—"doe's eyes."

He'd seen his daughter there, on the ground. He was certain.

The sick-sliding sensation in his gut wasn't unfamiliar. *In that place, again. The place of dread, horror. Guilt. His fault.*

And how: how was it his fault?

Lying on his back and his arms flung wide across the bed—(he remembered now: they'd brought him home, to his deep mortification and shame)—that sagged beneath his weight. (Last time he'd weighed himself he'd been, dear Christ, 212 pounds. Heavy and graceless as wet cement.)

A memory came to him of a long-ago trampoline in a neighbor's backyard when he'd been a child. Throwing himself down onto the coarse taut canvas that he might be sprung into the air—clumsily, thrillingly—flying up, losing his balance and falling back, flat on his back and arms sprung, the breath knocked out of him.

On the trampoline, Zeno had been the most reckless of kids. Other boys had to marvel at him.

Years later when his own kids were young it had become common knowledge that trampolines are dangerous for children. You can break your neck, or your back—you can fall into the springs and slice yourself. But if he'd known, as a kid, Zeno wouldn't have cared—it was a risk worth taking.

Nothing in his childhood had been so magical as springing up from the trampoline—up, up—arms outflung like the wings of a bird.

Now, he'd come to earth. Hard.

HE'D TOLD THEM like hell he was going to any hospital.

Fucking hell *he was not going to any ER.*

Not while his daughter was missing. Not until he'd brought her back safely home.

He'd allowed them to help him. Weak-kneed and dazed by exhaustion he hadn't any choice. Falling on his knees on sharp rocks—a God-damned stupid thing to have done. He'd been pushing himself in the search, as his wife had begged him not to do, as others, seeing his flushed face and hearing his labored breath, had urged him not to do; for by Sunday afternoon there must have been at least fifty rescue workers and volunteers spread out in the Preserve, fanning in concentric circles from the Nautauga River at Sandhill Point where it was believed the *missing girl* had been last seen.

It was the father's pride, he couldn't bear to think that his daughter might be found by someone else. Cressida's first glimpse of a rescuer's face should be *his face.*

Her first words—*Daddy! Thank God.*

HE'D HAD SOME "heart pains"—(guessed that was what they were: quick darting pains like electric shocks in his chest and a clammy sensation on his skin)—a few times, nothing serious, he was sure. He hadn't wanted to worry his wife.

A woman's love can be a burden. She is desperate to keep you alive, she values your life more than you can possibly.

What he most dreaded: not being able to protect them.

His wife, his daughters.

Strange how when he'd been younger, he hadn't worried much. He'd taken it for granted that he would live—well, forever! A long time, anyway.

Even when he'd received death threats over the issue of Roger Cassidy—defending the "atheist" high school biology teacher when the school board had fired him.

He'd laughed at the threats. He'd told Arlette it was just to scare him and he certainly wasn't going to be scared.

Just last month his doctor Rick Llewellyn had examined him pretty thoroughly in his office. And an EKG. No "imminent" problem with his heart but Zeno's blood pressure was still high even with medication: 150 over 90.

Blood pressure, cholesterol. Fact is, Zeno should lose twenty pounds at least.

On the bed he'd tried to untie and kick off the heavy hiking boots but there came Arlette to pull them off for him.

"Lie still. Try to rest. If you can't sleep for Christ's sake, Zeno— *shut your eyes at least.*"

She was terrified of course. Fussing and fuming over him to deflect her thoughts from the other.

That morning at about 4 A.M. she'd wakened him. When she'd discovered that Cressida hadn't come home. Since that minute he'd been awake in a way he was rarely awake—all of his senses alert, to the point of pain. Stark-staring awake, as if his eyelids had been removed.

A search. A search for his daughter. A search that was for a *missing girl.*

These searches of which you hear, occasionally. Often for a lost child.

A kidnapped child. Abducted.

You hear, and you feel a tug of sympathy—but not much more. For your life doesn't overlap with the lives of strangers and their terror can't be shared with you.

Was he awake? Or asleep? He saw the steeply hilly forest strewn with enormous boulders as in an ancient cataclysm and from behind one of these a girl's uplifted hand, arm—a glimpse of a naked shoulder which he knew to be badly bruised . . . *Oh Daddy where are you. Dad-dy.*

"*Lie still.* Please. If something happens to you at such a time . . . "

The voice wasn't Cressida's voice. Somehow, Arlette had intervened.

He knew, his wife didn't trust him. Married for more than a quarter of a century—Arlette trusted Zeno less readily than she'd done at the start.

For now she knew him, to a degree. To know some men is certainly not to trust them.

She was breathless, irritated. Not terrified—not so you'd see—but irritated. The house was crowded with well-intentioned relatives. There were police officers coming and going—their ugly police-radios crackling and squawking like demented geese. There were reporters for local media eager for interviews—they were not to be turned away, for they would be useful. And photos of Cressida had to be supplied, of course.

Coffee? Iced tea? Grapefruit juice, pomegranate juice? With a grim sort of hostess-gaiety Arlette offered her visitors refreshments, for she knew no other way to deal with people in her house.

Somehow, before she'd had a chance to call her sister Katie Hewett, Katie had come to the house. This was by 10 A.M. Katie had taken over the hostess-role and was helping Arlette answer phones—family phone, cell phones—which rang frequently and with each call, despite the evidence of the caller ID, there was the hope that the next voice they heard would be Cressida's.

Hi there! Gosh! I just saw on TV that I'm "missing"...

Wow. Sorry. Oh God you won't believe what happened but I'm OK now ...

Except the voice was never Cressida's. Remarkable, how it was never Cressida's.

Years ago Arlette would have crawled beside her husband in their bed, in a crisis like this; she would not have minded that her husband had sweated through his clothes, T-shirt and khaki shorts that were now clammy-cool, and smelled of his body; she would have held the anguished man in her arms, to shield him. And Zeno would have gathered his wife in his arms, to shield her. Shivering and shuddering and dazed with exhaustion but together in this terrible time.

Now, Arlette tugged at his hiking boots—so heavy! And the laces needing to be untied. Pulled the boots off his enormous feet seeing that, even in the rush of preparing to leave for the Nautauga Preserve, he'd remembered to put on a double pair of socks—white liner socks, light-woolen socks.

For all his careless-seeming ways, Zeno was a meticulous man. A conscientious man. The only mayor of Carthage in recent decades who'd left office—after eight years, in the 1990s—with a considerable surplus in the city treasury, and not a gaping deficit. (Of course, it was a quasi-secret that Mayor Mayfield had written personal checks for a number of endangered projects—parks and recreation maintenance, Little League softball, the Black River Community Walk-In Clinic.) One of the few mayors in all of upstate New York who, as he'd liked to joke, hadn't even been investigated, let alone indicted, tried and convicted, for malfeasance in office.

Arlette had asked the young man who'd driven Zeno home in Zeno's Land Rover what had happened to him in the Preserve, for she knew that Zeno would never tell her the truth.

He'd said, Zeno had gotten overheated. Over-tired. Dehydrated.

He'd said this was why it isn't a good idea, a family member to be searching for someone in his family who's been reported lost.

Zeno smiled a ghastly smile. Zeno managed to speak, for Zeno must always have the last word.

OK, he'd try to sleep. A nap for an hour maybe.

Then, he intended to return to the Preserve.

"She can't be there a second night. We can't—that can't—happen."

He stumbled on the stairs. Didn't hear Katie speak to him, and didn't seem to register that WCTG-TV was coming to the house to do an interview with the parents of the *missing girl* for the Sunday 6 P.M. news, later that afternoon.

Arlette had accompanied Zeno upstairs trying unobtrusively to slip her arm around his waist, but he'd pushed from her with a little snort of indignation.

He'd needed to use the bathroom, he said. Needed some privacy.

"I'm not going to croak in here, hon—I promise."

This was meant to be humor. Just the word *croak*.

She'd made a sound like laughter, or the hissing rejoinder to laughter, and turned away, and left the man to his privacy.

Almost, they were adversaries now. Grappling together each knowing what must be done, what should be done, annoyed with the other for being blind, stubborn.

Arlette had known he'd become overheated in the Preserve, he'd had no right to rush off like that tramping through underbrush while she was alone at the house. Waiting for a call—calls. Waiting for something to happen.

After a distracted hour she returned to check on Zeno: he was sprawled on the bed only partly undressed. As if he'd been too exhausted to do more than pull off his khaki shorts and let them fall to the floor.

Sprawled, breathing hoarsely and wetly, through his mouth, like a beached whale might breathe. And his face slack putty-colored, you'd never have guessed had been a handsome face not so long ago.

Unshaven. Wiry whiskers sprouting on his jaws.

Zeno Mayfield was a man who had to be prevented from pushing himself too hard. As if he had no natural sense of restraint, of normal limits.

As, when he'd been a young attorney taking on difficult cases— hopeless cases—unpopular cases; once, unforgivably, taking on a case so controversial, anonymous callers had threatened him and his family and Arlette had worried that some madman might mail a bomb, or affix a bomb to one of their cars. *In the name of God think what you are doing, man*—one of the anonymous notes had warned.

All Zeno had done, he'd protested, was defend a high school biol- ogy teacher who'd been suspended from his job for having taught Darwinian evolutionary theory to the exclusion of "creationism."

And when he'd been mayor of Carthage, an exhausting and quix- otic venture into "public service" that had paid a token salary—(fifteen hundred annually!)—he'd pushed himself beyond what even his avid supporters might have expected of him and saw his popularity plum- met nonetheless. The most controversial issue of Zeno's mayoralty had been a campaign to install recycling in Carthage—yellow barrels for bottles and cans, green barrels for paper and cardboard. You'd have thought that Zeno Mayfield was a descendant of Trotsky! His daughters had asked plaintively *Why do people hate Daddy? Don't they know how funny and nice Daddy is?*

Arlette hadn't lain down beside him. She hadn't held him tight in her arms. But she'd laid a cloth over his face, dampened with cold water, and he'd pushed it off and clutched anxiously at her hand.

"Lettie—d'you think—he did something to her? And now he's ashamed, and can't tell us? Lettie—d'you think—oh God, Lettie . . . "

YOUR MOTHER AND I *chose our daughters' names with particular care. Be- cause we don't think that either of you is ordinary. So an ordinary name isn't appropriate.*

He was solemn and dogged trying to explain. She was younger than the age she was now and rudely she laughed.

Bullshit, Daddy. That is such bullshit.

It was like Cressida to laugh in your face. Squinch up her face like a wicked little monkey. Her laughter was high-pitched like a monkey's chittering and her small shiny-black eyes were merry with derision.

They were in someplace Zeno didn't recognize. Not in the forest now but in a place meant to be this place—the Mayfield home.

Why is it, when you dream about a place meant to be "home"—or any "familiar" place—it never looks like anything you'd ever seen before?

He was trying to explain to her. She was making her silly-little-girl face rolling her eyes and batting away his words as she'd have batted away badminton birdies with both her balled-up fists.

Saying *Bullshit Daddy, except for her face Juliet is O-R-D-I-N-A-R-Y.*

Zeno took exception to this. Zeno was angered when his bright unruly younger daughter mocked his sweetly-serene and beautiful elder daughter.

And anyway it wasn't true. Or it was a partial truth. For Juliet's beauty wasn't exclusively her face.

The exchange between the father and Cressida was a dream. Yet, the exchange had taken place more or less in this way, years before.

The Mayfield girls were like the daughters of a fairy-tale king.

Bitterly the younger daughter resented the fact—(if it was a fact, it was unprovable)—that the father loved the elder, more beautiful daughter more than he loved her, whose twisty little heart he couldn't master.

I love both our girls. I love them for different reasons. But equally.

And Arlette said *I hope you do. And if you don't, or can't—I hope you can disguise it.*

All parents know: there are children who are easy to love, and children who are a challenge to love.

There are radiant children like Juliet Mayfield. Guileless, shadowless, happy.

There are difficult children like Cressida. Steeped in the ink of irony as if in the womb.

The bright happy children are grateful for your love. The dark twisty children must test your love.

Maybe Cressida was "autistic"—in grade school, the possibility had been raised.

Later, in high school the fancier epithet "Asperger's" was suggested—with no more validation.

If Cressida had known she'd have said, airily—*Who cares? People are such idiots.*

Zeno supposed that in secret, Cressida cared very much.

It was clear that Cressida resented how in Carthage, among people who knew the Mayfields, she was likely to be described as *the smart one* while her sister Juliet was *the pretty one*.

How much would an adolescent girl rather be *pretty*, than *smart*!

For of course, Cressida was invariably judged *too smart*.

As in *too smart for her own good*.

As in *too smart for a girl her age*.

When she'd first started school, she'd complained: "Nobody else is named 'Cressida.' "

It was a difficult name to pronounce. It was a name that fitted awkwardly in the mouth.

Her parents had said of course no one else was named "Cressida" because "Cressida" was her own special name.

Cressida had considered this. She did think of herself as different from other children—more restless, more impatient, more easily vexed, smarter—(at least usually)—quicker to laugh and quicker to tears. But she wasn't sure if having a *special name* was a good idea, for it allowed others to know what might be better kept secret.

"I hate it when people laugh at me. I hate it if they call me 'Cress'—'Cressie.' "

She was one of those individuals, less frequently female than male, whose names couldn't be appropriated—like a Richard who refuses to be diminished to "Dick," or a Robert who will not be "Bob."

When she was older and may have felt a little (secret) pride in her unusual name, still she sometimes complained that other people asked her about it; for other people, including teachers, were likely to be over-curious, or just rude: "'Cressida' makes me feel self-conscious, sometimes."

Or, with a downward tug of her mouth, as if an invisible hook had snagged her there, "'Cressida' makes me feel accursed."

Accursed! This was not so remarkable a word for Cressida, as a girl of twelve who loved to read in the adult section of the Carthage Public Library, particularly novels designated as *dark fantasy, romance.*

Of course, Cressida had looked up her name online.

Reporting to her parents, incensed: "'Cressida'—or 'Criseyde'—isn't nice at all. She's 'faithless'—that's how people thought of her in the Middle Ages. Chaucer wrote about her, and then Shakespeare. First she was in love with a soldier named Troilus—then she was in love with another man—and when that ended, she had no one. And no one loved her, or cared about her—that was Cressida's fate."

"Oh, honey, come *on*. We don't believe in 'fate' in the U.S. of A. in 1996—this ain't the Middle Ages."

It was the father's prerogative to make jokes. The daughter twisted her mouth in a wounded little smile.

The previous fall when Cressida was a freshman at St. Lawrence University in Canton, New York, she reported back that one of her professors had remarked upon her name, saying she was the "first Cressida" he'd ever encountered. He'd seemed impressed, she said. He'd asked if she'd been named for the medieval Cressida and she'd said, "Oh you'll have to ask my father, he's the one in our family with delusions of grandeur."

Delusions of grandeur! Zeno had laughed but the remark carelessly flung out by his young daughter had stung.

AND ALL THIS *while his daughter is awaiting him.*

His daughter with black-shining eyes. His daughter who (he believes) adores him and would never deceive him.

"Maybe she's returned to Canton. Without telling us."

"Maybe she's hiding in the Preserve. In one of her 'moods' . . ."

"Maybe someone got her to drink—got her drunk. Maybe she's ashamed . . ."

"Maybe it's a game they're playing. Cressida and Brett."

"A game?"

" . . . to make Juliet jealous. To make Juliet regret she broke the engagement."

"Canton. What on earth are you saying?"

They looked at each other in dismay. Madness swirled in the air between them palpable as the electricity before a storm.

"Jesus. No. Of course she hasn't 'returned' to Canton—she was deeply unhappy in Canton. She doesn't have a residence in Canton. That's insane." Zeno wiped his face with the damp cloth Arlette had brought him earlier, that he'd flung aside onto the bed.

Arlette said: "And she and Brett wouldn't be 'playing a game' together—that's ridiculous. They scarcely know each other. And I don't think that Juliet was the one to break the engagement."

Zeno stared at his wife. "You think it was Brett? *He* broke the engagement?"

"If Juliet broke it, it wasn't her choice. Not Juliet."

"Lettie, did she tell you this?"

"She hasn't told me anything."

"That son of a bitch! *He* broke the engagement—you think?"

"He may have felt that Juliet wanted to end it. He may have felt—it was the right thing to do."

Arlette meant: the right thing to do considering that Kincaid was now a disabled person at twenty-six.

Not so visibly disabled as some Iraq/Afghanistan war veterans in Carthage, except for the skin-grafts on his head and face. His brain had not been seriously injured—so it was believed. And Juliet had reported eagerly that doctors at the VA hospital in Watertown were saying that Brett's prognosis, with rehab, was "good"—"very good."

Before dropping out impulsively, after 9/11, to enlist in the U.S. Army with several friends from high school, Brett had taken courses in finance, marketing, and business administration at the State

University at Plattsburgh. Zeno had the idea that the kid hadn't been highly motivated—as Kincaid's prospective father-in-law, he had some interest in the practical side of his daughter's romance, though he didn't think he was a cynic: just a responsible dad.

(Juliet would never forgive him if she'd known that Zeno had managed to see Brett Kincaid's transcript for the single semester he'd completed at SUNY Plattsburgh: B's, B+. Maybe it was unfair but Christ, Zeno Mayfield wanted for his beautiful daughter a man just slightly better than a B+ at Plattsburgh State.)

He'd tried—hard!—not to think of Brett Kincaid making love to his daughter. *His* daughter.

Arlette had chided him not to be ridiculous. Not to be proprietary.

"Juliet isn't 'yours' any more than she's mine. Try to be grateful that she's so happy—she's *in love*."

But that was what disturbed the father—his firstborn daughter, his sweet honeybunch Juliet, was clearly *in love*.

Not with Daddy but with a young rival. Good-looking and with the unconscious swagger of a high school athlete accustomed to success, applause. Accustomed to the adoration of his peers and to the admiration of adults.

Accustomed to girls: sex. Zeno felt a wave of purely sexual jealousy. Nothing so upset him as glimpsing, by chance, his daughter and her tall handsome fiancé kissing, slipping their arms around each other's waist, whispering, laughing together—so clearly intimate, and comfortable in their intimacy.

That is, before Brett Kincaid had been shipped to Iraq.

Initially Zeno had wanted to think that the kid had had too easy a time, cutting a swath through the Carthage high school world with an ease that couldn't prepare him for the starker adult world to come. But that was unfair, maybe: Brett had worked at part-time jobs through high school—his mother was a divorcée, with a low-paying job in County Services at the Beechum County Courthouse—and he was, as Juliet claimed, a "serious, committed Christian."

It was hard to believe that any teenaged boys in Carthage were

"Christians"—yet, this seemed to be the case. When Zeno had been active in the Carthage Chamber of Commerce he'd encountered kids like these, frequently. Girls like Juliet hadn't surprised him—you expected girls to be religious. In a girl, *religious* can be *sexy.*

In a boy like Brett Kincaid it seemed like something else. Zeno wasn't sure what.

Recalling how Brett had said, at the going-away party for him and his high school friends, each enlisted in the U.S. Army and each scheduled for basic training at Fort Benning, Georgia, that he wanted to be the "best soldier" he knew how to be. (His own father had "served" in the first Gulf War.) Winter/spring 2002 had been an era of patriotic fervor, following the terrorist attack at the World Trade Center the previous September; it had not been an era in which individuals were thinking clearly, still less young men like Brett Kincaid who seemed truly to want to defend their country against its enemies. How earnestly Brett had spoken, and how handsome he'd been in his U.S. Army dress uniform! Zeno had stared at the boy, and at his dear daughter Juliet in the crook of the boy's arm. His heart had clenched in disdain and dread as he'd thought *Oh Jesus. Watch out for this poor sweet dumb kid.*

And now recalling that poignant moment, when everyone in the room had burst into applause, and Juliet's face had shone with tears, Zeno thought *Poor bastard. It's a cruel price you pay for being stupid.*

Difficult for Zeno Mayfield who'd come of age in the late, cynical years of the Vietnam War to comprehend why any intelligent young person like Brett Kincaid would willingly enlist in the military. Why, when there was no draft! It was madness.

Wanting to "serve" the country—whose country? Virtually no political leaders' sons and daughters enlisted in the armed services. No college-educated young people. Already in 2002 you could figure that the war would be fought by an American underclass, overseen by the Defense Department.

Yet Zeno hadn't spoken with Brett on this subject. He knew that Juliet didn't want him to "intrude"—Zeno had such ideas, such plans, for everyone in his orbit, he had to make it a principle to keep clear. And he hadn't felt close enough to the boy—there was an awkwardness between them, a shyness in Brett Kincaid as he shook hands with Zeno Mayfield, his prospective father-in-law, he'd never quite overcome.

Often, Brett had called him "Mr. Mayfield"—"sir."

And Zeno had said to call him "Zeno" please—"We're not on the army base."

Zeno had laughed, made a joke of it. But it disturbed him, essentially. His prospective son-in-law was uneasy in his presence which meant he didn't like Zeno.

Or maybe, didn't trust Zeno.

In the matter of the military, for instance. Though Zeno hadn't tried to talk him out of enlisting, Zeno hadn't made a point of congratulating him, either, as everyone else was doing.

Serve my country. Best soldier I can be.

Like my dad . . .

There was a father, evidently. An absent father. A soldier-father who'd disappeared from Carthage twenty years before.

Brett had been brought up some kind of Protestant Christian—Methodist, maybe. He wasn't critical, questioning. He wasn't skeptical. He wanted to *believe,* and so he wanted to *serve.*

Chain of command: you obeyed your superior officer's orders as he obeyed his superior officer's orders as he obeyed his superior officer's orders and so to the very top: the Administration that had declared war on terror and beyond that Administration, the militant Christian God.

None of this was questioned. Zeno wouldn't have wished to stir doubt. He'd defended the high school biology teacher Cassidy who'd taught Darwinian evolutionary theory to the exclusion of "creationism"—more specifically, Cassidy had ridiculed "creationism" in the classroom and deeply offended some students—and their parents—who were evangelical Christians; Zeno had defended Cassidy against the Carthage school board, and had won his case, but it had been a Pyrrhic victory, for Cassidy had no professional future in Carthage and had been soundly disliked for his "arrogant, atheistic" stance. And Zeno Mayfield had suffered a good deal of abuse, too.

Except that Brett Kincaid had become engaged to his daughter Juliet, Zeno had no wish to enlighten the boy. You had to learn to live with religion, if you had a public career. You had to know when to be quiet about your own skepticism.

Juliet belonged to the Carthage Congregationalist Church: she'd made a decision to join when she was in high school, drawn to the church by a close friend; after she and Brett began seeing each other, Brett accompanied her to Sunday services. No one else in the Mayfield family attended church. Arlette described herself as "a mild kind of Protestant-Christian-Democrat" and Zeno had learned to parlay questions about faith by saying he was a "Deist"—"In the hallowed tradition of our American Founding Fathers." Zeno found serious talk of religion embarrassing: revealing what you "believed" was a kind of self-exposure not unlike stripping in public; you were likely to reveal far more than you wished. Cressida bluntly dismissed religion as a pastime for "weak-minded" people—she'd gone to church with her older sister for a few months when she'd been in middle school, and been bored silly.

Strange how Cressida could be right about so much, and yet— (this was not a thought Zeno allowed himself to express aloud)—you resented her remarks, and were inclined to dislike her for making them.

Juliet's Christian faith had certainly been a great solace to her, since news had come of her fiancé's injuries—a hurried and incoherent phone message from Brett's mother had been the first they'd heard; she'd been grateful, and never ceased proclaiming her gratitude, that Brett hadn't been killed; that God had "spared him."

The shock to Juliet had been so great, Zeno thought, she hadn't altogether absorbed the fact that her fiancé was a terribly changed man—and the changes weren't likely to be exclusively physical.

Since Brett had returned to Carthage, and was living in his mother's house about three miles from the Mayfields, Juliet had spent a good deal of time with him there; the elder Mayfields hadn't seen much of him. When she could, Juliet accompanied Brett to the re-hab clinic attached to the Carthage hospital; she attended some of his counseling sessions, as his fiancée; eagerly she reported back to her parents that as soon as he was better able to concentrate Brett intended to re-enroll at Plattsburgh and get a degree in business and that there was talk—(how substantial, Zeno didn't know)—of Brett being hired by a Carthage businessman who made it a point to hire veterans.

See, Daddy—Brett has a future!

Though I know you want me to dump him. I will not.

Zeno would have protested, if Juliet had so accused him.

But, of course, Juliet had not.

Beautiful Juliet never accused anyone of such low thoughts. Least of all her father whom she adored.

But there came impish Cressida to slip her arm through Daddy's arm and to tug at him, to murmur in his ear in her scratchy voice, "Poor Julie! Not the 'war hero' she'd expected, is he." Cruel Cressida squirming with something like stifled laughter.

Zeno had said reprovingly, "Your sister loves Brett. That's the main thing."

Cressida snorted with laughter like a mischievous little girl.

"It *is?*"

Several nights later, on the Fourth of July, Juliet had returned home early—and alone—(the most gorgeous, gaudy fireworks had just begun exploding in the sky above Palisade Park)—to inform her family that the engagement was ended.

Her cheeks were tear-streaked. Her face had lost its luminosity and looked almost plain. Her voice was a hoarse whisper.

"We've both decided. It's for the best. We love each other, but—it's ended."

Zeno and Arlette had been astounded. Zeno had felt a sick sinking sensation in his gut. For this was what he'd wanted—wasn't it? His beautiful daughter spared a life with a handicapped and embittered husband?

When Arlette moved to embrace her, Juliet pushed past her with a choked little sob and hurried up the stairs and shut her bedroom door.

Even Cressida had been shocked. For once, her shiny black eyes hadn't danced with derision when the subject of Juliet and Brett Kincaid came up—"Oh God! Julie will be so unhappy."

At twenty-two, Juliet was still living at home. She'd gone to college in Oneida but had wanted to return to Carthage to teach (sixth grade) at the Convent Street School a few miles away from the family home on Cumberland Avenue. Planning her wedding to Corporal Brett Kincaid—guest list, caterer, bridal gown and bridesmaids, music, flowers, wedding service at the Congregationalist Church—had been the consuming passion of her life for the past eighteen months, and now that the engagement had ended Juliet seemed scarcely capable of speech apart from the most perfunctory exchanges with her family.

Though Juliet was always unfailingly courteous, and sweet. Tears welling in her eyes at which she brushed with her fingertips, as if apologetically.

There'd been no reproach in her manner, when the father gazed at her searchingly, waiting for her to speak. For never had Juliet so much as hinted *Are you happy, Daddy? I hope you are happy, Brett is out of our lives.*

Numbly Zeno said to Arlette: "She hasn't spoken to you—yet? She hasn't wanted to talk about it?"

"No."

"What about Cressida?"

"No. Juliet would never discuss Brett with *her.*"

In the issue of the sisters, it had often been that Arlette clearly sided with *the pretty one* and not *the smart one.*

"Maybe Brett wanted to talk about it with Cressida. Maybe that was why—the reason—they were together last night . . ."

If truly they'd been together—*alone together.* Zeno had to wonder if that was true.

It was totally out of character for Cressida to go to a place like the Roebuck Inn. Totally unlike Cressida, particularly on a Saturday night. Yet witnesses had told investigating officers that they were sure they'd seen Cressida there the night before, in the company of several people—mostly men; and one of them Brett Kincaid.

Saturday night in midsummer, at Wolf's Head Lake. There were a number of lakeside taverns of which the Roebuck was the oldest and the most popular, very likely the most crowded, and noisy; patrons spilled out of the inn and onto the decks overlooking the lake, and even down into the sprawling parking lot; on the deck was a local rock band, playing at a deafening volume. A drunken roar of motorboats on the lake, a drunken roar of motorcycles on Bear Valley Road.

Before he'd become a settled-down husband and father of two daughters, Zeno Mayfield had spent time at Wolf's Head Lake. He knew the Roebuck taproom. He knew the Roebuck men's rooms. He knew the sloshing of brackish water about the mossy posts sunk into the lake, that supported the Roebuck's outdoor deck.

He knew the "scene" on a Saturday night.

How puzzling, that Cressida would go to such a place, voluntarily! His sensitive daughter who flinched hearing rock music on the radio and who disdained places like the Roebuck and anyone likely to patronize them.

"Most people are so *crude*. And so *oblivious.*"

Such pronouncements Zeno's younger daughter had made from an early age. Her pinched little face pinched tighter with disdain.

Brett Kincaid acknowledged that he'd encountered Cressida at the lakeside inn. He'd acknowledged that she'd been in his Jeep. But he seemed to be saying that she hadn't remained with him. His account of the previous night was incoherent and inconsistent. Asked about scratch-marks on his face and smears of blood on the front seat of his Jeep he'd given vague answers—he must have scratched his face somehow without knowing it, and the blood-smears on the seat were his. There were other items of "evidence" a deputy had found examining the vehicle that had been found with its front, right wheel in a ditch on the Sandhill Road on Sunday morning.

The bloodstains would be analyzed, to determine if the blood was Kincaid's or someone else's. (As part of a physical examination the previous year, Cressida had had blood work done by a local Carthage doctor; these records would be provided to police.)

Zeno had been told about the bloodstains in Kincaid's Jeep that appeared to be "fresh" and "damp" and Zeno's brain had seemed to clamp down. Arlette, too, had been told, and had gone silent.

For they knew—they *knew*—that Juliet's fiancé, Juliet's ex-fiancé, who'd come very close to being their son-in-law, wasn't capable of hurting either of their daughters. They could not believe it, and would not.

As they could not believe that, at any minute, their missing daughter might not arrive home, burst into the house seeing an alarming number of vehicles parked outside—a mix of familiar faces and strangers in the living room—and cry: "What's this? Who won the lottery?"

The father wanted to think: it might happen. However unlikely, it might happen.

"Oh Daddy, for God's sake. You thought I was *lost*? You thought I was—*killed or something*?"

The daughter's shrill laughter like ice being shaken.

THAT MORNING, Zeno had wanted to speak to Brett Kincaid.

Zeno had been told no. Not a good idea at this time.

"But just to—see him. For five minutes . . ."

No. Hal Pitney who was Zeno's friend, a high-ranking officer in the Beechum County Sheriff's Department, told him this was not a good idea at the present time and anyway not possible, since Kincaid was being interviewed by the sheriff McManus himself.

Not *interrogated*, which meant arrest. Only just *interviewed*, which meant the stage preceding a possible arrest.

I need to know from him just this: Is Cressida alive?

" . . . only just to see him. Christ, he's like one of the family—engaged to my daughter—my other daughter . . ."

Zeno stammered, trying to smile. Zeno Mayfield had long cultivated a wide flash of a smile, a politician's smile, that came now unconsciously, with a look of being forced. He was frightened at the prospect of seeing Brett Kincaid, seeing how Brett regarded *him*.

Just tell me: is my daughter alive.

Pitney said he'd pass on the word to McManus. Pitney said it "wasn't likely" that Zeno could speak face-to-face with Kincaid for a while but—"Who knows? It might end fast."

"What? What 'might end fast'?"

Into Pitney's face came a wary look. As if he'd said too much.

"'Custody.' Him being in custody, and interviewed. It could end fast if he gives up all he knows."

A chill passed into Zeno, hearing these words.

He knew, Hal Pitney had told him all he'd tell him right now.

Driving east of Carthage into the hilly countryside, into the foothills of the Adirondacks and into the Nautauga Preserve to join the search team that morning, Zeno had made a succession of calls on his cell phone trying to learn if there were "developments" in the interview with Brett Kincaid. Like a compulsive cell phone user who checks for new calls in his in-box every few minutes Zeno could not shut off the flat little phone, still less could he slide it into his shirt pocket and forget it. Several times he tried to speak with Bud McManus. For Zeno knew Bud, to a degree, enough, he'd thought, to merit special consideration. (In the scrimmage of Carthage politics, he'd done McManus a favor, at least once: hadn't he? If not, Zeno regretted it now.) Instead, he wound up speaking with another deputy named Gerry Eisner who told him (confidentially) that the interview with Brett Kincaid wasn't going well, so far—Kincaid claimed not to remember what had happened the night before, though he seemed to know that someone whom he alternately called "Cress'da" and "the girl" had been in his Jeep; at one point he seemed to be saying that "the girl" had left him and gotten

into a vehicle with someone else whom he didn't know—but he wasn't
sure of any of this, he'd been pretty much "wasted."

Wasted. High school usage, guys boasting to one another of how
sick-drunk they'd gotten on beer. Zeno trembled with indignation.

During the interview, Kincaid had seemed dazed, uncertain of his
surroundings. He'd smelled strongly of vomit even after he'd been
allowed to wash up. His eyes were bloodshot and his skin-grafted
face made him look like "something freaky" in a horror movie, Eisner said.

You'd never guess, Eisner said, he's only twenty-six years old.

You'd never guess he'd been a good-looking kid not so long ago.
"Jesus! A 'war hero.'"

In Eisner's voice Zeno detected a tone of wonderment, part-
commiseration and part-revulsion.

It was pure chance that Corporal Kincaid had been apprehended
that morning at approximately the time the Mayfields were making
frantic calls about their missing daughter: taken into custody by a
sheriff's deputy at about 8 A.M. when he was found semiconscious,
vomit- and blood-stained sprawled in the front seat of his Jeep Wrangler on Sandhill Road; the front, right wheel of the Jeep had gone
off the unpaved road, that was elevated by about two feet above a
marshy area. Early-morning hikers in the Preserve had called 911 on
their cell phone to report the seemingly incapacitated vehicle with
an "unresponding" man sprawled in the front seat and both front
doors open.

When the deputy shook Kincaid awake, identifying himself as a
law enforcement officer, Kincaid shoved and struck at him, shouting
incoherently, as if he was frightened, and had no idea where he was—
the deputy had had to overpower him, cuff him and call for backup.

Still, Kincaid hadn't been arrested. Just brought to the Sheriff's
Department headquarters on Axel Road.

Zeno knew, Brett Kincaid wasn't supposed to be drinking while
taking medication. According to Juliet he was taking a half-dozen
prescription pills daily.

Zeno knew, Brett Kincaid was "much changed" since he'd returned from Iraq. It was not a new or an uncommon situation—it
should not have been, given media attention to similar disturbed,
returning veterans, a surprising situation—but to those who knew
Kincaid, to those who presumed to love him, it was new, it was uncommon, and it was disturbing.

Eisner said it did seem that Kincaid was maybe "brain damaged"
in some way. For sure, Kincaid remembered something that had
happened—he remembered a "girl"—but wasn't sure what he remembered.

"You see that sometimes," Eisner said. "In some instances."

Zeno asked, what instances?

Eisner said, guardedly, "When they can't remember."

Zeno asked, can't remember what?

Eisner was silent. In the background were men's voices, incongruous laughter.

Zeno thought *He thinks that Kincaid hurt her. Hurt her, blacked out
and now doesn't remember.*

The father's coolly-cruel legal mind considered: *Insanity defense.
Whatever he has done. Not guilty.*

It was the first thought any defense lawyer would think. It was
the most cynical yet the most profound thought in such a situation.

Yet, the father nudged himself: He was sure, his daughter had not
really been *hurt*.

He felt a flood of guilt, chagrin: *Of course*, his daughter had not
been hurt.

Sandhill Road was an unimproved dirt road that wound through
the southern wedge of the Nautauga Preserve, following for much
of its length the snaky curves of the Nautauga River. There were a
few hiking trails here but along the river underbrush was dense, you
would think impenetrable; yet there were faint paths leading down
an incline to the river, that had to be at least ten feet deep at this
point, fast-moving, with rippling frothy rapids amid large boulders.
If a body were pushed into the river the body might be caught imme-

diately in boulders and underbrush; or the body might be propelled rapidly downriver, leaving no trace.

It was perhaps a ten-minute drive from the Roebuck Inn at Wolf's Head Lake to the entrance of the Nautauga Preserve and another ten-minute drive to Sandhill Point. Anyone who lived in the area—a boy like Brett Kincaid, for instance—would know the roads and trails in the southern part of the Preserve. He would know Sandhill Point, a long narrow peninsula jutting into the river, no more than three feet across at its widest point.

Outside the Preserve, Sandhill Road was quasi-paved and intersected with Bear Valley Road that connected, several miles to the west, with Wolf's Head Lake and with the Roebuck Inn & Marina on the lake.

Sandhill Point was approximately eleven miles from 822 Cumberland Avenue which was the address of the Mayfields' home.

Not too far, really—not too far for the daughter to make her way on foot if necessary.

If for instance—(the father's mind flew forward like wings beating frantically against the wind)—she'd been made to feel ashamed, her clothes torn and dirty. If she had not wanted to be seen.

For Cressida was very self-conscious. Stricken with shyness at unpredictable times.

And—always losing her cell phone! Unlike Juliet who treasured her cell phone and would go nowhere without it.

Zeno was still on the phone with Eisner who was complaining about the local TV station issuing "breaking news" bulletins every half hour, putting pressure on the sheriff's office to take time for interviews, come up with quotable quotes—"The usual bullshit. You think they'd be ashamed."

Zeno said, "Yes. Right," not sure what he was agreeing with; he had to ask, another time, if he could speak with Brett Kincaid who'd practically been his son-in-law, the fiancé of his daughter, please for just a minute when there was a break in the interview—"Just a minute, that's all I would need"—and Eisner said, an edge of irritation in his voice, "Sorry, Zeno. I don't think so." For reasons that Zeno could appreciate, Eisner explained that no one could speak with Kincaid while he was in custody—(any suspect, any possible crime, he could call an accomplice, he could ask the accomplice to take away evidence, aid and abet him at a little distance)—except if Kincaid requested a lawyer he'd have been allowed that call but Kincaid had declined to call a lawyer saying emphatically he did not need or want a lawyer. Zeno thought with relief *No lawyer! Good.* Zeno could not imagine any Carthage lawyer whom Kincaid might call: in other, normal circumstances, the kid would have called *him.*

In a voice that had become grating and aggressive Zeno asked another time if he could speak with Bud McManus and Eisner said no, he did not think that Zeno could speak with Bud McManus but that, when there was news, McManus would call him personally. And Zeno said, "But when will that be? You've got him there, you've had him since, when—two hours at least—two hours you've had him— you can't get him to talk, or you're not trying to get him to talk—so when's that going to be? I'm just asking." And Eisner replied, words Zeno scarcely heard through the blood pounding in his ears. And Zeno said, raising his voice, fearing that the cell phone was breaking up as he approached the entrance to the Preserve, driving into the bumpy parking lot in his Land Rover, "Look, Gerry: I need to know. It's hard for me to breathe even, without knowing. Because Kincaid must know. Kincaid might know. Kincaid would know— something. I just want to talk to Bud, or to the boy—if I could just talk to the boy, Gerry, I would know. I mean, he would tell me. If—if he has anything to tell—he would tell me. Because—I've tried to explain—Brett is almost one of the Mayfield family. He was almost my son. Son-in-law. Hell, that might happen yet. Engagements get broken, and engagements get made. They're just kids. My daughter Juliet. You know—Juliet. And Cressida—her sister. If I could talk to Brett, maybe on the phone like this, not in person with other people around, at police headquarters, wherever you have him—just on the phone like this—I promise, I'd only keep him for two-three minutes—just want to hear his voice—just want to ask him—I believe he would tell *me . . .*"

The line was dead: the little cell phone had failed.

"DADDY."

It was Juliet, tugging at his shoulder. For a moment he couldn't recall where he was—which daughter this was. Then the sliver of fear entered his heart, the other girl was missing.

From Juliet's somber manner, he understood that nothing had changed.

Yet, from her somber manner, he understood that there'd been no bad news.

"Sweetie. How are *you.*"

"Not so good, Daddy. Not right now."

Juliet had roused him from a sleep like death. There was some reason for waking him, she was explaining, but through the roaring in his ears he was having difficulty hearing.

That beating pulse in the ears, the surge of blood.

Though his heart was beating slow now like a heavy bell rolling.

The girl should have leaned over him to kiss him. Brush his cheek with her cool lips. This *should have happened.*

"Be right down, honey. Tell your mother."

She was deeply wounded, Zeno knew. What had passed between her sister and her former fiancé was a matter of the most lurid public speculation. Inevitably her name would appear in the media. Inevitably reporters would approach *her.*

It was 5:20 P.M. Good Christ he'd slept two and a half hours. The shame of it washed over him.

His daughter missing, and Mayfield *asleep.*

He hoped McManus and the others didn't know. If for instance they'd tried to call him back, return his many calls, and Arlette had had to tell them her husband was sleeping in the middle of the day, exhausted. Her husband could not speak with them just now thank you.

This was ridiculous. Of course they hadn't called.

He swung his legs off the bed. He pulled off his sweat-soaked T-shirt, underwear. Folds of clammy-pale flesh at his belly, thighs like hams. Steely-coppery hairs bristled on his chest and beneath his arms dense as underbrush in the Preserve.

He was a big man, not fat. Not fat *yet*.

Mischievous Cressida had had a habit of pinching her father at the waist. *Uh-oh Dad-dy! What's this.*

It was a running joke in the Mayfield family, among the Mayfield relatives and Zeno's close friends, that he was vain about his appearance. That he could be embarrassed, if it were pointed out that he'd put on weight.

Dad-dy better go on that Atkins diet. Raw steak and whiskey.

Cressida was petite, child-sized. Except for her frizzed hair like a dark aureole about her head you might mistake her for a twelve-year-old boy.

Arlette said disapprovingly: "Cressida won't eat, because she 're-fuses' to menstruate."

The father was so shocked hearing this, he pretended he hadn't heard.

A couple of months ago when Brett Kincaid had come to the house in loose-fitting khaki cutoffs Zeno had had a glimpse of the boy's wasted thighs, flat stringy muscles atrophied from weeks of hospitalization. Remembering how Brett had looked a year before. It was shocking to see a young man no longer *young*.

Therapy was rebuilding the muscles but it was a slow and painful process.

Juliet helped him walk: had helped him walk.

Walk, walk, walk—for miles. Juliet's slender arm around the corporal's waist walking in Palisade Park where there were few hills. For hills left the corporal short of breath.

His arm- and shoulder-muscles were as they'd been before the injuries. When he'd been in a wheelchair at the VA hospital he'd wheeled himself everywhere he could, for exercise.

His skull had not been fractured in the explosion but his brain had been traumatized—"concussed."

A hurt brain can heal. A hurt brain will heal.

It will take time. And love.

Juliet had said this. She was gripping her fiancé's hand and her smile was fine and brave and without irony.

And so it had been a shock—a shock, and a relief—when only a few weeks later Juliet told them the engagement had ended.

Except, things don't end so easily. The father knew.

Between men and women, not so easily.

Christ! Zeno smelled of his body. The sweat of anxiety, despair.

Before bed that night he would change the bedclothes himself, before Arlette came into the room—Zeno had a flamboyant way with bed-changing, whipping sheets into the air so that they floated, as a magician might; tucking in the corners, tight; smoothing out the wrinkles, deft, fast, zip-zip-zip he'd made his little daughters laugh, like a cartoon character. In Boy Scout camp he'd learned all sorts of handy tasks.

He'd been an Eagle Scout, of course. Zeno Mayfield at age fourteen, youngest Eagle Scout in the Adirondack region, ever.

He smiled, thinking of this. Then, ceased smiling.

He staggered into the bathroom. Flung on the shower, both faucets blasting. Leaning his head into the spraying water hoping to wake himself. Losing his balance and grabbing at the shower curtain but (thank God) not bringing it down.

The sheer pleasure of hot, stinging water cascading down his face, his body. For a moment Zeno was almost happy.

In the bathroom doorway Arlette stood—beyond the noise of the shower she was speaking to him, urgently—*She's been found! It's over, our daughter has been found!*—but when Zeno asked his wife to repeat her words she said, anxiously, "They're here. The TV people. Come downstairs when you can."

"Do I have time to shave?"

Arlette came to the shower, to peer at him. Arlette didn't reach into the hot stinging water to draw her fingers across his stubbly jaws.

"Yes. I think you'd better."

Quickly Zeno dried himself, with a massive towel. Tried to run a comb through his hair, took a hairbrush to it, hoping not to confront his reflection in the misty bathroom mirror, the bloodshot frightened eyes.

"Here. Here are fresh clothes. This shirt . . ."

Gratefully Zeno took the clothes from his wife.

Downstairs were uplifted voices. Arlette tried to tell him who was there, who'd just arrived, which relatives, which TV reporters, but Zeno wasn't able to concentrate. He had an unnerving sense that his front door had been flung open, anyone could now enter.

The door flung open, his little girl had slipped *out*.

Except she wasn't a little girl any longer of course. She was nineteen years old: a woman.

"How do I look? OK?"

It wasn't unusual for Zeno Mayfield—being interviewed. TV cameras just made the interview experience more edgy, the stakes higher.

"Oh, Zeno. You cut yourself shaving. Didn't you *notice?*"

Arlette gave a little sob of exasperation. With a wadded tissue she dabbed at Zeno's jaw.

"Thanks, honey. I love you."

Bravely they descended the stairs hand in hand. Zeno saw that Arlette had tied back her hair, that seemed to have lost its glossiness overnight; she'd dabbed lipstick on her mouth and had blindly reached into her jewelry box for something to lower around her neck—a strand of inexpensive pearls no one had seen her wear in a decade. Her fingers were icy-cold; her hand was trembling. Another time Zeno said, in a whisper, "I love you," but Arlette was distracted.

And Zeno was disoriented, seeing so many people in his living room. And furniture had been moved aside in the room. TV lights were blinding. The female reporter for WCTG-TV was a woman whom Zeno knew from his mayoral days when Evvie Estes had worked in City Hall public relations in a cigarette-smoke-filled little cubicle office at the ground-floor rear of the old sandstone building. Evvie was older now, hard-eyed and hard-mouthed, heavily made-up, with an air of sincere-seeming breathless concern: "Mr. and Mrs. Mayfield—Zeno and Arlette—hello! What a terrible day this has been for you!"—thrusting the microphone at them as if her remark called for a response. Arlette was smiling tightly staring at the woman as if she'd been taken totally by surprise and Zeno frowned saying calmly and gravely, "Yes—a terribly anxious day. Our daughter Cressida is missing, we have reason to believe that she is lost in the Nautauga Preserve, or in the vicinity of the Preserve. She may be injured—otherwise she would have contacted us by now. She's nineteen, unfortunately not an experienced hiker . . . We are hoping that someone may have seen her or have information about her."

Zeno Mayfield's public way of addressing interviewers, gazing into TV cameras with a little frowning squint of the brow, returned to him at even this strained moment. If there was a quaver in his voice, no one would detect it.

Evvie Estes, hair bleached a startling brassy-blond, asked several commonsense questions of the Mayfields. In his grave calm voice Zeno prevailed when Arlette showed no inclination to reply. Yes, their daughter had spoken with them on Saturday evening, before she'd gone out; no, they had not known that she was going to Wolf's Head Lake—"But maybe Cressida hadn't known she was going to the lake, when she left home. Maybe it was something that came up later." Zeno wanted to think this, rather than that Cressida had lied to them.

But he couldn't shake off the likelihood that Cressida had lied. She'd lied by omitting the truth. Saying she was going to a friend's house, but not that, after visiting with her friend, she had plans to turn up at Wolf's Head Lake nine miles away.

It had been established by this time that Cressida had remained with her friend Marcy until 10 P.M. at which time she'd left for "home"—as she'd led Marcy to think.

Cressida hadn't driven to her friend's house which was less than a mile from the Mayfields' house, but walked. It was believed by Marcy that Cressida had then walked back home—having declined an offer of a ride from Marcy.

Or, it might have been that someone else, whose identity wasn't known to Marcy, had picked Cressida up, when she'd left Marcy's house on her way home.

Not all of this made sense (yet) to Zeno. None of this Zeno cared to lay bare before a TV audience.

Though he'd been thinking how ironic, when Cressida had been, as witnesses claimed, in the company of Brett Kincaid at Wolf's Head Lake, her sister Juliet had been home with their parents; by then, Juliet had probably been in bed.

That night, the Mayfields had invited old friends for dinner and Juliet had helped prepare the meal with Arlette. And Cressida had made it a point to explain that she couldn't come to dinner with them that night because she was seeing her high school friend Marcy Meyer.

Evvie Estes asked if there'd been anything to lead them to "suspect"—anything? When they'd last seen Cressida?

"No. It was an ordinary night. Cressida was seeing a friend from high school and she hadn't had to tell us, we would have known, she'd have been back home by eleven P.M. at the latest. It was just—an ordinary night."

Zeno hadn't liked Evvie Estes pitching that word to them— "suspect."

Zeno and Arlette were seated side by side on a sofa. Zeno clasped Arlette's hand firmly in his as if to secure her. Earlier, Juliet had helped Arlette locate photographs of Cressida to provide to police and media people, to be shown on TV and posted online through the day; Zeno assumed that these photos would be shown on the 6 P.M. news, during the interview. And he hoped that the interview, which was being taped, about fifteen minutes in length, wouldn't be drastically cut.

"All we can hope for is that Cressida will contact us soon—if she can. Or, if she's been injured, or lost—that someone will discover her.

We are praying that she is in the Preserve—that is, she hasn't been—taken"—Zeno paused, blinking at the possibility, a sudden obstacle like an enormous boulder in his path—"taken somewhere else . . ." His old ease at public speaking was leaving him, like air leaking from a balloon. Almost, Zeno was stammering, as the interview ended: "If anyone can help us—help us find her—any information leading to her—her whereabouts—we are offering ten thousand dollars reward—for the recovery of—the return of—our daughter Cressida Mayfield."

Arlette turned to stare at him. Ten thousand dollars!

This was entirely new. This had not been discussed. So far as Arlette knew, Zeno had not thought of a reward before this moment.

Uttering the words "ten thousand dollars" Zeno had spoken in a strangely elated voice. And he'd smiled strangely, squinting in the TV lights.

Soon then the interview ended. Zeno's white shirt was sticking to his skin—he'd been sweating again. And now he, too, was trembling.

Of course the Mayfields could afford ten thousand dollars. Much more than this, they could afford if it meant bringing their missing daughter home.

"ZENO? WHERE ARE YOU GOING?"

"Back to the Preserve. To the search."

"You are not! Not now."

"There's two hours of daylight, at least. I need to be there."

"That's ridiculous. You do not. Stay here with us . . ."

Zeno hesitated. But no no no *no*. He had no intention of remaining in this house, where he couldn't breathe, waiting.

FOUR

Descending and Ascending

I KNEW. AS SOON AS *I saw her bed wasn't slept-in.*
I knew—something had happened.

AT 4:08 A.M. that Sunday morning Arlette awakened with a start.

The strangest sensation—that something was wrong, altered. Though in the shadowy interior of her bedroom—her and Zeno's bedroom—here was comfort, ease. Though Zeno's deep raspy rhythmic breathing was comfort to her, and ease.

Must've been a dream that wakened her. A swirl of anxiety like leaves spinning in a wind tunnel. She'd been pulled along—somewhere. Waking dry-mouthed and edgy believing that something was changed in the house or in the life of the house.

Or—one of her limbs was missing. *That* was the dream.

What was the phenomenon?—"phantom limb"? In that case an actual limb is missing from the body but you feel the (painful) presence of the (absent) limb; in this case, nothing was missing from Arlette's body, so far as she knew.

It was mysterious to her, this loss. Yet it seemed unmistakable.

After this hour she would not ever feel otherwise.

WITHOUT WAKING ZENO she slipped from their bed.

Sometimes in the night when they awakened—through a single night, each woke several times, if but for a few seconds—Arlette kissed Zeno's mouth in playful affection, or Zeno kissed hers. These were kisses like casual greetings—they were not kisses meant to wake the other fully.

How's my sweet honey Zeno might mutter. But before Arlette could answer, Zeno would sink back into sleep.

Zeno was deeply asleep now. What subtle and irrevocable seismic shifting of the life of the house Arlette had sensed, Zeno was oblivious to. Like one who has fallen onto his back he lay spread-limbed, sprawled, taking up two-thirds of the bed in his warm thrumming sleep.

Arlette had learned to sleep beside her husband without being disturbed by him; whenever possible, her dreams incorporated his audible breathing in the most ingenious of ways.

Zeno's snoring might be represented, for instance, by zigzag-shapes like metallic insects flying past the dreaming wife's face. Sometimes, Arlette was awakened by her own surprised laughter.

That night, at dinner with friends, Zeno had consumed a bottle of wine himself, in the interstices of pouring wine for others. He'd been in very good spirits, telling stories, laughing loudly. He'd been tenderly solicitous of Juliet and refrained from teasing her, which was unlike the girls' Daddy.

Through their long marriage there had been episodes—there had been interludes—of Zeno drinking too much. Arlette understood, Zeno had been drinking tonight because he felt guilty: for the relief he'd expressed when Juliet's engagement had been broken.

Not to Juliet of course but to Arlette. *Thank God. Now we can breathe again.*

Except it wasn't so easy. It would not be so easy. For their daughter's heart had been broken.

Juliet had spent the evening with them. Instead of with her fiancé.

That is, her ex-fiancé.

Helping her mother prepare an elaborate meal in the kitchen, helping at the table, smiling, cheery. As if she hadn't a life elsewhere, a life as a woman elsewhere, with a man, a lover from whom she'd been abruptly and mysteriously divided.

It was a small shock, to see the engagement ring (of which Juliet had been so proud) missing from Juliet's finger.

In fact Juliet's slender fingers were ring-less, as if in mourning.

At the dinner table, three couples and the daughter. Three middle-aged couples, a twenty-two-year-old daughter.

And the daughter so beautiful. And heartbroken.

Of course, no one had asked Juliet about Brett. No one had brought up the subject of Brett Kincaid at all. As if Corporal Kincaid didn't exist, and he and Juliet had never been planning to be married.

It's God-damned sad. But not our fault for Christ's sake.

What did we do? Not a fucking thing.

He'd been drunk, muttering. Sitting heavily on the bed so the box springs creaked. Kicking a shoe halfway across the carpet.

Juliet should talk to us about it. We're her God-damn parents!

When he was in one of his moods Arlette knew to leave him alone. She would not humor him, or placate him. She would leave him to steep in whatever mood rose in him like bile.

It was an asshole decision, to enlist in the army. "Serve his country"— see where it got him.

Anyway he won't pull our daughter down with him.

Arlette didn't stoop to retrieve the shoe. But she nudged it out of the way with her foot so that neither of them would stumble over it in the night, should one of them rise to go to the bathroom.

Immediately his head was lowered on the pillow, Zeno fell asleep.

A harsh serrated breathing, as if briars were caught in his throat.

The air-conditioning was on. A thin cool air moved through the bedroom. Arlette pulled a sheet up over her sleeping husband's shoulders. At such moments she was overcome with a sensation of love for the man, commingled with fear, the sight of his thick-muscled shoulders, his upper arms covered in wiry hairs, the slack flesh of his jaws when he lay on his side. Inside the middle-aged man, the brash youthful Zeno Mayfield with whom Arlette had fallen in love yet resided.

In a man's sleep, his mortality is most evident.

They were of an age now, and moving into a more emphatic age, when women began to lose their husbands—to become "widows." Arlette could not allow herself to think in this way.

Remembering later, of that night: their concern had been for Juliet, and for Brett Kincaid whom possibly they would not ever see again.

Their thoughts were almost exclusively of Juliet. As it had been in the Mayfield household since Corporal Kincaid had returned in his disabled state.

Cressida passing like a wraith in their midst. On her way out for the evening to visit with a friend from high school who lived so close, Cressida could walk instead of driving. At about 6 P.M. she must have called out a casual good-bye—in the kitchen Arlette and Juliet would scarcely have taken note.

Bye! See you-all later.

Possibly, they hadn't heard. Cressida hadn't troubled to come to the kitchen doorway, to announce that she was going.

Zeno hadn't been home. Out at the liquor store, choosing wine with the fussy particularity of a man who doesn't know anything about wine really but would like to give the impression that he does.

It shouldn't have been anything other than an ordinary evening though it was a Saturday night in midsummer.

In upstate New York in the Adirondack region, the population trebled in summer.

Summer people. Campers, pickup trucks. Bikers' gangs. In the night, on even a quiet residential street like Cumberland, you could hear the sneering roar of motorcycles in the distance.

At the lakes—Wolf's Head, Echo, Wild Forest—there were "incidents" each summer. Fights, assaults, break-ins, vandalism, arson, rapes, murders. Small local police departments with only a few officers had to call in the New York State Police, at desperate times.

When Zeno had been mayor of Carthage, several Hells Angels gangs had congregated in Palisade Park. After a day and part of a night of drunken and increasingly destructive festivities local residents had so bitterly complained, Zeno sent in the Carthage City Police to "peaceably" clear the park.

Just barely, a riot had been averted. Zeno had been credited with having made the right decisions, just in time.

No one had been arrested. No police officers had been injured. The state troopers hadn't had to be summoned to Carthage.

The bikers' gangs hadn't returned to Palisade Park. But they congregated, weekends, at the lakes. Still you could sometimes hear, in the distance, at night, a window open, the sneering-defiant motorcycle-whine, mixed with a sound of nighttime insects.

Arlette left the bedroom. Zeno hadn't wakened.

In a thin muslin nightgown in bare feet making her way along the carpeted corridor. Past the shut door of Juliet's room—for she knew, Juliet was home—Juliet had been in bed for hours, like her parents—unerringly to the room in which she knew there was *something wrong*.

By this time, past 4 A.M., Cressida would have returned from Marcy Meyer's house. Hours ago, she'd have returned. She wouldn't have wanted to disturb her parents but would have gone upstairs to her room as quietly as possible—it was a peculiarity of their younger daughter, since she'd been a small child, as Zeno noted she could *creep like a little mousie* and no one knew she was there.

Even as Arlette was telling herself this, she was pushing open the door, switching on a light, to see: Cressida's bed still made, undisturbed.

This was wrong. This was very wrong.

Arlette stood in the doorway, staring.

Of course, the room was empty. Cressida was nowhere in sight.

They'd gone to bed after their guests left and the kitchen was reasonably clean. They'd gone to bed soon after 11 P.M., Arlette and Zeno, without a thought, or not much more than a fleeting thought, about Cressida who was, after all—as they'd been led to believe—only just visiting with her high school friend Marcy Meyer less than a mile away.

Maybe the girls had had dinner together. Or maybe with Marcy's parents. Maybe a DVD afterward. *Misfit girls together in solidarity* Cressida had joked.

In high school, Cressida and Marcy had been "best friends" by default, as Cressida said. *Friendships of girls unpopular together are forged for life.*

(It was Cressida's way to exaggerate. Neither she nor Marcy Meyer was "unpopular"—Arlette was certain.)

Slowly Arlette came forward, to touch the comforter on Cressida's bed.

With perfect symmetry the comforter had been pulled over the bedclothes. If Arlette were to lift it she knew she would see the sheets beneath neatly smoothed, for Cressida could not tolerate wrinkles or creases in fabrics.

The sheets would be tightly tucked in between the mattress and the box springs.

For it was their younger daughter's way to do things *neatly*. With an air of fierce disdain, dislike—yet *neatly*.

All things that were tasks and chores—"household" things—Cressida resented having to do. Her imagination was loftier, more abstract.

Yet, though she resented such tasks, she dispatched them swiftly, to get them out of the way.

Can't imagine anything more stultifying than the life of a housewife! Poor Mom.

Arlette was frequently nettled by her younger daughter's thoughtless remarks. Though she knew that Cressida loved her, at times it seemed clear that Cressida did not respect her.

But if you hadn't been up for it, Jule and I wouldn't be here, I guess.
So, thanks!

Arlette wondered: was it possible that Cressida had planned to stay overnight at Marcy's? As she'd done sometimes when the girls were in middle school together. It seemed unlikely now, but . . .

For God's sake, Mom. What an utterly brainless idea.

Arlette left Cressida's room and went downstairs. She was breathing quickly now though her heartbeat was calm.

From a wall phone in the kitchen downstairs, Arlette called Cressida's cell phone number.

There came a faint ringing, but no answer.

Then, a burst of electronic music, dissonant chords and computer-voice coolly instructing the caller to leave a message after the beep.

Cressida? It's Mom. I'm calling at four-ten A.M. *Wondering where you are . . . If you can please call back as soon as possible . . .*

Arlette hung up the phone. But immediately, Arlette lifted the receiver and called again.

The second time, she fumbled leaving a message. *Just Mom again. We're a little worried about you, honey. It's pretty late . . . Give us a call, OK?*

Now invoking *us*. For Cressida did respect her father.

It occurred to Arlette then that Cressida might be home: only just not in her room.

From earliest childhood she'd been an unpredictable child. You might look for her in all the wrong places as she watched you through a crack in a doorway, bursting into laughter at the worried look in your face.

Especially, Cressida had thought *scrunched-up (adult) faces* were funny.

So Arlette checked the downstairs rooms of the house: the TV room in the basement, which Cressida didn't often occupy, objecting that it was partially underground and, in very wet weather, wriggly little centipedes appeared on the (Sears, slate-colored, slightly stained) wall-to-wall carpeting to her extreme disgust; Zeno's cluttered home-office, with floor-to-ceiling bookshelves crammed with far more than just books, and an ancient rolltop desk Zeno liked to boast had been inherited from a Revolutionary War "quasi-ancestor" when in fact he'd bought it at an estate auction: a room in which,

when she'd been a moody high school student, Cressida had sometimes *holed herself away in* when Zeno wasn't there; and nooks and
crannies of the living room which was a long narrow room with
a beamed oak ceiling, shadow-splotched even when lighted, with
a gleaming black baby-grand Steinway piano which, sadly, to Arlette's way of thinking, no one played any longer, since Cressida had
abruptly quit piano lessons at the age of sixteen.

But why quit, honey? You play so well . . .

Sure. For Beechum County.

No one. Nothing. In none of these rooms.

But then, Arlette hadn't really expected to discover Cressida sleeping anywhere except in her bed.

At the rear sliding-glass door, which opened out onto a flagstone
terrace in need of a vigorous weed-trimming, Arlette leaned outside
to breathe in the muggy night air. Her eyes lifted to the night sky—a
maze of constellations the names of which she could never recall as
Cressida could even as a small child brightly reciting the names as if
she'd been born knowing them: *Andromeda. Gemini. Big Dipper. Little
Dipper. Virgo. Pegasus. Orion . . .*

Arlette stepped out onto the redwood deck. Just to check the outdoor furniture—and Zeno's sagging hammock strung between two
sturdy trees—but no Cressida of course.

Went to the garage, entering by a side door. Switched on the garage light—no one inside the garage of course.

Barefoot, wincing, Arlette went to check each of the household
vehicles—Zeno's Land Rover, Arlette's Toyota station wagon, Juliet's
Skylark. Of course, there was no one sleeping or hiding in any of
these.

Making her way then out the asphalt driveway which was a
lengthy driveway to the street—Cumberland Avenue. Though Cumberland was one of Carthage's most prestigious residential streets,
in the high, hilly northern edge of town abutting the old historic
cemetery of the First Episcopal Church of Carthage, Arlette might
as well have been facing an abyss—there were no streetlights on and

no lights in their neighbors' houses. Only a smoldering-dull light seemed to descend from the sky as if a bright moon were trapped behind clouds.

It was possible—so desperation urged the mother to think—that Cressida had made arrangements to meet someone after she'd spent the evening at Marcy's; they might now be together, in a vehicle parked at the curb, talking together, or . . .

How many times Arlette had sat with boys in their vehicles, in front of her parents' house, talking together, kissing and touching . . .

But Cressida wasn't that kind of girl. Cressida didn't "go out" with boys. At least not so far as her family knew.

I worry that Cressida is lonely. I don't think she's very happy.

Don't be ridiculous! Cressida is one-of-a-kind. She doesn't give a damn for what other girls care for, she's special.

So Zeno wished to believe. Arlette was less certain.

She did guess that it was a painful thing, to be *the smart one* following in the trail of *the pretty one*.

In any case there was no vehicle parked at the end of the Mayfields' long driveway. Cressida was nowhere on the property, it was painfully obvious.

With less regard for her bare feet, Arlette returned quickly to the house, to the kitchen where the overhead light shone brightly. You would not think it was 4:30 A.M.! The pumpkin-colored Formica counters were freshly wiped and the dishwasher was still warm from having been set into motion at about 10:30 P.M.; with her usual cheery efficiency Juliet had helped Arlette clean up after the dinner party. Together in the kitchen, in the aftermath of a pleasant evening with old friends, an evening that would come to acquire, in Arlette's memory, the distinction of being the last such evening of her life, Arlette might have spoken with Juliet about Brett Kincaid—but Juliet did not seem to invite such an intimacy.

Nor did either Arlette or Juliet speak of Cressida—at that time, what was there to say?

Just going over to Marcy's, Mom. I can walk.

Don't wait up for me OK?

Arlette lifted the phone receiver another time and called Cressida's cell phone number even as she prepared herself for no answer.

"Maybe she lost the phone. Maybe someone stole it."

Cressida was careless with cell phones. She'd lost at least two, both gifts from Zeno who wanted his daughters to be within calling-range, if he required them. And he wanted his daughters to have cell phones in case of emergency.

Was this an emergency? Arlette didn't want to think so.

She returned to Cressida's room—walking more slowly now, as if she were suddenly very tired.

No one. An empty room.

And now she saw how neatly—how *tightly*—books were inserted into the bookcases that, by Cressida's request, Zeno had had a carpenter build into three of the room's walls so that it had looked—almost—as if Cressida were imprisoned by books.

Some were children's books, outsized, with colorful covers. Cressida had loved these books of her early childhood, that had helped her to read at a very young age.

And there were Cressida's notebooks—also large, from an art-supply store in Carthage—in which, as a brightly imaginative young child, she'd drawn fantastical stories with Crayolas of every hue.

Initially, Cressida hadn't objected when her parents showed her drawings to relatives, friends and neighbors who were impressed by them—or more than impressed, astonished at the little girl's "artistic talent"—but then, abruptly at about age nine Cressida became self-conscious, and refused to allow Zeno to boast about her as he'd liked to do.

It had been years since Cressida's brightly colored fantastical-animal drawings had been tacked to a wall of her room. Arlette missed these, that revealed a childish whimsy and playfulness not always evident in the precocious little girl with whom she lived—who called her, with a curious stiffness of her mouth, as if the word were utterly incomprehensible to her—"Mom."

(No problem with Cressida saying "Daddy"—"Dad-*dy*"—with a radiant smile.)

For the past several years there had been, on Cressida's wall, pen-and-ink drawings on stiff white construction paper in the mode of the twentieth-century Dutch artist M. C. Escher who'd been one of Cressida's abiding passions in high school. These drawings Arlette tried to admire—they were elaborate, ingenious, finely drawn, resembling more visual riddles than works of art meant to engage a viewer. The largest and most ambitious, titled *Descending and Ascending,* was mounted on cardboard, measuring about three feet by three feet: an appropriation of Escher's famous lithograph *Ascending and Descending* in which monk-like figures ascended and descended never-ending staircases in a surreal structure in which there appeared to be several sources of gravity. Cressida's drawing was of a subtly distorted family house with walls stripped away, revealing many more staircases than there were in the house, at unnatural—"orthogonal"—angles to one another; on these staircases, human figures walked "up" even as other human figures walked "down" on the underside of the same steps.

Gazing at the pen-and-ink drawing, you became disoriented—dizzy. For what was *up* was also *down,* simultaneously.

Cressida had worked at her Escher-drawings obsessively, for at least a year, at the age of sixteen. Mysteriously she'd said that M. C. Escher had held up a mirror to her soul.

The figures in *Descending and Ascending* were both valiant and pathetic. Earnestly they walked "up"—earnestly they walked "down." They appeared to be oblivious of one another, stepping on reverse steps. Cressida's variant of the Escher drawing was more realistic than the original—the structure containing the inverted staircases was recognizable as the Mayfields' sprawling old Colonial house, furniture and wall hangings were recognizable, and the figures were clearly the Mayfields—tall sturdy shock-haired Daddy, Mom with a placid smiling vacuous face, gorgeous Juliet with exaggerated eyes and lips and inky-frizzy-haired Cressida a fierce-frowning child with arms and legs like sticks, half the height of the other figures, a gnome in their midst.

The Mayfield figures were repeated several times, with a comical effect; earnestness, repeated, suggests idiocy. Arlette never looked at *Descending and Ascending* and Cressida's other Escher-drawings on the wall without a little shudder of apprehension.

It was easier for Cressida to mock than to admire. Easier for Cressida to detach herself from others, than to attempt to attach herself.

For she'd been hurt, Arlette had to suppose. In ninth grade when Cressida had volunteered to teach in a program called Math Literacy—(in fact, this program had been initiated by Zeno's mayoral administration in the face of state budget cuts to education)—and after several enthusiastic weekly sessions with middle-school students from "deprived" backgrounds she'd returned home saying with a shamefaced little frown that she wasn't going back.

Zeno had asked why. Arlette had asked why.

"It was a stupid idea. That's why."

Zeno had been surprised and disappointed with Cressida when she refused to explain why she was quitting the program. But Arlette knew there had to be a particular reason and that this reason had to do with her daughter's pride.

Arlette recalled that something unfortunate had happened in high school, too, related to Cressida's Escher-fixation. But she'd never known the details.

On Cressida's desk, which consisted of a wide, smooth-sanded plank and aluminum drawers, put together by Cressida herself, was a laptop (closed), a notebook (closed), small stacks of books and papers. All were neatly arranged as if with a ruler.

Arlette rarely entered her younger daughter's room except if Cressida was inside, and expressly invited her. She dreaded the accusation of *snooping*.

It was 4:36 A.M. Too soon after her last attempt to call Cressida's cell phone for Arlette to call her again.

Instead, she went to Juliet's room which was next-door.

"Mom?"—Juliet sat up in bed, startled.

"Oh, honey—I'm sorry to wake you . . ."

"No, I've been awake. Is something wrong?"

"Cressida isn't home."

"Cressida isn't home!"

It was an exclamation of surprise, not alarm. For Cressida had not ever stayed out so late—so far as her family knew.

"She was at Marcy's. She should have been home hours ago."

"I've tried her cell phone. But I haven't called Marcy—I suppose I should."

"What time is it? God."

"I didn't want to disturb them, at such an hour . . ."

Juliet rose from bed, quickly. Since breaking with Brett Kincaid she was often home and in bed early, like a convalescent; but she slept only intermittently, for a few hours, and spent the rest of the night-hours reading, writing emails, surfing the Internet. On her night-stand beside her laptop were several library books—Arlette saw the title *Republic of Fear: The Inside Story of Saddam's Iraq.*

They tried to recall: what had Cressida called out to them, when she'd left the house? Nothing out of the ordinary, each was sure.

"She walked to Marcy's. She must have walked home, then—or . . ."

Arlette's voice trailed off. Now that Juliet had been drawn into her concern for Cressida, she was becoming more anxious.

"Maybe she's staying over with Marcy . . ."

"But—she'd have called us, wouldn't she . . ."

" . . . she'd never stay overnight there, why on earth? Of course she'd have come home."

"But she isn't home."

"Did you look anywhere other than her room? I know it isn't likely, but . . ."

"I didn't want to wake Zeno, you know how excitable he is . . ."

"You called her cell—you said? Should we try again?"

Nighttime cream Juliet wore on her face, on her beautifully soft skin, shone now like oozing oil. Her hair, a fair brown, layered, feathery, was flattened on one side of her head. Between the sisters was an old, unresolved rivalry: the younger's efforts to thwart and undermine the older's efforts to be *good*.

Juliet called her sister from her own cell phone. Again there was no answer.

"I suppose we should call Marcy. But . . ."

"I'd better wake Zeno. He'll know what to do."

Arlette entered the darkened bedroom, where Zeno was sleeping. She shook his shoulder, gently. "Zeno? I'm sorry to wake you, but—Cressida isn't home."

Zeno's eyelids fluttered open. There was something touching, vulnerable and poignant in Zeno waking from sleep—he put Arlette in mind of a slumbering bear, perilously wakened from a winter doze.

"It's going on five A.M. She hasn't been home all night. I've tried to call her, and I've looked everywhere in the house . . ."

Zeno sat up. Zeno swung his legs out of bed. Zeno rubbed his eyes, ran his fingers through his tufted hair.

"Well—she's nineteen years old. She doesn't have a curfew and she doesn't have to report to us."

"But—she was only just going to Marcy's for dinner. She walked."

Walked. Now that Arlette had said this, for the second time, a chill came over her.

" . . . she was walking, at night, alone . . . Maybe someone . . ."

"Don't catastrophize, Lettie. Please."

"But—she was alone. I think she must have been alone. We'd better call Marcy."

Zeno rose from bed with surprising agility. In boxer shorts he wore as pajamas, bristly-haired, flabby in the torso and midriff, he padded barefoot to the bureau, to snatch up his cell phone.

"We've tried to call her, Zeno. Juliet and me . . ."

Zeno paid her no heed. He made the call, listened intently, broke the connection and called immediately again.

"She doesn't answer. Maybe she's lost the phone. I'm just so terribly worried, if she was walking back home . . . It's Saturday night, someone might have been driving by . . ."

"I said, Lettie, please—don't catastrophize. That isn't helpful."

Zeno spoke sharply, irritably. He was stepping into a pair of rumpled khaki shorts he'd thrown onto a chair earlier that day.

In Zeno, emotion was justified: in others in his family, it was apt to be excessive. Particularly, Zeno countered his wife's occasional alarm by classifying it as *catastrophizing, hysterical.*

Downstairs, the lighted kitchen awaited them like a stage set. Zeno looked up the Meyers' number in the directory and called it as Arlette and Juliet stood by.

"Hello? Marcy? This is Zeno—Cressida's father. Sorry to bother you at this hour, but . . ."

Arlette listened eagerly and with mounting dread.

Zeno questioned Marcy for several minutes. Before he hung up, Arlette asked to speak to her. There was little that Arlette could add to what Zeno had said but she needed to hear Marcy's voice, hoping to be reassured by Marcy's voice; her daughter's friend was a sturdy freckle-faced girl enrolled in the nursing school at Plattsburgh, long a fixture in Cressida's life though no longer the close friend she'd been a few years previously.

But Marcy could only repeat that at about 10:30 P.M.—after they'd had dinner with her mother and her (elderly, ailing) grandmother—and watched a DVD—Cressida had left to return home as she'd planned, on foot.

"I offered to drive her, but Cressida said no. I did think that I should drive her because it was late, and she was alone, but—you know Cressida. How stubborn she can be . . ."

"Do you have any idea where else she might have gone? After visiting with you?"

"No, Mrs. Mayfield. I guess I don't."

Mrs. Mayfield. As if Marcy were a high school student, still.

"Did she mention anyone to you? Did she call anyone?"

"I don't think so . . ."

"You're sure she didn't call anyone, on her cell phone?"

"Well, I—I don't think so. I mean—I know Cressida pretty well, Mrs. Mayfield—who'd she call? If it wasn't one of you?"

"But where on earth could she be, at almost five A.M.!"

Arlette spoke sharply. She was angry with Marcy Meyer for allowing her daughter to walk home on a Saturday night: though the distance was only a few blocks, part of the walk would have been on North Fork Street, which was well traveled after dark, near an intersection with a state highway; and she was angry with Marcy Meyer for protesting, in an aggrieved child's voice *Who'd she call, if it wasn't one of you?*

THE RAPIDLY SHRINKING REMNANT of the night-before-dawn in the Mayfields' house had acquired an air of desperation.

Now dressed, hastily and carelessly, Zeno and Arlette drove in Zeno's Land Rover to the Meyers' house on Fremont Street, a half-mile away.

Freemont was a hillside street, narrow and poorly paved; houses here were crowded together virtually like row houses, of aged brick and loosened mortar. Arlette had remembered being concerned, when Cressida and Marcy Meyer first became friends, in grade school, that her outspoken and often heedless daughter might say something unintentionally wounding about the size of the Meyers' house, or the attractiveness of its interior; she'd been surprised enough at the blunt, frank, teasing-taunting way in which Cressida spoke to Marcy, who was a reticent, stoic girl lacking Cressida's quick wit and any instinct to defend herself or tease Cressida in turn. Cressida had drawn comic strips in which a short dark-frizzy-haired girl with a dour face and a tall stocky freckled girl with a cheery face had comical adventures in school—these had seemed innocent enough, meant to amuse and not ridicule.

Once, Arlette had reprimanded Cressida for saying something

rudely witty to Marcy, while Arlette was driving the girls to an event at their school, and Marcy said, laughing, "It's OK, Mrs. Mayfield. Cressie can't help it."

As if her daughter were a scorpion, or a viper—*Can't help it.*

Yet it had been touching, the girl called Cressida "Cressie." And Cressida hadn't objected.

At the Meyers' house, Zeno wanted to go inside and speak with Marcy and her mother; Arlette begged him not to.

"They won't know anything more than Marcy has told us. It isn't seven A.M. You'll just upset them. Please, Zeno."

Slowly Zeno drove along Fremont Street, glancing from side to side at the facades of houses. All seemed blind, impassive at this early hour of the morning; many shades were drawn.

At the foot of Fremont, Zeno turned the Land Rover around in a driveway and drove slowly back uphill. Passing the Meyers' house, he was now retracing the probable route Cressida had taken, walking home.

Both Zeno and Arlette were staring hard. How like a film this was, a documentary! Something had happened, but—in which house? And what had happened?

House after house of no particular distinction except they were houses Cressida had passed, on her way to Marcy Meyer's, and on her way from Marcy Meyer's, the night before. There, at a corner, a landmark lightning-scorched oak tree, at the intersection with North Fork; a block farther, at Cumberland Avenue, at the ridge of the hill, the large impressive red-brick Episcopal church and the churchyard beside and behind it. Both the church and the churchyard were "historical landmarks" dating to the 1780s.

Cressida would have passed by the church, and the churchyard. On which side of the street would she have walked?—Arlette wondered.

Zeno made a sound—grunt, half-sob—mutter—as he braked the Land Rover and without explanation climbed out.

Zeno entered the churchyard, walking quickly. He was a tall

disheveled man with a stubbly chin who carried himself with an aggressive sort of confidence. He'd thrown on a soiled T-shirt and khaki shorts and on his sockless feet were grubby running shoes. By the time Arlette hurried to join him he'd made his way to the end of the first row of aged markers, worn so thin by weather and time that the names and dates of the dead were unreadable.

Beyond the churchyard was a no-man's-land of underbrush and trees, owned by the township.

The churchyard smelled of mown grass, not fresh, slightly rotted, sour. The air was muggy and dense, in unpredictable places, with gnats.

"Zeno, what are you looking for? Oh, Zeno."

Arlette was frightened now. Zeno remained turned away from her. The most warmly gregarious of men, the most sociable of human beings, yet Zeno Mayfield was remote at times, and even hostile; if you touched him, he might throw off your hand. He prided himself as a man among men—a man who knew much that happened in the world, in Carthage and vicinity, that a woman like Arlette didn't know; much that never made its way into print or onto TV. He was looking now, in a methodical way that horrified Arlette, for the body of their daughter—could that be possible?—in the tall grasses at the edge of the cemetery; behind larger grave markers; behind a storage shed where there was an untidy pile of grass cuttings, tree debris, and discarded desiccated flowers. Horribly, with a clinical sort of curiosity, Zeno stooped to peer inside, or beneath, this pile—Arlette had a vision of a girl's broken body, her arms outstretched among the broken tree limbs.

"Zeno, come back! Zeno, come home. Maybe Cressida is home now."

Zeno ignored her. Possibly, Zeno didn't hear her.

Arlette waited in the Land Rover for Zeno to return to her. She started the ignition, and turned on the radio. Waiting for the 7 A.M. news.

"SHE'S SOMEWHERE, OBVIOUSLY. We just don't know where."

And, as if Arlette had been contesting this fact: "She's nineteen.

She's an adult. She doesn't have a curfew in this house and she doesn't have to report to *us*."

While Zeno and Arlette made calls on the land phone, Juliet made calls on her cell phone. Initially to relatives, whom it didn't seem terribly rude to awaken at such an early hour with queries about Cressida; then, after 7:30 A.M., to neighbors, friends—including even girls in Cressida's class whom Cressida probably hadn't seen since graduation thirteen months before.

(Juliet said: "Cressida will be furious if she finds out. She will think we've *betrayed her*." Arlette said: "Cressida doesn't have to know. We can always call back and tell them—not to tell her.")

Juliet had a vast circle of friends, both female and male, and she began to call them—on the phone her voice was warmly friendly and betrayed no sign of worry or anxiety; she didn't want to alarm anyone needlessly, and she had a fear of initiating a firestorm of gossip. She took her cell phone outside, standing on the front walk as she made calls; peering out at Cumberland Avenue, watching for Cressida to come home. Afterward she would say *I was so certain. I could not have been more certain if Jesus Himself had promised me, Cressida was on her way home.*

One of the calls Juliet made was to a friend named Caroline Skolnik who was to have been a bridesmaid in Juliet's wedding. And Juliet told Caroline that her sister Cressida hadn't come home the night before, and they were worried about her, and Juliet was wondering if Caroline knew anything, or had any ideas; and to Juliet's astonishment Caroline said hesitantly she'd seen Cressida the night before, or someone who looked very much like Cressida, at the Roebuck Inn at Wolf's Head Lake.

Juliet was so astonished, she nearly dropped her cell phone.

Cressida at the Roebuck Inn? At Wolf's Head Lake?

Caroline said that she'd been there with her fiancé Artie Petko and another couple but they hadn't stayed long. The Roebuck Inn had used to be a nice place but lately bikers had been taking it over on weekends—Adirondack Hells Angels. There was a rock band comprised of local kids people liked, but the music was deafening, and the place was jammed—"Just too much happening."

Inside the tavern, there'd been a gang of guys they knew and a few girls in several booths. The air had been thick with smoke. Caroline was surprised to see Brett there—"He wasn't with any girl, just with his friends," Caroline said quickly, "but there were girls kind of hanging out with them. Brett was looking—he wasn't looking—maybe it was the light in the place, but Brett was looking—all right. The surgery he's had—I think it has helped a lot. And he had dark glasses on. And—anyway—there came Cressida—I think it was Cressida—just out of nowhere we happened to see her, and she didn't see us—she seemed to have just come into the taproom, alone—in all that crowd, and having to push her way through—she's so small—I don't think there was anyone with her, unless maybe she'd come with someone, a couple—it wasn't clear who was with who. Cressida was wearing those black jeans she always wears, and a black T-shirt, and what looked like a little striped cotton sweater; it was a surprise to see her, Artie and I both thought so, Artie said he'd never seen your sister in anyplace like the Roebuck, not ever. He knows your dad, he was saying, 'Is that Zeno Mayfield's daughter? The one that's so smart?' and I said, 'God, I hope not. What's she doing *here*?' Brett was in a booth with Rod Halifax, and Jimmy Weisbeck, and that asshole Duane Stumpf, and they were pretty drunk; and there was Cressida, talking with Brett, or trying to talk with Brett; but things got so crowded, and kind of out of control, so we decided to leave. So I don't actually know—I mean, I don't know for sure—if it was your sister, Juliet. But I think it had to be, there's nobody quite like Cressida."

Juliet asked what time this had been.

Caroline said about 11:30 P.M. Because they'd left and gone to the Echo Lake Tavern and stayed there for about forty minutes and were home by 1 A.M.

"Oh God, Juliet—you're saying Cressida hasn't come home? She isn't home? You don't know where she is? I'm so sorry we didn't go over to talk to her—maybe she needed a ride home—maybe she got stranded there. But we thought, well—she must've come with some-one. And there was Brett, and she knows him, and he knows her—so, we thought, maybe . . ."

Slowly Juliet entered the house. Arlette saw her just inside the doorway. In her face was a strange, stricken expression, as if some-thing too large for her skull had been forced inside it.

"What is it, Juliet? Have you heard—something?"

"Yes. I think so. I think I've heard—something."

FOLLOWING THIS, things happened swiftly.

Zeno called Brett Kincaid's cell phone number—no answer.

Zeno called a number listed in the Carthage directory for *Kincaid, E.*—no answer.

Zeno climbed into his Land Rover and drove to Ethel Kincaid's house on Potsdam Street, another hillside street beyond Fremont: a two-storey wood frame with a peeling-beige facade, set close to the curb, where Ethel Kincaid in a soiled kimono answered the door to his repeated knocking with a look of alarmed astonishment.

"Is he home? Where is he?"

Fumbling at the front of the kimono, which shone with a cheap lurid light as if fluorescent, Ethel peered at Zeno cautiously.

"I—don't know . . . I guess n-not, his Jeep isn't in the driveway . . ."

Between Zeno Mayfield and Ethel Kincaid there was a layered sort of history—vague, vaguely resentful (on Ethel's part: for Zeno Mayfield, when he'd been mayor of Carthage and nominally Ethel Kincaid's boss, had not ever seemed to remember her name when he encountered her) and vaguely guilty (on Zeno's part: for he un-derstood that he'd snubbed this plain fierce-glaring woman whom life had mysteriously disappointed). And now, the breakup of Zeno's daughter and Ethel's son lay between them like wreckage.

"Do you have any idea where Brett is?"

"N-No . . ."

"Do you know where he went last night?"

"No . . ."

"Or with who?"

Ethel Kincaid regarded Zeno, his disheveled clothing, his metallic-stubbly jaws and swampy eyes that were both pleading and threatening, with a defiant sort of alarm. She had the just discernibly battered look of a woman well versed in the wayward emotions of men and in the need to position herself out of the range of a man's sudden lunging grasp.

"I'm afraid I don't know, Mr. Mayfield. Brett's friends don't come to the house, he goes to them. I think he goes to them."

Mr. Mayfield was uttered with a pointless sort of spite. Surely they were social equals, or had been, when Zeno's daughter had become engaged to Ethel's son.

Zeno remembered Arlette remarking that Brett's mother was *so unfriendly.* Even Juliet who rarely spoke of others in a critical manner murmured of her fiancé's mother *She is not naturally warmhearted or easy to get to know. But—we will try!*

Poor Juliet had tried, and failed.

Arlette had tried, and failed.

"Ethel, I'm sorry to disturb you at such an early hour. I tried to call, but there was no answer. It's crucial that I speak with Brett—or at least know where I can find him. This isn't about Juliet, incidentally—it involves my daughter Cressida." Zeno was making it a point to speak slowly and clearly and without any suggestion of the pent-up fury he felt for this unhelpful woman who'd taken a step back from him, clutching at the front of her rumpled kimono as if fearing he might snatch it open. "We've been told that they were together for a while last night—at the Roebuck Inn. And Cressida hasn't come home all night, and we don't know where she is. And we think—your son might know."

Ethel Kincaid was shaking her head. A tangle of graying dirty-blond hair, falling to her shoulders, uncombed. A smell as of dried sweat and talcum powder wafting from her soft loose fleshy body inside her clothing.

Now a look of apprehension came into her face. And cunning.

Ethel shook her head emphatically *no*—"I don't know anything that my son does."

"Could I see his room, please?"

"His room? You want to see his—room? In this house?"

"Yes. Please."

"But—why?"

Zeno had no idea why. The impulse had come to him, desperately; he could not retreat without attempting something.

Ethel was looking confused now. She was a woman in her mid-fifties whom life had used negligently—her skin was sallow, her eye-lashes and eyebrows so scanty as to be near-invisible, her mouth was a sullen smudge. She took another step back into the dimly lighted hall of the house as if the glare in Zeno Mayfield's face was such, she shrank from it. Stammering she said he couldn't come inside, that wasn't a good idea, and she had to say good-bye to him now, she had to close the door now, she could not speak to him any longer.

"Ethel—wait! Just let me see Brett's room. Maybe—there will be something there, that will help me . . ."

"No. That isn't a good idea. I'm going to close the door now."

"Ethel, please. I'm sure there is some explanation for this, but—at the moment—Arlette and I are terribly worried. And we've been told that Brett was seen with her, last night. It can't be a coincidence, your son and my daughter . . ."

"If you don't have a warrant, Mr. Mayfield, I don't have to let you in."

"A warrant? I'm not a police officer, Ethel. Don't be ridiculous. I'm not even a city official any longer. I just want to see Brett's room, just for a minute. How can you possibly object to that?"

"No. I can't. Brett wouldn't want that—he hates all of you."

Ethel Kincaid was about to shut the door in Zeno's face but he pressed the palm of his hand against it, holding it open. A pulse beat wildly in his forehead. He could not believe what Ethel Kincaid had so heedlessly uttered but he would never forget it.

Hates all of you. You.

"If your son has hurt my daughter—my daughter Cressida—if anything has happened to Cressida—I will kill him."

Ethel Kincaid threw her weight against the door, to shut it. And Zeno released the door.

He was stunned. He could not think clearly. He knew, he had better return to the Land Rover and drive home before he did something irrevocable like pounding violently on the God-damned door that had been shut rudely in his face.

Like breaking into the Kincaid house.

The spiteful woman would call 911, he knew. Give her the slightest pretext, she would fuck up Zeno Mayfield and his family all she could.

He returned to the Land Rover, that had been parked crookedly at the curb. He saw that a seat belt trailed out from the driver's seat, like something broken, discarded. A swift vision came to him of the pile of debris in the Episcopal churchyard. Driving away from the Kincaid house without a backward glance he thought *Maybe she didn't hear me. Maybe she won't remember.*

IN THE DRIVEWAY Arlette stood waiting for Zeno to return.

Waiting to see if he was bringing their daughter home with him.

And so in her face, as Zeno climbed out of the Land Rover, he saw the disappointment.

"She wasn't there?"

"No."

"Did you talk to—Ethel? Was Brett there?"

"Ethel was no help. Brett wasn't there."

Arlette hurried to keep up with Zeno, who was headed into the house.

Suddenly it had become 8:20 A.M. So swiftly, the night had passed into dawn and now into a sunny and shimmering-hot morning.

The privacy of the night. The exposure of the morning.

Arlette asked, in a shaky voice, "Do you think that Cressida and

Brett might have gone away together?—or, he took her somewhere? To hurt her? To embarrass us? Zeno?"

"Cressida is nineteen. She's an adult. If she chooses to stay away overnight, that's her prerogative."

Zeno spoke harshly, ironically. He had not the slightest faith in what he was saying but he believed these words must be reiterated.

Arlette clutched at his arm. Arlette's fingers dug into his arm.

"But—if she didn't choose? If someone has hurt her? Taken her? We have to help our daughter, Zeno. She has no one but us."

Unspoken between them was the thought *She isn't really an adult. She is a child. For all her pose of maturity, a child.*

There was no choice now, no postponing the call, even as Zeno stood in the driveway staring with eyes that felt seared, ravaged with such futile staring in the direction of Cumberland Avenue as into an abyss out of which at any moment—(feasibly! Not illogically and not impossibly!—for as a young aggressive attorney Zeno Mayfield had often conjured the attractive possibilities of alternate universes in which alternate narratives revealed his [guilty] clients to be "innocent" of the charges that had been brought against them)—his daughter Cressida might appear; no choice, he knew, except to contact law enforcement; calling the Beechum County Sheriff's Department and asking to speak to Hal Pitney who was a lieutenant on the force, not a close friend of Zeno Mayfield's but an old friend from Zeno's political days and, he wanted to think, a reliable friend. With forced calmness he told Hal that he knew, it might seem premature to be reporting his daughter missing, since Cressida was nineteen, and not a child, but the circumstances seemed to warrant it: she'd been gone overnight, she was definitely not a person to behave irresponsibly; they had learned that she'd been seen at the Roebuck Inn the previous night, alone; then, later, in the company of several men of whom one was Brett Kincaid. (Pitney surely knew of Corporal Brett Kincaid, from stories in the local media.) Zeno said they'd called Cressida's cell phone repeatedly and they'd called virtually everyone in Carthage who knew her, or might know of her—she seemed to have vanished.

Zeno said he'd gone to Kincaid's house. And Kincaid was missing, too.

Zeno spoke rapidly and, he hoped, persuasively. He was not prepared for Hal Pitney telling him that, though they knew nothing about his daughter, it had happened that Brett Kincaid had been brought into headquarters that morning, less than an hour before. He'd been reported by hikers seemingly incapacitated in his Jeep Wrangler, that appeared to have skidded partway off the Sandhill Road, just inside the Nautauga Preserve. There'd been no one with him but there'd been "bloody scratch or bite marks" on his face and bloodstains in the front seat of his vehicle; he'd been "agitated" and "belligerent" and tried to fight the deputy who restrained him, cuffed him and brought him into headquarters.

"He isn't cooperating. He's pretty much out of it. Hungover, and sick to his stomach, and scared. He didn't seem to know where he was, or why, or if anyone, like a girl, had been with him. We've sent two deputies back to investigate the scene, and his Jeep. We're questioning him now. You'd better come to headquarters, Zeno. You and your wife. And bring photographs of your daughter—the more recent, the better."

This news was so utterly unexpected, Zeno had to stagger into the house to fumble for a chair, a kitchen chair, and sit down, heavily; he felt as if he'd been kicked in the gut, the air slammed out of him. So weak, so frightened, he was scarcely able to hear Arlette pleading with him—"Zeno, what is it? Have they found her? Is she—alive? Zeno?"

→ ←

Time moved now in zigzag leaps.

Once Zeno made this call. Once what had been a private concern became irreversibly public.

Once their daughter was publicly designated *missing*.

Once they'd brought photographs of the *missing daughter* to law enforcement officers, to be shared with the media, broadcast over TV and on the Internet and printed in newspapers.

Once they'd described her. Once they'd described her in all ways they believed to be crucial to finding her.

Then, time passed with dazzling swiftness even as, perversely, time passed with excruciating slowness.

Swift because too much was crammed into too small a space. *Swift* like a nightmare film run at a high speed for a cruel-comic effect.

Slow because for all that was happening very little that was crucial seemed to be happening.

Slow because despite the many calls they were to receive in the course of a day, two days, several days, a week, the call they awaited, that Cressida had been found, did not come.

Alive and well. We have found your daughter—alive and well.

This call, so desperately wished-for, did not come.

(AND THEY KNEW, each hour that their daughter was missing there was more likelihood that she'd been injured, or worse.)

(Each hour that Brett Kincaid refused to cooperate, or was unable to cooperate, there was more likelihood that she'd been injured, or worse, and less likelihood that she would be found.)

PROVIDING LAW ENFORCEMENT OFFICERS with photographs of Cressida.

Spreading a half-dozen photos across a table.

Startling to see their daughter gazing up at them.

Wariness in Cressida's eyes, thin-lashed dark eyes gleaming with irony and the faintest tincture of resentment as if she'd known that strangers would be staring at her, memorizing her face, without her permission.

In none of the photos was Cressida smiling. Not since childhood had Cressida been recorded smiling.

Arlette had wanted to explain—*Our daughter was not an unhappy*

person. But she refused to smile when she was photographed. Not even in her
high school yearbook is she pictured smiling. And this is because . . .

But Arlette could not utter these words. Her throat closed, she
could not.

. . . she'd said, you know that one of the pictures will be for the obituary.
So you can't ever smile. You'd be a fool to smile at your own funeral.

IN THE LATE MORNING of Sunday, July 10, 2005, the search for the
missing girl in the Nautauga Preserve began and continued until
searchers were obliged to leave the park, at dusk; it was continued
the next morning, until dusk; and the next morning, until dusk.

The search differed considerably from more routine searches in
the vast Preserve for lost hikers, campers, mountain climbers, num-
bering quite a few in the course of an average summer: for it was
believed that this *missing girl* might have been assaulted—raped,
killed?—by a man.

The search was complicated by the possibility that the *missing girl*
had been dumped into the Nautauga River, and her body carried far
downstream.

Yet, morale was high. Especially among those volunteer searchers
who knew Cressida Mayfield and the (younger, female) park rangers
who were determined to find the *girl, missing* in their own territory.

It had been eleven years since anyone had been lost in the Preserve and had not been found alive; in that case, involving a young
boy believed to have run away from home, in the winter, the boy's
body wasn't found until the following spring.

In the course of the search a miscellany of castaway items was
found—rotted and desiccated articles of clothing including underwear (both men's and women's); single gloves, mittens; single shoes,
hiking boots, and belts; mangled hats; plastic bottles, cans, and Styrofoam; maps of the Preserve, hiking books, bird books, children's
toys, a single headless doll terrifying to the volunteer searcher who
discovered it believing it to be, for a moment, a headless human
infant.

Also, scattered bones determined to be the bones of animals or birds.

Here and there, a dead, rotting animal carcass like the partially devoured doe discovered by Zeno Mayfield, that seemed to have caused the father of the *missing girl* to collapse in a paroxysm of exhaustion and despair.

God if I could trade my life for hers. If that were possible . . .

SO MANY VEHICLES parked in the Mayfields' driveway, and along Cumberland Avenue, if the *missing girl* had arrived home she'd have thought it was a festive occasion.

Muttering out of the side of her mouth, a droll remark her mother could almost hear—*What's the big deal? Juliet's getting engaged—again?*

Bright TV camera lights in the living room as Arlette and Zeno Mayfield of Cumberland Avenue, Carthage, parents of the *missing girl,* were being interviewed by local TV personality Evvie Estes for WCTG-TV 6 P.M. news.

Arlette hadn't been able to speak. Zeno had done all the talking.

Of course, Zeno Mayfield was very good at *talking.*

His voice had quavered only slightly. His eyes pouched in tiredness were damp and seemed to have no clear focus.

But he'd showered, and shaved, and put on clean pressed clothes, and his thick-tufted hair had been brushed properly. He knew to speak to the TV audience by way of the TV interviewer and he knew not to be nettled or discomfited by certain of the woman's questions.

Arlette gripped in her right fist a wadded tissue. Her tongue had gone numb. Her eyes were fixed to the rapacious eyes of the heavily made-up Evvie Estes. Her terror was, her nose would begin to run, her eyes would leak tears, unsparingly illuminated in the bright TV lights.

Our daughter. Our Cressida. If anyone has any information leading to . . .

Then, there came the surprise of the ten-thousand-dollar reward.

Not one of the law enforcement officers who'd been interviewing the Mayfields had known this was coming. Judging by her confusion on camera, Arlette had not known this was coming. Zeno spoke in an impassioned voice of a ten-thousand-dollar reward for information leading to *the recovery of—the return of—our daughter Cressida.*

SURPRISING NEWS—*a reward.*
   Not a great idea.
   Many more calls will come in.
   Many more calls will come in.

FOR INSTANCE, from "witnesses" who'd sighted the *missing girl,* they were sure: in and near and not-so-near the Nautauga Preserve.

As far north as Massena, New York. As far south as Binghamton.

In a 7-Eleven. Hitchhiking. In the passenger seat of a van headed south on I-80.

Wearing a baseball cap pulled low on her forehead.

Wearing sunglasses.

Coming out of the Onondaga CineMax on Route 33, with a bearded man—the movie was The War of the Worlds *with Tom Cruise.*

As far north as Massena, New York. As far south as Binghamton.

Dozens of calls. In time, hundreds.

Most valuable were calls from "witnesses" claiming to have been at the Roebuck Inn on the night of Saturday, July 9.

Guys who knew Corporal Kincaid by sight. Women who'd seen a girl they suspected to be, or believed to be, or knew to be Cressida Mayfield, at the inn: in the crowded taproom, on the deck overlooking the lake, in the women's room "sick to her stomach"—"splashing water on her face."

One of the bartenders, who knew Kincaid and his friends Halifax, Weisbeck, Stumpf—"The girl came in from somewhere. Like she was alone, and kind of scared-looking. In jeans, a black T-shirt, and some kind of top, or sweater. Not the kind of girl who turns up at the Roebuck on Saturday night. Maybe she was with Kincaid, or just ran into him. I think they left together. Or—all of them left together. It was a pretty loud scene, with the band on the deck. But definitely, it wasn't any bikers she was with—this girl 'Cressida.' Hey—if other people call about Kincaid, and it turns out it's him, like if the girl is hurt—do we split the ten thousand dollars? What's the deal?"

And there was an ex-girlfriend of Rod Halifax, named Natalie Cantor, claiming to have been a "friend" of Juliet Mayfield's in high school, who called Zeno Mayfield's office phone to tell him in an incensed, just perceptibly slurred voice that whatever happened to his daughter, Rod and his buddies would know—"Once, the bastard got me drunk, slipped some drug into a drink, he'd been wanting to break up with me and was acting really nasty trying to pimp me to his disgusting buddies—Jimmy Weisbeck, that asshole Stumpf—out in his pickup. Right out in the parking lot, the son of a bitch. They're all mean drunks. I don't know Kincaid, but I know Juliet. I know your daughter, she's an angel. I'm not joking, she's an angel. Juliet Mayfield is an angel. I don't know the other one—'Cress'da.' I never saw 'Cress'da.' Anything you want to know about that poor girl, Rod Halifax will know. I wasn't the first girl he got tired of, and treated like shit. It was not 'consensual'—it was God-damn fucking *rape*. And I was sick afterward, I mean—infected. So, ask *him*. Arrest him, and ask *him*. Anything that's happened to that poor girl, like if they raped her, and strangled her, and dumped her body in the lake—you can be sure Rod Halifax was responsible."

ZIGZAG TIME ENTERED her head: hours moved slow as sludge while days flew past on drunken-careening wings.

Until she could think *A week. This Sunday is a week. And she hasn't been found* and it would have the ring of tentative good news: *She hasn't been found in some terrible place.*

He would never forgive himself, she knew.

Though it could not be his fault. Yet.

Arlette had long gotten over being jealous—at any rate, showing her jealousy—of her daughters. Particularly Zeno adored Juliet but he'd also been weak-minded about Cressida, the "difficult" daughter—the one whom it was a challenge to love.

At the very start, the little girls had adored their mother. As babies, their young mother was all to them. Which is only natural of course.

But quickly then, Daddy had stolen their hearts. Big burly bright-faced Daddy who was so funny, and so unpredictable—Daddy who loved to subvert Mommy's dictums and upset, as he liked to joke, Mommy's *apple cart*.

As if an orderly household—eating at mealtimes, and properly at a table, with others—walking and not running/rushing on the stairs—keeping your bedroom reasonably clean, and not messing up a bathroom for others—were a silly-Mommy's *apple cart* to be overturned for laughs.

But Mommy knew to laugh, when she was laughed-at.

Mommy knew it was love. A kind of love.

Except it hurt sometimes—the father siding with the daughter, in mockery of her.

(Not Juliet of course: Juliet never mocked anyone.)

(Mockery came too easily to Cressida. As if she feared a softer emotion would make her vulnerable.)

Arlette knew: if something terrible had happened to Cressida, Zeno would blame himself. Though there could be no reason, no logical reason, he would blame himself.

Already he was saying to whoever would listen *I wasn't even there, when she left. God!*

In a voice of wonder, self-reproach *Maybe she'd have told me—something. Maybe she'd have wanted to talk.*

COUNTLESS TIMES they'd gone over Saturday evening: when Cressida had left the house, on her way to the Meyers' for dinner.

Casually, you might say indifferently calling out to her mother and her sister in the kitchen—*Bye! See you later.*

Or even, though this was less likely given that Cressida wouldn't have stayed very late at Marcy's—*Don't wake up for me.*

(Had Cressida said that? *Don't wake up for me?*—intentionally or otherwise? *Wake up* not *wait up*. That was Cressida's sort of quirky humor. Suddenly, Arlette wondered if it might mean something.)

(Snatching at straws, this was. Pathetic!)

Certainly it was ridiculous for Zeno to reproach himself with not having been home at that time. As if somehow—(but how?)—he might have foreseen that Cressida wouldn't be returning when she'd planned, and when they'd expected her?

Ridiculous but how like *the father.*

Particularly, *the father of daughters.*

EACH TIME the phone rang!

Several phones in the Mayfield household: the family line, Zeno's cell, Arlette's cell, Juliet's cell.

Always a kick of the heart, fumbling to answer a call.

Deliberately Arlette avoided seeing the caller ID in the hope that the caller would be Cressida.

Or, that the caller would be a stranger, a law enforcement officer, possibly a woman, in Arlette's fantasizing it was a woman, with the good news *Mrs. Mayfield!—we've found your daughter and she wants to talk to you.*

Beyond this, though Arlette listened eagerly, there was—nothing.

As if, in the strain of awaiting the call, and hearing Cressida's voice, she'd forgotten what that voice was.

DRIVING TO THE BANK, fumbling with the radio dial, in a panic to hear the "top of the hour" news—almost colliding with a sanitation truck.

Recovering, and, in the next block, almost colliding with an SUV whose driver tapped his horn irritably at her.

And, in the bank, bright-faced and smiling in the (desperate, transparent) hope of deflecting looks of pity, waiting in line at a teller's window *exactly as she'd have waited if her daughter was not missing.*

This fact confounded her. This fact seemed to mock her.

Wanting to hide. Hide her face. But of course, no.

"Arlette? You are Arlette Mayfield—aren't you? I'm so sorry—really *really* sorry—about your daughter . . . We've told our kids, one is a junior in high school, the other is just in seventh grade, if they hear anything—anything at all—to tell us right away. Kids know so much more than their parents these days. Out at the lake, and in the Preserve, there's all kinds of things going on—under-age drinking is the least of it. All kinds of drugs including 'crystal meth'—kids don't know what they're taking, they're too young to realize how dangerous it is . . . I don't mean that your daughter was with any kind of a drug-crowd, I don't mean that at all—but the Roebuck Inn, that's a place they hang out—there's these Hells Angels bikers who are known drug-dealers—but parents have their heads in the sand, just don't want to acknowledge there's a serious—tragic—problem in Carthage . . ."

And not in the bank parking lot, can't let herself cry. Not with bank customers trailing in and out. And anyone who knew Arlette Mayfield, including now individuals not-known to her who'd seen her on WCTG-TV with her husband Zeno pleading for the return of their daughter, could stare through her car windshield and observe and carry away the tale to all who would listen with thrilled widened eyes *That poor woman! Arlette Mayfield! You know, the mother of the missing girl . . .*

CALLS CONTINUED TO COME to police headquarters.

Though peaking on the second day, Monday, July 11: a record number of calls following the front-page article, with photos, in the *Carthage Post-Journal*. And the notice of the ten-thousand-dollar reward.

Myriad "witnesses" claiming to have sighted Cressida Mayfield—somewhere. Or to have knowledge of what might have happened to her and where she was now.

In some cases, making veiled accusations against people—(neighbors, relatives, ex-husbands)—who might have "kidnapped" or "done something to" Cressida Mayfield.

Zeno had wanted these calls routed through *him*. It was his fear that a valuable call would be overlooked by someone in the sheriff's office.

Detectives explained to Zeno that, where reward money is involved, a flood of calls can be expected, virtually all of them worthless.

Yet, though likely to be worthless, the calls have to be considered— the "leads" have to be investigated.

The Beechum County Sheriff's Department was understaffed. The Carthage PD was helping in the investigation though this department was even smaller.

If kidnapping were suspected, the FBI might be contacted. The New York State Police.

Was offering a reward so publicly a mistake? Zeno didn't want to think so.

"Maybe the mistake is not offering enough. Let's double it— twenty thousand dollars."

"Oh, Zeno—are you sure?"

"Of course I'm sure. We have to do *something*."

"Maybe you should speak with Bud McManus? Or maybe—"

"She's our daughter, not his. Twenty thousand will attract more attention. We have to do *something*."

Arlette thought *But if there is nothing? If we can do nothing?*

There was Zeno on the phone. Defiant Zeno on two phones at once: the family phone, and his cell phone.

"Hello? This is Zeno Mayfield. We've decided to double the reward money to twenty thousand dollars. Yes—right. *Twenty thousand dollars for information leading to the recovery and return of our daughter Cressida Mayfield. Callers will be granted anonymity if they wish.*"

IN CRESSIDA'S ROOM. Drifting upstairs in the large empty-echoing house as if drawn to that room.

Where, if she'd been home, and in the room, Cressida would have been surprised to see her parents and possibly not pleased.

Hey, Dad. Mom. What brings you here?

Not snooping—are you?

"Her bed wasn't slept-in. That was the first thing I saw."

Arlette spoke in a hoarse whisper. They might have been crouched in a mausoleum, the room was so dimly lighted, so stark and still.

In the center of the room Zeno stood, staring. It was quite possible, Arlette thought, that he hadn't entered their daughter's room in years.

Detectives had asked Arlette if anything was "missing" from the room. Arlette didn't think so, but how could Arlette know: their daughter's life was a very private life, only partially and, it sometimes seemed, grudgingly shared with her mother.

Detectives had searched the room, as Arlette and Zeno stood anxiously by. As soon as the detectives were finished with any part of the room—the closet, the old cherrywood chest of drawers Cressida had had since she was six years old—Arlette hurried to reclaim it, and re-establish order.

With latex-gloved hands they'd placed certain articles of clothing in plastic bags. They'd taken a not-very-clean hairbrush, a toothbrush, other intimate items for DNA purposes presumably.

Cressida's laptop. They'd asked permission to open it, to examine it, and the Mayfields had said yes, of course.

Though reluctant even to open the laptop themselves. To peer into their daughter's private life, how intrusive this was! How Cressida would resent it.

The detectives had taken it away with them, and left a receipt.

Almost Arlette thought *I hope they return it before Cressida comes back.*

Almost Arlette thought, unforgivably, *I hope Cressida doesn't come back before they return it.*

Zeno said, falsely hearty: "It's good that you woke up, Lettie. That something woke you. Thank God you came in here when you did."

"Yes. Something woke me . . ."

That sensation of a part of the house missing. A part of her body missing. *Phantom limb.*

Arlette's thought was, seeing the room through Zeno's eyes, that it didn't have the features of a girl's room, as a man might imagine them.

Cressida's clothes were all put away and out of sight—neatly folded in drawers, on shelves, hanging in closets. And her small stubby-looking shoes, neatly paired, on the floor of the closet.

One of the detectives, meaning to be kind, had remarked that his teenaged daughter's room looked nothing like this one.

Zeno had tried to explain, their daughter had never been a *teenager*.

Years ago Cressida had cast away the soft bright colors and fuzzy fabrics of girlhood and replaced them with the stark black-and-white geometrical designs and slick surfaces of M. C. Escher, that so strangely entranced her. She had so little interest in colors—(her jeans were mostly black, her shirts, T-shirts, sweaters)—Arlette could wonder if she saw colors at all; or, seeing, thought them sentimental, softhearted.

Zeno was peering at the labyrinthine *Descending and Ascending* as if he'd never seen it before. As if it might provide a clue to his daughter's disappearance.

Did he recognize himself in the drawing?—Arlette wondered. Or were the miniature humanoid-figures too distorted, caricatured?

Zeno's eye was for the large, blatant, blinding. Zeno had not a shrewd eye for the miniature.

Arlette slid her arm through her husband's. Since Sunday, she was always touching him, holding him. Very still Zeno would stand at such times, not exactly responding but not stiffening either. For he dared not give in to the rawest emotion, she knew. Not quite yet.

"Whatever happened, with Cressida's math teacher, Zeno? Remember? When she was in tenth grade? She never told me . . ."

"'Rickard.' He was her geometry teacher."

Arlette recalled days, it might have been weeks, of veiled exchanges between Zeno and Cressida, about something that had happened, or hadn't happened in the right way, at school. It might have been that Cressida had brought a portfolio of drawings to school—beyond that, Arlette hadn't known.

When she'd asked Cressida what was troubling her, Cressida had told her it was none of her business; when she'd asked Zeno, he'd told her, apologetically, that it was up to Cressida—"If she wants to tell you, she will."

Their alliance was to each other, Arlette thought.

She'd hated them, then. In just that moment.

She'd asked Juliet, out of desperation. But Juliet who wasn't living at home at the time—who was a freshman at the State University at Oneida—had soared so far beyond her tenth-grade sister, she'd had little interest in the sister's emotional crises—"Some teacher who didn't appreciate her enough, I think. You know Cressida!"

Arlette didn't, though. That was the problem.

Zeno said hesitantly, as if even now he were reluctant to violate any confidence of their daughter's, that when Cressida had first become so interested in M. C. Escher she'd created a portfolio of pen-and-ink drawings using numerals and geometrical figures, in imitation of Escher's lithographs.

"This one—*Metamorphoses*"—Zeno indicated one of the pen-and-ink drawings displayed on Cressida's wall—"was the first one I'd seen, I think. I didn't know what the hell to make of it, initially." Arlette examined the drawing: it was smaller than *Descending and Ascending* and seemingly less ambitious: moving from left to right, human figures morphed into mannequins, then geometrical figures; then numerals, then abstract molecular designs; then back to human figures again. As the figures passed through the metamorphoses from left to right their "whiteness" shaded into "darkness"—like negatives; then, as negatives, as they passed through reverse stages of metamorphoses, they became "white" again. And some of the scenes were set on Carthage bridges, with reflections in the water that underwent metamorphoses, too.

"It's based upon an Escher drawing of course. But how skillfully it's executed! I remember looking at it, *Metamorphoses,* following with my eyes the changes in the figures, back and forth . . . It was the first time I realized, I think, that our daughter was so *special.* You can't imagine Juliet doing anything like this."

"Juliet wouldn't want to do anything quite like this."

"Of course. That's my point."

"Cressida's drawings are like riddles. I've always thought it was too bad, her art is so 'difficult.' Remember when she was a little girl, not four years old, she drew such wonderful animals and birds with crayons. Everyone adored them. I'd always thought I might work with her, I'd thought we could create children's books together. But . . ."

"Lettie, come on! Cressida isn't interested in 'children's books'—not now, and not then. Her talent is for something more demanding."

"But she seems to have quit doing art. There's nothing new on the wall here, that I can see."

"She didn't take art courses at St. Lawrence. She said she didn't respect the teachers. She didn't think she could learn anything from them."

How like Cressida! Yet she didn't seem to have made her way otherwise.

Arlette asked what had happened with Mr. Rickard?

From time to time Arlette encountered the rabbity moustached Vance Rickard on the street in Carthage, or at the mall. Though Arlette smiled at him, and would have greeted him warmly, the high school math teacher invariably turned away without seeming to see her, frowning.

"That bastard! He'd seen some of Cressida's drawings in her notebook, and praised her; he said he was an admirer of Escher, too. So Cressida put together a portfolio of her new work and brought it to school to show him, and the son of a bitch wounded her by saying, 'Not bad. Pretty good, in fact. But you must be original. Escher did this first, so why copy him?' Cressida was devastated."

Arlette could well understand, their sensitive daughter would be devastated by such a heartless remark.

Yet, she'd wanted to ask Cressida something like this herself.

"He might have meant well. It was just—thoughtless . . . I'm sorry that Cressida was so upset."

"That was why she did so poorly in geometry that semester. She stayed away from class, she was so ashamed. She'd ended with a barely passing grade."

Arlette remembered: that turbulent season in their daughter's life.

"Cressida came to me and told me what he'd said. She was utterly demolished. She said, 'I can't go back. I hate him. Get him fired, Daddy.' I was furious, too. I made an appointment to speak with Rickard who professed to be totally unaware of what he'd said, or even if he'd said it; he told me that if he'd made such a remark to Cressida it must have been meant playfully. He said he'd been impressed with her drawings and with her work in his class though he worried that she was 'inconsistent'—'too easily discouraged.'"

Arlette thought yes, that is so. But Zeno was still indignant.

"I wouldn't have tried to get the bastard fired, of course. Even if—maybe—I could have. The man was just crude, and thoughtless. Cressida changed her mind, too: 'Maybe we should just forget about it, Daddy. I wish we would. I don't deserve any higher grade than the one I got, really.' But that was ridiculous, she'd certainly have earned an A, if the damned Escher misunderstanding hadn't happened."

Zeno didn't need to add: Cressida's grade-point average would have been considerably higher without a D+ in sophomore math.

For often it happened that Cressida did well in her high school courses through a semester and then, unaccountably, as if to spite her own pretensions of excellence, she failed to complete the course, or failed to study for the final exam, or even to take the final exam. She was often ill—respiratory ailments, nausea, migraine headaches. Her high school record was a zigzag fever chart that culminated in her senior year when, instead of graduating as class valedictorian, as the teachers who admired her observed to her parents, she graduated thirtieth in a class of one hundred sixteen—a dismal record for such a bright girl. Instead of being accepted at Cornell, as she'd hoped, she was fortunate to have been accepted at St. Lawrence University.

Her first year away from home, in the small college town of Canton, Cressida had been homesick, lonely; a girl who'd scorned conventional "clichéd" behavior, yet she'd found herself missing her home, the routine and safety of her home. Still, she hadn't emailed or called her parents often and when Arlette tried to contact her, Cressida was elusive; if Arlette managed to get her to answer her cell phone, Cressida was remote, taciturn.

"Honey, is something wrong? Can you tell me? Please?" Arlette had pleaded, and Cressida had made a sound that was the verbal equivalent of a shrug. "You aren't having trouble with your courses, are you?" Arlette asked, and Cressida said coldly, no. "Then what is it? Can't you tell me?" Arlette asked, and Cressida said, mimicking her, " 'What is'—what?" Arlette had been reading about suicidally depressed undergraduates, and Cressida's reaction worried her. (When she mentioned the subject to Zeno he'd laughed at her. "Lettie! You never fail to catastrophize." When she'd seen a TV documentary on suicide among adolescents, in which the word *epidemic* was used, she dared not mention it to Zeno.)

When she returned home at winter break, and again at spring break, Cressida had been listless and withdrawn; she'd barely made the effort to visit with high school friends like Marcy Meyer who'd had to call Cressida repeatedly, and finally to come to the house to see her. She'd been stricken with fugues of depression, angry melancholy. She'd spent much of her time in her room with the door pointedly shut. While Juliet basked in the happiness of her engagement to Corporal Brett Kincaid, and the Mayfields and their friends spoke of little else except the upcoming wedding, Cressida was detached and indifferent. And when news of Brett's injuries came, she'd said, after a moment of surprise and shock, "Well—Brett is a soldier after all and he was *at war.* You can't always expect to be the one who does the killing."

Fortunately, Cressida hadn't made this remark within Juliet's hearing.

When Brett re-entered their lives, however, badly damaged, initially in a wheelchair, Cressida had been visibly shocked, and subdued; her usual habit of irony was suspended.

To Arlette she said: "Juliet will never marry him now. I predict."

Arlette, annoyed, had told Cressida that she was mistaken. She didn't know her sister, clearly.

"Well, just wait! I predict."

Another time, when Arlette and Cressida happened to be alone together in the house, she'd said suddenly, almost angrily: "What's the point of all this?" and Arlette had said, "The point of all—what?" Cressida had waved her hand irritably, as if brushing away flies. "All this *effort.*"

As if she'd meant the entire world. And its history.

Arlette had gathered, though not directly from Cressida, that college had been a surprise to her. From earliest childhood Cressida had taken for granted her intellectual superiority and, though she'd have ridiculed the very notion, her social status as the daughter of Zeno Mayfield who'd bought for his family a handsome old Colonial on Cumberland Avenue; she'd taken for granted the very air she breathed, in her family's house. But in Canton, amid strangers of whom many belonged to sororities and fraternities, living away from her comfortable home with no one who knew her, loved her, and fretted over her slightest whim or unhappiness, Cressida must have been unmoored: lost.

If she'd made friends, Arlette knew nothing of them. If she went without eating properly, if she stayed up through a night, if she went outdoors lightly dressed in freezing winds; if she was careless about her health, or cut classes; if she perceived herself at the edge of the university world, not by choice or design but helplessly—no one took any special notice, no one *cared.*

Poor Cressida! In Canton, no one even knew her as *the smart one.*

"When she came home from college, and was keeping to herself so much, I should have tried to talk with Cressida more. She isn't a child technically but she has the sensitive feelings of a child. She's never gotten over having done so poorly in high school where she should have been a star."

Zeno spoke broodingly. Zeno's monologues were all of Cressida now where previously, he'd been obsessively concerned with Juliet in the aftermath of the broken engagement.

A ringing phone interrupted. Zeno moved hurriedly to answer it—the Mayfield family line—in the bedroom next to Cressida's.

"HE'S OUT? He's—home? Just like that—*out on bail?*"

Zeno was incredulous to learn that Brett Kincaid had been released from police custody after three days.

Yet more furious to learn that Brett hadn't been released *on bail*—he'd never been arrested, no charges had been filed against him.

Preliminary bloodstain tests were inconclusive: Kincaid's blood type was A positive, and some of the bloodstains in the passenger's seat of his vehicle were type B positive, which was Cressida's blood type; but there was no way to determine if the bloodstains were Cressida's. Several hairs found in the front seat of the vehicle were "almost certainly" a match with Cressida's hair and at least one fingerprint on the passenger's door handle, though smudged, did appear to be a match with a print of Cressida's taken from surfaces in her bedroom.

Bud McManus telephoned to explain why Kincaid had had to be released. Zeno slammed down the receiver.

"Fuckers! 'Not enough evidence' to hold him! That's bullshit."

Brett had been interviewed at length by detectives but had insisted that he didn't remember much of what had happened on Saturday night at the Roebuck Inn, or afterward. He did seem to remember—vaguely—that someone had been with him in his Jeep; he thought he remembered having been drinking with his friends Halifax, Weisbeck, and Stumpf earlier; with the air of one straining to recall a disturbing and chaotic dream he managed to recall that whoever had been with him in his Jeep, a girl, or a woman, had wanted at some point to get out of the vehicle, that had skidded off a road—(he thought)—but he had not thought it was safe for her to climb out of the Jeep and into the wilderness at night and so—maybe—he'd had "some kind of struggle" with her.

Except maybe this wasn't so. Maybe—that had happened some other time.

If it had happened, or whenever it had happened—he was *very sorry*.

His remarks were rambling and incoherent. His behavior was "erratic." Several times he broke down sobbing. Several times he flew into a rage. He attempted to terminate the interview, and had to be forcibly restrained.

In the struggle, the chair he'd been sitting in, in the interview room, skidded out beneath him. He fell, heavily, onto the floor. Like a dead weight he lay for some stunned seconds with his stitched-together face pressed against the floor until police officers hauled him up.

O Christ he was sorry he was very sorry didn't remember what had happened or which one of them but he was sorry and wanted to go home.

Still, he did not want a lawyer. He had not done *anything wrong* and so he did not want a *God-damn lawyer*.

He refused to eat. Or could not eat. He was able to drink Diet Coke in small careful swallows.

What he most wanted he said was to brush his teeth.

Except he didn't have his toothbrush and he had no toothpaste.

His mother Ethel Kincaid arrived at the sheriff's headquarters on Axel Road in a high state of excitation and protest. She'd brought with her a supply of the prescription drugs her son was obliged to take— (at least a dozen different medications, most of them more than once a day), medical reports and U.S. Army discharge documents. She brought her son's Purple Heart and the Iraq campaign medal, in a chamois drawstring bag. In a loud voice she insisted that her son was innocent of any wrongdoing and that he should not be questioned as a "criminal suspect"; he was "unwell"—"under doctors' care"—he'd been discharged with a "medical disability" from the army. He was a "corporal" and a "war hero" who should be treated with respect and he should certainly have a lawyer, a "free" lawyer, even if he seemed to think that he didn't want one.

Mrs. Kincaid was allowed to confer with her exhausted and near-delirious son, who was still wearing the blood- and vomit-stained clothing in which he'd been apprehended early Sunday morning, and to weaken his resolve not to request a lawyer.

For Corporal Kincaid seemed to believe that only a guilty man would need a lawyer.

And if he had a lawyer, he would have admitted guilt.

Mrs. Kincaid succeeded also in convincing detectives that her son should be examined by a doctor; and that he must be released soon, to return to the rehab clinic for his prescribed therapy.

On Sunday afternoon and again on Monday detectives had come to Ethel Kincaid's house to question her about her son and now that she'd come to headquarters, they took the opportunity to question her again. By this time the corporal's mother had settled upon the phrase *My son is innocent of any wrongdoing and this will be proved in a court of law if necessary.*

Returned home, Ethel Kincaid made numerous phone calls on her son's behalf. She contacted Elliot Fisk, the local businessman who'd publicly pledged, since 9/11, to do "all that he humanly could" to help support Beechum County veterans of the Afghanistan and Iraq wars, and convinced him to hire a lawyer for her son: a "real" lawyer and not a public defender.

And so, as it turned out, Corporal Kincaid's lawyer was a Carthage criminal defense lawyer of some esteem named Jake Pedersen. Zeno was incensed, for he and Pedersen had often been allies on county bond-issue campaigns and Pedersen had helped campaign for Zeno when he'd run for mayor. Each man was prominent in the Beechum County Democratic party.

Within an hour of Pedersen's arrival at sheriff's headquarters on Tuesday afternoon, Brett Kincaid was released into the custody of his mother and his attorney and allowed to return home. No charges had been filed against him but he was forbidden to leave Beechum County and "under no circumstances" was he to contact the Mayfields.

He'd become less excitable by this time. He was walking with a cane his mother had brought him. He'd taken his meds, and in a lavatory at headquarters he'd been allowed to change into the fresh clothes his mother had provided. He'd brushed his teeth so vigorously his gums bled.

"Now I want to help. I want to help, too."

They asked him, help how? Help who?

"Look for the girl. 'Cress'da.' I want to help, too."

BY WAY OF his zealous friends in the Sheriff's Department it was reported back to Zeno Mayfield what Brett Kincaid had said.

"God damn him, he'd better not. He'd better not come anywhere
near any of us."

Zeno was trembling with rage, indignation. His hands clenched
and unclenched like the claws of spastic sea-creatures.

On TV news, there was Corporal Kincaid flanked by his fierce-faced
mother Ethel and his lawyer Jake Pedersen hurrying to a vehicle waiting near a rear door of the Beechum County sheriff's headquarters.

Reporters rushed at the young man. Mrs. Kincaid waved them
away with windmill motions of her arms, furious. The corporal
walked unsteadily with a cane, ducked into the backseat of the vehicle driven by Jack Pedersen. He wore dark glasses that obscured half
his face but TV cameras picked up, in lurid and unsparing detail, the
scarred and flushed mannequin-face and the small stitched-looking
mouth.

*Questioned in the disappearance of nineteen-year-old Carthage resident
Cressida Mayfield believed to be last seen late Saturday night in the Wolf's
Head Lake–Nautauga Preserve area.*

On WCTG-TV this video played, and replayed.

It was followed by an edited version of the Sunday evening interview with Mr. and Mrs. Mayfield with an addendum, by bright-eyed
Evvie Estes, that the "Mayfield reward" had been doubled to twenty
thousand dollars.

And by an aerial shot of rescue workers and volunteers searching
the pinewoods of the Nautauga Preserve.

A five-second interview with a husky blond park ranger who said
if Cressida Mayfield is in the Preserve, they would find her for sure!

Another time, photos of Cressida were shown. The high school
yearbook photo which was earnest and unsmiling as if the plain-

featured young girl was staring into the viewer's eyes with an expression of subtle contempt.

"So far, there has been no trace reported of the missing girl. If anyone believes that he or she has information to share about the whereabouts of Cressida Mayfield, the number to call is . . . And if any caller wishes anonymity, that will be granted."

"I HAVE TO SEE HIM. To speak with him. I promise—I won't become emotional."

Zeno had been warned against attempting to see Brett Kincaid. He'd been warned against returning to Ethel Kincaid's house.

Outrageously, Ethel had reported him to Carthage police claiming that Zeno had tried to convince her that he had a "warrant" to search her son's room and he'd "made threats and threatening gestures" against her when she refused to let him into her house. And that he was "spreading malicious lies" about her son Brett who was a wounded war veteran, a hero, and had had nothing to do with his daughter.

Because he'd "broken off a bad engagement" with Zeno Mayfield's other daughter, that was one of the reasons Zeno had come to her house to threaten her.

Zeno was informed of these charges by a Carthage police lieutenant he knew who dropped by the house to visit with him. Avoid the Kincaids, the lieutenant said. Avoid any situation where he was likely to be over-excited.

Zeno, who knew the law, or should have known the law, understood the principle here. He was the father of the *missing girl,* he must not blunder into breaking the law himself.

"But how can they just let him *go*? Not even *out on bail*? Why didn't they arrest him?"

"Because they can't, yet. But they will."

Zeno felt a chill, hearing these words.

"You mean, if Cressida is—isn't—if she . . ."

Zeno didn't know what he was saying. He covered his face with his hands. His jaws had grown stubbly again, his breath smelled sour in his own nostrils.

The Carthage PD lieutenant placed his hand on Zeno's shoulder. This pressure, meant to be kindly, manly-kindly, remained with Zeno after the lieutenant himself had slipped away eager to escape the strained static air of the Mayfield household.

Arlette was required to calm her ranting husband. Arlette who'd scarcely slept since 4 A.M. of July 10, now days ago, feared for the man's high blood pressure, his audible shortness of breath, the quivering of his hands.

"The fingerprints in the Jeep were hers. The hairs, for Christ's sake! The bloodstains—probably. And 'witnesses' at the Roebuck . . ."

"Yes. We know."

" . . . how can they just *let him go*! And now he has a lawyer, and that self-promoting asshole Fisk will pay for his defense!"

"Yes. But there's nothing to be done right now, Zeno. Come here, sit down, let me hold you. Please."

They were regressing, in their marriage, long a marriage of mature and nimbly wise-cracking adults, to an earlier stage of wayward and desperate surges of raw emotion, even sexual need. Indignant and belligerent in public, Zeno was susceptible to weakness and trembling in the privacy of his home, in his wife's consoling arms.

Arlette thought *I will have to prepare him for the worst. He can't prepare himself.*

The blood test was inconclusive because, unluckily, there was no way to determine if the blood was Cressida's. The single smudged fingerprint and the stray hairs were also "inconclusive" because there was no way to establish that these had been left in the Jeep on Saturday night, and not at another, earlier time.

That was the point which Kincaid's lawyer Pedersen was using, to argue that Cressida had been in Brett's Jeep on an earlier occasion, and not on Saturday night.

That is, not *demonstrably* on Saturday night.

Because the scene had been crowded and confused, witnesses contradicted one another. Some claimed that they'd seen Cressida, or someone who closely resembled her, crossing the cinder parking lot at about midnight with Brett Kincaid limping and leaning against her, on their way to his vehicle; others claimed that they'd seen Cressida, or someone who closely resembled her, on the outdoor deck of the Roebuck, in the company of others, including, or not including, Brett Kincaid.

No one would *absolutely claim* to have seen Cressida in Brett's Jeep Wrangler.

Witnesses spoke of "bikers" at the Roebuck. Deafening roars of their motorcycles, drunken shouts.

Women who'd claimed to have seen Cressida in the restroom splashing water onto her face could not claim to have actually spoken with her—"It wasn't like she was asking for anybody to help her, see. And she isn't the kind of person you just tap on the shoulder to ask if she's 'all right'—you know she'd be offended."

Kincaid's friends Rod Halifax, Jimmy Weisbeck, and Duane Stumpf, all in their mid-twenties, lifetime residents of Carthage who'd known Brett Kincaid at Carthage High School, were interviewed individually by Beechum County detectives. Of the three, Halifax and Stumpf were known to local law enforcement: already in high school they'd been arrested for fighting, destruction of property, petty theft and public drinking but their cases had been adjudicated in the county court without recourse to incarceration. Halifax and Weisbeck had been cited in complaints by young women claiming they'd been "harassed" and "abused" by them—but here too, charges were dropped or had evaporated.

Halifax had enlisted in the Marines in November 2001 but had been discharged after twenty-three days at the Marine basic training at Camp Geiger, North Carolina.

At about that time, in the fall of 2001, when Brett Kincaid had enlisted in the army, Weisbeck and Stumpf had applied to enlist too, but hadn't completed their applications.

With something of the earnest clumsiness of amateur actors whose scripts have been memorized Halifax, Weisbeck, and Stumpf gave accounts of Saturday night at the Roebuck Inn with their friend Brett Kincaid that were near identical: they'd arrived at the Roebuck in separate vehicles, they'd been drinking together since about 10 P.M., they'd moved from the outdoor deck into the taproom to be closer to the bar, at one point there'd been maybe a dozen guys with them, and girls; some of them old friends, and some virtually strangers; by midnight the place was really crowded and it was sometime then that "the Mayfield girl" showed up, alone; or it looked as if she was alone; nobody knew her (except Brett) since she'd been a few years behind them at Carthage High, and nobody had ever seen her before at the lake—"Like, she wasn't the type to hang out there."

How long "the Mayfield girl" remained talking with Brett in a corner, maybe twenty minutes, or a half hour, they didn't know. Or when she left. Or with who.

Might've been bikers—there was a gang of them, Adirondack Hells Angels in the parking lot tearing up the cinders.

But definitely it wasn't Brett Kincaid she left with. Because they'd all left at the same time.

And it wasn't any one of *them*.

"IF I COULD get my hands on them. Get them alone. For just five minutes. Just one of them. Just one."

"Yes but you can't, Zeno. You know that. You can't."

"Stumpf is the one who'd break first. Less than one minute. If I could just . . ."

"Yes, Zeno. But you can't. Please tell me you know this—you can't."

Like a wounded buffalo, poor Zeno. Arlette tried to hold him, stroke his snarled hair, kiss his bristling cheek. She understood how sick at heart her husband was, how terrified of what awaited them, when he failed to push her away.

FIVE

ENDANGERED MISSING ADULT

CRESSIDA CATHERINE MAYFIELD

If you believe you have any information regarding this case
that will be helpful in this investigation please contact Beechum
County (NY) Sheriff's Department (315 440-1198) or City of
Carthage (NY) Police Department (315 329-8366)

$20,000 reward for information leading to the recovery
and return of Cressida Mayfield.

Callers will be granted anonymity if requested.

Name: CRESSIDA CATHERINE MAYFIELD

Classification: Endangered Missing Adult

Alias/Nickname: None

Date of Birth: 1986—04—6

Date Missing: 2005—07—10.

From city/state: Carthage, NY

Missing from (country): USA

Family: Arlette Mayfield (mother), Zeno Mayfield   (father)

Age at Time of Disappearance: 19

Gender: Female

Race: White

Height: 61 inches

Weight: 100 pounds

Hair Color: Dark brown

Eye Color: Dark brown

Complexion: Pale

Glasses/contacts description: Clear contacts/ wire-rimmed glasses

Identifying characteristics: Short, "frizzy"-curly dark hair, prominent dark eyebrows, non-raised faded strawberry birthmark on left forearm, faded (childhood) scar on right knee

Medical history: Migraine headache, bronchitis, (childhood) chicken pox, measles, mumps, scarlet fever.

Jewelry: None known. Ears not pierced.

Attire at time of Disappearance: Black jeans, black T-shirt, black/white striped cotton sweater, sandals.

Circumstances of Disappearance: Unknown pending police investigation. Cressida was last seen by witnesses at midnight July 9 in the parking lot of the Roebuck Inn & Marina, Wolf's Head Lake, New York, but is believed to have been later in the Nautauga State Forest Preserve.

Investigative Agency: Beechum County Sheriff's Department, City of Carthage Police Department

Investigative Case # 04-29374

NCIC #: K-84420081

Through July, that nightmare month, and into August 2005.
        Waiting for the phone to ring.
    "The news will come by phone. No other way—phone."

He'd ordered six thousand flyers. A first printing.

This was a replica of the national endangered missing adults Web site for *Cressida Catherine Mayfield*.

He'd arranged for a massive mailing to households in Beechum, Herkimer, and Hamilton counties.

Volunteers affixed flyers to telephone poles, trees, public walls and the sides of buildings in Carthage and in the villages of Wolf's Head Lake, Echo Lake, and Black River. In post offices in these places and as far away as Watertown, Fort Drum, Sackets Harbor, and Ogdensburg.

And everywhere in the Nautauga State Forest Preserve—restrooms, the ranger stations, every one hundred feet along popular trails.

Walking in the Preserve, along the Sandhill Road where—(he persisted in thinking)—he might yet discover some inexplicably overlooked article of clothing or item belonging to his daughter he stared at the ENDANGERED MISSING ADULT CRESSIDA MAYFIELD flyers stapled to trees making his way from one to the next—to the next—and the next—like a man with a single leg, stumbling on a crutch.

Where a flyer appeared to be missing, or was torn, or rain-ravaged, he stapled another. In a backpack he carried an infinite supply.

"Someone will recognize her. Someone will have information. We have faith."

Through July, that nightmare month, and into August, and early September—the expectation prevailed in the Mayfield household.

Waking in a place she had no idea she'd been—(slumped on a sag-bellied sofa in the basement TV room, sunshine glaring through narrow horizontal not-very-clean windows)—or when—to a sudden piercing pain at the back of her skull. A phone ringing upstairs!

Stumbling upstairs to grab at the receiver.

For always there was the expectation that the next call would be Cressida.

Or news of Cressida.

Mrs. Mayfield? Arlette? We have good news . . .

Are you Mrs. Mayfield? The mother of Cressida? At last we have good news for you and your husband . . .

"Yes. I mean no—we don't give up waiting. We will never give up waiting. We are convinced that our daughter is alive and will contact us . . ."

Or: "It's a matter of *faith*. We know that Cressida is—somewhere. And sometime, we will see her again."

They were being interviewed: TV cameras.

They were being photographed: flashbulbs.

They were the Mayfields, Arlette and Zeno. And sometimes, Juliet. Family of the *missing girl*.

"No. We are not bitter. We understand that the detectives are 'investigating'—'collecting evidence.' They can't arrest him—anyone—until they have 'built a case.'"

And: "We know that he knows. Everyone in Carthage knows that Brett Kincaid knows what has happened to Cressida—but he's protected by the law, for the time being. Until the detectives have 'built their case.'"

Stalwart Zeno seemed oblivious, that faith in his daughter being alive after more than forty days did not compute with faith that Brett Kincaid would soon be arrested for a crime involving his daughter.

Arlette understood the illogic. Arlette sensed the pity of others in the face of the Mayfields' obdurate faith.

And there was Juliet, with her stunned smile. Beautiful Juliet Mayfield, elementary school teacher at the Convent Street School, prom queen of Carthage High Class of 2000 and ex-fiancée of Corporal Brett Kincaid believed to be the "last person" to have seen Cressida Mayfield in the early morning hours of July 10.

"I know that my sister Cressida is alive and well—somewhere. I know that Brett did not harm her but I think that Brett might know who did harm her and where she is. All my prayers are with her and with Brett also . . . I do believe in the power of prayer, yes. No, we don't see each other now—Brett Kincaid and me. Not right now. But I pray for him, too—I pray for his troubled soul."

SHE WAS FIFTY-ONE years old! A few months ago, she'd been a *girl*.

Something skeletal had taken root inside her, not soon to be shaken.

What she'd come to dread: opening her eyes in the morning.

For once her eyes were opened, she could not close them again until nighttime.

Once the thoughts of her lost daughter were unleashed, like a landslide, like a flash flood, they could not be curtailed. They could not be contained.

Oh God. Cressida! Tell us where you are, honey.

If we can come to you—tell us . . .

Nor could Arlette avoid acknowledging her husband lying exhausted in sleep beside her like a winded, wounded beast that groaned and muttered in its sleep; or, worse, lay awake; having been awake for hours, thoughts churning in his head like laundry in a washer.

It had long been their custom to kiss in the morning—casually aimed kisses like greetings. But now, Arlette lay very still not wanting to move in the hope that Zeno wouldn't know she'd wakened.

Yet, Zeno always knew. His brooding monologue, that had rumbled through the night inaudibly, now surfaced:

"God damn I'm going out to see McManus this morning. Bastard never returned my call yesterday and I think—I've been thinking—there is something they know, they're hiding from us. Some reason they haven't arrested Kincaid yet."

Or: "I'm going over to the Meyers' this morning. I think—I've been thinking—there is something more Marcy knows, she hasn't told anyone. But maybe I can prevail upon her to tell *me*."

Wordless Arlette moved to kiss her husband on his mouth, that had so little to do with her, only with the continual monologue, the argument.

A kiss is a way of not-speaking. A way of cowardice.

Arlette was thinking of Cressida's pen-and-ink drawing—*Meta-morphoses.*

White humanoid figures that evolved by degrees into abstract shapes and became "black"—then evolved back to their original shapes, and their original "whiteness"—but profoundly altered.

JULIET TOO WAS QUESTIONED by detectives.

Absent from the house for more hours than Arlette would have considered reasonable.

Arlette called Juliet on her cell phone, repeatedly—*Honey? This is Mom. Just wondering how you are. When you're coming home. Give me a call, will you?*

But no call. Which wasn't like Juliet.

Arlette was beginning to be afraid that Juliet, soon, would move away from home.

A feeling of terror, her only remaining daughter would leave.

And then: just Arlette and Zeno in the large house.

When she'd been so happy for Juliet previously. So happy at the prospect of Juliet marrying Brett Kincaid—*What a nice, gentlemanly, handsome young man! Except he's in the army, Lettie—you're damn lucky.*

The newlyweds would live in Carthage. That had seemed to be the plan. Juliet was teaching at the Convent Street School just two miles from Cumberland Avenue and Brett would be working for El-liot Fisk, if all went well. No reason to think that all would not go well. Zeno had spoken with the couple, he'd said, in the most diplo-matic way, suggesting that he could help them finance a house, help with a mortgage, anytime they were interested . . .

After her interview with the detectives Juliet returned home in the early evening subdued and evasive and with an excuse that she wasn't hungry, hurried upstairs to her room and shut the door. And when Arlette knocked Juliet might have said *Oh Mom please—go away* but Arlette seemed not to hear. Pushing open the door, saying she just wanted to know how the interview went, what did the detectives ask her, and Juliet who was lying on her bed, fully clothed lying on her bed with her arm over her face to shield her face from her anxious-smiling mother, did not reply at first saying then that the interview had been very tiring, questions about Brett she had not wanted to answer . . . Arlette came to sit on the edge of the bed stroking her daughter's hair, which was lovely glossy honey-brown hair, unsure what to ask Juliet for Arlette knew she must not pry, even with her unfailingly sweet-natured daughter she knew she must not pry; until Juliet said, with a little sob, "The questions they asked me about Brett! I was just so—ashamed . . ."

"'Ashamed'? Why?"

"Because—because there are things about him, of course there are 'personal' things, 'intimate' things, you don't tell about anyone you've been so close to . . . You just don't."

Arlette said in what she hoped wasn't a voice of complaint or alarm: "Your father warned us, there will be nothing 'personal' or 'private' in our lives, once there's a police investigation. They have to ask questions—all kinds of questions. About Brett, they would have wanted to know"— Arlette spoke carefully—"if he'd ever been, you know—threatening or abusive to you."

"Yes. I know."

"'Yes'—what? He wasn't was he?"

"No. I told them no."

"Well—it's the truth, isn't it?"

"Yes."

But Juliet had hesitated so long, Arlette wondered what this reply meant.

"They asked me also about what he'd told me about being in Iraq. What kinds of things he'd done there. What might have happened to him, or to men in his platoon. And I told them, I didn't know—Brett wouldn't talk about that."

When he'd first been shipped to Iraq Brett had emailed Juliet frequently and sent her countless pictures from his cell phone, which Juliet shared with everyone in the families and with mutual friends. Then, these had dropped off. Shortly before he'd been injured and hospitalized, Brett was sending no more than an email every two or three days, ever more terse and evasive.

Zeno had said about the early emails and pictures—*If the kid has other kinds of war-news, he isn't sending it to his fiancée.*

Arlette had said to Ethel Kincaid, on one of several occasions when she'd tried to befriend her daughter's fiancé's standoffish mother *It's like holding your breath—just waiting for Brett to get back.*

And Ethel Kincaid had looked at Arlette with an expression that had seemed to suggest that Arlette and her family hadn't any right to be waiting for her son—even to say such inane remarks.

Now, Ethel Kincaid was their enemy. In an interview with WCTG-TV she'd accused the Mayfields of "exaggerating" and "falsifying" things about their son—"slandering a war hero." Pressed by Evvie Estes, shameless in her zeal to stir up local excitement and controversy, she'd claimed, unforgivably, that "both Mayfield daughters" had "chased after" her son.

How Juliet felt about such terrible things being said, Arlette didn't know. She hoped that Juliet's Christian faith was helping her—in some region of the soul where not even her loving mother could follow her.

Though she knew that Juliet wanted to be alone, Arlette lingered in her bedroom. She was reluctant to break off the conversation which was the most intimate conversation she'd had with Juliet since before the engagement had been broken.

"Well, honey! You didn't have anything much to tell the detectives, did you? If Brett hadn't ever been 'threatening' or 'abusive' with you."

"Yes. That's right."

"So—you didn't tell them that. You didn't . . ."

"Nothing 'personal' or 'intimate.' I did not."

"Because—there was nothing to tell. Is that it?"

"Yes. I've told you, Mom."

Arlette looked closely at Juliet. A just perceptible edge of impatience in the daughter's voice so that the mother knew, for the moment, she had better back off.

⇥ ⇤

On the day following Labor Day 2005 another massive mailing of the ENDANGERED MISSING ADULT CRESSIDA MAYFIELD Web site flyer to households in Beechum, Herkimer, Hamilton counties.

What the price was, for such desperate mailings, fourth-class bulk mail regulated by the U.S. Postal Service and distributed to thousands of anonymous "homeowner" addresses Zeno never told Arlette and Arlette never asked.

Nor did Arlette ask what proportion of such mailings yielded any measurable responses at all—telephone calls, emails.

She didn't remind Zeno of how ruthless he was, disposing of the fourth-class mail that crammed their mailbox. Such flyers, mixed with throwaway advertisements and local shopping weeklies, Zeno Mayfield would never have condescended to glance at, himself.

As if Arlette had voiced such uncertainties aloud Zeno said, defensively: "Granted, most of these are thrown away unread. But of thousands of flyers, if just one yields some crucial information—that will be worth it!"

OTHER LOCAL INCIDENTS seized headlines and *breaking news* bulletins in Beechum County.

Drunks in a boating accident on Echo Lake. A domestic fracas spilling out onto a South Carthage street, three adults and a ten-year-old child killed in a blast of gunfire. Adirondack Hells Angels arrested in a methamphetamine lab raid by New York State Police at Independence River and of seven individuals taken into custody, three had been sought for questioning by Beechum County sheriff's detectives in the Cressida Mayfield investigation.

"YES. IT HAS BEEN HARD. It has been . . ."

" . . . but we're hopeful, and very grateful . . ."

" . . . so many people, many of them strangers, expressing support for us—for Cressida. So many volunteers, searching the Preserve . . ."

" . . . do have faith, yes. Our daughter returning to us . . ."

"Yes it's sad—the fall term is beginning at St. Lawrence, and she isn't there . . ."

" . . . Cressida loved her classes . . ."

" . . . yes, they've promised . . . there will be a 'breakthrough' soon. They've been interviewing . . ."

" . . . interviewing many people, they've said . . ."

" . . . following 'leads' in other parts of the state . . ."

" . . . people who've 'sighted' our daughter . . ."

" . . . they mean well, but . . ."

" . . . the police have brought Brett Kincaid back twice more to interview him . . . 'Building a case' takes time and if there's a premature arrest . . ."

" . . . will undo the work of months . . ."

" . . . faith of course. We are not 'religious' but . . . we do have faith that . . ."

" . . . our daughter will be returned to us."

And there came Zeno, subtly corrective: " . . . our daughter *will return* to us."

Photographed close together, seated on a sofa in the living room of their Cumberland Avenue house, Zeno Mayfield's heavy arm around his wife's shoulders so that she had to brace herself against the weight.

And which interview was this?—of numerous "follow-up" interviews in the local media? The *Carthage Post-Journal*. *Watertown Journal-Times*. *Black River Valley Gazette*.

Zeno smiled stiffly for the cameras. Arlette could not bring herself to smile any longer—thinking of Cressida's refusal to smile, for photographs.

One will be your obituary. Can't smile for your obituary!

IN THE LOCAL MEDIA there was a brief flurry of excitement when the Hells Angels bikers with their outstanding warrants and previous police records for aggravated assault, drug trafficking, and theft were taken into custody by Beechum County deputies for "questioning"— but nothing seemed to have come of this, either.

HERE WAS A SECRET: Arlette Mayfield did not truly *have faith*.

That is, faith that her daughter would be returned to her.

Almost from the start, after the first-day's search had yielded so little, and certain facts had been revealed of Brett Kincaid's involvement with Cressida, the boy's facial wounds, the "fresh" bloodstains in the front seat of the Jeep, the boy's guilty behavior, Arlette had thought *The worst has happened. He has killed her, because of Juliet. Because he hates us. He has killed her and hidden her away. And so maybe it would be a mercy not to find her.*

Arlette dared not reveal such terrible—perverse—unmotherly thoughts to anyone: certainly not to Zeno, or to Juliet.

Not even to her sister Katie Hewett who was three years older than Arlette, the most sensible of women, an assistant superintendent of Carthage public schools whose ability to perceive subterfuge, obfuscation, and deceit in the most guileless of individuals was legendary.

Katie squeezed Arlette's hand, frequently.

Katie hugged Arlette, so hard her ribs ached.

Katie kissed Arlette on the side of the face, a hot wet kiss that seared.

As if wanting Arlette to know: she understood.

Only once did Arlette say to Katie, in the fifth or sixth week of the search, in a weak abashed voice as the two sisters prepared a meal in the Mayfields' kitchen while in another room Zeno was speaking rapidly on his cell phone, in the tone of a man accustomed to giving orders: "Oh Katie, I am trying, Katie. You know, I am trying. I won't ever give up. He would never forgive me, if I did."

→ ←

Still, Arlette placed calls to the missing cell phone.

Just to punch in the numbers. Just to listen, breath withheld, for the ghost-ring.

In the *Carthage Post-Journal* there were ever briefer articles, on inside pages, on the "ongoing search" for nineteen-year-old Cressida Mayfield, and at the conclusion of these articles was the reiterated statement that "no arrests have yet been made" and that the police investigation was "continuing."

Rumors flourished: that Brett Kincaid had been arrested finally, not on suspicion of having had something to do with the disappearance of his former fiancée's sister, but on a complaint of a neighbor that the young man had "shoved him and shouted at him" outside their house on Potsdam Street; that a "young girl's body" had been found in a landfill, near Wild Forest, eight miles east of Wolf's Head Lake where a sprawling enclave of Adirondack Hells Angels lived; that Juliet Mayfield, former fiancée of Corporal Brett Kincaid, had resigned her position at the Convent Street Elementary School and was moving away from Carthage—*Couldn't bear the shame.*

So far as Arlette could determine, none of these rumors was true.

Though it was true, Juliet was thinking of enrolling in a master's degree program in education, at Plattsburgh—sometime.

Not giving up her teaching job in Carthage but commuting, once a week to a night-school class.

And very possibly it was true, Brett Kincaid had gotten into some sort of shouting match with a neighbor.

And very possibly—"a young girl's body" might have been found in a landfill near Wild Forest, if not at the present time, sometime ago. Or sometime to come.

ANOTHER RUMOR WAS that Marcy Meyer had had some sort of "nervous collapse" in Ogdensburg, in the week following her return for her second year in the nursing school.

This was in late August. The nursing school term began earlier than the university.

Arlette called the Meyers' home, and Marcy's mother answered.

Mrs. Meyer said that Marcy had had an "accident"—she'd fallen down a flight of stairs dragging a suitcase up to her room on the third floor of the nurses' residence.

She'd been unconscious for several minutes. She'd sprained an ankle and dislocated a shoulder bone. She'd been in such pain, even with painkillers, the nursing school had insisted that she take off the fall term and return home.

Arlette stammered how sorry she was to hear this terrible news!

"Should I come over to see her? Is there anything I could do to help?"

Linda Meyer, whom Arlette had known in high school, not well, for they'd belonged to very different circles, hesitated a moment before saying, with finality, "No. That isn't necessary, Arlette. Seeing you would just remind Marcy of Cressida and she's had enough of that."

ZENO HAD SPOKEN with Marcy Meyer several times.

Arlette had had the idea—(she hadn't wanted to ask her husband)—that his visits were upsetting to Marcy, who'd been questioned for more than one session by police detectives.

Marcy had been "devastated" by her friend's disappearance. But Marcy had been "shocked" and "bewildered" when she'd learned that Cressida hadn't returned to her home, but had gone to Wolf's Head Lake, seemingly to meet with Brett Kincaid, after leaving the Meyers' house.

There was the possibility, you would not want to label it a fact, that Marcy Meyer's closest friend had lied to her.

The last time Zeno had spoken with Marcy, soon before she'd left for nursing school at Ogdensburg, he'd returned to Arlette to say that, he might be imagining it, but it had seemed to him that Marcy was *just slightly jealous of—someone—or something—in Cressida's life.*

Arlette had thought of course: Brett Kincaid.

Zeno was sitting on a leather sofa in the living room. Rubbing his face so vigorously, thumbs against his eyes, Arlette could hear the eyeballs moving in their sockets in a way to make her shiver.

"Get me a beer, Lettie. Please! I'm just too—God-damned—fucking—tired to get one myself."

Yet, fired with a new idea, a new and not yet demonstrably futile idea regarding their lost daughter, Zeno spoke rapidly, even zestfully.

"Marcy finally told me—which I don't think she'd told the police—that, that night at her house, she'd thought that Cressida might have made a call on her cell phone at one point, or possibly the cell phone had been set on vibrate, since it didn't ring, and Cressida might have had a call on the phone, which she took in another room—(they'd been in the dining room, at dinner, with Marcy's parents and her grandmother, and Cressida had excused herself as if she were going to the bathroom)—but since she wasn't at all sure, and was so confused trying to remember, answering questions put to her by the police and trying to remember every desperate thing, she didn't think that she could tell them this. 'It's like I might have imagined it. It's like I have been thinking about that night so much, my brain is spilling over with false memories, I don't dare tell the police, they tape every word, it would become permanent and could never be erased.' And Marcy was trying not to cry, you know how we always think of Marcy as so healthy, sturdy, what is Cressida's description—*stalwart and true of heart, like a wildebeest*—but here was poor Marcy looking as if she'd lost ten pounds, and so anxious—'You know how furious Cressida would be with us, if she knew we were talking about her like this . . . Trying to remember every syllable of what she'd said, and every kind of speculation . . . ' And Marcy did start to cry, and I held her hands to comfort her. And I guess I cried, too."

"NOTHING CONCLUSIVE. But probably, nothing significant."

For weeks police kept Cressida's laptop. Presumably a computer forensics specialist was examining it.

But at last the laptop was returned to the Mayfields with a report that their daughter didn't seem to have been involved in any unusual or risky Internet activities. She'd used her laptop for academic research primarily; her school papers were neatly filed by course titles;

her email correspondence was nothing out of the ordinary—much of the mail was impersonal, from St. Lawrence University. She seemed to have few friends, and these were young women—predominantly, Marcy Meyer.

No secret life! Somehow, this saddened Arlette.

But really, no: this was a relief.

"Your daughter has a limited social life, judging from the email record. Does she have a boyfriend, that you know of?"

Arlette shook her head, no. Zeno frowned and did not reply.

Arlette was grateful for the detective speaking of their daughter in the present tense: *Has. Does. Is.*

"What about here in Carthage, in high school maybe—was there anyone?"

Arlette hesitated as if having to think. But the answer was no.

"Was Cressida interested in—involved with—girls? Would you know about that, if she was?"

Arlette hesitated again. A flush rose into her face.

Zeno said, in a neutral voice: "You mean—'lesbians'? You think my daughter is a 'lesbian'?"

"Would you be in a position to know, if she was?"

"That's a hard question to answer, officer! As you've phrased it."

"Arlette, what do you think?"

What Arlette thought was *No. My daughter could not love anyone like herself.*

"I really don't think so. Cressida has girlfriends as other girls her age do. In some ways, as we've tried to explain to you, she was—is—a very young nineteen. She's always been smart, precociously smart, but she spends most of her time inside her own head—she isn't so aware of people, as her own thoughts. She isn't—I guess you'd say—very mature."

Arlette spoke haltingly. It was a terrible thing for a mother to so betray her daughter, to strangers!

A swift vision of Cressida's pale furious face, lifting to Arlette.

"Mrs. Mayfield, apart from Kincaid and his friends, one of the last people who saw your daughter that night is this girl 'Marcy Meyer.' How close are they?"

"They've been friends since grade school. But not really—from Cressida's perspective, certainly—*close*."

"And you would know that, Mrs. Mayfield, how? Exactly how would you know that?"

How did Arlette know anything about her daughter! The detective's questions were unanswerable.

"From remarks Cressida has made. From the fact that Cressida seems to forget Marcy for periods of time. It's Marcy who has to contact *her*."

"And if they were in contact now—just assuming, for a moment, that your daughter is alive, somewhere"—how frankly Detective Silber spoke, how matter-of-fact the leverage of *if*—"is it possible that Marcy Meyer would keep this contact secret? If Cressida asked her not to, she wouldn't tell *you*?"

Arlette and Zeno turned to each other, confounded.

No idea how to reply.

ENTERING CRESSIDA'S ROOM. *She'd knocked—but too lightly for Cressida to hear, evidently. Which was a mistake. And there was Cressida in flannel pajamas half-lying/half-sitting on her bed with her back against the headboard and her knees awkwardly apart, and raised; and a notebook—more precisely a journal with a marbled cover, which Arlette hadn't ever seen before—positioned in such a way, against Cressida's knees, so that she could write in it. And Cressida glared at Arlette, and dropped the journal onto the bed, partly hiding it with a comforter; in that instant, Cressida was furious, saying rudely: "Go away! You're not welcome here! No snooping here!"*

Cressida had been eleven or twelve at the time.

Arlette had retreated, stung.

She'd never seen the hard-covered journal again. She'd rarely entered Cressida's room again. And this was so embarrassing to her, like the accusa-

tion of snooping, the rudeness of her own daughter for which (she believed) she was herself to blame, she'd never told anyone: not a woman friend, not her sister Katie, not her husband Zeno.

NINE WEEKS, TWO DAYS after her disappearance it was revealed: in the afternoon of July 9, a physical therapist at the Carthage Rehabilitation Clinic named Seth Seager, who'd worked with Brett Kincaid at the clinic for several months and was on friendly terms with him, happened to see Cressida Mayfield in the Carthage CVS on Main Street. Cressida didn't know Seth Seager but he knew her, or knew something of her, as *the smart one* of Zeno Mayfield's two daughters. He called out hello to her—she seemed suspicious of him at first—but then, when he identified himself as a new friend of Brett Kincaid's, from the rehab clinic, her manner changed.

"There was something about Cressida—I really liked her. She reminded me of a cousin of mine, a girl, kind of a tomboy-type, but smart—and smart-mouthed. And that's a kind of girl I like. I mean, a kind of girl that's cool. Like, she isn't waiting for you to compliment her or say nice things to her—she knows a guy isn't going to do that. Most guys are not going to do that. 'Cause she isn't the kind of girl a guy would be attracted to, in that way. But I liked Cressida a lot, and I think she liked me. And I told her, Brett Kincaid plans on going out that night, to the Roebuck Inn with some friends, he'd invited me and I told him no thanks, that scene wasn't for me. (Sure, I'd told Brett it wasn't a great idea, drinking while he was taking those meds, but Brett just shrugged and laughed, 'What the hell. I'll be OK. And if not—what the hell.') And Cressida asked this funny question—if Brett was 'celebrating'—and I said I didn't know, what would he be 'celebrating'?—and Cressida said, 'He's not getting married.' Well, I'd heard about this, but not from Brett; Brett would not ever talk to anybody at the clinic about any personal thing, so I didn't know what to say. And Cressida said, like she'd had a change of heart, and was sorry what she'd said to me, 'I didn't mean it, I know Brett must feel bad—both of them must feel bad. I'm sorry what I said.' And she was looking like she'd start to cry, which is not what you expect from such a cool girl, the kind that never cries, or anyway not when you can see her. 'He wouldn't do harm to himself, would he?' she asked me, which was a weird thing to ask, something we don't talk about, like, y'know, you don't talk about guys who kill themselves after they start to get better, lost their legs, or have to wear a colonoscopy bag, or brain-damaged so they can't speak a sentence anyone can comprehend, and once they get a little more in control of their lives they kill themselves, or have an 'overdose' or a 'fatal accident'—so I said, 'Hell, no. Not Corporal Kincaid, no way.' And she said, 'So he will get through it, you think?'—she wasn't being sarcastic, or joking, but looking at me like I could really answer this question for her; and I said what we all say in rehab, 'Sure he will! One day at a time.' "

The detectives to whom he'd made this statement asked Seth Seager why he'd waited so long to contact them.

Shamefaced he said, he didn't know.

He said, well maybe—he hadn't wanted to "make things worse" for Brett Kincaid who'd already been fucked-over in Iraq.

He said: "Then I was always thinking, telling myself—Cressida would come back. She'd have been away somewhere, and she'd come back. And she'd explain what had happened. And Brett wouldn't be blamed, or arrested. And I wouldn't have to get involved, myself."

Detectives asked Seager how he thought Cressida had gotten to the Roebuck Inn from Fremont Street in Carthage, a distance of approximately nine miles. He'd laughed saying, "If she's anything like my cousin Dorrie she'd have stuck out her thumb and hitched a ride on Route 33. Seems like everybody's going out to the lake, Saturday night in July."

⇥ ⇤

September 15, 2005. Caught amid rocks and rusted iron pipes beneath a bridge in Sackets Harbor, thirty miles west of Carthage where the Nautauga River emptied into Lake Erie, a curious mummified object was found by a twelve-year-old boy who hauled it to shore with a pole: it would turn out to be a girl's sweater, mud-colored, stiff as a board. The boy brought the mummified sweater home to show his mother—he'd known about the *missing girl* and the twenty-thousand-dollar reward.

Next day, one of the Beechum County detectives called the Mayfields and asked them to please come to headquarters. An article of clothing had been found in Sackets Harbor, on a bank of the Nautauga River, they hoped the Mayfields might examine, to see if it might have belonged to Cressida Mayfield.

In Zeno's Land Rover they drove to the building on Axel Road: Zeno, Arlette, Juliet.

Zeno said: "It's too far away—Sackets Harbor. That isn't likely."

When Arlette didn't respond Zeno said: "Sackets Harbor is too far away. This is a waste of time."

In the backseat of the Land Rover Juliet sat with her arms folded tight across her chest, shivering, yet uncomplaining, in the blast of air-conditioning Zeno had released.

It had been weeks since the Mayfields had entered the Beechum County Sheriff's Department. Detective Clement Lewiston was waiting for them, to escort them into a room where, on a table, the mummified sweater had been placed. Whatever its original color had been, the sweater was the color of dried mud now. It was too small for an adult woman—too small, Arlette saw with relief, to have belonged to Cressida. Zeno peered at it, frowning: he'd never seen it before, he was sure. Arlette touched it with a forefinger, undecided. It wasn't a woolen sweater—hardly a "sweater" at all—only just something with sleeves, a cardigan, of some synthetic material like nylon, Orlon. It scarcely had stitching. It was obviously very cheap. Only two little broken buttons remained and its buttonholes were caked with mud. Arlette said, relief in her voice: "No. This is nothing of Cressida's."

But Juliet, who'd removed her dark glasses when she stepped into the windowless room, leaned over the mummified sweater for some seconds, staring. Since her younger sister's disappearance, Juliet had lost weight: her cheeks were thinner, her eyes were ringed with strain. In an undertone Zeno was speaking with Detective Clement Lewiston, words Arlette couldn't hear. She'd been feeling faint since entering the room and decided it was the brackish river-smell of the mummified sweater that was making her sick.

Almost, it was time to depart. Arlette would have liked to grab at her husband's arm, to pull him to the door. And she'd have liked to haul Juliet away, too.

"Yes. This is it. This is Cressida's sweater—the one with the black-and-white stripes." Juliet spoke slowly, thoughtfully. "If you look close enough you can see the stripes. It used to be my sweater—I gave it to Cressida. Or, Cressida took it from me. It was too small for me. So I'm sure. This is Cressida's. There's no doubt about it, Detective—this is my sister's sweater, she was wearing the night she was taken from us."

SIX

The Corporal in the Land of the Dead

July 2005–October 2005

JESUS! WHAT THEY'D DONE.

What they'd done *was*.

Held her down. Jammed a rag into her screaming mouth.

Taking turns with her. Grunting, yelping like dogs.

Then afterward one of them sliced her face.

Sliced halfway up her face on both sides. Corners of her mouth he'd sawed-at with a Swiss Army knife.

So she was grinning. Like a crazy clown.

And her eyes open, staring.

THEY WERE ASKING *What had he done to her. Had he hurt her, and where had he left her.*

They were saying *If you were provoked. If you confess now, and lead us to her. Where you left her, Corporal.*

DIDN'T WANT A LAWYER. A lawyer meant guilt.

A lawyer meant shame, and a lawyer meant guilt.

His mouth tasted of vomit, he'd tried to rinse the sour taste away. And where he'd bitten his tongue, or maybe it was a mouth ulcer. In

Iraq he'd had them—mouth ulcers. Staring in the mirror seeing the tiny white dots thinking it was cancer.

A terrible death by cancer, eaten alive. From the mouth outward.

It was a worse death because slower, than the other.

He'd heard—felt—the explosion. Heard screams, and then curses.

In their combat outpost, a deserted school. Battered and the windows like gouged-out eyes and behind it a bomb inside a drainage pipe that'd exploded blowing off the hands of Private Hardy and killing Private Quinn outright.

He'd run to them. Blindly running, thinking he could help.

What he saw was—███████████████████.

When it came to be his turn to die later and in another place. Shouldn't have been so totally surprised but fact is, he was.

For always you think, can't help but think *God would not let that happen to me. Jesus would not. I am a good person, I will be spared.*

He'd been a good person, Corporal Kincaid. All his life tried.

Boy Scout for Jesus the Sergeant called him sneering with one-half his face like a side of beef grinning.

This was in Salah ad Din province. Dusty, sandy, nasty.

Daily patrols were fifteen, sixteen hours—the record was eighteen hours. Your brain turned off, legs and feet continued like a windup zombie-toy. Boots so damn heavy like lifting weights or leg shackles and the socks not thick enough to prevent the skin scraping off his heels or a sharp toenail cutting into an adjacent toe feeling like a shard of glass driven into the toe. *Infantrymen are particularly warned to be careful of infections which can happen easily in a combat zone and which can be life-threatening.* The object was to protect the army base—(but why the hell was the base in such a dusty sandy nasty place requiring protection)—from fragmentation grenades, sniper fire, insurgent assault.

Move! No matter how exhausted if you stand still for more than four seconds—you're a candidate for a Ziploc bag, kid.

Fucking snipers never slept.

Or maybe it had been somewhere else—the names were strange

and dreamlike riddles you can't be sure you've heard right, you feel a pressure inside your head not wanting to fuck up and be laughed-at.

In emails home he'd tried to be accurate. As a student he'd tried to be accurate. It was the least you could do, he'd thought, to prevent things from being more fucked-up than they were, yet still he couldn't have sworn it had been Salah ah-Din and not Diyala or As Sadah. And there was Kirkuk.

They'd shoveled him up in pieces there—Kirkuk.

Guys joked about *donor organs*. Like for instance, *cock, testicles*.

There was a rumor, wealthy Saudis bought kidneys, livers, lungs, hearts, eyes, bone marrow on the black market. Their own kind—"Arabs"—"Muslims"—were cheap to be harvested.

In the U.S. that was illegal. In the U.S. you could not sell or purchase any body part or organ, this was against U.S. standards of morality.

The fight against terror is a fight against the enemies of U.S. morality—Christian faith. Somewhere in this God-forsaken place were the *imams* of the Al Qaeda terrorists who'd blown up the World Trade Center. Out of a pure hateful wish to destroy the Christian American democracy like the pagans of antiquity had hoped to do, centuries before. Ancient imperial Rome in the time of the gladiators—you would be required to die for your faith. It had been explained to them by their chaplain—this is a crusade to save Christianity. General Powell had declared there can be no choice, the U.S. has been forced to react militarily. The U.S. will never compromise with evil. No choice but to send in troops before the *weapons of mass destruction* are loosed by the crazed dictator Saddam—nuclear bombs, gas and germ warfare.

Only a very foolish and cowardly country would "wait and see" what developed. In the chapel the minister told them, Our ancestors are those brave enough to take the pre-emptive strike.

The insurgents were terrorist-enemies. The other Iraqis—"civilians"—were friends of the U.S., dependent upon the U.S. military to protect them.

Some were Kurds, not Iraqis. Kirkuk was the site of a vast oil field.

Some of this the guys knew, or had known at one time.

Soon, you began to forget. Following orders you forget what was the day before.

Names of places were easy to forget. Drifted in sand. And sand in eyes, nostrils, mouth. Sand inhaled in lungs so each breath you took, you drew the desert deeper into you.

Later in the hospital he'd tasted the sand-grit in his mouth. In his lungs. Coughing-choking trying to clear his lungs and what came up was a thick syrupy mucus tinged with blood.

In his brains, something squirming and teeming like—maggots?

A titanium implant, to secure the broken skull.

In his mangled left eye and the soft-matter (brains) behind the eye a minuscule intraocular lens (guaranteed to withstand melting at temperatures below 1000 degrees Fahrenheit) was implanted.

Vision is in the brain. The "eye" is the lens of the brain.

From one of the (dead, blasted) insurgents they'd taken trophies: eyes, thumbs, ears. Entire faces sliced off though rarely in one piece.

Wrapped in gauze and secured then in hand-sized Ziploc bags.

You figure why not. Fucking earned it.

Not Kincaid the Boy Scout. But others.

Private Muksie was the Jokester of the platoon.

"Coyote" Muksie who was Sergeant Shaver's right-hand man.

Insurgents. Insurgent snipers. These were an army of shadows, no way to fight shadows except to obliterate them in waves like flame.

There were *counterinsurgency measures* since before Corporal Kincaid had arrived. Yet, the memory of an earlier strategy issued by the brigade commander Colonel T___ remained fresh and was preferred: KILL THEM ALL AND LET GOD SORT THEM OUT.

He'd lost his meds. These were antibiotics to keep the death-bacteria from eating him alive.

Begin in the blood, then soft-tissue. Then, the brain.

He was prone to seeing things *not-there* and hearing things *not-there* since the explosion inside his head.

Problem is, you can't distinguish.

Telling them he didn't know. The girl—he'd forgotten her name.

Never knew her name. Any of their names. Civilians.

The interrogation continued through the night. He'd been one of the younger men assigned to the detail. It was thrilling to enter the little houses of the Iraqi civilians in which insurgents were suspected of hiding. Ducking your head to step through one of the dwarf-doorways next thing you know you might be shot—your head might explode. That could happen.

Later, he'd been sick with shame. At the time, there was no high like it.

Sure he'd smoked dope. He'd never tried cocaine, heroin. He'd never (yet) tried crystal meth. But he knew, there could be no high like this *because it was a natural high.*

"Kill board"—Sergeant Shaver was the overseer.

Muksie was the expeditor.

They hadn't asked him. Hadn't invited him. Knowing he'd snitch on them. Fucking Boy Scout Kincaid should've shot *him.*

Fragmentation grenade. Should've fragged *him.*

It wasn't a secret. "Coyote" told lots of people.

Anything that is done by one in the company, is done by all.

An army is *ants.* Essentially.

He'd been sick for two, three days. He'd felt his brain soften and drift bobbing like an embryo in formaldehyde, in a glass jug.

Went to the chaplain. His throat was so dry from the sand, almost he couldn't speak.

Are you sure, son. Take your time, son.

What passes between us is confidential.

They'd asked: who did the shooting.

He was trying to remember: she'd run from him.

Couldn't understand why—she'd run *from him.* He'd called after her but she'd run *from him.*

Hadn't wanted to hurt her. She'd said *I am the only one who understands you. No one else can know what we know, they are beloved of God.*

His guts were like concrete. The only way for him to shit was if it turned to liquid, fiery liquid, scathing as it poured out of him.

Otherwise, it was concrete.

So fucking ashamed, pain in his bowels. Rocking with pain. Breaking out into sweat. And trying to piss, after the catheter. You have to learn how, it isn't an instinct.

He was trying to tell them he hadn't seen. Hadn't been anywhere near.

Or maybe he'd been there and hadn't seen—exactly—what the guys were doing, or had done. Maybe by then it was over. Maybe it was hours over. Days over.

Or maybe he'd blundered into it. Staff Sergeant Shaver calling him: KIN-CAID! CORP'L FUCKING KIN-CAID! like the surprise was for him.

Bring your cell phone, Kin-caid! Photo op!

THEY'D THOUGHT SHE WAS OLDER—for sure. Hadn't known she was so *young*.

And the younger brother, eight or nine.

And the parents—so small they'd look like children back in the States.

And the old ones—grandparents . . .

After they'd dragged the girl out and were done with her Sergeant Shaver said disgusted *No witnesses! Wipe 'em.*

It hadn't been what they'd planned. None of it felt right. The girl was just a child not a teenaged girl like they'd been expecting, of which so many had been speaking *A girl! Sexy babe!* like it was MTV and rap music accompanying and if somebody was raped, or beaten bloody and dead, it wasn't like MTV where they came back laughing. It wasn't like any of that it was like—it was like a *sad, stupid mistake* . . . In the culvert they dragged her about one hundred feet from the end of the village road and tried to bury her beneath mud-chunks and rocks and slats of a broken fence. One more Goddamned task to be done once the high was over. *Essentially it was hard to take the Iraqi civilians seriously. Hard to see why they cared if they lived or died. If one of their kids died, or some old people. Anyone.*

Muksie, Broca, Mahan, Ramirez. Not Kincaid.

How many feet separated him from Shaver and his "kill crew" he'd be asked to estimate later. At the time in confusion and alarm he'd had no idea for he'd had no idea what the men were doing exactly.

Then, he'd seen Muksie with the shears. He'd heard the guys laughing kind of scared and breathless like kids in his high school daring to climb out onto the school roof and run stooped across the roof during school hours. *Wild!*

He'd raised his voice to protest. But no sound came.

Sick to his stomach. Puking out his guts.

Photo op, dudes! Lookit!

HE'D BROUGHT IT BACK with him, that last time.

The new cell phone, a gift from his prospective in-laws.

The Mayfields are snooty people living up there on the hill. They will look down on you like a dog—trained little mongrel-puppy. Don't come whining to me when you find out.

Fact is he was crazy for them. Zeno, Arlette.

Any resentment he'd had, his mother's bitterness, something about how the mayor had treated her, or hadn't treated her—it might have been that Ethel had wanted more attention from the mayor, as a reasonably good-looking woman (single) with a little kid (boy, needing a dad) might expect from a man like Zeno Mayfield giving off heat just entering a room—*Hel-lo! Ladies, good mornin'!*

What he was, was a phony. God-damn phony politician.

She'd been a file clerk. Worked in the front office. High heels, lipstick. Never got promoted. Eleven years.

Took her revenge, brought home office supplies in her Shop-Rite bag.

Paper she had no use for, reams of paper. Ballpoint pens by the fistfuls. Even printer cartridges. (But she had to be careful: the cartridges were expensive. Didn't dare take more than a single one every week or two.) Even rolls of toilet paper from the storage closet, unopened. So they had all the God-damn toilet paper they'd ever need.

He'd said, Jesus Mom! If they catch you what're you going to say?

I'll say *You owe me! Cheating bastards owe me.*

Embarrassed of his mother. Yet there was something crazy and thrilling about Ethel, too.

As in a quasi-public place for instance the food court at the shopping mall where you could take sugar packets, miniature salt and pepper packets, paper napkins of a particular coarseness, plastic cutlery. Grim-faced with stealth Ethel would stuff these in the deep pockets of her nylon parka. Even Styrofoam cups, though these were more difficult to conceal. Never know when you might have use for supplies, she'd said. It didn't feel like stealing to Ethel just what she called *evening things out.*

The world was a God-damned unjust place, for some people. Single mothers, women-left-behind treated like shit by men. You had a right to take revenge where you could.

From those who have, you take. You take, and you take.

So long Ethel had been complaining bitterly of Brett's father. Then with startling abruptness she would speak in praise of his father.

Brett tried so hard to remember him! A blurred memory like something smudged with an oily cloth though he'd been six years old when his father had left—old enough to remember, in a normal child.

Without both parents you don't feel confident you know what *normal* is. Like walking on a tilting floor but you can't gauge in which direction the floor is tilting.

Brett's father had been a noncommissioned officer in the U.S. Army: Sergeant First Class Graham Kincaid who'd served in the first Gulf War, May 1990 to March 1991. In the keepsake album were photos, fading and dog-eared. Sergeant Kincaid appeared to have been a handsome man despite a thick jaw, squinting eyes, an unnerving habit of smiling with half his mouth.

In each of the army photos Sergeant Kincaid was with other soldiers in his platoon, in uniform: you could see a family likeness among the men, from the oldest to the youngest. Here was a mysterious family of *soldier-brothers.*

You felt—if you were a young child, fatherless—a profound envy of this family, like nothing in your own diminished life.

Brett Kincaid: what do you want to be when you grow up?

A sergeant! Like my dad.

After Sergeant Kincaid had been discharged from the army he'd been too restless to remain in Carthage working at Klinger Auto Parts as production foreman. He'd driven west with a promise that he was "looking for work" and would send for his family when he found a suitable job and in the interim he sent postcards to "Ethel & Brett"—(these postcards were still in Brett's childhood room affixed to the wall beside his bed with yellowing Scotch tape)—and the last of these was Yosemite Park, jagged and streaked-looking mountains across which vaporous clouds trailed.

Ethel would have torn these postcards into bits except Brett prevented her *No, Mommy! Please don't.*

It was like his father had been secretly wounded, crippled—and that part of him, that was broken and defeated, had been left behind.

Ethel was boastful of Graham Kincaid at times and at other times furious with him. He was a *natural-born leader of men—should've been a major, or a captain.* Or, he was a *God-damn son of a bitch. Period.*

They'd met when she was just seventeen. He'd *taken advantage* of her, she said. He'd *made her get pregnant,* she said.

Hadn't wanted to marry her, but it had happened.

(Brett knew, from his careless-talking grandmother, Ethel's mother, that this first pregnancy had ended in a miscarriage. And a second pregnancy had ended in the birth of a "preemie" who'd lived only a few days. And so by the time Brett was born Ethel had become *kind of crazy* and Graham had *kind of turned himself off, like men do.*)

Ethel felt keenly the injustice of the world: snatching up a magazine to hold beside her face and there on the glossy cover was the face
of a woman—film actress? rock star?—and Ethel demanding *She's
better-looking than me? Like hell!*

Or she'd demand of Brett *What's the difference between her and me,
d'you know?* and Brett wouldn't know; and Ethel would say *She got all
the breaks, that's what. And what did I get?—shit.*

The Mayfields were not the only "snooty" Carthage family whom
Ethel scorned but her proximity to Zeno Mayfield earned him a particular notoriety in her life. As a boy Brett had heard repeatedly of
how the mayor would invite city employees out for drinks on Friday
afternoons—and never got around to inviting *her.*

Never even remembered her God-damned name, the hypocrite
son of a bitch!

Except when Brett was older and in high school on the varsity
football team. And his picture in the newspaper. And people talking
of him. And Zeno Mayfield wasn't too snooty to take note of *that.*
And one day in the office he'd stopped to say to her *Are you Brett Kincaid's mother? You must be very proud.*

She'd said *Yes, Mr. Mayfield, I am.*

And God-damn if that wasn't the end of it! Hypocrite bastard
never said five more words to her, for years.

Until two years ago it turned out that Brett was "dating" one of
Mayfield's daughters.

Ethel hadn't ever seen the daughters. But she knew from what
people said that one of them, the elder, was *the pretty one;* the other
was *the smart one.*

When Brett told Ethel about Juliet she'd been astonished, disbe-
lieving. *Mayfield? You're going out with a—Mayfield?*

Ethel had been so savagely critical of the luckless girls Brett had
occasionally brought home to be introduced to her, he'd given up
bringing them home; but now, with Juliet, he had no choice.

You can't be serious. She'll make a fool of you.

Or—is she the homely one? He's got two daughters.

By this time Brett had learned not to be upset or annoyed by his eccentric mother. He'd warned Juliet that his mother was "difficult" but "good-hearted" though he wasn't sure that that was an accurate description of Ethel Kincaid.

He'd felt a curious little thrill of vindication, satisfaction—bringing Juliet Mayfield together with Ethel, not at Ethel's sour-smelling house but on neutral territory, at a riverside café in Carthage.

The first glimpse Brett had had of Juliet Mayfield, all his resentment of the Mayfield family had faded. The quick connection between them—like a match struck into flame.

He'd seen her smiling eyes on him. He'd felt lighted-up inside.

In Brett's young life there had been a succession of girls, and more lately women. He'd moved out of his mother's house on Potsdam Street after graduating from high school, despite his mother's protests; he'd needed to live alone, to *breathe*.

When he'd enlisted in the army, he'd given up his rented apartment in South Palisade Park. When he'd returned from the army, discharged and disabled, like trash tossed off the rear of a speeding truck, he'd had to move back into the house on Potsdam Street, which was like a death sentence to him. Back into his old, boyhood room which Ethel had left as it had been, the room of a dead child.

But that was in the future: when he'd first met Juliet Mayfield, he'd had a place to bring her to, where they could be alone.

Fuck he'd try to explain anything of the way he felt to Ethel. He would not.

He was crazy for Juliet and for her family, that was a fact. And they seemed to like him, too.

His heart leapt, when Zeno strode forward to shake his hand.

Hiya, kid! Great to see ya.

The Mayfields were the nicest people he'd met. Ever.

Even the funny little sister with the funny name—Cressida.

Which he'd heard wrong, at first—thought they were calling her something like *Cressita, Cressika*—the name of a foreign country.

Little dark-eyed girl with almost Afro-style hair, inky-dark hair,

frizzing out from her head. Wiry little body like a child of eleven
or twelve and with a deadpan-face, you couldn't guess what she was
thinking.

Of the Mayfield girls, the smart one.

But even Cressida was nice to him! Shaking his hand with a solemn smile that quickly faded though her inky-dark eyes remained on
his, searching, startled.

*We all love you, Brett. Mom, Dad, Cressie. You are the most wonderful
person to walk into our lives—I swear!*

Juliet slipping her hand into his. Juliet squeezing his fingers with
hers. Juliet nudging him gently with her shoulder, to alert him to—
something . . .

The guys never asked Brett about Juliet Mayfield. Guys he'd gone
to high school with, and he'd outgrown—to a degree: Halifax, Weisbeck, Stumpf.

There was no vocabulary with which they could speak of girls or
women who meant anything to them. And so, they did not try to
speak of women except in the crudest terms. *Cunt, tits, ass. Hot as
hell. Slut.*

So how could he speak of Juliet to them. He could not.

Just to say her name—to risk hearing her name repeated in the
mouths of Halifax, Weisbeck, Stumpf—he could not.

Like a flower she'd opened to him. One of those roses with many
petals wrapped around one another, enclosed in a tight little bud
and then, who knows why, the warmth of the sun maybe, the petals
begin to open, and open.

He'd been *so happy.* He'd said stammering *I guess I love you, is it too
soon—is it too soon to say? Don't laugh at me, OK?*

HE COULD NOT COMPREHEND, why he'd hurt her, then.

This girl he loved, he'd hurt—had he? (*Had* he?)

First, knocked her away from him. A sharp little cry like an animal
kicked.

And her jaw bruised, dislocated.

No: in fact not dislocated.

At the ER they'd taken an X-ray. The bone hadn't been dislodged. She'd said.

Explaining how she'd slipped, fallen. Clumsy! Her own fault, no one else's.

Weird how everyone accepted this. Believed this.

Beautiful Juliet with a faint bruise like a purple iris rising from beneath the left side of her jaw into her cheek laughing insisting she'd slipped, she'd fallen, it didn't hurt at all and anyway she could cover it with makeup—and no one had noticed.

Not even the parents. Hadn't seen.

See what you have eyes to see. All else, you are blind to.

Then, another time. Why she'd provoked him teasing him with— who the fuck was it—one of the guys he'd known from high school: *Bisher.* Teasing him *Where's Corporal Kincaid that cool dude.*

Or she'd provoked him saying *The only person who can understand you in Carthage is me. Because we are both freaks.*

In a nightmare trying to resuscitate her. Pushing on her chest with the flat of one hand, as he'd been trained, leaning on her chest, trying to revive her breathing, sobbing and whimpering begging *No no no no no don't die.*

Later, he'd found a shallow place for her amid marshy soil, rocks. Tried to cover her with rocks and handfuls of muck. Trying to think *A body must be buried. A body must not be left for animals and birds.* He wasted precious time searching for a marker—a cross.

Why was this, Corporal?

Because—it is the Christian burial.

→ ←

Elephants bury their dead too. He thought this was so.

Maybe on Discovery Channel. Maybe he'd seen a documentary there.

Except elephants could recognize the bones of their dead, years later. A matriarch elephant bellowing and agitated seizing the great curved bones of her grandmother lying in the dried-up earth.

But no human being could recognize the bones of a relative. Could not recognize his own fucking bones set before him on a platter.

Of earthly creatures only *Homo sapiens* and elephants buried their dead. Out of anguish, and out of respect.

And out of a wish that the dead remain *dead*.

In one place, where you'd left them. Covered with mud-chunks, rock, earth. *Dead*.

IN THE LETTER to Juliet he'd asked her never to open except if he did not return from the war he'd written in the careful stiff handwriting of one who rarely wrote by hand *Knowing a thing should give you the strength to do it but sometimes you are not strong enough. God does not make you strong enough.*

Do unto others. Love thy neighbor.

Thou shalt not kill.

Confused he'd thought possibly he had buried the letter with her in the shallow marshy grave beside the river! In which case the (wet, torn) letter would be deciphered in his handwriting, signed *Love, Brett* and traced back to him.

Maybe this was meant to be so. Maybe this was why God had guided his hand writing the letter.

ANOTHER TIME ASKING the corporal what he'd seen. Whom he'd seen.

How close he'd been, and when.

Number of rifle shots. How many times the AK-47 fired.

If he'd seen the bodies inside the house. The body in the culvert.

Each pronouncement of *Corporal* was a mockery in his ears.

WHAT ARE YOU CLAIMING, *Corporal. Did you witness.*

You were not there, yet you claim.

You were there, yet you claim.

How can you be certain. These are serious allegations.

Not what you have heard from others but what did you see.

Not what they told you. Not what you told the chaplain or what you remember. Not the pictures you saw or believed you saw.

Serious allegations, Corporal. Accusations.

EXACTLY WHAT DID YOU SEE. *Exactly which men.*

Not which men you "knew" were there but which men you saw and in what relationship to one another and to you and when. Not which men you "were told" were there but which men you saw.

Did you see the faces, Corporal. Can you identify each individual.

Did you witness.

Were you there. If there, why did not you not intervene.

Why were you there if you could not witness.

Serious allegations. Accusations.

Corroborators?

THEY WERE SAYING *Sure you did, Brett.*

Corporal? Just tell us how it happened.

They were not uniformed. Their hair was not shaved at the sides.

He was confused, how his interrogators had altered themselves. Like they'd moved into a blurred patch in the center of his head and emerged on the other side and were different people and the fascination of this so drew his concentration he had no clear idea what was being asked of him still less how to truthfully reply.

Didn't mean to hurt her—eh? Just, got out of control.

. . . led you on? These things happen.

And she's the sister of the other one.

Fuck anybody'd blame you, son. After what you went through in the U.S. Army treating you like shit your own fiancée blowing you off you're "disabled" then the sister in your face—hell man, you were provoked.

Wasn't he provoked? The corporal? Sure he was—shit!

Want to tell us how? And what you did with her—with the body—after? We know you put her in the river. See we found some of her clothes at

*Sackets Harbor. That far away, Corporal—hard to believe but happens to
be true.*

*See, this is it—her sweater. That poor little girl's sweater, some kids
found in the rocks at Sackets Harbor too bad for you, Corporal, it didn't get
carried out into the lake like maybe her body is there—in the lake? Or maybe
her body is in the river, sunk? You know anything about that?*

*We can find the body, you don't cooperate and tell us, Corporal. It will
take a while but we can find it, state troopers will help us drag the river
and out into the lake. Poor little girl didn't weigh one hundred pounds and
her blood was in your Jeep and on your shirt and her hairs in your Jeep
where you yanked at her head—that what you did, Corporal? Grabbed her
by her hair and smashed her face against the windshield so there's blood
there? And her fingerprints, too. Just will take time for us to find her so
you could save us the time and it will be a credit to you, the judge will be
impressed if you cooperate, see Corporal—not like asshole meth-heads and
fuckups too stupid to cooperate with the D.A. wind up on Death Row at
Dannemora in a cell the size of a shitter and rot there for ten, twenty years
till they wish they were dead and by that time their brains have rotted like
Alzheimer's. But if you say what you did with her could be the D.A. will
drop the charge to manslaughter not homicide, that's his call, could be the
judge will give you twenty to life so you could be paroled in nine years—a
pretty good deal considering what you did to that poor little girl, Corporal.
You know and we know and you need to acknowledge it. And the girl's
family needs to be told and their minds put at ease. Everybody in Carthage
is saying Corporal Kincaid was a good decent American kid got fucked up
by the Iraqi-enemy—not your fault, Corporal. No one will blame you, or
hardly.*

HE WAS SICK with shame. Sick with guilt. Backed-up in him like a
drain. He couldn't purge himself.

Better to die. To have died—"in combat."

Now it was too late. He'd been killed but hadn't died—exactly.

Felt to himself like something carelessly made to resemble a human being—a mannequin-mummy. Scraps of original skin dried like

leather, swaths of hair like something you'd see in a natural history museum exhibit.

In D.C. he'd visited museums—Smithsonian, National Gallery.

It was calming to think of a museum, for a museum housed dead things. People stared at the dead things which were appropriate in such places and did not arouse emotion or even much interest. It was a kind of embalming—cool air, marble floors, high ceilings.

During "exodus" break at Christmas—midway in basic training at Fort Benning—he'd had ten days he might've been home in Carthage but instead flew to D.C.

Alone he'd gone. Alone he'd wanted to see the Vietnam Veterans Memorial he'd been reading about for years. He knew the monument had been considered "controversial" initially. He wanted to see for himself.

He knew of an older relative—father's cousin—who'd died in Vietnam. There'd been others in Carthage but he wasn't sure of their names.

The first name was *Tom*, or *Tim*. A name he hadn't paid much attention to, as a child.

He wished his father knew he'd enlisted in the army. That in BCT—basic combat training—he'd excelled, so far.

The drill sergeant seemed to like him. The other guys seemed to like him. He'd been chosen "platoon leader" in his training class.

Wished his father could know, he'd enlisted twelve days after 9/11.

Scared him to think, maybe his father would never know.

He'd be sent to the Middle East, probably. Infantry. That was his choice. Iraq, Afghanistan—he didn't care which. It was a secret from Juliet, his mother and the Mayfields—how eager he was to *go*.

Eager to finish basic training. Then to advanced training also at Fort Benning, Georgia. With a part of his mind he knew it was crazy yet he hoped—like a child, desperately hoped—the war(s) would not end before he joined the U.S. troops there.

It wasn't normal behavior, he knew. Every guy in basic training was desperate to get home after six weeks of exhausting boot camp but Brett Kincaid opted to spend the first weekend alone in D.C. where he didn't know anyone. There was his fiancée waiting for him in Carthage, waiting to love him, not even knowing he wasn't coming home directly.

Might've taken Juliet with him. He had not.

Cold-raining Saturday morning yet there were visitors to the memorial. Most were families, a few couples hand in hand, but apart from Private Brett Kincaid, not one other person there alone.

Juliet didn't know where he was. No one knew.

Moving with others facing the long horizontal monument-walls down a gradual descent you didn't realize was meant to suggest a communal grave in the shape of a V. No wonder he'd begun to feel strange—halting and breathless.

So many names!—stretching beyond his range of vision.

Visitors—had to be relatives of dead soldiers—searched for names then stopped to stare for long minutes like sleepwalkers. With a childlike sort of wonder they touched the names engraved in the black granite. Some had to stand on their toes straining to touch names almost out of reach. There was a stepladder you could use, to climb higher. For it was not enough to *see,* you had to *touch.*

In the ground at the base of the memorial were small flags wet from the rain, photographs, flowers both artificial and real. He'd read that, each evening, these precious objects were cleared away.

When had his father's cousin died? Brett wasn't sure but he believed it was nearer the end of the long war than the beginning.

Scanning columns of names seeking out KINCAID.

His father's name would not be here of course. Brett knew that. His father hadn't served in Vietnam but in the first Gulf War and in any case his father hadn't died in any war.

More than fifty-eight thousand soldiers had died in Vietnam! You could not comprehend such a sum, your brain was struck blank at the prospect.

Passing years 1959, 1963, 1967, 1970 . . . His eyes blurred with moisture, it was difficult to see. No name leapt to his eye as familiar until near the end of a column beneath 1971 there was TIMOTHY KINCAID.

That was him!—his father's cousin.

Brett stopped dead. He stared at the name, that was at about the height of his shoulder. He leaned forward to touch it—to move his fingers over it.

He swallowed hard. He had no idea why he was so deeply moved by what was essentially a stranger's name.

"Excuse me?"—a woman was speaking to him. An older woman walking with a cane, in a transparent raincoat, younger people accompanying her—must've been asking Brett who TIMOTHY KINCAID was to him and he murmured something vague and polite to her even as he turned away blinking tears from his eyes.

"God bless."

Quickly moving away. Not a backward glance.

He hadn't even taken a picture with his cell phone as he'd planned.

When he returned to Carthage he would tell no one about his visit to D.C. Often he would recall the name TIMOTHY KINCAID as one might recall the name of a lost relative, a brother not seen in many years.

Even his fingertips recalled—TIMOTHY KINCAID.

IN THAT PLACE, the Land of the Dead.

His mother, his fiancée and her parents. His friends.

High school buddies/brothers. Soldiers in his platoon.

They are all silent, the color has drained from their faces.

Like faded Kodak snapshots in his grandmother's old photo-album.

Brett? Come here.

Yes you are in the right place.

Yes we have been waiting.

PORNOGRAPHY, CHEAP CANDY, tooth-rotting candy.

Drugs. Dope. Smoking joints like shit. Dog-shit. Dried, mummi-fied. Sandstorms.

He'd died when the grenade exploded. When the wall exploded.

He'd been called. Commanded to hurry forward. With his rifle at the ready cradled in his arms rifle butt pressed into his shoulder hard and firm, prepared to fire. *Enemy sighted!* The last voice he'd heard was braying Sergeant Shaver—*Get here, Kincaid! Get here! Jesus Christ get here fast!*

He'd died and gone to *that place.* There, he'd seen figures huddling together for warmth.

Still, they'd shoveled and swept the parts of him together. Ingeniously stitched and glued and inserted wires to hold him together. He saw a pattern of figures—shapes like clouds passing high overhead—and knew he had to deduce, from this ever-shifting pattern, a focal point, a *self,* that saw it; a *self* that possessed the mechanism that registered it.

Call this *self* some convenient name—*Brett Kincaid. Timothy Kincaid.*

Trying to trick him asking him to "lift" his right leg, left leg, right arm, left arm he couldn't figure out how to do this, how you could manage to "lift" whatever it was they were asking you to "lift"—how could a part of the body "lift" a part of the body?—trying to explain *You would not have leverage.*

And they'd touch you with a rod or a stick that was sharp?—meant to tickle?—like the sole of a foot—(but which foot?)—and you'd have to guess what this was. And was something "hot" or "cold"—was the texture "smooth" or "rough"—wildly he guessed or sometimes just said *Whatever* to signal it was OK with him whatever—whatever it was.

Loyalty. Duty. Respect. Selfless Service.

Honor. Integrity. Personal Courage.

Army Core Values.

Corporal Brett Graham Kincaid Property U.S. Army.

Intraocular lens in his mangled left eye. Titanium implant holding together the broken skull. The skin/skins of his face stitched together and a rash like stinging ants itching like hell but you must not scratch the stitches for you might tear them out and the skins would loosen and bleed and become infected. Tight-strung wires in the lower part of the body (bowels, groin) and a *cath-EEE-ter* stuck up inside his limp-rubber cock to drain the poison-piss so he wouldn't turn mustard-yellow like some of the guys in the hospital you couldn't guess how old they were—his age, or his father's age.

Jesus, he'd been a happy kid! Didn't realize at the time, his mother suffered such misery and bitterness backed up in her like a stopped toilet—(and their toilet on Potsdam Street was always getting stopped up, Ethel complained and wept trying to unstop it herself with a filthy toilet plunger)—but Brett made friends easily, in grade school; one of the taller boys, quick on his feet, a natural athlete but not a bully or boastful for the sadness in him, his father had *gone away*. People were likely to say that he took after Graham, good-looking, wavy fair-brown hair and pale brown eyes and a quick smile, rarely sulked or brooded or talked-back to adults for adults naturally liked and trusted him.

Basically Brett was just a nice guy. Everybody liked him—kids, adults. He never mouthed off like the other guys, he'd be quiet thinking his own thoughts. He didn't judge people, he never made fun of people. A cripple-kid—Brett would be nice to him. A teacher having trouble keeping the kids in order, Brett would help maintain discipline. He'd had to work at school like with math and English but actually he got pretty good grades—mostly B's. He'd be loyal to his friends like Duane Stumpf, Rod Halifax and what's-his-name—Weisbeck. They'd been little kids together in the neighborhood along Potsdam so it was like they were brothers. Why he'd defend Stumpf when Stumpf got into trouble, you'd have to know their background. Duane Stumpf had this round pudgy face, little-boy-face when he was a young kid, he'd break you up saying some crude really dirty things like he had no idea what the words meant.

Those guys didn't act toward Brett Kincaid the way they acted toward other kids. They sort of sucked up to Brett, they were admiring of him. None of them was any kind of athlete like Brett.

Brett was the kind of guy you'd ask for a favor if you needed it. And he'd do it if he could—wouldn't ask questions or act like it was some kind of imposition on him or afterward make some joke or snotty remark.

He wouldn't lend money but he'd lend other things—his bike, for instance. He worked after school at least two jobs—grocery store bagging, tree farm—had to save what he could, his mother didn't have any money she was always saying. Why Brett enlisted in the army—he'd get paid, he was going to apply to be an officer and take courses at one of the SUNY colleges, after a few years. He'd give his mother what money he could.

Brett's crazy mother Ethel! She'd come outside front of their house in just a bathrobe—something like you'd see in a movie all shiny and silky and nothing beneath so you'd have a glimpse of her breasts and thighs shaking like Jell-O, and a snatch of hair between her legs you'd look away from quick not wanting to see.

In a porn magazine or video you'd want to see this but in actual life—another guy's mother!—no.

Brett was embarrassed of her. But Brett was protective of her, too.

This time we were in tenth grade. Things were fucked-up at my house. My father was drinking and sick and my mother was always saying how she'd like to swallow all the pills she could get her hands on and I'd been missing school a lot. And Brett didn't say much just kind of hung out with me. On his way home from work or football practice he'd drop by our house. He wouldn't come inside, I didn't ask him inside—we'd hang out in the driveway, or on the street. Or we'd go over to the 7-Eleven parking lot. Brett wouldn't ask why I hadn't been in school. He never asked any questions. He never wanted to smoke a joint with me—just said no thanks. He never criticized other people much. One day I was feeling pretty shitty and he said hey why didn't I come over to his place for supper. He seemed to know there wasn't likely to be any supper at our house, my mother wasn't in any condition to make a meal, or even to eat a meal. I said no thanks! Nobody had ever invited me to supper at their house—not before, and not since. Brett said his mother would be OK with having me. So I said OK—it was, like, the nicest thing anybody'd ever asked me to do. The surprise was, that night Brett's crazy mother wasn't like what you'd expect. Maybe because it was just me alone and not other guys, too. Maybe she felt sorry for me, Brett must've told her about me.

We had frozen pizza Brett brought home from the ShopRite where he worked. Pepperoni and cheese and tomatoes and Mrs. Kincaid mashed up some canned tomatoes to add to it, so it wouldn't dry out in the oven. The three of us sat watching TV—ER which was Brett's mom's favorite TV show. She liked seeing people worse off than her and how they dealt with it and later I thought—That's why Mrs. Kincaid likes me around. But that was OK, I could relate to that.

That year I went over to Brett's place maybe five times. It wasn't always supper, sometimes we'd just hang out. One of those times Mrs. Kincaid was drinking beer and she said to me, Your name is Budny, isn't it?—and I said yes—and she said this strange thing, I always remembered: Your mother used to be a friend of mine in high school. But I don't hold that against her now.

Meaning I guess she was angry at my mom for not staying friends with her. I think that's what she meant. But if Mrs. Kincaid had known my mom then, she wouldn't have said such a thing. My mom was so fucked-up anybody was a friend of hers, or a relative, they'd run like hell in the opposite direction.

There never was anybody married and in a family, that we knew of, that didn't get fucked-up sooner or later.

Brett was, like, a real Christian I guess you could say. He never talked about things like religion, he'd have been embarrassed as hell but maybe that was it. "Do unto others—" like they say. He tried that—why he got in over his head in Iraq, maybe. And then, "disabled" like he was, and taking some kind of powerful drugs—also drinking, which you aren't supposed to do taking the drugs. This is what people are saying. But his main weakness was, he couldn't say no to his old friends like Stumpf and Halifax and Weisbeck—just couldn't.

If anybody wants testimony like in a trial—a "character witness"—I will do that. If there is a trial.

Somebody said you can't arrest anybody for murder if there isn't a body so maybe there will never be a trial. But if there is, I will stand up for Brett

Kincaid no matter what they're saying he did. Or even if he says so himself finally. Because Brett Kincaid who is my friend would not ever have hurt anyone and if it turns out he hurt that Mayfield girl, then that wasn't Brett Kincaid but somebody else not known to me.

AMID THE EARTH/RUBBLE spilling off a shovel you'd see miniature bits of colored glass, might be "gems"—meant to signal *There is beauty within ugliness. There is good within evil. Have faith!*

Hard to believe this wasn't so. In his innermost heart, he could not believe otherwise.

As in basic training he hadn't been scared like the others. Seeing how the drill sergeant cast his steely gaze over the recruits determining which ones are OK, reliable, mature, focuses his attention on the weaker recruits it's his responsibility to toughen, plus a few inevitable fuckups he can humiliate, beat down and break in the presence of the others the way a triumphant boxer will keep hitting, bloodying his opponent's face until the poor sap goes down, flat on his back, *out*. Seeing how the sergeant observed *him*—he knew he was OK, a man among men.

So when it was time, knowing, or guessing, that the guys in his platoon who knew what he knew about what they'd done to the Iraqi girl and her family and (possibly) what he'd been telling the chaplain were conspiring to kill him if not outright then to set up circumstances in which (possibly) he'd be killed—"in combat"—yet on patrol at the northern edge of rubble-strewn Kirkuk he'd come forward when summoned by his sergeant, obeyed his superior officer's command as he'd been trained for he had seen no alternative as a soldier.

And now he'd died, he didn't have to testify at the hearing. *Army Criminal Investigation Command.*

Neurologically impaired—"retrograde amnesia"—incapable of remembering with any degree of clarity, accuracy, confidence what had/had not happened in the early evening of December 11, 2004, at the northern edge of rubble-strewn Kirkuk, Iraq.

Not even who'd taken the knife, sliced the girl's cheeks. No-face and no-name.

Wouldn't need a lawyer.

Wouldn't need to travel—to be "shipped"—to D.C.

Wouldn't need an attendant to accompany him on the plane, in taxis and to the hearings in the Pentagon. Help him walk, count out his meds, keep him from alcohol and from killing himself in a hotel bathroom, wipe his leaky ass.

NOR DID HE NEED to beg Juliet to take him back so that she could accompany him to D.C.—help him walk, count out his meds, keep him from alcohol he'd lap like a dog if he could, wipe his sad sick leaky hemorrhoidal ass insisting she loved him, would always love him, sickness and in health and in the life to come if only he'd let her.

WHAT DID I TELL THEM *honey I told the truth—it was an accident.*

Slipped and fell and struck the door—so silly.

At the ER they took an X-ray. My jaw is not dislocated.

It's sore, it's hard to swallow but the bruises will fade.

I know, you did not mean it.

I am sorry to upset you.

I am not crying, truly!

We will look back on this time of trial and we will say—It was a test of our love. We did not weaken.

HE'D SAID NO. He didn't think so.

Grinning-clown face so close to her, she was spared seeing it.

SERIOUS CHARGES. *Better be certain what you are claiming, Corporal.*

Your safety and security can't be guaranteed if you pursue these charges.

Lieutenant C_ staring at Corporal Kincaid as if a bad smell were leaking from him.

THE JEEP WRANGLER had been impounded by police immediately. Every inch of the vehicle was examined. Only Jake Pedersen's persistence resulted in the Jeep being returned to its owner who after all hadn't (yet) been arrested.

Gathering evidence. Ongoing investigation.

Now it wasn't clear that Brett Kincaid should have been driving. Or should drive now.

His therapist-friend Seth had said he thought it might be OK. If someone else was always in the vehicle with him.

Vision corrected to twenty-forty in the right eye. In the left eye ███████████. Which met the minimum state requirement for a driver's license.

Left leg wasn't strong but right leg OK—the crucial leg: foot, gas, brake.

It was (possibly) true: the corporal's reflexes were not so coordinated as they'd once been. Peripheral vision you could say frankly *shot to hell.*

Still, he could drive a vehicle. Had the right to drive a vehicle.

Wasn't going to beg. Ethel would beg for him.

Saying *You can't take my son's driver's license from him, too!*

All that you already took from him, his health, his life—the rest of his life—capit'list bastards can't take that, too.

MUST'VE BEEN A DREAM he had buried her alive.

Mouth filled with earth but trying to scream.

He woke screaming in terror struck at her with the shovel.

Threw rocks onto her until she was still. Then more rocks, pebbles, clumps of mud carried in his two hands and dumped onto the little body until it was still and the face covered.

OR MAYBE IT WAS STUMP fooling around. You had to laugh at Stumpf—Stump. One day in ninth-grade civics which was on the second floor of the school they looked out the windows—across a concrete walkway—and there, on the roof, was Stumpf! He'd climbed some stairs only the custodian was supposed to use. Found a way out onto the school roof where he was walking kind of stooped-over so he wouldn't be detected, or detected too quickly. "Hey! Look!"—Rod nudged Brett.

At the front of the room Mrs. Nichols was talking. Or some girl was giving a presentation at the blackboard. And out the window, and on the tar paper roof across the way, there was Duane Stumpf and what does the crazy fuckhead do, crouched behind a brick chimney it looks like *he's pissing down the side of the building.*

Before he got to high school, Stumpf—"Stump"—was famous.

Senior yearbook he'd be voted class clown.

Sometimes Stump wasn't so funny. But sure, Stump was *fun-ny!*

The guy with the sewer-mouth. The guy who farts in class.

Dead maggoty squirrel he'd carried on a shovel, dumped in the front seat of Mr. Langley's car behind the wheel.

Things he did to girls. Female teachers.

Some of it Stump did with other guys but mostly alone.

Some of it was never revealed. No one ever knew.

One of the stuck-up girls in their class. Good-looking, cheerleader, beautiful face, fluffy angora sweaters. Her daddy owned the Cadillac dealership. They lived up on Cumberland Avenue near the fancy limestone church. Valentine's Day Stump left for "Debbie" a clump of *actual dog shit* in a velvet wrapping tied to her locker.

Mrs. Gordiner, tight little drum of a (pregnant) belly clearly visible through her clothing they'd tried not to stare at, and some of them resented, some of the guys resented, but also some of the girls. So anyway—lots of jokes about Mrs. Gordiner who taught junior-senior English and advised the Drama Club. Crazy Stumpf downloaded a photo of an *actual human fetus in formaldehyde* he'd found on the Internet and this, in a pink envelope, also a quasi-Valentine, he'd left on Gordiner's desk on Valentine's Day.

Pictures of girl classmates—girls' faces on nude female bodies—some of the bodies *really fat, really nude*—Stump emailed, posted on the Web. Still, Stumpf had girlfriends, later in high school. And later, after high school. Mostly *pigs,* he called them. *Sluts.*

Brett didn't think Stump was so very funny. Didn't think "Coyote" was funny.

Once, they were alone together, Duane Stumpf told Brett something he'd never told anyone else, he said.

"When I was a little kid, my father taught me words like *shit—cocksucker—motherfucker*—to make people laugh. He'd take me with him drinking, like we'd go to Herreton Mills and get some things for the house or the yard and afterward he'd drive out to Wolf's Head and he'd lay me out in the backseat of the car so I could sleep, sometimes he'd forget me—wouldn't get home till way after dark. My mother didn't know where the fuck we were, she'd be real upset. The summer before I started school they'd had a fight and Pa walked out and took me with him—like he'd just thought of it and hadn't made any plans. He'd call her, he hadn't kidnapped me exactly, but we didn't get home much. I cried a lot at first then it got so I really dug it, surprising people and making them laugh. I mean—really shocking them, like. And women, too. Girls. They'd call over other people to hear me, a crowd would gather around us at the bar, Pa was really into it, like somebody on TV, and I felt so—it was so—great . . . A little kid saying these 'dirty' words like he didn't know what he was saying, that's really funny. There was a joke we did together kind of—forget how it went but I was 'little cocksucker'—people laughed like hell. Pa said, my little cocksucker's gonna be on TV someday, you wait.

"'Course other times, Pa would get drunk and just kind of forget me out in the car. And forget to feed me, too. And this was the opposite of that."

ASKING WHAT HE'D DONE with her. What he'd done with *her body.*

And he'd said what was true: he didn't remember.

Some things he remembered, a swirl of things like dirty water rushing down a drain, but it was not possible to attach names to these; and it was not possible to shape the words, the sounds of the words, with his mouth.

Between somewhere in his brain and his mouth/tongue there was slippage.

. . . *make things easier for us, and for you. The judge would be lenient considering your service to the country. And the girl's family you would allow them to bury the body it's the only decent thing and you are a decent person corporal and still young—out on parole in eight, nine years.*

What do you say, son?

Here was a surprise: they released the corporal.

Could not comprehend this! Had to be a mistake.

For now, there was a lawyer—"representing" Brett Kincaid.

He'd been adamant: he hadn't wanted a lawyer. Thinking if his father knew, if Staff Sergeant Graham Kincaid found out, that his son had a lawyer, required a lawyer, in this situation he was in, his father would be disgusted. He believed that retaining a lawyer is an admission of guilt and so was ashamed to have a lawyer "representing" him—like a criminal.

Shaver, Muksie, Broca, Mahan, Ramirez—all had *legal counsel*.

Army prosecutors had negotiated with Ramirez, only nineteen and the youngest of the men: plead guilty, inform on the others, sentence will be less than twenty years.

Ethel had been furious claiming her *disabled hero-son* was being *railroaded* into prison—to *Death Row*.

She'd made arrangements. There were many who supported Corporal Kincaid. Not a public defender but a *first-rate* private lawyer.

See what Zeno thinks now. Trying to destroy us!

Brett refused to speak with what's-his-name—Pedersen. His brain just shut off.

The guys were staying away from him now. His old friends. Maybe they were anxious—he'd inform on *them*.

Fuckhead snitch. Got what he deserved.

It was astonishing, he'd been released by the Beechum County police. Allowed to leave the building, make his way outside leaning on Ethel and what's-his-name—Pedersen.

Photographers, TV camera crews outside in the parking lot. Nothing to be ashamed of, Ethel said. In the TV lights, Ethel's eyes flared like cat's eyes.

It was an indeterminate time he was sick part-collapsed on the soiled old sofa in Ethel's living room. Days now, a week couldn't move his bowels like concrete. Screamed with pain. Screams like hyena laughter.

"Coyote" laughter—Muksie sawing at the girl's face with the knife. Sergeant Shaver had cut off the little finger, with the trauma shears.

Broca took pictures. Little cell phone flash in the shadows.

A smell of oil pervading everything here. Oil, heat and sand.

The corporal hadn't seen, really. Hadn't been within twenty feet was the estimate.

Yes but—he could not swear. Under oath you must *swear.*

Under oath you could not speak vaguely. You could not speak emotionally.

It was an open secret it would happen to him: Kincaid.

His friends warned him. His friends were anxious for him. One of his friends sent emails home to his father, retired navy officer, telling him of *the situation in Kirkuk.*

He'd been a fuckhead snitch. Motherfucker snitch. They'd warned him, he hadn't listened.

Well, he'd listened—he'd told the chaplain. Turned out to have been a mistake maybe.

But he had not known how otherwise to behave.

Later, after the explosion, after the hospitalizations, when he hadn't been paying attention they'd released him from military service—"honorably discharged."

Purple Heart. Iraq War Campaign medal. And the beautiful Infantry Combat Badge that was the special sign of his bravery and his sacrifice.

Proudly Ethel displayed these in the living room. Giving interviews to the press and to TV, Ethel held these in cupped hands for the camera.

The investigating committee wouldn't be subpoenaing the corporal.

His testimony was inconsistent. His testimony was impaired.

Strange to him now, he was being released again. During his days in custody at sheriff's headquarters he'd considered *If I reach for a gun. One of their guns. They will shoot me point-blank, put me out of my misery.*

For the plainclothes detectives wore their revolvers, inside their coats. On duty, a man must never be without his firearm.

He'd lost his rifle somewhere—that was a painful fact. All his gear, sixty pounds—seemed to have been lost. Where?

In a sweat awaiting the drill sergeant's infuriated voice.

Kincaid. What the fuck have you been doing.

You little shit Kincaid what the fuck d'you mean letting the army down. You disgust me.

His lawyer had negotiated the terms of his release which was that Brett Kincaid could not leave Beechum County without notifying law enforcement officials. The corporal hadn't been arrested on charges of homicide, kidnapping, unlawful disposal of a body, obstruction of justice—yet.

Detectives were circumspect, how close they were to making an arrest. It was known that they were investigating the Adirondack Hells Angels bikers, too.

In the house on Potsdam Street he had time to think about these matters except his brain was awash with debris as in a muddy inlet of the Nautauga River after a heavy rainstorm.

Ethel's relatives came to visit. A few of Brett's father's relatives whom he hadn't seen in years.

They spoke together incensed of how "shitty" was the treatment of a *war hero* in Carthage.

The enemy was perceived to be Zeno Mayfield who'd been the one to accuse Brett from the start. The matter of the broken engagement was seen to be the motive.

Some of Brett's friends from high school came by. Guys he'd known years ago and a few girls including one who was married now, and pregnant, and had come to see him defiant of her husband's objections, as she'd made sure Brett knew.

Halifax, Stumpf, Weisbeck came by. Awkward in Brett's company since Brett lapsed into silences while they talked, guzzled beer and greedily ate potato chips Ethel set out for them in front of the TV.

Real shitty, Brett. What the fuckin cops are tryin to do.

People sayin crazy things. Assholes . . .

. . . we weren't there, you tell them that? None of us, we weren't there, whatever happened, wherever you took her, or—whatever it was . . .

After the Roebuck Inn. Wherever it was . . .

It was just you, Brett, OK? That girl climbing all over you, had to be crazy-high, asking for—whatever it was, that happened.

Overhearing, Ethel stormed into the room, screamed at them to get the hell out of her house. If they were Brett's friends God damn they had to *help him.* Fuck them all they wanted was to cover their fucking asses well how's about *helping him,* Brett was the one in *need of fucking help.*

Neighbors came over. Not many. Others, sighting wild-eyed Ethel by the curb, or Brett Kincaid limping to his Jeep to drive to rehab, turned quickly away without a greeting.

Interviewers ceased coming to the house. Visitors ceased.

Not what Ethel Kincaid had expected! When the phone rang it wasn't relatives, friends, neighbors wishing them well, assuring them they believed that Brett was *innocent,* but strangers calling to accuse Ethel of harboring a murderer. *Aren't you ashamed! You're his mother—tell him to confess.*

Cards came to the house addressed to Corperal Kinkaid: *You disgusting killer. You are a rapest killer of that young girl, you are a coward to confess.*

Jesus sees into your heart you are both Sinners & will be brougt to justice.

In the house on Potsdam Street he stayed inside most days. In his old boyhood room with yellowing postcards from his father still taped to the wall, he never saw any longer. He could not leave the house without being observed. He could not enter the rehab clinic without being observed. Seth Seager who'd been his therapist/friend until he'd broken up with Juliet and for a while afterward had quit the clinic and moved away without saying good-bye. Sessions at the clinic were arduous, painful. A shimmering coil of pain ran up and down his spine like electricity. His breathing was labored, his lungs were yet acrid with fine filaments of sand, like death; tears ran down his cheeks, he could not brush away fast enough; his new therapist, replacing Seth, was a middle-aged woman named Inge who smiled tightly at him as if she could not bear to touch him, despite their physical intimacy.

Sometimes, Inge called him "Corporal"—he gave no sign of hearing.

On bad days Ethel had to take off work to drive him to the clinic and home again which was a round-trip of about six miles. Where in mid- and late summer Ethel Kincaid had been triumphant at the fact of her son being *out of police custody* now in the fall, as time passed, she was becoming ever more resentful of her situation as the mother of a *disabled Iraq War veteran under nonstop police surveillance.* In her mood of embittered strain she was likely to swerve, skid, hastily brake and sideswipe the now-battered Jeep Wrangler against rails or even other vehicles stationary or in motion.

Out of nowhere as in a TV movie a girl Brett had known (before Juliet Mayfield) reappeared in his life to drive him to rehab and to the doctors in Watertown and anywhere else he wished but one day when Gayle Nash called him it was Ethel who answered the phone saying tersely *No more. He can't see you no more. He says to tell you. Thanks for all you done but—no more.*

Last thing the grieving mother wanted was another man-crazy

female grabbing hold of her son. The last one that did that, stuck-up Mayfield bitch, see how *that* turned out.

It was rare that Brett ventured outside now. Drinking with his friends at the lakeside taverns on weekend nights had ended abruptly that night in July.

Occasionally, he went with Ethel to the mall. It was Ethel's idea: *get out of the house, show your face, nothing to be ashamed of, they're the ones should be ashamed!—sonsabitches.*

At the mall, Brett walked haltingly. He was still tall—but curiously asymmetrical, as if his spine were twisted and his hips out of alignment. He wore a baseball cap pulled down over his forehead, loose-fitting shirts with long sleeves, khaki pants with drooping cuffs. At first glance you thought his face was a gauze mask, or parts of a gauze mask. Dark-tinted glasses hid the upper half of his face.

He stared straight ahead. He walked with his arms close against the sides of his body. Ethel gripped his arm, to steady him. She was trembling with indignation even when no one stared at them.

What are you looking at, you?—take a good look.

Know who this is?—a wounded veteran of the Iraq War.

Sacrificed himself for you—now look at him!

What's the matter—can't face us? Asshole!

Once, Ethel gave a little rush in the direction of several young teenagers who were gaping at her and her tall lanky son who looked fitted-together out of mismatched parts, hissing—*Get away! Go to hell! Think your turn won't come—it will!*

No one asked Brett about Cressida Mayfield. No one spoke of *the girl, that girl—the girl they say is missing.*

Ethel did not ask him about Cressida. It was a long time before Brett realized she'd never asked him anything about that night, or about what had happened to him in Kirkuk.

He'd overheard her on the phone, speaking with a relative very likely one of her sisters.

This place Kik-kik it's called—in Ir-wack—turns out there's a big oil field there—like, really big. So the U.S. government, you can figure, there's big-business oilmen paying them off, so they go into the Arab states to take over the oil. Capit'lists laying some damn big pipeline. That's why Bush declared war! Poor Brett, he didn't know none of this, nobody did, but you wise up fast. Poor dumb kid is what you call col-late-ral damage nobody gives a shit for, once they're out of uniform like his sonuvabitch old man that disappeared into the West like who's-it—Clint Eastwood.

You bet, they owe us big-time. Once this trial is out of the way we're going to sue the U.S. government for "liability." Department of Defense. Rumsfield. Everybody says we'd be fools to take the first offer of a settlement, like only a million or two when the papers and TV gets hold of Brett's story and the shit hits the fan of America.

EACH CUT OFF A FINGER, and each an ear.

From other bodies they'd cut other bits of flesh. A small square of skin dries swiftly in the desert heat—instant "mummification."

An almost-entire face. He'd had a glimpse of a pouch made of three civilian faces, looked like male faces, carelessly sewn together. Muksie had said it was something the Sioux and the Iroquois did.

Cell phone pictures of corpses, and guys goofing off. Secret pix you wouldn't want to get into the wrong hands.

Don't show Kincaid. Not for the corporal!

Still he'd seen. Had to see. No way not to see.

Everybody in the platoon knew. Mostly it was just—*Jesus that's sick. You assholes are kind of disgusting y'know?*

But you wouldn't inform. Not even the chaplain. You just wouldn't, you *would not.*

Except, Kincaid believed in his heart he must. Could not sleep knowing *I must.*

Like sand sifting through your fingers. Nothing to grab onto. Nothing to give a name to. When you return home you will confide in just your special friends, possibly a brother, but no one else in the family. Guys who understand, know what you endured and why these matter—*trophies.*

Your mom, your girlfriend or wife, sister, cousin—you don't show these trophies which are private. No female could understand. Even a female pretending not to be one of her sex like Juliet's fierce-faced younger sister could not understand. You don't show them any trophies just "picturesque" photos, trinkets, mementos, souvenirs. Nobody knew where Iraq was or had any knowledge of the country, you could buy Middle Eastern–looking jewelry or miniature African animals carved out of ivory in the Frankfurt airport, Indian shawls—who'd know the difference?

First deployment, on his return home he'd bought things like that for Juliet, for his mother and Mrs. Mayfield. Second deployment, on his way home he was shipped in an airtight Ziploc body-bag.

In Halifax's car they drove out to Route 31 to score some pot.

God-damn strong dope, does weird things to your brain.

He's wheezing like asthma. Halifax thumps his back.

Jesus Christ! Don't fucking die on me Kincaid!

THE FANCY LAWYER who'd taken on his case had a way of speaking of Corporal Kincaid in the third person even when he was present like you'd speak of a brain-dead person, or a corpse.

My client acknowledges the girl might have been in his vehicle which accounts for the prints, the blood and the hairs. But not that night. Another night.

My client is neurologically impaired. That is a medical fact. Medical records are here provided. He cannot remember clearly since he was injured in Iraq—"traumatic brain injury." No jury would ever convict him.

IN THE BARRACKS lavatory at the post north of Kirkuk. He did not think *I will kill him now. This must be done.* In his hands he was wielding his rifle with just enough space to raise and swing and so that the butt struck Private Muksie on the side of the head, one, two, three swift strokes as with a look of utter surprise Muksie grunted and sank to his knees, sank to the befouled cement floor spouting blood. Not thinking *God has directed me. This is the first.*

But somebody had seen him. One of the guys hurrying to help him—to help Brett—taking the rifle from him, wiping the butt clean.

Gone to hell. This is the first.

He was laughing. Stumbling. His friends were hauling him back to the barracks.

Later seeing Private Muksie—"Coyote"—returning from patrol.

Fully awake then rubbing his temples feeling the fat arteries inside beat, beat, beat close to bursting.

Can't guarantee your safety, Corporal. Take precautions.

SHE'D WANTED HIM to tell her these things—*Secrets you can't tell anyone else. I know—you have them.*

In her lowered voice assuring him *I am the only one who understands you, Brett. No one else can know what we know, they are beloved of God and we are—misfits.*

In the Jeep he was driving. Gripping the wheel tight in both hands because he'd been drinking and a nasty buzz permeated his skull like a hive of hornets.

Crucial to him—to get the girl home: Juliet's sister.

Saying desperate things to him, even drunk he knew to be embarrassed—*Juliet didn't deserve you. Juliet is one of those who "lives in light"—hasn't a clue what we know. I am the one who can love you, Brett— please believe me.*

He was shocked. Juliet's sister!

Didn't know what to say to her. Though feeling a stirring of— remotely—as if at a distance—what might've been, in another lifetime, sexual yearning.

. . . the one who can love you. Brett please.

His first thought was—too young.

And Juliet's sister who would've been, if they'd gotten married, like a sister of his.

Desperately he wanted to be rid of her.

Safely rid of her—take her home.

If Juliet knew . . . Juliet would be shocked.

He'd never felt at ease with the younger sister. Possibly he'd never once spoken her name: *Cres-sida*.

He'd gotten along with her OK at the start. He'd known her, encountered her, when she'd had a bicycle accident a few years before—seemed like she'd been another person then.

Younger, then.

Later, she'd changed. Held herself apart from others, observing, judging; never quite smiling or laughing when Brett spent time with them. Thought herself *superior*.

Frequently in Brett's presence she seemed to be looking at *him*—in a way he hadn't wanted to decode.

For Cressida's *will* was a force in the Mayfield household—Brett had gathered.

From remarks Juliet had made, Brett had gathered that this was so.

Even bossy Zeno deferred to her. Arlette rarely contradicted Cressida and often in her company grew quiet as if hoping to avoid a sharp or sarcastic remark from the "precocious" younger daughter.

Cressida rarely helped in the kitchen. If she was inveigled into helping clean up after a meal she slung dishes and cutlery into the dishwasher without troubling to rinse them, with a kind of spiteful glee.

Once, in the wake of a meal, when even Zeno was helping in the kitchen, Cressida drew Brett away upstairs to her room, insisting upon showing him her "Esch-er drawings" on display on a wall, and in a portfolio on a shelf. He hadn't known what to expect and he'd been surprised and impressed by these highly detailed, obviously very skillful works of art like nothing he'd ever seen executed by anyone in Carthage.

In her room which he would remember as crammed with books and weird drawings, nothing at all like Juliet's feminine room, Cressida told him that her drawings were a way of exploring the "interior" of her own brain.

When you pick up a pen, dip it into ink, there's a kind of thrill like an electric current that runs up your arm. You go into a kind of trance. Like dreaming with your eyes open. Pausing then to add, with a shrug of her small shoulders *Oh but—it's lonely there.*

She told him what she hadn't told her family: when she'd been away in Canton, she was surprised how she'd missed them. And him.

I missed you all. I guess I was homesick! It sounds so banal, corny. You were in Georgia—yet I felt close to you. Closer than to my ridiculous suite mates. Juliet forwarded your emails and cell phone pictures, or most of them . . .

Brett thought it was odd, Cressida had been surprised by being homesick. He'd been wracked with what must've been homesickness—and missing Juliet—for most of boot camp at Fort Benning.

Cressida had emailed Brett, too. Terse and coy and he hadn't taken much time to puzzle over her riddle-like letters. Probably he hadn't answered most of them. Boot camp had been exhausting and intense and when he had time to think it was Juliet of whom he thought—Juliet whom he missed.

He hadn't wanted to think that Cressida had been jealous of Juliet and him. Jealous of her beautiful older sister whom everyone adored. It was in mockery she spoke of those *beloved of God*—which certainly included Juliet.

Yet he couldn't believe she was serious now, claiming to love him!

Seeing her at the Roebuck Inn, in that crowd—what a surprise it had been to him! Then realizing she'd come to see *him.*

He hadn't encouraged her. He hadn't responded to her. Yet he'd felt responsible for her.

She'd insisted upon sitting with him in one of the booths, alone.

He'd told her that he wanted to drive her home and she said *Oh thank you Brett but not immediately—oh please.* Shyly, daringly, she'd laid a hand—a small, tremulous hand—on his arm.

Which he should have eased off, or shaken off—but didn't.

He was used to girls and women coming on to him—or had been, until recently. But this was different.

It was hard to look at her, he was so—shocked.

Disapproving, embarrassed.

Yet he'd complied with her wish. Her will.

He'd decided to leave the lakeside tavern and not return. Take the girl home, as he told his friends.

They'd stared at Cressida. Only just waiting for Brett to take her away so that they could make crude jokes Brett didn't want to hear repeated.

He'd had to help her up into the cab of the Jeep. She'd been excited, anxious. Unsteady on her feet as if a single can of beer had gone to her head.

In the Jeep he'd driven a little too fast.

Windows rolled down so the rushing wind made it difficult to hear what she was saying.

She seemed to be pleading *We have so much to say to each other Brett. I don't think you know me at all, I am not really one of them—the "May-fields."*

Behind the wheel of the Jeep he felt slightly better. Fresh air in his face and lungs, a smell of the lake, pinewoods.

. . . had to see you. If you want to talk about Juliet, or . . . about us. What I think I could bring to you, how I could help you . . . not "adjust" . . . I don't mean any silly cliché like "adjust" . . . I mean in your life now your life is so changed and I am the only one who understands, I think.

He'd listened to her: that was the mistake.

He'd listened, he'd been persuaded. Not that what she said was attractive to him, or that she was attractive to him, but that the surprise of her words was *hopeful* to him, who did not believe—(he would have claimed)—in anything so unlikely as *hope*.

She'd asked him please not to drive back to Carthage. Not yet.

She'd asked him please to drive into the Preserve, and along the river—by moonlight.

(It hadn't been a clear moonlight but muggy, hazy. A smudged-looking sickle-moon past which thin fingers of clouds moved like dazed fish as if self-propelled. Beyond the Jeep's headlights was a penumbra of faint, faded light like blindness in which the straight tall trunks of pines emerged with dramatic suddenness.)

He'd wanted to warn her—*What's between Juliet and me—I'm not talking about. But I can't be near people, I will hurt them.*

Somehow it happened, though he knew it was a mistake, the Jeep turned into the Preserve.

Somehow it happened, the Jeep turned onto Sandhill Road.

Making its way along the rutted dirt road by moonlight. And the river only a few yards away, beyond the passenger's window, frothy white water in glimmering patches, the sound of the water confused with wind rushing through the Jeep's windows.

She'd asked him please to stop the Jeep. Just—stop.

He would remember this—(not immediately, not when he'd been questioned by the Beechum County sheriff's detectives, but weeks later)—but not what he'd said trying to reason with her while not looking at her, as in boot camp you learned not to look at the drill sergeant who was yelling at you, it was forbidden to look, to lock eyes, as if you were his equal; whatever she was saying to him, touching his arm, causing the hairs on his forearm to stiffen; leaning closer to him, frightened of him, trembling with her own audacity—*Of course she's a virgin: she's terrified. But of course this has to happen, for her it is time. Can't turn back.*

More forcibly he wanted to tell her—he couldn't risk it, hurting her. She was his fiancée's sister. He could not hurt *her.*

Fuck fuck fuck this is such a fucking mistake Kincaid. Get out before it's too late.

There were tears on Cressida's cheeks. She was heedless, distraught. Pushing herself at him as if, having made a decision in violation of all that she believed and was, it was not comprehensible that he could deny *her.*

How long she'd planned this, or something like this, rehearsed and plotted, feverish, silly and sad—he couldn't have guessed.

How many weeks, months. Sick with jealousy which she'd have denied was jealousy.

And now, Juliet was out of his life. So far as she knew.

. . . *two of us understand each other. Misfits, freaks—now you know what it's like and it has deepened you and made you more like me. What has happened to you is visible, what happened to me is* . . .

They were parked on Sandhill Road near the Point. He hadn't been here in, how long?—not since Iraq.

Not since he'd died. This frantic buzz at the base of his skull.

The girl was clutching at him at first lightly, playfully—you could still interpret what she was saying as provisional. Then, with more force.

He understood: the girl had no idea what she was doing. What she was inviting. No idea what sex *was*.

For all her superiority, her exalted sense of herself, she was a child, basically.

Never had touched anyone as she was touching Corporal Kincaid. Never dared, for she'd feared being rebuked.

Trying to laugh telling her *Hey no—better not.*

He was pushing her away. Not hard but hard enough so she'd know he was serious. And at once she pushed him back laughing, a wild sort of laughter, hurt, angry—*Brett please I know this: no one can love you like I can, now. Now you are—changed. I promise I can love you enough, I can love enough for two, it won't matter if you don't love me.*

SEVEN

The Corporal's Confession

October 12, 2005

H E'S CONFESSED."

" 'Confessed'—what?"

"About Cressida. What he—you know . . . What he did to her."

But Zeno was having trouble comprehending. *Confessed what?*

In the interregnum between a late supper and bedtime sprawled in his leather chair in the comfortably cluttered room that was his study Zeno glanced up over bifocal glasses at his wife who'd appeared breathless in the doorway but had not stepped inside.

In his hands an old college ethics text he'd been examining curious at the many highlighted passages in yellow, green, and red like faded neon—in the margins of Plato's *Symposium* for instance were *How proved? Doubtful! Bullshit!*

How earnest he'd been, Zeno Mayfield at the age of nineteen or twenty. How involved with these revered old philosophers as if any critique of his, any remark, any query could have the slightest bearing on their philosophies or reputations.

In the doorway Arlette stood uncertainly. Zeno registered a sudden strangeness in his wife: a look in her face stricken yet dreamlike as her lips trembled in a semblance of a smile.

No one would mistake his dear wife for a girl now, even at a distance.

Since July her hair had begun quite conspicuously to turn gray. Her face for so long young had begun to crinkle like parchment.

"McManus called. He's coming over. He told me he had 'news'—I made him tell me over the phone. He wanted just to come here, to talk to us—first. I think that's what he wanted. He was emotional . . . You don't expect Bud McManus to be emotional, do you."

Zeno was fumbling to set aside the paperback. On the armrest of the leather chair glazed with age like varicose veins a can of luke-warm pilsner, that toppled onto the floor spilling beer.

Arlette stared at the fallen can, the wetted rug, without a word of reproach.

IT WAS 11:08 P.M., October 12, 2005. The Mayfields would note—the twelfth of the month.

Her ghost had been everywhere, these months.

Almost, so long *missing,* she'd come to assume a kind of ubiquity—imperviousness to harm.

Abruptly now, that had ended.

HE'D HURT HER, yes.

Hadn't meant to but he had. Yes.

Oh God he was sorry. God have mercy on his soul he was sorry.

HE'D HURT HER *he thought.*

Seemed to think yes—he'd *hurt her.*

Couldn't remember—why . . .

Why he'd hurt her, then tried to bury her, couldn't remember *why.*

AT SHERIFF'S HEADQUARTERS. In custody.

He'd been arrested out on Route 31. An altercation in a tavern parking lot, police were called, two men were fighting and one of them was Brett Kincaid, face bloodied, staggering and aggressive and in a rage initially attributed to alcohol, then to marijuana laced with phencyclidine—PCP.

Police backup was required. Three officers to subdue the corporal despite his injuries, throw him down onto the dirty pavement and cuff him.

And in the back of the police cruiser being taken into custody trying to tell the officers *I did it, I'm the one. I killed her. I want to make a full confession.*

REFUSED TO SEE HIS LAWYER. Refused to see his mother.

They would tell him to lie, he said. He was finished with lying.

SEVEN HOURS' INTERROGATION. Videotaped.

Couldn't remember exactly why, the quarrel between them.

It had been his idea—to drive her home.

They had not been at the Roebuck Inn together. She had come later, alone.

Somehow, in the Nautauga Preserve.

She'd slapped at him, maybe. Pushed at him and he'd lost control, he understood now that's what had happened.

Lost control. Didn't mean to hurt her. Then, it was over.

How?—he wasn't sure. His fists maybe. Or she was so small like a child he'd maybe just pushed her too hard against something, the windshield, the passenger door window, like a lighted match tossed into something you don't anticipate is going to explode and it explodes and you can't retract the match nor even a clear memory of why you'd done such a thing—who it was who'd made such a mistake.

Many mistakes he'd made. Can't retract.

Or maybe he'd strangled her. Now it seemed possible, his hands had done *that*.

WHY?—THIS WAS HARD to compute.

Like an object too large and sharp-edged being shoved inside his head making him wince.

On the videotape the corporal's young-ruined face like layers of onionskin beginning to peel, scabby with dried blood.

Saying maybe it was—why he'd killed her—because she wasn't happy.

Or maybe—he'd killed her because she was saying he was a freak like her, she loved him that he was a freak like her.

And he could not stop himself.

He'd warned her, he might hurt a civilian.

Why a civilian, why would you hurt a civilian, he wasn't sure. Except civilians are afraid of you. In their eyes you can see they expect you to hurt them.

He had warned her. And her sister—his fiancée.

He'd hurt *her*—Juliet. He hadn't meant to but it had happened.

She'd made him angry never judging him, never seeing who he was, what he'd done, terrible things he'd done, he'd witnessed but also he'd done and she had not wished to see or to acknowledge. What was unbearable to him, *she did not know what he'd done but forgave him anyway as if none of it mattered and if none of it mattered then nothing mattered including her and what there was between him—Juliet and Brett. Like it was a sacred marriage, Jesus had blessed them. And if what he'd done or witnessed over there was bullshit then this other too was bullshit which was why he had to laugh, his mouth hurt with that special twitchy laughter.* So Christ he'd hit her, or maybe he'd shoved her. She'd fallen the way they all do, that look of surprise but also embarrassment, even shame—*Oh! this is not happening to me.* Struck her jaw against the edge of a table and stumbled away crying and he'd wanted to drive her to the— what's the name of it—"ER"—the hospital he'd wanted to drive her but she'd said no no she would drive herself, she'd run from him afraid of seeing in his freaky face what their life together would be and he'd hoped she would not return to him but she had for she forgave him you could see the forgiveness and the fear shining in her eyes.

But—he hadn't strangled *her*.

YOU HAVE TO ASCERTAIN if an enemy combatant is actually *dead*.

It isn't enough to shoot him you must shoot him *dead*.

The sergeant would give the command usually. Or any officer at the scene.

Finish him.

Finish! It was a word to lodge in your brain. A word at the back of the throat like the rotted date he'd almost swallowed. And at the checkpoint. The command to fire and several rifles had been discharged into the (fleeing?) vehicle, unclear whose shot or shots actually struck any of the Iraqi family though all were dead or dying by the time the gunfire ceased.

These are the *rules of engagement.*

Operation Iraqi Freedom.

SOME OF THE INTERROGATORS had come to his room, he was saying.

Which interrogators?—he thought they were the military police.

In fact they were—(he realized now)—the Beechum County police.

In his room on Potsdam Street. Where they hadn't a warrant.

Or maybe he was mixing them up with—wasn't sure . . .

One of them, he'd wakened the corporal in his Jeep, where he'd passed out. Scared the shit out of him he'd thought he was back in Iraq he'd fallen asleep on patrol.

No idea where he was except it wasn't Iraq. Taste of vomit in his mouth making him want to puke again.

Vomit and bloodstains on the front of his shirt that was pulled out of his pants. Every joint and muscle in his God-damn body aching and that dull pulsing ache behind his eyes—as soon as he awakened, it returned.

An officer in a gray-blue uniform was asking to see his driver's license, car registration. He was trying to wake up but didn't move fast enough for the officer and so somehow it happened, the officer had drawn his billy club and was prodding the corporal with it, then restraining him with it, laid against the corporal's straining left forearm.

Don't want to do that, son. Don't want to force me to cuff you.

Here was a surprise: the Jeep was at an acute angle partly off the road. Right front wheel in a ditch. And it appeared to be morning—in some wilderness place, the corporal didn't recognize.

Didn't know the name of the road though later he would learn it was the Sandhill Road. And he was in the Nautauga Preserve not far from the front entrance.

The Jeep's front doors were open as if they'd been flung wide. The door on the passenger's side had opened downward into a tangle of briars.

In the other vehicle, the sheriff's deputy's cruiser, a two-way radio was emitting a crackling noise you might confuse with the fierce cries of jays.

The river was about twenty feet from the Jeep, on the passenger's side. The water level was high, the river was rushing splashing and glittering in the early-morning sun.

The deputy commanded the corporal to step away from the vehicle. Step away from the vehicle and kneel on the ground, hands on his head and elbows pointing out.

The deputy glanced into the vehicle, front and back.

Anything here he should know about? Guns, drugs, needles?

Somebody with you in this vehicle? Was there?

Looks like—what's this—blood? Blood on the windshield?

Who scratched your face and why are your clothes torn?

The deputy called for backup. The Jeep was secured and the corporal silent, dazed and unresponsive was taken into custody like one of the enemy not understanding the words shouted at him, something in his eyes *gone out.*

FINISH HER! *Finish the job.*

No. He'd tried to resuscitate her. He knew CPR: in basic training he'd learned.

Then, he tried to bury her in a grave but could only dig with his hands. There was no shovel or any other implement in the Jeep. Tried to use flat moderately sharp rocks but these were awkward. He could not dig a grave deep enough. The land here was marshy, yet pebbly as you approached the river. The water level was not predictable. In early spring as snow melted in the mountains there could be flooding, in late summer it could be only a few inches deep. But now after last week's thunderstorms the depth was ten, twelve feet close to shore.

Finish! Asshole did you finish her.

The grave was too shallow with stones and pebbles he'd placed on top of her. He did not want to cover her face with dirt (for possibly she was breathing, she would inhale the dirt) so he placed a rag over her face he'd found in the Jeep. There was the fear too that birds would come at daybreak and peck out her eyes—hawks, crows. Or in the nighttime, owls. But as soon as the filthy rag was in place, he felt better.

Then, he wasn't sure who the girl was. The girl who'd come to the Preserve with him against his wishes.

Laying a hand on his arm, rousing him to desire.

The angry desire of the cripple, whose potency is fury charged hotly in the throat.

In any case the grave was too shallow. A poorly dug grave, a fuckup of a grave. He hadn't been so stupid, so clumsy and such a general asshole in Iraq. He'd been one of the reliable guys, look an officer in the eye when he responded, always a reliable soldier but now, he'd been fucked up bad, wasn't thinking logically he knew. But—anyway—this was good: he'd found a broken tree limb, that could be broken again to fashion a crude sort of cross.

Christian burial. It was the decent thing to do.

The Mayfields would appreciate this. The mother, and Juliet. They would know what the cross meant.

He didn't believe any longer. Tried to explain to the chaplain who'd seemed bored. Or maybe he believed there was God, and there was Jesus Christ, but not for *him.*

Not for the girl, either: God had not "succored" her.

Why God did for some, and not for others, you could not know.

The girl was so still now. She had infuriated him with her heedless words and she had dared to touch him, who could not bear to be touched any longer. Her eyes were beautiful eyes but the life had drained from them. He lifted the greasy rag to see—yes, the life had drained from them.

So ashamed! He could not ever face the Mayfields again, who had loved him.

It was good, he would not see any of them again. Their love for him was a burden. Their love for him choked and suffocated him. Made him nauseated. In civilian eyes you see the fear, there is no remedy for this fear except to kill them.

If one civilian is killed, why not all.

Why would you stop with *one*. And why with *two*.

Why with *three, four, five* . . . Why the fuck would you *stop*.

HOPED HE MIGHT DIE by firing squad. In the interstices of his seven-hour confession to Beechum County detectives he spoke of this wish.

Only in Nevada, son. This is New York State not Nevada.

In New York State at Dannemora, he would sit on Death Row forever.

Few Death Row prisoners were executed any longer in New York State.

Lethal injection. Not electric chair. Not firing squad.

THROUGH THE NIGHT he spoke with detectives. Sporadic, rambling, not-always-coherent confession to having killed *the girl*.

If they asked him are you speaking of *Cressida Mayfield* he would say yes. But he did not once utter the name *Cressida Mayfield* in his own words.

Had he forgotten the name? Could he not bring himself to speak the name?

The girl. Juliet's sister.

The one who came to the Roebuck Inn for me.

Like being infected—AIDS, HIV. You can't help but infect others you touch. That is the nature of evil.

The other one—his fiancée—had spoken of babies. Her he was badly frightened of hurting yet she continued to love him. Or to claim that she loved him.

Wanting to place a pillow over her face when she slept. (For instance.) So he would not harm her.

Her face was very beautiful. He could not harm her beautiful face.

She would help him, she'd said. They would have a baby: she would become pregnant. There were ways. There were "techniques." They would learn.

He'd come to realize, killing her might be more merciful than disappointing her.

You do not want to disappoint those who love you or whom you love. Always it is the easier thing to kill them as it is easier to kill a civilian who might fuck you up with a complaint, easier than to negotiate a deal, once a person is dead there are no longer two sides to a story.

This was Sergeant Shaver's advice. All the guys repeated it like you'd repeat a joke that gets funnier each time you tell it.

IN THE MORNING they drove him to the Preserve. Five police vehicles accompanying.

At Sandhill Point he walked unsteadily. He was cuffed in front—still, he walked unsteadily.

He paused to cough, a violent hacking cough. Tears started from his eyes running down the onionskin face in tiny drops.

Couldn't locate the grave. Wasn't sure in which direction it was.

Detectives were skeptical, there could be anything resembling a grave out here. The narrow spit of land had been examined many times. The search had been practically inch by inch.

After a while the corporal seemed to have located the grave-site.

All you could see was marshy soil, a few rocks. No evidence of a body having been laid in this area but a photographer took pictures.

He'd had to place her in the river, he said.

The grave had been a mistake. Wild animals would have found her, devoured her. He could not bear the desecration of her body.

He'd carried her, he said. Led them along the bank of the Nautauga River in underbrush, stumbling over boulders, rocks. Where the river was approximately fifty feet across, where a stand of birch trees emerged startlingly white and beautiful out of the morning haze on the farther shore, there he thought he'd placed her in the river, making his way out into the boulders near shore.

He crouched, he demonstrated how he'd done it.

And where had the Jeep been, he was asked.

The Jeep! Must've been somewhere close by.

She was carried away by the river, he said.

What would happen to her then, how far downstream her body would be carried, all the way to Lake Ontario maybe—he would not know.

In the hands of God. I guess.

He'd stumbled back then to the Jeep and blacked out.

Sometime in the night he'd wakened, a terrible gut-cramp and he'd begun to vomit.

Like battery acid the vomit tasted in his mouth. He'd thought possibly the things in his brain, in his eye, possibly one in his heart to control the micro-valve, one or all of these might be malfunctioning as a result of the vomiting but had no way of knowing.

Next he knew, the deputy was shaking him.

Son! Son! Wake up.

MUCH OF THIS, the Mayfields witnessed.

Fascinated and scarcely daring to breathe, the Mayfields witnessed.

Like what you would never imagine—the way the world is without you in it.

In the interrogation room, through the camera we could watch.

We could hear, and we could watch.

Except Brett's head was so low, so bowed. All we could see was the base-ball cap part-sideways on his head he'd pulled down in shame.

It would require some time to realize what they were seeing and hearing and it would require even more time to realize that those long weeks, months they'd been searching for their daughter, making telephone calls, on the Internet twelve hours a day, sending out ENDANGERED MISSING ADULT to thousands of households, their daughter had not been alive.

If Brett Kincaid's testimony was truthful their daughter had not been alive even at the time she had become, to them, *missing*.

Each of the Mayfields had been deceived: self-deceived.

Arlette had believed that she'd been prepared for this terrible news. How many times she'd instructed herself *You must prepare Zeno. He will not be able to prepare himself.*

Zeno had believed that, of the two of them, obviously he was the stronger, the more responsible. He would have to protect Lettie—and Juliet as well. *They can't. They aren't strong enough. It will be me.*

Yet, Zeno hadn't really believed that Cressida could be dead.

Arlette hadn't really believed that Cressida could be dead.

A *missing person* cannot be a *dead person*. For a *dead person* is not really a *missing person* even if the body has not been discovered.

FINALLY THEY WERE allowed to see him.

Twelve hours after the taped confession finally they were allowed to speak with the ravaged young man who had almost become their son-in-law.

Zeno asked *Why?*

Kincaid said *Don't know, sir. I don't know.*

How tired he was, suddenly!

His head fell onto his crossed arms on the table before him. In an instant like a lighted match snuffed out, he was asleep.

EIGHT

The Corporal's Letter

BENEATH SILKY SATINY THINGS in a bureau drawer in her bedroom she'd placed it. The letter her fiancé had given her when he'd departed for Iraq—"Only open this if you will never see me again."

She'd known what he meant, at once.

She'd taken the envelope from him quickly, so that no one might see.

She'd kissed him good-bye. Hugged him, kissed him, pressed her tear-streaked face against his.

"Of course I will see you again, Brett! Don't say such a thing."

NOW IN THE EVENING of October 13, 2005, when it was becoming known through Carthage that the young corporal so long suspected of having murdered Cressida Mayfield had confessed to police, now when it was known to the Mayfields that Cressida was gone utterly, and would not ever return to them, and that Brett Kincaid too was dead to them, and would not ever return to them, quietly Juliet entered her bedroom, went to the bureau and slid open the drawer and removed from it the envelope she'd hidden away nearly two years ago in the hope that she would not ever be drawn to seeking it let alone opening and reading it.

Downstairs, a murmur of voices. Relatives and friends were gathering, to console.

How to mourn, a death so bodiless? Forever *missing*.

Yet there would be a church service of some kind for Cressida—a funeral rite for the *missing*. Arlette in despair could not be consoled, otherwise.

On the envelope was written, in Brett's careful, slightly back-tilting handwriting: JULIET MAYFIELD MY FIANCÉE.

Blindly now she opened the envelope. She was sitting on the edge of her bed, fumbling to open the envelope.

Dear Juliet,

If you are reading this then something has happened to me.

I will not see you again I guess. I love you so much!

Sometimes I believe in the "after life"—where we will meet again. It is not always possible to believe but I am trying.

Some thing will happen to us all in time. There is no great sorrow really in losing me at this time and not another. If you read this Juliet, do not look back. If you can help it.

It is strange how knowing a thing should give you the strength to do it but sometimes you are not strong enough. God does not always make us strong enough.

Do unto others. Love thy neighbor.

Thou shalt not kill.

If you are a soldier you must do certain things, you would not do if you had a choice.

You must acknowledge, you may not return safely to your home & loved ones.

Dear Juliet I am hoping that when we are married one day I will discover this letter hidden away where you forgot it. And I will put it back in its hiding place & not say a word.

For I love you so, Juliet. That is the one true thing that I know. I don't feel young now. I think I am old in my heart.

It will do no good to grieve with Ethel. She will grieve in her own way angry & alone. You & your mother should not try to help her, she will resent it.

Look to the future now Juliet. Marry somebody who deserves your love & have the kids we would have had (I know that is crazy to think, I am not serious really)—& God bless you most of all be happy my darling Juliet. Know that I will be thinking of you always.

I wonder where I will be right now—when you read this.

I love you. Always you will remain—my darling Juliet.

Love, kisses & hugs

Brett

PART II

✦ ➤ ✦

Exile

NINE

Execution Chamber

Orion, Florida, March 2012

W HO CAN OPEN THIS DOOR? Any volunteer?"

The door looked heavy. Set in the stone wall. A look as of the grave, ancient and weathered. The visitors were hesitant. A thin damp wind rippled in their hair like ghost-fingers.

In his loud bullying voice the Lieutenant repeated: "No volunteer? There must be a volunteer."

The Intern dared not glance in the direction of the Investigator, who was her employer. The Intern dared not call attention to herself, whose hope was to remain diminished and invisible as a plain brown-speckled hen is invisible in a dense underbrush.

It was the Intern's first journey as the Investigator's assistant. The Intern desperately hoped, it would not be her last.

"Anyone? I'm waiting."

The Lieutenant was an affable-seeming man with smudged-Caucasian skin and a quick sly smile like a razor flash. He might have been any age between forty-nine and sixty-nine and he was of moderate height, about five feet nine. He had the look, at about 180 pounds, of a stolid-bodied man who has lost weight recently.

He wore the dun-colored guards' uniform of the Orion Maximum

Security Correctional Facility for Men at Orion, Florida. He carried no firearm, but attached to his leather holster was what appeared to be a mean-looking billy club or baton. His face was weather-creased and totemic. His pebbly eyes scraped over the faces of his listeners.

The tour had begun nearly ninety minutes ago. The execution chamber was the last stop on the tour, at the farther end of the dour cinder block building designated Death Row. The Lieutenant had just led the tour group through Cell Block C which had been a harrowing experience but they had not visited the Death Row cell block, off-limits to civilians. Of the fifteen visitors most had begun to stagger with exhaustion and apprehension.

In the dining hall which had been the stop before Cell Block C there'd been two volunteers to sample the prisoners' food and these young people stood now abashed and silent.

"We will not enter if the door is not opened, my friends. *There must be a volunteer.*"

The restless eyes passed over them, rapidly. Since the start of the tour, even before the Lieutenant had led the fifteen civilians through the first of the prison gates and inside the high wire-mesh walls, it seemed that he'd been counting them compulsively. With his eyes, counting. *One, two, three . . . six, seven . . . twelve, thirteen, fourteen . . . fifteen.*

You could figure that inside the prison facility guards were trained to count. They were trained to account for.

All individuals in the corrections officers' vicinity inside the prison walls were their responsibility. Fifteen civilians had been processed through security checkpoints to be guided through the prison by the Lieutenant and so fifteen civilians had to be released at the end of the tour.

Otherwise, as the Lieutenant had genially informed them, the entire prison would go into *lockdown.*

At such a time no one would exit or enter the prison until all individuals known to be inside the facility were *accounted for.*

The Intern swallowed hard. The Intern stepped forward out of invisibility to volunteer.

"Sir, I will."

Was this a surprise? The Lieutenant might have preferred another civilian.

Of the fourteen other civilians all were taller, stronger-looking, more mature in appearance and bearing than the Intern who could not have been taller than five feet one and who didn't look the age she must have been—(that is, twenty-one)—to have been allowed into the prison.

The Lieutenant knew, or should have known, that the Intern was a twenty-five-year-old female, since he'd seen her ID at the start of the tour; but the Lieutenant had forgotten this detail, for he'd paid very little attention to the Intern during the tour, addressing most of his provocative remarks to the half-dozen young women sociology graduate students from Eustis and their female professor as well as to the most distinguished of the civilian visitors, a tall straight-backed white-haired gentleman in a proper suit, white dress shirt and tie, of an age beyond seventy, who resembled a retired professional man, or a judge, and who'd been taking notes in a little notebook through the tour.

There were several men who might have volunteered. But they'd avoided the Lieutenant's questing eye.

Since the dining hall visit, and particularly since the visit to Cell Block C, even the sturdy-bodied male civilians were looking as if they'd strongly preferred to be elsewhere.

Several times on the tour the Lieutenant had winked at his charges saying, "Damn hard to breathe in here, eh? And you folks have just arrived at Orion. Think if you'd never again depart for the rest of your life!"

The Lieutenant was just slightly vexed that the volunteer who'd stepped forward wasn't at all a volunteer he'd have chosen. You could see that the prison tour was the Lieutenant's public life and that each stop was like a station of the cross culminating with, at this farther end of the ugly cinder block Death Row, the execution chamber.

"Well! You don't hardly look like you weigh one hundred pounds, fella, but—step right up."

In fact, the Intern had weighed ninety-seven pounds the last time she'd been weighed on any proper scale which had not been recently in her haphazard and pieced-together life. The Intern ignored the condescending *fella*.

The Intern did not mind that the issue of her *sexual identity* would seem to be, for the Lieutenant, and for others very likely, at this moment, gazing not at her but at the effort she represented as she tugged at the door in their place, not an issue at all.

Damn heavy door.

"Try again."

The Intern tried, harder. Clearly the Intern wished to refute any notion that she/he was a runty little fella.

Yet still, the damned door did not budge.

One of those miserable public situations in which you pose as a good sport. You *persevere*.

In others' eyes, strangers' eyes, you are judged kindly—capable of taking a joke.

Was this a joke? The Intern tugged so hard at the door her arms felt as if someone were trying to yank them out of their sockets.

"Is it locked, sir?"

"No. It is not locked."

The Lieutenant laughed, irritably. As if he were playing some sort of cruel crude trick on the civilian!

Though the Lieutenant quite liked the acquiescent *sir*. For a tour-group is a heterogeneous and unpredictable gathering of individuals of whom a certain number are sure to be *not on the tour guide's side*.

Another time the Intern tried to open the door. She was panting now, embarrassed and self-conscious. Perhaps the Lieutenant wasn't punishing the Intern so much as those others, seemingly more ca-

pable, who'd held back in dread, and allowed the runty little fellow
to step forward in their place.

The Intern perceived that power over generations of confined men
had corrupted and deformed the Lieutenant as the hardiest of trees is
deformed by a pitiless wind.

Why had the Intern volunteered to try to open the damned door,
when no one else had stepped forward?

No one could know: the Intern had been prodded into action because the Investigator, who was the tall white-haired gentleman with
the little notebook, had cast her a significant glance a moment before.

Well, the Investigator hadn't cast her a look she'd actually *seen*.
She had sensed it.

Go ahead, McSwain! Step forward.

In such circumstances, in public places, it was to be their protocol:
without a word the Investigator might signal an order to the Intern,
who was not to question his motives.

This signal had come swiftly and deftly as a neutrino passing between them. For the two were not strangers as they appeared to
be—(they'd taken care to keep a little distance from one another
on the tour but they'd come to Orion in the same vehicle, driven by
the Intern). But no one, even the sharp-eyed Lieutenant trained to
intercept covert glances among his charges, seemed to have noticed.

"Sir, I think the door must be locked, or stuck . . ."

"One more try, fella! Then you can give up if you wish."

In dark corduroy trousers, long-sleeved shirt and corduroy jacket,
and hiking boots the size of a child's boots, the Intern resembled a
precocious sub-species of schoolboy virtually non-existent in central
rural Florida. She wore glasses with round dark plastic rims. Her
long-sleeved shirt was white cotton, and not entirely clean. Her face
was small-boned, plain and fiercely intent. Her dark hair was razor-
cut at the nape of her neck, short as a boy's. A premature furrow
wavered across her forehead and a bluish vein throbbed at her right
temple.

A final try, and still the door would not budge.

"All right, then! I will open it. Excuse me."

The Lieutenant positioned himself in front of the ancient-looking door, grasped the knob and tugged and lifted—(the Intern saw: this was the trick)—until the door swung open like a gaping mouth.

The point of the Lieutenant's demonstration would seem to be: *Death is not easily approached.*

In a matter-of-fact voice, as if to suggest how effortless the task had been for him, the Lieutenant explained that, in fact, the door to the execution chamber was always kept locked—of course. "It's opened only for occasions like this and when an execution is being prepared."

But now, were they expected to shuffle inside? Inside and *down*? No one edged forward. Already the visitors could smell an overripe earthy-chemical odor wafting from the opened doorway.

"Step inside, friends! I advise you to take a deep breath beforehand." Like a cruel impresario the Lieutenant stood beside the doorway, beckoning.

Of course, no one wanted to step forward. Especially the young female graduate students hung back, flurried and frightened as birds.

"Oh!—if people have died inside here . . ."

"Can some of us w-wait outside . . ."

The Lieutenant laughed, not unkindly. "No. No one can wait outside. The tour won't conclude, and you won't be released to the outside, except through the execution chamber—that is our tradition at Orion."

Was this true? The Lieutenant rubbed his hands which were large stubby-finger hands, with a zestful air. The pebbly eyes continued to rake the faces of his captives.

"But if human beings have d-died in here—"

"*Of course* human beings have died in here. What would be the purpose of a taxpayer-supported execution chamber, if no one died in it?"

Several of the visitors laughed. As they'd been laughing since the start of the tour, nervously.

It seemed quite natural, the dignified Investigator was the first to enter the cave-like chamber. A tall straight-backed man, he stooped to enter. He set his foot on a grimy stone step, the first of three that descended to a grimy concrete floor as in a crude and unimproved cellar.

The Intern saw: the Investigator's slender feet were shod in shiny-black-leather dress shoes. No one else in the tour had dressed so *particularly.*

Amid the civilians in the tour group this elderly white-haired gentleman had kept to himself from the start. He had resisted efforts to "befriend" him—he'd resisted the instinct, powerful in such a group as a rush of piranha after prey, to participate in the edgy banter between the Lieutenant and the others. He had not been observed to be disdainful or aloof—he'd been intent upon taking notes in his little notebook, which was not forbidden in the prison facility, like taking photographs or videotaping. (Any kind of camera equipment, however small and ordinary, was forbidden to bring into the prison.) You had the sense, seeing the Investigator scribbling into his small spiral notebook, that, if you looked over his shoulder, you'd discover he was writing in code.

The Investigator passed by the Intern without a glance. The Intern was looking not at the Investigator—she was too professional for such a slip—but toward the Investigator with the expression of a young person who both reveres and fears an elder.

Please don't make me do anything more—sir! Not in this terrible place.

One by one the others followed the Investigator into the execution chamber. Stepping out of the overcast March morning that was yet a dull glowering-white as if in a cataclysm of the Florida sun in which only an afterglow remained, but that powerful and even blinding in contrast to the dimly fluorescent-lit interior of the execution chamber.

The Intern hung back. How the Intern would have liked to flee, back to the front gate of the prison! But the prison grounds were labyrinthine, and dangerous: no civilian was allowed to wander off from the tour group.

The Intern swallowed hard. The Intern had seemed to know, before she and the Investigator had left their vehicle in a remote corner of the visitors' parking lot, that accompanying her employer to Orion prison was a mistake she would regret.

Beside the doorway the Lieutenant was waiting for her. With a smile to indicate that, if he didn't keep a sharp eye, the little *fella* would slip away.

The Intern took a deep breath, and stepped inside. But already it was too late, the dank air of the execution chamber had entered her lungs.

"Go all the way in, please. Plenty of room. Those in front move forward, *please.*"

The Lieutenant spoke chidingly. The Lieutenant spoke with an air of grim jocularity. The Lieutenant assured the visitors that there was room for as many as thirty people in the cramped space.

"In recent years, with lethal injection, there are sometimes double executions. The demand for seats is doubled too, as you can imagine."

No one was eager to move forward. The frightened young women and their professor had stopped dead in their tracks a few yards from the front of the room. Even those men who'd been bravely stoic about marching around the entirety of Cell Block C to the hoots and shouted obscenities of prisoners were balking now, pushing to the side where there were two rows of straight-backed chairs in front of a grim windowless cinder block wall.

At the center, rear of the low-ceilinged chamber was a bizarre structure: it appeared to be a diving bell, painted an incongruous robin's-egg blue. It was octagonal in structure with several Plexiglas windows in its sides. Inside, you could see two straight-backed chairs positioned side by side.

The ceiling of the diving bell, at the apex of its curve, looked as if it could not be even six feet high.

An airtight structure, the Intern reasoned. Since gas had been a means of execution in the state of Florida until recently.

The Intern was feeling faint-headed like one who has ignored a warning, and has approached danger—but what was the warning?

She could not recall any warning.

Accompany me to the maximum-security facility at Orion. I will pay you one and a half your usual salary.

The Intern had been grateful for the Investigator's invitation. The Intern was in need of employment and was, at the present time, financially dependent upon the Investigator. It may have been, the Intern was emotionally dependent upon the Investigator as well.

In his grating voice the Lieutenant was chiding: "Those of you in front—please move out of the aisle. Please sit in those chairs! Those chairs are the most prized seats in the house, reserved for the family of the victim and for law enforcement officers with a particular interest in the execution."

The members of the tour group murmured and whispered together. The witness-viewing area of the execution chamber was so *small*—you would always be in close proximity to the condemned man, no matter where you were seated.

Could scarcely draw a breath that wasn't contaminated by—death.

The Lieutenant was saying, in his bullying-teasing manner, that, when a condemned individual was "obstructurous" as they were being, he was *forcibly carried* into the chamber.

Had the Lieutenant *chuckled*? No one laughed with him.

A mistake to have come here, the Intern was thinking. For—was something awaiting her, *here*?

At last the visitors were spread out into the room, some of them uncomfortably close to the diving bell. A few had reluctantly taken seats in the prized chairs facing the Plexiglas windows and could not help but stare inside.

The Investigator was still standing, in the aisle. The Investigator may have switched on a (miniature) recording device carried in a fountain pen, in his lapel pocket; the Investigator would want to see and record all that he could.

The Lieutenant said, gloating, with a zestful rubbing of his hands, "Now, folks, if you are settled— I will shut the door."

Panic rippled through the low-ceilinged room! In a flock of birds such an alert would provoke all to fly away at once, flutter their wings and escape but these visitors had no wings and were trapped in a windowless cave.

Voices lifted, protesting. "Shut the door? Oh but why—"

The room was ventilated by a chill, mineral-smelling rattling overhead like the breath of a great sinuous serpent. It was not entirely subterranean but felt so. You felt the dark earth surrounding you, the gravity-tug of death and dissolution.

In his way that was part-sneering, part-sincerity—part reproach and part genuine pride—the Lieutenant was saying, to his captive audience: "The experience of our execution chamber at Orion is a closed one. Very few individuals are allowed into this place. And of these, not all leave again. You will have the wrong impression if you think that the open sky, fresh air, and a quick means of exit have anything to do with *execution*."

The Lieutenant strode to the door and shut it.

THE INTERN THOUGHT *Eternity has no conjunction with time. This— where we are—is but a place, and a time. It will not prevail and cannot confine me.*

He'd said with a doubtful look, you will do.

He'd been sifting through applications, candidates. He had not wanted, he'd said, a *merely academic* assistant of whom there were dozens available, and eager to work with *Professor Cornelius Hinton of the Institute for Advanced Research in Social Psychology, Criminology, and Anthropology, University of Florida at Temple Park, Florida.*

PROF. CORNELIUS HINTON—this was the name on the little plaque affixed to the Investigator's door at the Institute.

She'd assumed at the outset that yes, this was the white-haired gentleman's name—"Hinton." Later, she would learn that "Hinton" was one of several working-names the Investigator used when he was *incognito*.

Not only was the Investigator other than "Hinton" but he was older than "Hinton" whose birth date on his laminated Institute ID card was 1941.

From a remark he'd let slip, the Intern understood that the Investigator was a few years older than the fictitious *Cornelius Hinton*. But so youthful-looking, for a gentleman of his age, and so resembling the slightly blurred, bespectacled and bewhiskered white-haired professor in the little photo ID, who would have suspected?

She hadn't been searching among the Investigator's files. She would not have wished to perceive herself that way—furtive, deceitful.

In her former lifetime lost to her now as the scattered and faded remnants of a photo album tossed among anonymous trash she'd created a wickedly witty pen-and-ink drawing in the style of her obsessive master M. C. Escher depicting small humanoid figures spying on one another in a landscape of dense vertiginous symmetries like impacted wallpaper. There were starkly white humanoid figures and starkly black humanoid figures in a Gestalt pattern so that, if the eye saw "white," the eye could not simultaneously see "black"; if the eye saw "black," the eye could not simultaneously see "white." The trick of the drawing was that all these foolish/hapless figures spied upon one another yet were oblivious of being spied-upon. The wit of the drawing was that no humanoid figure differed in the slightest from any other: all were identical.

She'd been thirteen at the time of the drawing, in the first thrilled flush of inspiration.

Spying, snooping—she felt a moral revulsion for such human activities. She would not have wished to snoop among the Investigator's private files as much for her own sake as for his.

She was a convalescent, still. She'd been convalescing for how many years, she'd lost count.

She'd fled, she was in exile. *Back there* was a way of naming the unnameable.

Essentially in life you are at Point X—*this, where we are*—continuously. It's a delusion to think that you can travel *back there*—from which you've been expelled.

And so, she hadn't been searching among the Investigator's files for anything other than the misplaced file he'd been looking for. (The Investigator was a methodical man for whom scrupulosity and order were sacrosanct: he'd been known to turn white-lipped with rage if a small item on his desk were out of place.) Yet she'd found, in an older filing cabinet, in a creaking lower drawer, a much-creased manila envelope that contained several laminated ID cards for several "identities"—all male, birth dates 1938 to 1943, and all associated with academic or research institutions in Minnesota, Illinois, New York State, Washington, D.C., Bethesda, and Florida.

These IDs dated back to another era, clearly. Might've been the 1980s. The Investigator at that time had had dark blond hair, a sharp-boned but whiskery face, shrewd eyes hidden behind tinted lenses.

Unless, the Intern speculated, the photos weren't of the Investigator himself but of someone who resembled him enough to pass for him, should the ID have been inspected at a checkpoint. The more she peered at the little ID photos, the less they resembled the man whom she knew, and the less they resembled one another.

There is a thriving business in manufactured-to-order IDs including driver's licenses. The Intern, whose own identity was not entirely fixed, understood this.

Still, you could stare at the Investigator's numerous ID photos and not be sure if they were, or were not, *him*. As you could observe the man himself, seemingly placid, always preoccupied, humming under his breath, quizzical, bemused, beguiled, absently gazing out a window at a sky streaked with opalescent cloud above the Atlantic Ocean miles away as—(it seemed)—a tempest of thoughts raged in his brain—and not have the slightest idea who he *was*.

To the Orion Maximum Security Correctional Facility for Men in the flatlands of central Florida the Investigator had brought a laminated ID card identifying him as *Professor Cornelius Hinton* of the

Institute for Advanced Research in Social Psychology, Criminology, and Anthropology, State University of Florida, Temple Park, Florida. The Institute was an actual place, as the Temple Park branch of the State University of Florida was an actual place in one of the older palm-tree-lined suburbs of Fort Lauderdale. There, as a non-degree-enrolled student named "Sabbath Mae McSwain" the Intern had taken night school courses over a period of several semesters—courses chosen less for their subjects than for the convenience of scheduling; she'd become one of those individuals who dwell at the edges of large university campuses, attached to the universities in the way that a scattering of small treeless islands is attached to the mainland.

Derailed. In exile. Deeply ashamed, despised. Yet she had so little pride, she was grateful most days simply to be alive.

There is Minimalist art: there are Minimalist lives.

By default she'd become a certain kind of student—older, solitary. The ideal camouflage for one in exile—it wasn't camouflage at all. And she was sure by this time, no one was pursuing her.

She'd lived in Miami for a while, at various addresses. She'd had her "friend"—her "protector." And they'd moved to Fort Lauderdale, and now in Temple Park where she was living alone, and was content to be living alone, or told herself so. Temple Park was a residential suburb north of Fort Lauderdale, partly bordering the ocean, but only partly. In all these places—Miami, Lauderdale, Temple Park— she'd worked at a motley succession of minimum-wage jobs—(store clerk, kitchen worker, waitress [a single, humiliating evening]), veterinary assistant, "lab tech," fresh-produce market hand; valiantly she'd managed a secondhand bookstore for several haphazard weeks as the doomed and dust-ridden store ("Gay & Lesbian Pride, New Rare & Used Books") sank into bankruptcy, and beyond. At the same general time, in Temple Park, she'd begun a circuitous progress, as she thought it, into the State University which in its labyrinthine interstices provided work-study scholarships for students, for which she believed she might one day qualify. She imagined for herself a university career of credits accumulated slowly and painstakingly as

precious pebbles on a beach; somehow, a B.A. degree would mate-
rialize out of this earnest effort, then a graduate fellowship, a Ph.D.
and a teaching position—in some subject, somewhere. She could envision for herself only college-level teaching, or a research position
in a laboratory; she could not think of public school teaching, high
school or lower, without a wince of dread and shame.

Already in her young girlhood, she'd failed at *that*.

She could not even recall. But she knew, she'd failed.

Back there, she'd been stripped of all pride. She'd been exposed as
contemptible, debased. And so it had been, but she was no longer
back there.

Here, where no one knew her, and cared nothing for her, she felt
a small residue of hope. She'd had friends of a kind, and had drifted
from them, preferring to live alone. Her "progress" at the university
resembled the motions of a rock-face climber who inches upward so
close to the rock face that he's blind to it, as he is blind to the spec-
tacular view behind his back.

You must have faith, your efforts are *upward*. You are *ascending*.

As she worked in a succession of nondescript and anonymous jobs
mostly without complaint as she was without expectations so she
lived in a succession of nondescript and anonymous residences far
from the Atlantic Ocean, dazzling sand beaches and causeways and
glittering high-rise hotels. In the great tourist cities of Florida it is
possible to live within a mile or less of the ocean and to never see
it, and to never think of seeing it, or of caring to see it. She'd made
her way like flotsam floating upon a haphazard tide for months,
and years; in so wayward a life, one year blends into the next, and
that into the next; until in Temple Park where she seemed to have
washed ashore, at least temporarily, she found herself living in a
small single room in the slant-roofed attic of a rotting flamingo-pink
Victorian house across the street, Pepperdine Avenue, from a multi-
ethnic residence for undergraduate and graduate students called
International House where in the cafeteria she ate inexpensive ethnic meals at long communal tables, was befriended by strangers, at-

tended films, lectures, discussions; especially, she was befriended by a feminist group called Females Without Borders which had a center in the building. In such milieus her identity as *Sabbath McSwain* was never questioned:

Sabbath Mae McSwain, birth date August 15, 1986. Breathitt, MD.

This was not a laminated ID but an actual birth certificate replica much folded and creased. With it came a Social Security card— *Sabbath Mae McSwain* whose number was 113-40-3074.

A woman she'd met at Female Without Borders, a post-doc in clinical psychology who'd befriended her, had been the one to put her into contact with Cornelius Hinton at the Institute—"He's a nice guy. He's eccentric. He's *old*—he won't hassle you."

Hinton was looking for an assistant, an "intern"—except the work paid well, significantly higher than the university rate for student assistants. His previous intern—(also a young woman: Hinton described himself as a feminist and tried always to hire women)—had had to give notice suddenly, leaving him bereft. The intern was expected to drive Hinton's vehicle for him, short and long distances; assist Hinton in making appointments, buying groceries and picking up prescriptions at the pharmacy; if Hinton was flying, the intern would make plane and hotel reservations, and oversee each detail of the schedule; often the intern would travel with Hinton when he went to give lectures, teach seminars—whatever it was Cornelius Hinton did, as a self-described *cultural anatomist*.

"He investigates things and writes about them—like sub-standard care for mentally ill children, or nursing homes where patients are mistreated. He travels *incognito*. He might use different names. People say he writes best-selling books under pseudonyms and there's no author photo on the jackets. Everything's secret about him. He'd been arrested, back in the 1960s. He'd demonstrated against the Iraq War, too. He's what they call an 'old Leftie'—not sure what that means. Like, a Communist. Anyway, a Socialist. He's kind of pissy and stand-offish at first but later, one day, he turns into a great guy— generous. He's given us money for our center here. He's helped me out personally, with my girlfriend. He kind of forged documents for us, on Institute letterheads. The thing is, he's generous if you don't ask him, and if you don't expect it. He likes to surprise you. He's a great guy—mysterious. *Weird*."

Chantelle paused, thoughtfully.

"Might be rich, too."

"YOU ARE—'SABBATH MCSWAIN'?"

Yes. She was.

"And you're applying for the 'internship'—my assistant?"

Yes. She was.

"Recommended by Chantelle Rios."

Yes. That was so.

The Investigator peered at her, curiously. She saw that his fair-blue eyes weren't those of an older man but youthful, sharp and acute. His beard was close and neatly trimmed, dazzling-white as his hair, but dense and wiry as his hair was soft, airy, and flowing. His face reminded her of an old, faded-bronze coin. His manner was brusque, matter-of-fact. His posture suggested a military bearing. Yet he was courtly, elegant. He wore a tweed sport coat over a dark turtleneck sweater that gave him the look of an older male actor in a British film of some bygone era—eagerly you would spill to such a man all your secrets, except of course such a man would not want to hear all your secrets.

On his left wrist was an aluminum stretch-band watch with an ungainly large face, of a kind popular with sporty young men—a digital watch likely to be waterproof and to glow in the dark, to tell the tides, the date, the hours of sunrise and sunset.

And on the third finger of his right hand, a thick silver ring in the shape of a star.

"'Sabbath McSwain'—you are—*female*?"

She laughed, the question was so unexpected.

"Yes. I think so."

"You only 'think so'? Indeed?"

It was true, she preferred boys' clothes—not men's clothes but boys' clothes which were likely to fit her slender hipless body. Boys' shirts, boys' pullover sweaters, boys' khakis and jeans. Boys' running shoes, hiking boots. Of colors she preferred beiges, browns, black— but a dull matte-black. *Small, drab, minimal and inconsequential.*

She had no serious fear of being recognized any longer. Anyone who might recognize her, who might have known her *back there*, would have forgotten her by now, she was certain.

Forgettable, forgotten. Good!

"When required, I check the box 'F.' It seems more appropriate than the box 'M.' But it isn't, I guess, what you'd call *significant.*"

"And why is that, Miss McSwain?"

"Because I think that our sexual identity is no more significant than the color of our eyes—to some of us, at least. It doesn't *weigh heavily.*"

"Doesn't it! You seriously think that there are no essential, biological differences between female and male?"

"I am speaking of culturally-mandated differences."

"And these spring from—what?"

"Culture."

"And culture springs from—what?"

This was a familiar academic-intellectual riposte but Sabbath McSwain was at a loss how to reply—she was distracted by the Investigator's pale-blue gaze upon her, that was impertinent and bemused, and strangely intimate. It had been years since she'd engaged with any professor—with any adult—in this sort of intellectual dialogue, that lifted her heart as in an impromptu Ping-Pong game.

She said, "Dr. Hinton—I know that there are many essential biological differences between the sexes, of course. But not so many 'culturally-mandated' differences. In First World countries we've evolved beyond mere biology—it isn't the fate of the human female to be pregnant continuously until she wears out and dies."

It was a heated little speech. It was a heated, breathless, utterly un-

original and obvious speech. Yet the Investigator fixed the Intern—
(for so she wished to think of herself, however prematurely)—with
something like sympathy.

"You are right, of course! No one should expect you—or any other
'female'—to have a succession of babies until she wears out and dies.
I think that is a quite plausible wish. But I only hoped to ascertain
whether in fact you *are female*—I've found that, as interns, *females* are
just more competent."

Abashed Sabbath McSwain murmured *yes*, she was *female*.

A wave of hot shame washed over her. She could not have said
why, in her deepest being, she felt such *sex-shame*.

As she was repelled by glimpsing her own diminutive body, unclothed, exposed, in a mirror or reflective surface. *Ugly that's the ugly
one* a jeering voice assailed her.

"But I like it that you aren't—in the slightest, and by choice, I
think—'feminine.' That no one, glancing at you, would take a second glance. Which is not the case, I'm afraid, with 'Prof. Hinton.'"

The Investigator enunciated the words *Prof. Hinton* with such
quaint disdain, the Intern was moved to laugh.

"And I like your laugh, Sabbath: it's inaudible."

The Intern laughed again inaudibly. It had to be the first time she'd
laughed in such a way, as if she were being tickled, in memory.

"Chantelle says you are a very *solitary* young woman. And a *mysterious* young woman—with no evident attachments."

The Intern ceased laughing. *Was* this funny, or not-so-funny?

It made her uneasy, as it was unexpected and surprising, that anyone should be talking about *her*.

"'Sabbath McSwain'—a curious name. It strikes me as invented,
somehow."

"Did you say—'invented'?"

"Is it?"

The Intern stared at the Investigator, as if he'd slapped her: not
hard but, as it's said in martial arts, hard enough to capture one's
attention.

"It's a real name. A family name. I have an older sister—Haley Mc-Swain. We're both—we both—we live in the Fort Lauderdale area—though we aren't so close as we were, once."

"So you do have family? Chantelle was mistaken?"

The Investigator was frowning. Not so good!

"No. Not really. Haley is my—half-sister. I mean—*step*sister. I never see her any longer, now—we're estranged."

"But 'Sabbath McSwain' is your name?"

"Yes. 'Sabbath McSwain' is my name."

(It was so, "Sabbath McSwain" wasn't a name she'd have chosen for herself. The name was a gift, it had been a freely given and loving gift, she could not ever repudiate, for it had helped to save her tattered and fraying life at the time.)

(To Haley she owed this remnant-life. Yet, in speaking so expeditiously of her, she'd betrayed Haley.)

Fumbling in her backpack for those crucial documents without which she could not make her way blind and groping across the treacherous rock face.

So long as she was *ascending*. Any effort, any danger was justified.

"I have—an ID. I have two IDs. A birth certificate and a—a Social Security card. I can show you, if . . ."

These documents, carried in a manila folder, she presented to the Investigator, who examined them closely. The Intern wondered if it was the name and birth date of "Sabbath McSwain" that piqued his interest so much as the literal nature of the documents—the very paper with which each was made.

Did he think they were *forged*? But why would he think so?

"They're legitimate, Dr. Hinton! You can examine them under a microscope if you wish. The seal of the State of Maryland—I'm sure that's legitimate. You can go to the place of issue, in the county court of records in Breathitt, Maryland. Same with the Social Security number. It belongs to *Sabbath McSwain—8/15/86.*"

"No photo ID?"

"Yes. I have a—a driver's license, somewhere. I don't have it with me because I—I don't have a vehicle right now. I don't drive. I mean—right now."

"The internship would require driving, you know. That's a principal requirement. *I* don't drive if I can avoid it."

"I said, Dr. Hinton, I do have a driver's license. Not for the state of Florida but—another state. I can look for it when I get back—to where I live."

"And where do you live?—I see, '928 Pepperdine Avenue, Temple Park.' That's your *home*?"

"No. Just where I live, temporarily. While I take classes here at the university."

Though in fact, this semester, she wasn't taking classes. She'd fallen out of the bottom of the big, rotted net—something small and squirmy that yet clung to the underside of the net, desperately.

"And where is your home, 'Sabbath'? Not around here, eh?"

"I—I don't have any permanent home, Dr. Hinton. I've lived in various places—I've moved, a lot, in recent years. My parents are—aren't—living . . . My family is 'scattered' . . ."

"Where were you born?"

"B-born? You mean—"

"Where was your mother, literally, when you were born? Where in the United States?"

"I think—well, obviously—Breathitt, Maryland. It's just a—a small town in a—mostly rural county. I've never actually lived there, except as an infant. And my mother—my mother and my father—are not any longer living there, either."

"And where did you grow up?"

"*Grow up*? I've told you—I think it's in the application letter . . ."

"No. Not here."

"We moved from Breathitt to a small town in Pennsylvania, when I was just a few months old. No one has ever heard of it—'Ephrata.' Then, we moved to East Scranton where I went to school. Then—the family kind of broke up. Then—I went to college—a community college—then, I was out of school for a while—I'd left home by that time, and—I was working, and I was traveling."

Her voice was slow, halting and struck with wonderment.

Is this my life? This—my life?

But this is not a life—is it?

"I have no inner life. I have no 'intimate' life. I am just what I— what I *do*. I move from one habitation to another like one of those—is it hermit crabs? Taking up residence in others' shells."

If the Intern had thought that the Investigator might be impressed by this solemn recitation, he wasn't. He said, with a shrug: "Others' shells are fine. You come, and then you go. *They're* gone."

Quickly she said, as if the aim of the interview were to entertain: "And then I came to Florida, to Miami first—with friends. Not 'friends' exactly but—people I knew. Used to know."

"Why Miami?"

"It wasn't my choice. It was just—where I was taken."

Not very vividly she recalled those days. Months?

Things had happened to her then, in that place. But not intimately. Easy to pick off, like scabs, scaly encrustations.

"You're twenty-four?"

The Investigator seemed faintly incredulous, whistling thinly through his teeth.

Grayish-white teeth they were, not big, broad and gleaming-white.

Set in the neat-trimmed dazzling-white beard, these teeth exuded an air of sincerity, even modesty.

"I guess so—yes. Twenty-four."

So little had happened to *her*, it was hard to comprehend how twenty-four years had passed in her presence.

"You look younger. You look," the Investigator said, slightly sneering, "like a *teen*."

The Intern shook her head, *no*.

"You've never lived in upstate New York?"

"Upstate New York? W-why do you ask?"

"Why do you think I would ask, Sabbath?"

"I—I'm not sure."

"Not that I am a linguistic expert. I am not. But my inexperienced ear can detect certain regional accents, like upstate New York. Somewhere in the north of the state, and the west—near Lake Ontario. You've lived there—for a long time."

"Well. I don't r-remember exactly, but . . . Maybe, after Ephrata, my father took us somewhere, maybe it was upstate New York, until . . ."

"You don't sound like you've lived in Florida very long. Maybe you've forgotten the exact dates."

Bemused, the Investigator read through Sabbath McSwain's application letter another time. The entire letter was a single, brief paragraph with the letterhead *Females Without Borders Temple Park, FL* stating the applicant's wish to work as Dr. Hinton's assistant on the recommendation of Ms. Chantelle Rios.

Included also was Chantelle Rios's letter of recommendation, extravagant with praise for *my sister and my friend Sabbath McSwain.* Thoughtfully if not altogether accurately Chantelle had indicated that Sabbath had been a "lab technician" in her psychology lab at the university and that, at Females Without Borders, she'd helped with "crucial" administrative tasks; Sabbath McSwain was a "zealous, tireless, idealistic & 100 % reliable" worker whom Dr. Hinton would not regret hiring for such a "sensitive & confidential" position.

Also with the letter was a list of Sabbath's paltry minimum-wage jobs—clerk, kitchen worker, etc.—and two pages, stapled together, of photocopied transcripts of courses and grades issued by the registrar of the State University of Florida at Temple Park.

Just faintly smudged, all the grades were A and A-. All had been issued to *Sabbath McSwain, Continuing Education School.*

The Investigator peered at the photocopied transcripts as if, just possibly, they were forged documents.

Which they were *not.*

"You don't have a B.A. degree, I gather?"

The hot wave of feeling came over her again, a sensation like angry nausea. She hoped that the little blue vein in her right temple wasn't visibly beating.

"Many things I don't have, Dr. Hinton. A degree is one of them."

The Investigator laughed. This was a good answer.

So far as she'd been able to gather, Cornelius Hinton had several distinguished degrees—Harvard, Cambridge University, Columbia University. He'd written a number of books published by academic presses on obscure topics in semantics, social psychology, cognitive psychology and philosophy of mind. His *Text/Subtext/Encoded "Meaning": An Existential Theory of Semantics* (Oxford University Press, 1979) was his most acclaimed academic book, that had won an award from the National Academy of Science; since that time, his interests seemed to have shifted elsewhere, and if he continued to publish it was under another name or names. At the Institute, he was a prominent name and yet an elusive figure who was invariably "on leave"—he hadn't taught his popular undergraduate course "An Anatomy of American Civilization" in years, and his graduate seminars on obscure subjects ("Charles Sanders Peirce: Semiotics & Visionary Madness") were limited to a small, select number of graduate students. Hinton was the most coveted of dissertation advisors, as he was likely to be the most absent of advisors—Chantelle claimed that there were individuals writing dissertations under his guidance who had not seen the man, face-to-face, in years. Hinton had come to prefer emails to personal conferences and had acquired a distaste for "copious hard copy" that took up too much room on his desktop and in his life. His preferred way of professional academic reading had become, he'd said, *scrolling*.

Behind the Investigator was a floor-to-ceiling bookcase crammed with books both horizontal and vertical, in no discernible order—semantics, linguistics, political philosophy, novels by Upton Sinclair, John Dos Passos, Willa Cather and William Faulkner; oversized books of drawings by Käthe Kollwitz, George Grosz, Ben Shahn, and (unexpectedly) Saul Steinberg; books of photographs by Mathew Brady, Edward Weston, Dorothea Lange, Robert Frank, and Bruce

Davidson; David Hume's *An Enquiry Concerning Human Understanding* and Thomas Hobbes's *Leviathan* beside Noam Chomsky's *Problems of Knowledge and Freedom*, Frantz Fanon's *The Wretched of the Earth*, Dostoyevsky's *The Insulted and Injured*, John Rawls's *A Theory of Justice*, Peter Singer's *Animal Liberation* and a vivid-red paperback anthology titled *Striking Back: Animal Rights Activism for the 21st Century*. On a shelf with Aristotle's *Politics* and Descartes's *Meditations* was a slender yellow book—*The Art of Paradox: Zeno of Elea*.

The Investigator saw the Intern staring past his shoulder, turned and looked at the shelf—"Which of these are you interested in? *Zeno of Elea?*"

"No."

"No—you're not?"

The Intern shook her head, no. Quickly now looking from the bookcase to the Investigator who was regarding her with a quizzical expression.

"No one knows much about 'Zeno of Elea.' He was a contemporary of Socrates and very like Socrates, essentially. They were men who provoked others to *think*—in that way they made enemies."

The Intern continued to stare at the Investigator's desktop.

Her eyelids were lowered, impassive. Moisture filled her eyes but did not spill over onto her cheeks.

Staring at the Investigator's hands which were narrow, long-fingered—a man's hands yet graceful, with short-trimmed nails. And the star-shaped silver ring on the right hand, that looked like a talisman.

The Investigator returned to the subject of the interview.

"I've had several assistants—'interns'—in the past. Each worked out very well, once we understood each other. Basically I am looking for a trustworthy and reliable person. I am somewhat impractical-minded—I forget things, misplace things—rarely do I actually *lose* things, because my intern will find them for me—that may be her greatest challenge! I'm not looking for an intellectual—I'm certainly not looking for an 'original' or 'creative' personality for whom working for another is a mere sideline. I'm looking for an individual who will, in a sense, *belong to me* and will not resist me—my assignments, I mean. And these will be exciting assignments! And risky, at times. So I need a fearless intern, yet not a foolhardy intern. An intern who scrupulously follows directions, anticipates problems, and solves them without involving *me*. An intern who is clear-minded and articulate but who speaks very little—as if each word costs her. (My first intern chattered so much, meaning to be 'charming,' I warned her that I would dock from her check a dollar-a-word for all words that were inconsequential. She caught on, quickly!) Particularly I am looking for an intern who draws no attention to herself—who can slip into places in which I'd be detected at once. I'm not looking to be 'charmed'—I've had enough of being 'charmed,' believe me. The only seductions practiced in my vicinity will be my own—my 'seductions' of my subjects, to get them to talk imprudently, and not in their own best interests. An intern must be alert to the quagmire of 'transference'—as in a psychoanalysis—and I never encourage any sort of 'confessing.' The intern will not call me 'Cornelius'—(in fact, that dowdy old name isn't my actual name nor, at the present time, my *nom de guerre*)—but 'Dr. Hinton'—or 'sir'—will do. The intern will not fall in love with me—even in fantasy. Or imagine that I am her father, still less her grandfather. We have work to do which I consider urgent work, exposing the sick underbelly of the American soul—if you'll allow a surreal twist of speech—and so we may have to take risks. We must be impersonal as missiles, and we must be efficient. *I do not give a damn about the intern's inner life.*"

The Intern smiled, uncertainly. Had she confided to the Investigator that she had no *inner life*? She had.

"Ms. McSwain—'Sabbath.' Tell me, do you respect the law?"

"No."

"No?"

"Well, I'd have to ask—which law? Is there a single, singular *law*?"

The Investigator nodded approvingly. "Good! I like your skepticism. I like even that prissy little way you curl your lip—'Is there a single, singular *law*?' I have here"—quickly, almost abashedly, yet surely boastfully, the Investigator lowered his head, indicated a part amid snowy-white hair on the left side of his head—"a commemorative scar from a cop's billy club, the 'siege of Chicago 1968,' to suggest the brutality of the *law*. So I take *law* with a grain of salt, indeed." The Intern had a fleeting view of a startling zipper-track of serrated scalp—then the flowing-white hair, a testament to masculine vanity so refined as to approach abnegation, obscured the old, bitter hurt like a caress.

"You look like one who has lived—not 'outside' the law but, in some way, orthogonal to it. Is this correct?"

Orthogonal. She took a plunge, guessing: parallel? perpendicular? proximate but irrelevant?

"Yes, sir."

"Always good to ask 'which law'—'law for *who*.' Sometimes it's a moral imperative to break such a law—a more noble imperative to work to abolish it. So I have a criminal record, of a kind—not as 'Cornelius Hinton,' however. And you, Ms. McSwain?"

"And me—what?"

"Do you have a criminal record?"

"N-no . . ."

"You haven't been a political activist? Like Chantelle and her friends? 'Code Pink'?"

"No."

"And in all your travels—your years of drifting about Florida—vague as they were made to sound—you were never, as it's said, 'busted'?"

"No. I was not."

The Intern laughed. She wondered if she should feel offended, or flattered.

"Quite innocent and naïve people find themselves arrested, often," the Investigator said, "if for instance a Republican convention comes to town, and the local PD turns out its mounted storm troopers. Especially people of color, and people of ambiguous sexual identity. So my question shouldn't strike you as rude."

The Intern was sure, *Sabbath McSwain* had no criminal record, she'd died so young.

She'd never typed the name in any computer. Out of superstition she wouldn't have wished to research the name any more than she'd have wished to research her old, lost name—the self she'd been *back there.*

She had no curiosity about the past, to the degree to which it touched upon her. An impersonal past, the "historical" past—social, political, cultural—this interested her far more than her own past which was befouled like a summer sweater of some light, delicate material dragged through a mud puddle.

The Investigator was saying: "So—would you be willing, if necessary, to 'break the law'—to 'trespass'—even to 'steal'? By which I don't mean any sort of common theft of property, but evidence that has been hidden away from the public, which we might require to expose deviousness and fraud."

"Y-yes, sir."

"You'd be willing to go, with me, into unpleasant places, even dangerous places, at my request? And if you were detected, I couldn't help you."

"Y-yes, sir. I mean—yes. I would be willing. I would try."

She liked it, being asked to *trespass.* She liked the idea of an outlaw life, in which deceit in the service of righteousness was the prevailing logic.

A subversive life for which she would be paid. A *life.*

"And salary. Have we discussed 'salary'?"

As if casually the Investigator quoted a weekly sum several times what the Intern might have expected.

The Intern smiled, uncertainly.

"Well—would that salary *do?*"

The Intern smiled yet more uncertainly. Was the proper answer— *yes?*

"Know what I like about you, Sabbath McSwain? You don't waste breath. You take up damned little space."

The interview seemed to be winding down. Perhaps the interview was over.

The Investigator had begun to glance toward his computer screen, as if distracted by new email. The Intern wondered if she'd been dismissed? Rejected? *Had she missed something crucial?*

"I—I should leave now, Dr. Hinton? Is that—what comes next?"

Very clumsy this was. The Intern could think of no other words.

So often she went for days without speaking to anyone, at length. And seeing those few people whom she knew, she was likely to duck away from them, in a kind of shame.

The Investigator said, "Yes. Good. You can leave now of course. But return tomorrow at seven-fifteen A.M."

"Return tomorrow?"

"Yes. How otherwise would you work as my intern, if you aren't on-site?"

"Do you mean—I'm hired?"

"I think I mean—you will do for the time being."

The Intern stood, stunned and dazed. The Investigator more languidly stood, looming above her. He did not see her to the door. He did not mean to be gallant—that would not be a feature of their relationship. *Truly he did not want a personal connection,* the Intern understood.

Yet clumsily she thrust out her hand. A child's hand, a boy's hand—with ragged nails, dirt-edged nails, bitten-nails. The cuff of her plaid shirt was stained, the toes of her boys' winter shoe-boots were stained. The Investigator shook the Intern's hand with a perturbed little smile, not rising to the level of exasperation, not rising to the level of an indulgence, fleeting, kindly, to send her on her way out of his office and out of the Institute that, positioned at an edge of the university campus that fronted a busy avenue, suggested its peripheral and orthogonal relation to the campus, much of its funding from private sources. Outside, the Intern walked quickly away.

Began to run, was running in a light-autumn rain out of an opaque sky, hearing herself laughing, an inward-laughing, not-audible, rapidly blinking in the rain that cooled her warm face—*You will do for the time being. I think I mean. You!*

THE INTERN'S FIRST TASK under the Investigator's tutelage was to master the "crafty art" of photographing an (ignorant, oblivious) subject from a distance of just a few feet.

"Observe. From yesterday."

The Investigator invited the Intern to look at the screen—large, flat, state-of-the-art—of his desk computer.

She was astonished to see there eighteen pictures labeled MCSWAIN—*her?*

She winced to see herself head-on, innocently unsuspecting, with that little frowning-furrow in her forehead, and what the Investigator had called the prissy little set of her mouth. The photos were slightly out of focus but unmistakably *Sabbath McSwain.*

The Intern was too surprised to be disturbed, or offended. The Intern had to marvel.

"How did you do it, Dr. Hinton? I had n-no idea . . ."

"Of course you had 'no idea.' That is the point of the mini-camera."

The Investigator laughed, as if the Intern had uttered a very naïve remark.

He explained: deftly and inconspicuously he'd snapped these pictures during their conversation with a Sony mini-camera hidden in his watch, that operated with a tiny battery charged like a cell phone.

The Investigator showed her how it was done. The Investigator reminded her how he'd engaged her fullest attention as he'd spoken with her, distracting it from his wristwatch.

The Investigator smiled with a corner of his mouth. Clearly, the Investigator was pleased with himself.

"The mini-camera-watch is a new purchase. I'm still experimenting with it. I've used pen-cameras, which are also good. None of these produce as sharp images as, for instance, a not-extraordinary cell phone. It does take skill. It takes practice. It takes *sangfroid—chutzpah*. As my intern you must possess both, while seeming to possess neither." The Investigator paused. He could not have known—(could he?)—that no one had addressed the Intern in such a tone, at once so intimate and so aggressive, in a very long time; and that the very sound of his voice left her mildly shaken.

She did not speak of course. She knew as much of *sangfroid* as she did of *chutzpah*—from reading, and not from experience. But she did not speak. The Investigator continued:

"In the world of high-tech surveillance espionage for instance, these aren't very sophisticated tools, but my subjects don't seem to have caught on just yet. And of course, Professor Cornelius Hinton is *so unassuming.*"

The Investigator laughed, out of pride at his own cleverness.

The Intern marveled at the watch, and the tiny camera contained within the watch. The Intern despaired that she would ever master such a delicate operation, under the gaze of a subject.

"My fingers are too clumsy, Dr. Hinton. I could never do that—what you did. I'd get caught, I—"

"You will not 'get caught.' You will take mini-pictures as well as I do, eventually better. You will begin. Here."

The Investigator gave the Intern her first Sony mini-camera, a feminized version of his big-faced digital watch, to slip onto her slender wrist.

Her eyes filled with tears. So beautiful!

→ ←

That was eight months ago. Since then, the Intern had come to know the Investigator intimately.

Not *inwardly*—but intimately.

To know, for instance, that when the Investigator worked at his computer, transcribing scribbled notes from his tiny notebook into a file as he did obsessively, hour following hour, day following day—he listened to Mozart.

Mozart piano sonatas, primarily.

The simplicity of an early sonata—Sonata no. 15 in F Major.

The more powerful C Major Sonata, K. 330, played by Horowitz.

Out of the computer these notes swelled in a fluid cascade. Utter clarity. Perfection.

Working nearby in the Investigator's office, involved in more mundane secretarial tasks, the Intern would find herself listening entranced. The Investigator's prose was often raw, rough-textured in indignation—the *savage indignation* of Jonathan Swift, as he described it—but his ideal was classic clarity.

"Nothing truly matters but social justice," the Investigator said. "Even to know that we can make very little headway against injustice, still—" His voice quavered, the challenge was thrilling to him.

The Intern wondered if the "personal life" had failed the Investigator—he'd been hurt, he'd been crippled, or had hurt others, crippled and disappointed others, who could not shape their (personal) lives to an (impersonal) life of service. The Intern wondered but would not ever have asked.

Long ago the Intern had played Mozart. The early piano pieces, composed by the child-Mozart. She smiled to recall—but no, she could not recall.

That little kick in the heart—the thrill of memory! No.

All that was *back there* was closed to her now. They had cast her away in shame and derision. She was the *ugly one,* unloved.

Almost, she could recall her (near-naked) body covered in muck, excrement. Her hair, her eyes. They'd laughed in derision.

Ugly ugly ugly. There's the ugly one.

Her family she had shamed. Their name, debased. She could not bear to think of it and so she did not, she had not and would not *ever.*

Except: listening to the piano notes of Mozart lifting out of the Investigator's computer, she was compelled to recall.

Listening entranced, staring at the back of the Investigator's head—airy-white hair, grown just slightly long over his collar—the intelligent cast to his head, as if cocked, to hear more accurately, what another, more coarse-eared, could not hear.

At such times feeling that her soul had been vaporized. Sucked from her. The crystalline piano notes, the clarity and beauty and the ease that was without haste or urgency, and in a way anonymous—as if the composer-Mozart were not an individual, a mere man, mortal, who had died centuries ago, but the voice of humankind itself, re-fined of all that is crude, gross, debased and ugly.

"McSwain!"—the Investigator was calling to her. (Often now omitting the honorific *Ms.* because *McSwain* was so much more ef-ficient and so much more suited to the occasion.)

"Yes, sir?"

"Not busy, are you?"

"I—n-no . . ."

Of course, the Intern was busy. The Investigator had many times more work for the Intern to do than she could possibly do in a single day.

Between interns, the Investigator had "fallen behind"—it seemed.

There were ordinary household and office bills to be paid—gas, electric, taxes. There were royalty checks to be sent to the bank(s) in which the Investigator had his account(s). There were bank state-ments to be recorded, there were IRS documents to be filled out and sent to the Investigator's accountant in Fort Lauderdale. More myste-riously, there were checks—some of them monthly—to be made out to numerous individuals and services. Above all there were files—manila folders stuffed with notes, documents, newspaper articles, email printouts—to which the Intern had been assigned.

"Will you get me some tea? Green tea. A large mug. And some honey. And for yourself, if you wish. Please."

The Investigator's natural mode of communication was giving orders to others—matter-of-fact, just slightly bossy. He'd been a PI—"principal investigator"—in experimental psychology laboratories at the Institute and at previous universities where his role had been to give orders to younger assistants, post-docs, graduate and under-graduate students.

But there was the *please,* that mitigated.

"Yes, sir."

SOON THEN THE INTERN KNEW more of the Investigator than the Investigator could have guessed she might know.

She knew his name(s). His birth name, his early professional name, the "Investigator"-name(s) under which he published. And his bank-account name(s).

Not only could the Intern forge the Investigator's signature(s), it was her task, as the Investigator bid her, to forge these signatures when he was too busy to be interrupted for such mundane tasks.

"The only thing we can't 'forge' is a legal document. For that, we need witnesses and a notary public."

Here was a surprise: for all that the Investigator was famously secretive and reclusive, "impossible to interview"—(as the author of the *SHAME!* series was described on the Internet, for instance)—contacting even his distinguished New York City and London pub-lishers and his agents through a maze of fictitious email identities, he was astonishingly casual with the Intern once he'd determined that he could trust her.

He'd seemed to know, by the set of the Intern's impassive little face in which her eyes appeared large and stark and shrewd and yet uncertain, that she was guileless as she appeared, and could have no motive for betrayal. And perhaps he took for granted that, like previ-ous young female interns in his employ, she adored *him.*

The Intern was not one to *adore.* Not for a very long time.

Neither would have acted upon this adoration. It was just *there*—like a talisman dangling about the Intern's neck which you could choose to see or not-see.

The Intern had been surprised to learn that the Investigator, born *Andrew Edgar Mackie Jr.* in St. Paul, Minnesota, on March 1, 1938, had been a seminarian at the Jesuit seminary at Rockland, Minnesota, from 1958 to 1959; he'd dropped out of the seminary to attend the University of Minnesota, from which he graduated in 1963 with a B.A. in psychology and anthropology. Ever afterward the Investigator was known to say that he'd never abandoned the Jesuit imperative—*Love God, and do what you will.*

God he interpreted as the "most exalted" of all human projects—as the German philosopher Ludwig Feuerbach had believed. Human will, human love, human hope, human desire—a gigantic image projected upon a screen, a sky-screen of blue opacity.

The Intern supposed that this must be so. She had no religious beliefs of her own.

The Investigator had been a scornful unbeliever—a "militant atheist"—after he'd left the seminary and the Roman Catholic Church; now, decades later, he was still contemptuous of religious institutions, but sympathetic with individuals for whom religious faith was a necessity of life.

The Investigator had abandoned the Midwestern *Andrew Edgar Mackie Jr.* sometime in the 1960s.

Soon then, there appeared *Cornelius Hinton*, with advanced degrees from Harvard, Cambridge University, and Columbia University.

Hinton was an energetic and seemingly ambitious academician. His fields were semantics, social psychology, cognitive psychology and philosophy of mind—the least penetrable of disciplines. In the 1970s *Hinton* began to be published widely in academic journals and to be offered professorships at distinguished universities—Columbia, Duke, Yale, Cornell. He moved about as a visiting professor. As a visiting fellow at research institutes. He had no interest in academic rank or in tenure—often, he stayed at a university for only a single semester. He lived in the (rented) homes and apartments of professors on leave. In Ithaca he'd lived much of the time at a campsite in Lebanon State Park a half-hour's drive from the Cornell campus. He wore his hair long. He ceased shaving. He leased cars, when necessary. He preferred bicycles even in cold weather which, in upstate New York, can be very cold, blustery and snowy indeed.

In 1991 he accepted a fellowship at the National Science Foundation in Arlington, Virginia. Soon after that, a permanent and high-paying position at the Institute for Advanced Research at Florida State University–Temple Park where multi-millionaire Fort Lauderdale donors were hoping to establish a world-class research institution. Yet, strangely, *Cornelius Hinton* seemed to have ceased publishing at about the time he arrived in Temple Park.

The Investigator's first, controversial bestseller in what would be the *SHAME!* series had actually been published in 1979: this was *SHAME! ARCADIA HALL 1977–78*, a vividly narrated undercover account of the largest state-run home for mentally ill adolescents in Pennsylvania, Arcadia Hall in Philadelphia. This was a psychiatric medical facility in which attendants routinely harassed, beat, and sexually abused their charges while medical staffers and administrators ignored complaints until serious injuries and a death occurred. *SHAME! ARCADIA HALL 1977–78* was presented in diary form by the Investigator who remained anonymous within its pages; according to the book cover, the author was "J. Swift"—the Investigator's homage to his great predecessor Jonathan Swift. From a brief biographical note on the book's dust jacket you learned little of "J. Swift" except that he'd been born in the Midwest "at the end of the Great Depression" and had "traveled widely, and deeply, within U.S. borders"; there was no jacket photo. From the diarist account itself you surmised that "the Investigator" was an impassioned individual who had once intended to become a Jesuit but who'd dropped out of the seminary to become involved in the civil rights movement. Preparing to write *SHAME! ARCADIA HALL 1977–78* the Investigator had trained as a medical attendant at the University of Pennsylvania School of Nursing; he'd worked twelve-hour days for nine increasingly stressful months at Arcadia Hall, recording and photographing his experiences, until he was fired for "insubordination"—trying to intervene between patients and fellow attendants.

It was a part of the controversy of *SHAME! ARCADIA HALL 1977–78* that the author had been beaten, injured, and hospitalized himself;

his assailants had eventually been arrested, tried and found guilty of criminal assault and battery. His life had been threatened numerous times but by the time *SHAME! ARCADIA HALL 1977–78* was published, and climbing bestseller charts following a sensational front-page review in the *New York Times Book Review* by the distinguished psychiatrist and Harvard professor Robert Coles, the mysterious "J. Swift" had disappeared from Philadelphia with no plans to return.

In 1979, this had occurred. Not until seven years later would the Intern be born.

Of course, already in high school she'd heard about the *SHAME!* series, which eventually included nine books, each a blunt, shocking, and meticulously researched diarist account by the individual who called himself "the Investigator"; on book covers, the author remained "J. Swift." Over the years, J. Swift's biographical information scarcely expanded except to include an ever-growing list of awards— National Book Award, National Book Critics Circle Award, Anisfield-Wolf Award, Pulitzer Prize. The Investigator/J. Swift seemed to have no private life—no wife, no family, no fixed place of residence. And no photo.

The zealous Investigator had gone undercover to visit horrendous factory farms in the Midwest, and dispiritingly understaffed V.A. hospitals in New England; he'd infiltrated slaughterhouses supplying fast-food chains—(in forthright homage to one of his heroes, Upton Sinclair, of *The Jungle*); he'd infiltrated medical research laboratories experimenting on chimpanzees, dogs, and cats—(managing to take terrifying photographs, released on the Internet to much protest and outrage). Under a name other than "J. Swift" he'd been arrested in San Francisco as an animal rights activist—("terrorist" was the official charge)—and as an "eco-terrorist"—but charges were eventually dropped for lack of evidence. (The Intern would learn, when going through the Investigator's finances, that he'd been a generous donor to such animal rights organizations as PETA, Animal Rights Liberation Front, and Animal Rights Militia, as he'd been a generous donor to leftist-activist organizations like Code Pink and feminist organizations like Females Without Borders.) The Investigator's most recent best-selling book was *SHAME! YOUR (DIS)HONOR*, published in 2009, a harrowing exposé of several corrupt family court judges in Nassau County, Long Island, who'd accepted more than two million dollars in bribes since 2005, to send as many as three thousand first-time offenders to privately owned correctional facilities. Most of the first-time offenses had been misdemeanors and not felonies, which would have resulted in probation if the judges hadn't shunted the youthful offenders into the prison system; the defendants had had no lawyers, since their parents had been talked into signing away their legal rights by family court officers who were also receiving bribes. In one of the notorious boot-camp facilities, a squalid barracks in the Poconos, young inmates had been harassed, beaten, and sexually abused by corrections officers and fellow inmates, resulting in the suicide of a seventeen-year-old girl who'd been arrested for having shoplifted less than twenty-five dollars' worth of merchandise from a Rite Aid store—her first offense! The Investigator had gathered his sordid material by posing as "Hank Carpenter," a representative of the privately-run correctional service PioneerAmerica Corrections, Inc., who'd bluntly offered the Nassau County family court judges "five thousand a head" for each youthful offender they sent to the facility; he'd recorded their astonishing conversations, to be replicated verbatim in *SHAME! YOUR (DIS)HONOR*.

Before the book was officially published, the Investigator had turned his findings over to the Nassau County prosecutor and the New York State federal attorney general; excerpts published in *The New Yorker* had stirred a national firestorm of protest and outrage.

Eventually, the corrupt judges pleaded guilty to charges of accepting bribes, lost their positions and were sentenced to prison terms varying from seven to fifteen years.

Seven to fifteen years! With time out for "good behavior," in moderate-security (state-run) prisons, the ex-judges would serve just a fraction of their sentences.

With the bribes from the private-prison facilities they'd bought expensive cars, a yacht, new homes; they'd built swimming pools, taken luxury cruises to the Bahamas, sent their children to expensive private schools. (None of the bribe-money had been returned.)

So far, the private-prison facilities hadn't been charged with any wrongdoing.

In totalitarian China, government officials like the corrupt judges might have been executed.

Out of disgust with the Nassau County judiciary, the Investigator was turning his attention to capital punishment in the United States in the past several years following the highly publicized successes of the Innocence Project—specifically, to those states in which the frequency of executions had not slowed despite revelations of wrongly convicted individuals on Death Row, through DNA testing. While states like Illinois, New York, and New Jersey had acted immediately to suspend all executions pending further investigations, such states as Texas, Georgia, Alabama, Mississippi, Louisiana and Florida had hardly reacted to the disclosures of the Innocence Project at all. "It's as if they don't give a damn, whether a convicted person is 'guilty'— once he's been found 'guilty' by a jury or a judge. Whether a person is *innocent* isn't a factor in whether the state kills him." The Investigator was incensed, indignant.

It was for this project that the Investigator had hired the Intern.

He'd warned her that it could be "stomach-turning"—"possibly even dangerous." They would try to be admitted into maximum-security Death Row prisons in disguise as lawyers, criminologists, or university professors in sociology, psychology; if prison officials knew who the Investigator was, the muckraking author of the notorious *SHAME!* series, he would never be granted admittance. The Intern would be less carefully scrutinized, he was sure—"As my assistant, you can go virtually anywhere I can go. No one will look at *you*."

"MCSWAIN! DEAL WITH THESE."

A stack of envelopes, not-yet-opened.

It was one of the Intern's tasks to cash the Investigator's checks and to pay the Investigator's bills for him, for the Investigator had a fastidious dislike of what he called *finances*.

Envelopes containing the Investigator's royalty checks—(to "J. Swift" as well as "Cornelius Hinton" and several others)—he could not bring himself to open, or, if he did, he could not bring himself to glance at the figures, as if to see the extent of his income might be an act of immodesty. Even "Cornelius Hinton's" monthly checks from the Institute, he could barely bring himself to examine.

Such tasks, as well as paying bills, the Investigator gave over entirely to the Intern, surprisingly soon after the Intern came to work for him. (Not at the Institute but in the Investigator's stucco town house on the Rio Vista Canal connecting Temple Park with Fort Lauderdale, which the Investigator was leasing from a colleague on leave at the university. As if incidentally, the town house had a two-storey living room mostly glass-walled, with a view, dazzling in the morning, of the Atlantic Ocean and the misty sky above the ocean a mile and a half to the east.)

So this is what *bestseller* means!—the Intern whistled thinly through her teeth.

"He's rich! Money spilling out of bank accounts, he doesn't know what to do with."

And there were translations and foreign sales, reissued paperback editions of old titles, as well as new titles; adaptations of several of the *SHAME!* titles into TV and film documentaries, in Europe; even, in Sweden, a proposed stage adaptation of *SHAME! YOUR (DIS)HONOR* to be produced by a major Stockholm theater.

The Investigator dressed well, in a gentlemanly fashion, when he wanted *Professor Cornelius Hinton* to present a convincing image to the public; but overall, so far as the Intern could determine, the Investigator lived well within his means, owned no property and only grudgingly leased a high-end vehicle, in the late winter of 2012 a steel-colored Acura MDX, of practical use for his trips by car to Death Row prisons.

(The Intern had not been misleading when she'd assured the Investigator that she had a driver's license—somewhere. Since she'd been hired by him, she had managed to acquire, through a Fort Lauderdale acquaintance with a contact in the Broward County Motor Vehicle Department, a laminated driver's license with a photo ID issued to *Sabbath McSwain born 8/15/86.* For the Investigator would not drive any vehicle, for any purpose, if he could avoid it.) Along with routine bills—gas, electricity, insurance—the Intern paid bills to a number of services each month, one of them a long-term-care hospital in Minneapolis called Mount Saint Joseph. Also, a check for fifteen hundred dollars went out each month to *F. J. Mackie,* of St. Paul; another, for a slightly lower sum, to *Denise Delaney,* of Chicago; still others, for varying amounts of money, to a dozen individuals of whom most lived in the Midwest. (Relatives, former spouses, children? *Did the Investigator have children? Grandchildren?*) One of the accounts, to which the Investigator had paid more than thirty-five thousand dollars between 2005 and 2011, to a party named *Hollis Whittaker,* resident of White Plains, New York, had been closed in 2011; in red pencil, the Investigator had written F I N I across the name in his handwritten bank account record.

At several colleges and universities including the University of Minnesota, Wake Forest College, Ithaca College, Loyola College of Chicago, and the College of Arts and Sciences at Temple Park, Florida, the Investigator had established scholarship funds for undergraduates with endowments ranging from $500,000 to $900,000. At Cornell University, in addition, there had been established, in 2007, the *J. Swift Fellowship in Bioethics and Investigative Reportage,* with an endowment of $900,000, for graduate and post-doc students.

Which meant, as the Intern rapidly calculated, that the Investigator had given away several million dollars within the past decade—a fact no one else could know since no one had tabulated and made a note of it and very likely, the Investigator couldn't have named the numerous scholarships he'd endowed.

In a spare room of the rented town house, on a white Parsons table that stretched the length of the room, were accordion-files of letters:

typed and even handwritten letters. Hundreds of these dating back
to the late 1960s. (A note from a previous intern, on a Post-it, stated
Sorting & filing to 1991. Incomplete.)

And there were files of more recent, email letters. Most of these
were from editors, some were from readers, a scattering were from
friends and acquaintances, former academic associates of the Investigator, students. Salutations were to *J. Swift, Cornelius Hinton, "Andy."*
(Could "Andy" be an affectionate diminutive of "Andrew Edgar
Mackie Jr." who'd disappeared decades ago?) The Intern skimmed
this miscellany, alert to such phrases as *Love, Much love, Love always.*

Mixed with letters were cards. Savage-beautiful art postcards, re-
productions of paintings by Matisse, Derain, Rousseau . . . The most
gorgeously gaudy cards appeared to have been sent by the same individual whose scrawled name might have been *Isabel,* or *Inez.*

The last of these cards was dated 2/22/08 and the postmark was
Brussels, Belgium.

The Intern had been instructed to "tidy things up"—"identify,
with labels"—"dispose of duplicate books, galleys, etc." in the rented
stucco town house. Less than a year's lease remained on the town
house and the Investigator hadn't given a thought—of course—to
where he might move next. (The Investigator was notoriously careless about planning for an immediate, domestic future: his concentration was focused upon the current project.)

Previous interns had sorted, filed and labeled much of the Investigator's materials. The Intern discovered, in cardboard boxes neatly
labeled by years—(1970–1980; 1980–1990, etc.)–publications in which
the Investigator's work had appeared, *New York Review of Books, The
Nation, The New Yorker, Harper's* and *TLS;* copyedited manuscript
pages and galleys for the *SHAME!* books; print interviews with the Investigator, under the name *J. Swift;* swatches of reviews, some lauda-
tory and some not. In a folder marked SUMMER 1981/ASPEN were
photographs of a festive outdoor wedding in which the Investigator,
in his early forties, didn't appear to be the groom but—possibly—the
best man. He was wearing a tie-dyed suit of some eccentric mate-

rial like burlap; on his feet were sandals, and on his head dark bristling snaky braids like dreadlocks; his beard wasn't close-trimmed
as it was now but wide, dark, and curly. He didn't look so much like
himself—rather more like a ruddy American-simulacrum of the revolutionary Che Guevara.

The wedding photos were haphazard. The camera was scarcely
in focus. On a mountainside in the background were wildflowers in
vivid bloom, as in a fauve painting. The Intern smiled to think—*They
are all stoned. They are all so happy! What has become of them now, three
decades later?*

There was the girl-bride—in white tattered-silk, long silky blond
hair, barefoot. And there was the groom—a young guy in his thirties, with a sunburnt face, hair in a ponytail—clean-shaven, and barefoot also.

How handsome the Investigator was, in the summer of 1981! In
that long-ago time when he'd been young, still. When he'd been
amid a circle of celebrating friends, with whom he was, you could
see, emotionally close.

The Intern hadn't yet been born, in 1981. She felt a stab of jealousy
seeing in several photographs the Investigator standing with a young
woman: not a beautiful young woman but attractive, snub-nosed,
with wavy chestnut-colored hair, in a long lacy skirt to her ankles.
The two were laughing together, relaxed. There was—you could see
it—a sexual ease between them, a physical radiance.

The Intern brought these photographs to a window, to examine
them more closely. She thought *I have never had a life. What would it
be, to have a life?*

The Intern felt no bitterness, only curiosity. An almost scientific
curiosity.

Thinking too *But he has given up this life—of the emotions. He has
moved on, he has abandoned these people. Those are the terms on which we
can be together.*

→ ←

The new project was tentatively titled *SHAME! CRUEL & USUAL PUNISHMENT: Publicly Sanctioned Murders in the U.S.*

Though the Investigator was meticulous in his research, the Investigator did not care for a subtle, Jamesian prose style in his writing— his aim was to surprise, to shock, to dismay, to disgust, to *convince* and to *emotionally involve.*

The Investigator had been amassing information on death-penalty cases since the highly publicized successes of the Innocence Project in the first decade of the new century, in which more than 260 convicted individuals, many on Death Row, were found innocent through DNA testing. In his computer-files were hundreds of pages of documents including lengthy law journal articles by such specialists in the field as Barry Scheck, Austin Sarat, and Leigh Buchanan Bienen. It was sobering—more than sobering, appalling—to speculate how many individuals, a high percentage of them dark-skinned, had been sentenced to death, though in fact they were not guilty of the crimes for which they'd been sentenced; to speculate how many such individuals were incarcerated in Death Row cell blocks at the present time, who might be freed, if the Innocence Project had access to their cases.

The Investigator characterized himself as a "skeptic"—"since the age of twenty, a cynic in the tradition of Swift and Voltaire"—yet he was astonished and outraged by the fact that in a distressing number of states, virtually nothing had been done to reduce death-penalty judgments, despite the possibility of DNA exoneration. The Investigator raged to the Intern: "Even the Supreme Court of the United States doesn't seem to care if an innocent person is executed, once he's been found 'guilty'!"

The Investigator particularly detested the "right-wing-leaning" chief justices of the Court. His bêtes noires were Scalia and Thomas. He'd have dearly loved a *SHAME!* exposé of the (secret, concealed) lives of the Supreme Court justices, but these American citizens were so far removed from accountability to anyone, it was all but impossible for "J. Swift" to imagine exposing them.

"Oh God! If I could live forever. If I never slowed down. If I could go back in time, enter law school, manage to get myself appointed a law clerk for Scalia or Thomas! So much of contemporary evil springs from the Court, as from the White House and the Pentagon, dripping down like a shit-stained ceiling . . ."

The Intern was flattered that the Investigator should speak to her so openly. The Investigator had no fear that his Intern hadn't been hired by his enemies to spy on *him*.

Often she heard him on the telephone talking to old friends, colleagues and comrades in his activist organizations—she heard his aggrieved voice, his harsh laughter.

She felt a thrill of pride. She was the Investigator's *intern*.

Though unknown to anyone except the Investigator, at the present time, perhaps sometime, after the new *SHAME!* project was completed, the name "Sabbath McSwain" might be linked with his name, and their names.

Naively thinking *Maybe we will make a difference. What we expose to the world—will change the world.*

THE FIRST VISIT to a Death Row facility had been arranged: March 11, 2012, at 10 A.M., at the Maximum Security Correctional Facility for Men at Orion, Florida. Orion was a small town in the flatlands of Central Florida north and west of Lake Okeechobee approximately a two-and-a-half-hour drive from Temple Park.

"The tour is arranged, McSwain? Good work!"

The Investigator never failed to express pleased surprise when the Intern accomplished something of a kind he found difficult to undertake: simple telephone requests, reservations and bookings, filling a prescription at the local drugstore, querying a bill that had already been paid. The Investigator was temperamentally *vexed* at having to execute such ordinary tasks, as a musical prodigy would be vexed having to play "Chopsticks."

The Intern had long been "shy"—that is, not-very-sociable—inclined to extreme taciturnity, even to sullenness—but had quickly assumed, as Dr. Cornelius Hinton's assistant, a confidence, a kind of hearty arrogance, befitting her position. Her ordinary voice was hesitant and scratchy and near-inaudible but her telephone voice was sharp and forthright; the impressively pompous *Professor Cornelius Hinton, Institute for Advanced Research at the State University of Florida at Temple Park* rolled off her tongue as if she'd been uttering it for years, to intimidate others.

From a contact of the Investigator's in the University of Florida Law School at Gainesville the Intern had managed to secure two places in the Orion tour, which was reserved for individuals in the field of criminal justice, professors and educators and psychologists, politicians, social welfare workers, clergy. In theory, background checks were to be made of all visitors to Florida prison facilities; in practice, the Intern gathered, such checks were cursory and random. Since a professor at the Law School had vouched for Dr. Hinton, neither Hinton nor his young assistant was likely to arouse suspicion in the Orion authorities.

On the morning of March 11, 2012, the Intern came early to the Investigator's office at the Institute. The plan was that the Intern would drive them in the Investigator's leased Acura SUV to the prison facility north and west of Lake Okeechobee. On the drive—on U.S. 27, along the North New River Canal—the Investigator studied Death Row documents he'd downloaded from the Internet, made cell phone calls and rehearsed with the Intern what their strategy should be during the guided tour—"I will be recording when I can. What seems valuable. Just the tour-guide talking, if he's a corrections officer, is the sort of thing I want. Death Row anecdotes. 'Off the record' kind of things—he'd never say in an interview. And in the execution chamber, if the tour takes us there—we'll both want to take pictures, if we can. The closer to the execution site, the better. But don't worry: I won't expect you to do anything risky, this first time. Though you're my 'assistant' we won't acknowledge any connection during the tour. The tour has been organized through the warden's office, it's doubtful that the guide would even know that

'Sabbath McSwain' is 'Cornelius Hinton's' assistant. I'll signal you if I want you to do something in particular but don't try to anticipate anything—just behave naturally. Fit in with the others. You look like a student—you won't attract attention. I will take as many photos as I can, that seem to me pertinent to our project. But we should both be *sparing*."

The Intern smiled uneasily. *Sparing!*

The Intern had no wish to call attention to herself. The Intern had a strong wish to remain invisible for as long as possible.

At the Orion exit, all signs led to the prison facility.

At the Orion exit, already you could see the flatland-acreage of the prison grounds bordered by a fifteen-foot electrified wire-mesh fence topped with coils of razor wire. You could see, at regular intervals along this fence, guard-tower stations. And beyond, only just visible, the ugly fortress-like buildings of the prison. The Investigator said thoughtfully: "I've been 'jailed' a few times but not yet 'imprisoned.' There's a profound psychological difference, it's said. And only just imagine—a sentence of *life behind bars*. A sentence of *death*."

The Intern detected an air of excitement and apprehension in her employer's voice. The Intern did not wish to think *He is anxious, too—but will never show it.*

On the two-and-a-half-hour drive from Temple Park, the Intern had thought *If something goes wrong now—an accident—we would be spared. The worse danger would be averted.*

But the Intern was a careful driver. The Intern was a precise driver. The Intern was something of an obsessively careful and precise and *law-abiding* driver in the very face of a (secret) wish to sabotage the morning's project, to spare the Investigator and herself the risk of entering the maximum-security prison and confronting what lay within.

By 9:45 A.M., the prison facility was bathed in the dull-winter-glower of central Florida in late winter: no visible sun, a sky of coarse clouds, yet a shadow-less light everywhere. The Intern could recall— vaguely, as one might recall a childhood movie never seen in its entirety, or consciously—a very different sort of late-winter, in another, more northerly climate.

Especially in the mountains, snow would lie everywhere in mid-March—in heaps, in layers, in rivulets, some of it gritty and discolored and some of it fresh, freshly-fallen and dazzling-white.

Here in Florida, snow never fell. No startling surprise out of the sky—*snow*.

By 9:45 A.M., the prison facility was well into its day. Very likely, the prison-day began, for corrections officers and other employees who came into the facility, at dawn.

The employees' parking lot was nearly full. The visitors' lot, which had to be at least an eighth of a mile beyond, was already about one-third full.

Before they were allowed into the prison, the Investigator and the Intern had to lock away personal items in their car trunk or glove compartment: wallets, credit cards, cash, all electronic equipment including cell phones, laptop computers, iPads. They were forbidden to bring inside *contraband*—cigarettes, for instance, or any sort of medication. Any sort of instrument or weapon, anything that might be fashioned into a weapon, a toothbrush for instance, house or car keys, gold-chain necklaces, any sort of conspicuous jewelry. They were allowed to wear wristwatches and they were allowed to bring inside with them a single pen and a single small notebook—no recording devices or cameras, of course. They were forbidden to wear any shade of blue for blue was the prisoners' primary color, nor could they wear denim of any color, including black, for denim was the prisoners' primary fabric. They were forbidden to wear orange—orange jumpsuits were the uniforms of a certain cadre of prisoners who were not-yet-sorted into the general population. And they were forbidden to wear brown, or beige-brown, for these were the colors of the COs' uniforms.

Visitors were forbidden to wear shorts, sleeveless shirts or pullovers, open-toed shoes like sandals. Female visitors in particular were not to wear "provocative" clothing no matter the heat. (Some administrative offices were air-conditioned at Orion but, overall, the facility sweltered and baked in the heat of the sun through April to October and beyond: if you believed you could not bear temperatures in the mid- or high 90s, or higher, it was not recommended that you visit Orion during these months.) On this chilly day, the Intern wore dark corduroy trousers and the Investigator surprised her by wearing a quite striking suit, dove-gray, pinstripe, of a light flannel wool, with a white shirt and a silk necktie, which she'd never seen before.

He'd even trimmed his white beard. He'd trimmed his fingernails.

Of course, visitors were forbidden to speak with—"signal to"—any inmate. They were not to drift away from the tour-group under any circumstances. They were not to attempt to pass notes to any inmate—or corrections officer. If the tour-guide introduced them to a trustee—an inmate-worker—they could speak to this man, but not otherwise; and they could not ask him any personal questions, whatsoever.

"It will be like taking a tour through a 'factory farm,' or a slaughterhouse, which I've already done and which can be pretty ghastly. Essentially, our aim is to soak up as much information as we can, and take pictures when we can, and get back out alive." The Investigator laughed, as if he'd said something witty.

The Investigator instructed the Intern to please walk ahead of him, to catch up with a half-dozen other visitors who were making their way up a flight of crude stone steps to the roadway above. The Investigator remained at the SUV for a few minutes longer, before following after her. And when he joined the group of fourteen visitors assembled outside the prison gate it was 9:58 A.M., he did not so much as glance at her.

THOUGH SCHEDULED TO BEGIN promptly at 10 A.M., the tour did not begin until 10:38 A.M. when the tour-guide—the Lieutenant—arrived, from inside the prison facility. He was a tall fit-looking man of indeterminate age, not old, yet certainly not young, in the dull-brown uniform of the Orion correctional officers; his shoulders were

muscular, yet slightly slumped, as his chest seemed just slightly con-
cave, as if he'd been ill recently and had not yet regained his lost
weight and strength. His jaws looked as if they hadn't been shaved
recently—at least, not clean-shaven. His eyes crinkled at the corners
with an unpredictable sort of merriment. He checked the IDs of the
tour-visitors and passed them back without comment except to say,
apropos the "sociology of crime" class and their (female) professor
from the Florida State University–Eustis—"Might be, I could learn
something from *you*." His tone was somewhere between sneering
and flattery.

Just inside the prison gate was a metal-detector checkpoint
through which the Lieutenant drove his visitors like a herd-dog driving sheep. Again they showed their laminated ID cards, this time to a
frowning guard who stared at them suspiciously as if he'd never seen
a tour-group before. The guard stamped their wrists with invisible
ink warning them that, if they washed the ink off, the entire facility
would go into lockdown—"Nobody *in,* and nobody *out.*"

Other guards were moving through the checkpoint with them.
It was protocol, the Lieutenant said, for visitors to allow COs to go
ahead of civilians.

The Intern moved without hesitation. Her heart was beating
calmly. In such times of wonderment it is good to recall *I am not really meant to be alive—this is all posthumous. I will endure.*

"Step along, folks. This way. *Don't stray from my side.*"

Now they were inside the facility, or rather in an interior courtyard
of the facility. Underfoot was a scrubby open area of cobblestones
edged with weeds and, to the right, a weatherworn stucco building
upon which a rainbow mural had been painted, very likely by inmates. The Intern glanced back at the others in the tour-group—the
students of whom all but two were female, the (female) professor,
several middle-aged men, all white—and, in his distinguished pinstripe suit, the Investigator who'd already begun taking notes in his
little pocket notebook.

The Investigator's Sony watch, with the large state-of-the-art face in which dates, tides, sunsets and sunrises were registered, was visible on his wrist, and set to take instantaneous mini-pictures, the Intern knew.

Her own Sony watch, a gift from the Investigator, wasn't so conspicuous on the Intern's wrist, nor did she feel comfortable about using it. The Investigator had rehearsed picture-taking with her—numerous times—but the Investigator had told her not to take pictures inside the facility if she was anxious about doing so: to take pictures here was in violation of Florida law, and she could be arrested.

He had no intention of being caught, or arrested. *He* prided himself on never once having been discovered when he'd gone undercover on a project, since the late 1970s.

The Lieutenant was telling them about the history of the Orion Maximum Security Correctional Facility for Men, founded in 1907, on just twenty acres of land. In subsequent decades the prison was enlarged and in 1939 the current Death Row unit was built, holding thirty-five prisoners. In 1982, other maximum-security facilities were built in central Florida, to accommodate a "growing increase" in the prison population—"Due mainly to drugs and drug-trafficking in the Miami area." In the state of Florida there were three other Death Row institutions—Florida State Prison, or Starke Prison; Union Correctional Institution in Raiford; and Lowell Correctional Institution Annex, where women on Death Row were housed.

From her research the Intern knew most of this. The Lieutenant's voice was brisk and hearty and grating to her ears. The Intern saw how the Lieutenant's pebble-colored eyes moved over the individuals of the tour-group, compulsively. He had no need to listen to himself speak—he'd said these words many times, and knew to pause when he expected smiles, or nervous laughter. For it seemed that the Lieutenant was always counting the members of the tour-group—he couldn't help himself.

The Intern sometimes found herself counting—people, figures, objects. Who knows why?

A way of fixing the infinite. Stopping time before it flows—away.

It was an M. C. Escher predilection, maybe. A compulsion.

Badly she wanted to draw—something. Her fingers twitched, as the Investigator's fingers twitched, with the need to collect, to record. In this forbidden place, in particular. Where they moved like wraiths, *undercover.*

The Intern, as "Sabbath McSwain," had had an art exhibit, with two other young women artists, at the Females Without Borders center at the Temple Park. After a long absence of creating art—of feeling the wish to create art, still less the energy and hope of such effort—the Intern had worked for several exhilarated weeks on intricately rendered pen-and-ink drawings, not of Escher-like visionary subjects but of individuals she'd observed close-up, and intimately: some of them had been customers in the failing bookstore, faces that had appealed to her, a kindred loneliness in them as in herself, and that peculiar *yearning.*

The instinct for abstraction had waned in her. The instinct for a witty acquisition of being, through quantification and repetition. Now, she seemed to care mostly for individual faces: quirky, homely, unself-conscious, unique. Millions of individuals, very few of any particular distinction yet all of them unique. Here was the mystery!

The Investigator hadn't wanted an assistant who was *creative.* The Intern would hide from him this impulse, never would she confide in him that she'd had an exhibit at the Females Without Borders center. (Which possibly the Investigator had seen, though he wouldn't have remembered her name attached to twenty-five pen-and-ink portraits of extreme simplicity.)

The Intern smiled: overhearing one of the young women in the tour-group murmur to a companion that the Investigator—"that man, there—with the white hair"—was "some kind of retired chief justice"—a remark which, the Intern thought, would amuse her employer when she told him.

"Any questions, folks? If not, follow me!"

The Lieutenant had finished the opening passages of his tour-speech.

Now he was leading his fifteen visitors across the courtyard and into the stucco chapel.

"This is our 'non-denominational' house of worship, folks. We are very proud of our chapel."

The interior was spartan, with pinewood pews, a low ceiling, sputtering candles against a wall and a plain T-cross, not a crucifix, elevated at the front of the room. There was a pulpit banked with artificial calla lilies and behind the pulpit stood a light-skinned black man in blue prison uniform, about thirty-five years old, nervously waiting to address the group. He had a boyish face, eager eyes. The Lieutenant introduced him as "Juan-Carlos"—a "lifer"—that is, the inmate had been given an indeterminate prison sentence—"thirty years to life"—from which he might, at some point in the future, be paroled.

Juan-Carlos spoke rapidly, staring out into the pews with shining eyes. His voice had a gospel-lilt. Telling of how he'd made a "bad choice" as a boy, joining a gang, in Miami, drug-dealing-gang—"thown my own life away like garbage"—and ever after, "tryin to retrieve it through the help of Christ Our Lord."

Aged fifteen he'd been initiated into the gang. He'd been involved in a "cutting"—later, a "killing"—though he hadn't killed anyone himself he'd been present at an execution of two men and so he was guilty—"felony murder."

Also his own loving mother, he'd stolen from, and struck in the face—she'd died, of some junkie beating on her, he understood it was *his fault.*

Every day praying, Juan-Carlos said, for the men he'd seen die. Bled to death on the street. For the families of the boys. Every day praying for his momma. And for himself, his soul. Every day twenty-two years, eight months since the men died.

The New Year of that year, that followed, when he was seventeen years old and Jesus had come into his soul like a "blinding comet."

The Intern was moved by Juan-Carlos's words. The Intern would have liked to press her hands against her ears, not to hear more.

Thown my life away.

Garbage.

The chapel-talk was ending. The Lieutenant stood in the aisle asking the tour-visitors if they had questions for Juan-Carlos.

At first no one spoke. Then, the woman professor lifted her hand to ask what had been Juan-Carlos's "gang-affiliation" but the Lieutenant interrupted—"Sorry, ma'am! That can't be revealed."

Several others asked questions, about parole. Juan-Carlos said that he'd been interviewed by the parole board twice, and turned down twice, but that he would not give up—he would re-apply, next year.

"Every day I pray to God, to thank Him, I was not sentenced to death. For it might have happened—and I would be on Death Row this morning, and not here speakin with you. Amen!"

The Investigator raised his hand to ask a question. All looked at him—the white-haired gentleman in the expensive-looking suit, white shirt and tie, of whom it was rumored he was a retired judge.

But the Investigator's question was not a sensational one. He asked only if Juan-Carlos was taking courses in the prison? High school courses, vocational courses?

Juan-Carlos shook his head, *no*. There were no courses for inmates in Orion, right now.

"So you don't have a high school diploma, obviously. So if you are paroled—what will you do, outside?"

Juan-Carlos smiled at the Investigator. Juan-Carlos said he'd worked in the "license-plate" shop, he had experience *there*.

"Reading skills? Writing? Math?"

Juan-Carlos would have attempted an answer except the Lieutenant interrupted, irritably: "Thank you, sir, for your question. It's a very good question, we will think about it. But now—time to move on."

Juan-Carlos was ushered from the pulpit by a guard in a dun-colored uniform. The Lieutenant led his tour-group out of the chapel in two columns, back to the cobblestone courtyard. Overhead the sky remained white-glowering and opaque. Like a thin rubber film stretched tight.

The Intern shielded her eyes with her fingers. The inmate's words had been moving to her, she'd had a wish to draw his face, his lanky figure. Along his right leg were the white vertical letters $PRISONER$ which rendered all that the man said somehow diminished, as if a clown were speaking, to entertain his captors.

The Intern didn't want to glance at her watch, to see how little time had passed in the chapel. Already she could see that time moved with infinite slowness inside the prison walls.

The Lieutenant herded his visitors in the direction of a squat dull-granite memorial stone with a double column of engraved names—"COs who died in the line of duty here at Orion. From 1907 to 2010."

Beside the memorial stone was an American flag hanging at perpetual half-mast.

Many questions were asked about these deaths in the line of duty. The Lieutenant said that he had himself seen, with his own eyes, fellow COs attacked, beaten, even killed by prisoners "on a rampage"—narrowly he'd escaped being taken hostage, in the 1980s, in a "prison uprising."

The Lieutenant told of the "most violent ten minutes" in the prison's history, in 1969—an attempted breakout when a Black Panther defense attorney smuggled an automatic revolver into the prison, to leave with his client who smuggled it inside his clothing and, as he was being escorted back to his cell block, suddenly began shooting wildly, killing several COs and fellow inmates until he was rushed by tower-guards and shot down dead.

"Ten minutes, and ten people killed. That's what we live with every hour of every day in this facility—what can happen to us at any time."

One of the visitors asked what had happened to the defense attorney? Had he been arrested for smuggling the weapon into the prison?

"No. He was not arrested. He fled the country—went to Cuba. Far as I know, he's still there."

The Lieutenant spoke bitterly, vehemently. The Intern knew that the Investigator would have liked to question the man further: how did the "Black Panther defense attorney" smuggle the weapon through the metal-detector? How had the attorney so easily escaped the country? There had to be more to the account than what the Lieutenant had said.

But the Investigator allowed the moment to pass. It was not his strategy to arouse antagonism, still less suspicion, in any individual whom he confronted while *undercover*.

In one of the newer buildings was the infirmary, but the Lieutenant wasn't going to lead the tour-group inside.

"It ain't the safest place. It don't smell good. Like, lots of germs from sick people. 'Infections.' Last November there was swine flu, then shingles, and chicken pox—half the facility was quarantined. Lots of COs were hit—including me. Sick as a dog and lost like twenty pounds. But worst you can get in here is T.B.—some new kind of strain, there ain't the medicine to combat it."

Visitors asked how many "physicians" were on call at Orion.

Visitors asked if "seriously sick" prisoners were removed from the facility, to hospitals.

The Lieutenant answered these questions with a sly razor-flash of a smile. The Lieutenant said it was the "most usual thing to expect," a man would die in the infirmary if he was an old man, a lifer.

"That's what you have to expect, folks. If you 'do the crime, you gotta do the time.' If you are sent to Orion ain't unreasonable to expect you might-be gonna die in Orion."

Someone began to object—there should be "health and medical options" for all prisoners—but one of the older men who'd been silent until now, though grimly nodding at every remark of the Lieutenant's, interrupted to say that it was "ridiculous" to expect maximum-security prisoners to have first-rate medical treatment any more inside prison than they'd have had outside prison.

"Taxpayers are tired of coddling these people. One in one hundred U.S. citizens is 'incarcerated'—or will be—and one in less than ten—males—in the 'African-American' community is incarcerated, or will be. You can see it here at Orion—in the 'Yard' . . . Can't blame the prison-system for that that's to do with breakdown in families, family-values . . ."

The speaker was fleshy-jowled and flush-faced and had the righteous-exasperated look of a school superintendent in a troubled school-district or maybe the look of a minister of a Protestant sect just-this-side-of-respectable-middle-class. The chuckling Lieutenant agreed with the fleshy-jowled man as if to pique the more liberal-minded of his visitors—(the university professor and her students? The white-haired gentleman scribbling in his little notebook?).

"Sir, you are absolutely correct. Can't blame the prison-system for the population that's crammed in it."

They were being led along a coarse-gravel path that pained the Intern's feet, even in hiking boots. At the rear of a building they stood observing inmates working with metal—"license-plate manufacture"—and with wood—"furniture-manufacture." The inmates were of all ages including surprisingly old—"lifers" in their fifties, sixties—some of them with straggling beards, bald heads and canes; amid the younger men, of whom the majority were dark-skinned, here and there were "disabled"—canes, walkers, even wheelchairs. The Intern was distracted from the Lieutenant's words staring at these men who were oblivious—(or wished to give that impression)—to being rudely observed by civilian-strangers.

Her heart beat rapidly. She hoped they would not—would not turn, to see *her*.

Criminals, they were—"convicts." Yet she had to suppose they were very likely veterans—"wounded in action."

The woman professor standing close beside the Intern turned to her, with a look of concern.

"Excuse me? Are you—feeling faint?"

The Intern had been breathing strangely. The Intern had been feeling very shaky.

As if blood were draining from her head. Sensation draining downward out of her brain.

"Yes. No. Thank you. I am—fine."

The Intern made an effort to listen to the Lieutenant questioning his fellow COs in charge of furniture-and-license-plate manufacture in the facility. Their exchanges had the air of much-repeated words yet were not uninteresting nonetheless.

The tour-group civilians were lavish in their praise like doting parents or grandparents confronted with the work of brain-damaged children.

"Gosh this is very good work! This is just—excellent work."

"This is—these are—pieces of furniture I would buy myself. I could imagine, buying . . ."

". . . this table, is it maplewood? It looks really solid . . ."

". . . for our sons' room, I would buy a bureau like this. Good and solid and . . ."

"So smooth and *shiny*. It's like, shellacked?—no slivers . . ."

They were informed that most government offices in the state of Florida were furnished by furniture-makers at one or another of the prison facilities. A number of schools, community colleges.

"Y'see, prison is a 'learning opportunity.' It ain't just taking courses like how to read, write—it's learning a trade, too."

The Lieutenant seemed to be addressing the Investigator who was inspecting the furniture at close hand, with an expression of affable scrutiny.

"Some men get paroled from Orion, they're hired right-away by furniture companies—ain't no problem them getting back in the job market."

Next, the Lieutenant led his charges on a hike uphill. Soon a number of the tour-visitors were panting. At the corner of a high gaunt building they were led abruptly left, and down an incline—in front of them, a sudden expanse of open land, part-pavement and part-scrubby grassland, the "Yard."

The civilians stared. Hundreds—could it be *hundreds*?—of inmates were in the Yard, under the supervision of what appeared to be, to the casual eye, a very few guards.

Though there were guards in the watch-towers of course. Stationed at intervals along the fifteen-foot electrified wire fence.

The Lieutenant explained how gangs of inmates—African-Americans, Puerto Ricans, Dominicans, Cubans, "whites"—with now, more recent in past decades, "Chinese"—had taken possession of particular parts of the Yard, that were off-limits to all other gangs. "Inside, it's your skin-color that matters. Not one other thing so much. *That never changes.*"

They were surprised to see a number of older inmates—the Investigator's age, at least. Several had long white wispy beards and walked with canes on the dirt track while younger inmates jogged past them. Elsewhere inmates were shooting basketballs at netless rims, lifting weights, doing exercises; standing about, pacing—restless. You were aware of "race"—skin color. It was as the Lieutenant had said, the men were self-segregated by skin color and the fact was a depressing one yet unmistakable, unarguable. The Intern would have liked to confront the Investigator: *Where is your idealism about race blindness now?*

For the Investigator was far more idealistic than the Intern. The Investigator placed his faith in the future—in "a" future—in which social justice had at last been eradicated as one might wish to eradicate, in the state of Florida, for instance, a particular plant- or animal-invader that was devastating native species.

The tour-group was quiet now as they followed the Lieutenant blindly through the Yard. Not all of the inmates had noticed the tour-group but those who had were staring, some of them openly, others covertly like children. In the Yard, on the scrubby ground, cloud-shadows passed swift and fleet as the shadows of predator birds.

"Folks, this way. Don't stare, ain't po-lite to stare, ain't that been explained to you? 'No-eye-contact'—'no fraternization with inmates'—you got it, right?"

Briskly the Lieutenant led the visitors along another rough-gravel path. This one was protected by the open expanse of the Yard by a ten-foot wire-mesh fence. In the near distance were open urinals— the Intern was astonished to see, as other (female) individuals in the tour-group were astonished to see—about which the Lieutenant said, chiding, " 'Open urinals'—don't look. It's a protocol—*don't look*. The inmates know to keep their eyes to themselves, but visitors have got to be reminded of good manners. *Just don't look*. Any man using any open urinal, he's invisible, like. Monkey-don't-see, monkey-don't-do."

What did this mean? Was the Lieutenant teasing, scolding? Threatening? Quickly the Intern looked away from the open urinals.

"Anyway just step-along here, folks. No need to linger here."

Yet the Intern saw: inmates' eyes shifting in their sockets, across a considerable distance. They were noting the presence of females.

How, the Intern wondered, were they counting *her*?

Ugly ugly ugly. That one.

Gloating to think that *ugliness* is a shield.

Ugliness attracts no sex-desire.

"Inmates allowed in the Yard like this, their daily exercise, they value it highly and would not jeopardize it. Dangerous felons you will not see, mostly—they are in solitary, or a special cell block, or Death Row. To get Yard rights, a man has got to show good behavior. There's gangs out there but not the worst members. Long as nobody pushes in anybody else's territory, there won't be trouble. Don't worry they're looking at us—they don't want nothing to do with us. The prison don't negotiate hostages—that's known. A CO like myself, I am not carrying a firearm. You will note, I am not carrying a firearm. So that a firearm can't be taken from me. And if anybody tried to get around this fence, the tower-guards would see them right away. I mean, a half-second. The tower-guards call in a bullhorn—EVERYBODY DOWN! EVERYBODY DOWN! And if they do, you throw yourself down. You don't think twice, you don't try to figure what the hell it is, is it serious danger, or whatever it is, you hear that command and you throw yourself down and if you don't, folks, if you're still standing, you're a candidate for getting shot down. That's why we tell visitors not to wear anything remotely like blue, you don't want to be confused with an inmate in a time of emergency. A tower-guard will shoot you down, that is his authority. The fact is—'No Warning Shots.' A civilian can be killed out of ignorance. If some kind of uprising started, and no warning. But look—chances are, nothing is gonna happen, see they're just watching us without making any move, they're too smart to make any move, broad daylight like this is. Like I said the worst guys are not out in the Yard—they're lucky they get one hour in forty-eight for 'exercise' outside their cell—and it ain't in any Yard—and a shower—and that's it. Some of them, sheer animals, crazy-like, they'd tear your throats out with their teeth if they could, so you don't see them, a visitor is spared the sight of them. So ladies, don't worry! Truth is no tour-group has ever been threatened at Orion. No hostages! Not on my watch. And I been leading tours for—hell, twenty years now. Not that this is the main CO work I do, it is not, but guided-tour is what I guess not everybody at Orion is suited for, or has the talent for, so the warden counts on me and I ain't gonna let him down. Any questions?"

The Investigator asked the Lieutenant which of his numerous assignments at Orion did he value most.

"Death Row. I prefer Death Row."

"And why is that, Lieutenant?"

"Well, say. Nobody ever asked me that question before. And the answer is—Death Row because the men are mostly all settled in. Not like the new recruits that haven't been sorted out yet and haven't figured it out yet, they're *inside*—could be a guy twenty years old, he's in for life, just getting to catch on, that's a guy so wild and desperate he'd kill anybody he could get his hands on and that includes himself—why the new guys hang themselves, the first few days you really have to watch them. Not one percent of them is what you'd call 'sane'—once they get inside. But a Death Row inmate, he's different. He could be 'crazy' too—but it's a more settled kind of crazy. He'd be trying to figure legal briefs, writing letters to lawyers, judges, news-papers, TV—his mind would be crazy but not violent-like. And there's just enough of them on Death Row whose sentences are commuted, or there's some history of it, the average Death Row inmate can have hope. Some of them been here like twelve, fifteen—eighteen years. The lawyers keep filing appeals and the 'anti-capital-punishment' people keep showing up out front to demonstrate when there's an execution. It's like a carnival, with TV cameras. Now, it's on the In-ternet. This old guy Pop Krunk, that was executed last month, he'd been on Death Row here since 1987. Walked with a cane, then in a wheelchair—his legs just went. He had a white beard, like some kinda crazy Santa Claus, so it was like real interesting to talk with him. They accumulate wisdom on Death Row. You kind of grow old together. They're more thoughtful, the majority. They don't have to share a cell like the rest of the population—most of them now, it's three to a cell, and supposed to be just two. But it's three. So they're crammed together like animals and when they get sick, like swine flu, Christ!—it ain't a pretty sight. Even if they don't kill one another they can infect one another, bad. But Death Row is like, the elite. And their cells are bigger too, six feet by nine feet by nine-and-a-half (in height). I never thought about it before—till you asked me, sir—I mean, Professor. My answer is Death Row."

The Intern, listening intently, did not turn to glance at the Inves-tigator.

She admired her employer for his methodical ways: he inveigled people into saying far more than they believed they were saying; vol-unteering to confide in him, as to a friend. He was an artist of words as another might be an artist of music: he could "play" compositions to evoke emotions in others, and this was the purpose of the *SHAME!* series. He was an emotional man, himself—yet it was an intellectual outrage he wanted to evoke in his audience, a sense of the terrible violation of a moral contract with other individuals, different from themselves. (And in the case of animals, of a species different from their species.) He chose to write bluntly and directly—not "calculatedly." When he could, he allowed others to speak in his place, like the Lieutenant whose words he was recording, without the Lieutenant knowing.

"Through here, folks! Best to hold your breath as long as you can."

The Lieutenant led the tour-group into a vast room like an airplane hangar, filled with long tables and chairs—a dining room. Adjacent to this vast room was a second vast room similarly furnished. Though the dining rooms were empty it was not difficult to imagine inmates crammed at the tables—a buzz and mutter of male voices, a clattering of plates, cafeteria trays. The smells were a mix—garbagey, rotted, rancid, gaseous, excretory. Old, stale, spilled food, and old, stale, spilled urine. The Intern felt a little leap of nausea.

"Staggered lunch-hours, the inmates feed. Cell Block A, Cell Block B, Cell Block C, Cell Block D—they all come through here like cattle through a chute."

Each wall of each room was covered in a highly detailed, bizarre and hallucinatory mural, or mosaic of murals, executed by an amateur artist with but a primitive sense of perspective, the human face and the human body. Heads were over-large on dwarf-torsos, arms were spindly and legs foreshortened. The faces were pasty-pale, dull-blank like the faces of the dead. Were the murals a peek into Hell, or a mirroring of the dining halls?

At a height of about ten feet above the floor, catwalks circled the dining hall, for guards to overlook the scene. Prominent on the catwalks were signs NO WARNING SHOTS.

With evident seriousness the Lieutenant was praising the "prison-artist" who'd been paroled from Orion in 1981 but had died not long afterward in a detention house in Tampa where he'd been picked up for vagrancy in a squatters' village under Interstate 75. The Intern wanted to shut her eyes, she could not bear to see the deformed heads and faces, the blank dead eyes.

The Lieutenant was praising the deceased artist, unless the Lieutenant was mocking the claims of others of the deceased artist— "DeVuonna is compared to 'Michael-angelo'—the Italian artist—in his use of wall-space and parts of the ceiling, too. There was a special fund for 'preserving DeVuonna' . . ."

The Intern shut her eyes for just a moment. How delicious, yet how dangerous! She was afraid of falling asleep on her feet.

The Lieutenant then seemed to be chiding his visitors, urging them farther into the room—"We are not leaving quite so soon, folks! Relax." The young-woman sociology students were seated at one of the long tables, the Intern and the Investigator and others at a nearby table, a trapped audience for the Lieutenant who continued to regale them with tales of episodes that had happened in the dining rooms, not so long ago. By this time the females in the tour-group had grown quiet. The men had removed their jackets, beginning to perspire. Only the white-haired Investigator maintained an air of curiosity, and gave no sign of feeling ill or faint.

The Lieutenant was showing his audience a box of items— homemade weapons discovered in the possession of inmates in the dining room within the past month. These were a toothbrush whittled sharp as an ice pick, a rusted razor blade attached to a cardboard handle, a metal hook fashioned out of large paper clips, a spike with a duct-tape grip that looked as if it were ideal for eye-gouging. "We keep 'em like in a museum, locked in here. Any weird thing you can think of, that could be a weapon, our inmates have already thought of at Orion."

Almost proudly the Lieutenant spoke.

Suddenly a door was opened at the rear of the dining hall. Two burly COs entered ushering before them several inmates in blue uniforms—the intrusion was startling, and distracting; the tour-group visitors stared at the inmates only a few yards from them, who stared back at them. Their eyes were stark and glassy and dead-seeming like eyes in the mural, except they were moving. Three of the inmates were dark-skinned, the fourth a light-skinned Hispanic in his mid- or late twenties who wore his hair in a tiny braid at the nape of his neck and who swung himself along on crutches with a grim little wince of his jaws.

Quickly the Intern looked away from the young Hispanic not wanting to lock eyes with his.

Wounded. A veteran.

A recent veteran: Iraq? Afghanistan?

She felt a wave of sickness, guilt. A guilt so profound, it was a sickness in the gut.

She did not look after the young man who was of her age, her generation. She felt the fury in his shoulders, that were muscled, and in his upper arms, his forearms and strong hands gripping the crutches that allowed him to move with a kind of stealthy swiftness, far faster than one would expect of a crippled boy.

That is, a wounded veteran.

It seemed to the Intern that no one in the tour-group wished to acknowledge the wounded inmate, nor even the other inmates. The Lieutenant called out a greeting to his fellow COs who saluted him with deadpan protocol—"*Sir!*"

Where the COs and the inmates had come from at this time and where they were going wasn't explained. The Intern was made to feel, as the others surely felt, how easily it could happen that inmates might break loose from their captors, for there were so many more inmates than corrections officers . . .

Probably, the inmates were kitchen-workers. They were headed for the kitchen to prepare for the massive upcoming lunch.

The Lieutenant was saying, "Most people are curious about how we feed two thousand six hundred sixty-eight inmates in general population—maximum security—three times a day. Well—it ain't easy! First, a bell goes and they're marched out of their cell blocks into the dining hall and along the walls—there, and there—and through the cafeteria line, get their trays and food, return to the dining hall here, and *sit*. And I mean *sit* in their designated places, only. If they sit at some table not designated for them there's the danger of retaliation—like, their throat cut. Anybody fucks around—(excuse me, ladies)—he's stripped and tossed into solitary. Twenty minutes in and out—a bell goes—they're marched back to their cells. It's like cattle through a chute—they're going in one direction, one at a time. And the food ain't bad, either—the inmates are damn hungry, the way they eat."

Though the vast dining halls were empty it wasn't difficult to envision prisoners crammed together at the tables, and to hear their muffled, surging voices, the clatter of plates and cutlery. It wasn't difficult to imagine an intensification of smells—food, spillage, unwashed flesh, intestinal gases. It was not difficult to sense the prisoners' desperation, and the danger in that desperation.

From somewhere in the building, possibly from the kitchen area at the rear, into which the inmates and COs had disappeared, there came a sound of raised voices, a door shut hard, clanging pot-lids. The Intern felt uneasy, apprehensive; a touch of panic, that inmates would swarm into the dining room, their voices booming, echoing. Yet the Lieutenant continued his maddeningly matter-of-fact speech, a kind of harangue—making some point about "mass-food."

"Folks! Two volunteers are needed."

The Lieutenant snapped his fingers. At the signal a kitchen-worker inmate, a smiling young black man in a hairnet, long-sleeved blue T-shirt, blue pants with $P R I S O N E R$ in white on the right leg, appeared with a tray of "sample food" on a platter: something breaded and nubby—chicken nuggets?—a small slab of grayish-fatty meat, mashed potatoes and gravy; a burrito, French fries; melted "American cheese" sandwich, a jelly-glaze donut.

"You must all be hungry," the Lieutenant said, teasing, to the tour-group. "Lunch is yet far off. So—volunteers?"

So swiftly the sample-food had appeared, obviously this was a part of the tour. Between the Lieutenant and the smiling young black man with oily-kinky hair flattened by a hairnet there passed a side-long glance of complicity.

"Yo, Harman? You fix up a pretty-good samplin' for us, for today?"

"Yessir sure has. Yessir Loo-t'nent."

The Lieutenant spoke with excruciating comic-condescension. Yet, Harman seemed to mind not at all and fell in immediately with the banter.

No one wanted to come forward. The Intern hoped that the Investigator wouldn't glance over at her, to signal her.

At last, two of the younger visitors—both sociology students—a girl with a long swishing ponytail, a young man in a Marlins baseball cap—came forward, with apprehensive smiles.

"Good, good! Thank you! Just a few bites of each! I think you will be favorably impressed by the quality."

The Lieutenant—smirking, or sincere—seated the volunteers in front of the tray. Slowly and self-consciously they began to eat.

The girl ate chicken nuggets with her fingers, the young man speared a piece of "beef-steak" and ate. Mashed potatoes and gravy, fries—burrito . . . The volunteers bravely chewed, swallowed. "Not bad, eh? Compliments to the chef?" The Lieutenant laughed.

Like a watchful parent he stood over the volunteers seeing that they sampled a bit of everything. It seemed to the Intern that the girl-student was beginning to look sick, and the boy-student's jaws were grinding with grim tenacity.

The Intern knew enough of what kitchen-conditions might be in an institution like this, to feel a shudder of dread at the prospect of eating such food. The Investigator would know, too. Of course. She didn't dare glance in his direction. Toxic bacteria breeding, invisibly swarming as in a petri dish . . .

What a joke, those admonitions in restaurant restrooms— *Employees are required to wash their hands thoroughly with soap and water before returning to work.* How much more ironic, in this maximum-security prison.

The Lieutenant was answering less painfully clinical questions from visitors about food preparation at Orion. "Well, see—as you'd expect—ninety-three percent of the prison services are provided by inmates. Couldn't afford the luxury of 'incarceration' otherwise."

The volunteers were eating more slowly. More slowly chewing, and swallowing. With a wink of merriment the Lieutenant said, "Not bad, eh? Compliments to Harman-yo, here—*he the chef.*"

The black boy in the hairnet laughed showing a flash of teeth.

The ponytail girl smiled faintly. The young man in the Marlins cap wiped at his mouth with the back of his hand.

"See, if you're hungry, you eat. If you ain't eating, then you ain't hungry. Law of nature."

The Lieutenant offered the other visitors the remains of the prison-food sample. When no one accepted he picked up a chicken nugget—turned it in his fingers but with a mysterious chuckle decided not to pop it into his mouth.

"Harman-yo. You turnin' into a real pro, once you get outta here you're gonna cut some swath through South Beach, yo. Take my word for it, son."

At last, led out of the dining hall. Outside, the Intern drew a deep breath of fresh air.

How badly she wanted to detach herself from the tour-group, and escape back to the entrance. So exhausted, she could have crawled back to the entrance.

Except, the Investigator would be terribly disappointed in her.

Disapproving, disgusted with Sabbath McSwain.

A few yards away oblivious of her. Scribbling notes in his little notebook. The dining-hall episode hadn't bothered the Investigator, much. Or, he'd put it quickly out of his mind.

Next, the Lieutenant led the group on a brisk little hike.

Cell Block C in a fortified stucco building that, to enter, required passing through another checkpoint. The (invisible) ink code on the civilians' wrists was checked in ultraviolet light. The Intern's laminated driver's license issued to *Sabbath McSwain* was examined closely if to no particular purpose. The sociology professor asked the Lieutenant why they were going through another checkpoint, since they'd already gone through two checkpoints, and the Lieutenant retorted with none of the affability he'd been beaming on his charges for the past ninety minutes or more: "Ma'am, it's how it *is.* You don't wish to comply, I can find a CO to take you back to the entrance and you can take yourself home with no further ado."

The woman was rebuffed, red-faced. No more flirty exchanges with the Lieutenant, for her!

This was a crazed place, the Intern was beginning to see. You could not fully comprehend the craziness for you saw only surfaces, edges and outlines of things. You saw *faces* not what was *beneath*.

The slightest infraction upon another's sense of himself—his pride, his integrity—his *power*—and you felt the immediate opposition, the leap of madness.

Yet somehow, the Intern wasn't prepared for Cell Block C. After the proximity of the inmate-workers in the furniture-and-license-plate factory who'd seemed oblivious of their civilian visitors and had seemed among themselves friendly, cooperative and non-threatening. And Harman exchanging banter with the white Lieutenant.

As soon as they were ushered out of the checkpoint area and into the squat building housing Cell Block C the Intern sensed the difference. A powerful smell of men's bodies. A sensation of strain as if the very air were viscous, vibrating.

In his mock-affable tone the Lieutenant introduced the tour-group to the cell block officers who glanced at them with barely concealed contempt. Nor did these officers exchange friendly greetings with the Lieutenant who seemed in their company suddenly fatuous, foolish. There was a high din in the air as of a thrum of angry hornets—the first tier of cells seemed to stretch away for as much as a city block, and above it—overhead—a second tier, which you could barely glimpse from the ground. As the Lieutenant spoke to the group about Cell Block C—a "new-recruit cell block mainly"—"before the men are sorted out and their gang affiliations determined"—the Intern became slowly aware of a chilling sight: on a catwalk around the cell block guards were stationed at intervals, holding automatic rifles in the crooks of their arms; the nearest guard, a severe-looking black man, was standing almost directly above the Lieutenant and his gathering of civilians, one foot up on a railing, rifle grasped in his hands as if he were prepared to fire at any moment.

Behind him and prominent on the stucco wall in full view of both tiers of cells was the ominous sign NO WARNING SHOTS.

The Intern wanted to pluck at the Investigator's sleeve, to make sure he'd noticed the guard overhead. The Investigator would have wanted to take pictures of this guard, the Intern was sure.

(But maybe that wouldn't be a prudent idea, to take pictures of the armed COs. If the Investigator was caught violating prison policy, and arrested—what then?)

Before they'd come to Orion, the Intern and the Investigator had done a good deal of research into the facility. The degree of "prisoner-on-prisoner" violence—"CO-on-prisoner" violence—unsatisfactorily explained "accidents" resulting in deaths—"suspicious suicides"—was high; though no higher than comparable correctional facilities in the state of Florida, and elsewhere in the United States.

But only in Cell Block C did the Intern *feel*—a sense of personal helplessness and dismay so powerful, it could not be named . . .

The area in which the civilians were standing ill at ease and self-conscious was cramped. There was no space here for a tour-group. You could see that the Lieutenant was barely tolerated in Cell Block C and his questions, put to his fellow COs for the benefit of the civilians, were met with sullen mumbles. Like several young-woman sociology students the Intern found herself standing only a few yards from three inmates in blue uniforms who were, for some reason, not in their cells but in the aisle, and not handcuffed or shackled together. Two of the inmates were dark-skinned Hispanics and the third, the tallest, had a Caucasian-demon face threaded with broken capillaries and a blunt bald head covered in tattoos; on his bulging biceps, swastika-tattoos, a green-snake tattoo, a bloody little heart impaled upon a dagger. Seeing such a figure you would want to smile—*can this be real?* The men were staring at the Intern, and past the Intern at the uneasy university students, their faces blank as faces stitched out of leather.

What were these men doing out of their cells? No one thought to explain. The Lieutenant seemed oblivious of them.

Next, the Lieutenant herded his tour-group onto a walkway that spanned the full length of the first-tier block of cells. It seemed to be the Lieutenant's intention to march them, single-file, around the cell block—past the cells, within a very few inches of the cell bars, and the men huddled inside.

"A word of caution, folks! Not just the ladies but gents, too. Try to stay as far to the left as you can, by this railing—do not walk too close to the cells. If one of the inmates reaches out to grab you— could be hard to extricate you from his grip. Got it?"

The Lieutenant chuckled meanly. The Intern was shocked: did the tour-guide think this was amusing? A joke? Was marching his civilian tour-group around the cell block a good idea? The young women students were looking terrified. Their professor was looking terrified. Even the several men who'd tried to affect an air of reasonable calm in the dining hall were looking concerned.

Only the Investigator was unperturbed. Stately-tall, courtly-mannered, with airy-floating white hair and an expression of just-perceptible disapproval, the oldest member of the tour-group took the Lieutenant aside to say: "Don't you think this is a little risky, Lieutenant? Provocative? That the prisoners might get over-aroused? And your visitors endangered?"

"No one is 'endangered'—that's ridiculous. The men are secured in their cells. They can't possibly break out. Don't linger looking into the cells, and don't linger making conversation with them. This is one of the concluding features of our tour through Orion. Everybody agrees afterward, you won't know the 'feel' of a maximum-security prison without the 'march around the block.'"

But the Investigator had nettled the Lieutenant, who felt his authority challenged.

The Intern had sized up the situation with the three inmates outside their cells: they were being marched off, taken away to another part of the prison; though looking like parodies of maximum-security prisoners, it seemed likely that they were being escorted to parole hearings, or had even been granted parole, or had "maxed-out"—for they weren't handcuffed or secured in any way. This was a relief—was it? The Intern had never seen close-up anyone quite like the tattooed Nazi: a member of the notorious Aryan Brotherhood.

When they'd researched the Death Row prisons, the Intern had also looked into the Death Row prisoners and the crimes they'd been convicted of committing.

The Intern had come to realize, as the Investigator had suggested, that, if you were a foe of capital punishment, it was a good idea not to know what condemned prisoners had been convicted of doing to their victims. Good not to temper mercy with too much information.

Despite her anxiety the Intern was clear-minded enough to position herself at the very head of the line. She was small, agile, quick on her feet—no problem to her, to slip past slow-moving others.

Her instinct was to save herself. It was immediate, and primitive. It had nothing to do with conscience, duty, or "good." She knew what was coming now and hoped to escape the worst of the punishment.

The Lieutenant was taking up the rear—he would drive the tour-group forward. But the Intern would walk first, and fast; she would press to the left, against the railing, and would not glance into any of the cells, if she could prevent herself; she didn't wish to provoke any of the inmates, particularly she didn't wish any of the inmates to grasp that she wasn't a slight-bodied young man but a young woman in boy's clothing.

Several of the young-woman sociology students were asking the Lieutenant if they could stay behind but the Lieutenant told them no, absolutely not.

"This is the full-tour of Orion! You signed up for the full-tour! You will not leave Orion without completing the full-tour, girls! Let's begin."

A cruel merriment shone in the pebbly eyes. The Intern thought *He hates us. As much as the inmates hate him.*

The march began. The Intern, at the head of the line, managed to pass by most of the cells before the inhabitants, crowded inside, realized what the situation was—a tour-group being marched around the cell block by the Lieutenant—and let out howls of excitement and derision particularly directed toward the females.

The Intern strode forward, swiftly. The Intern bit her lower lip.

The Intern thought *I am not "female"—not as the others are. These men have no interest in me.*

Yet the Intern felt the men lunging at her. The Intern felt the air agitated by their arms thrust through the bars, their outstretched fingers grabbing at her. The Intern could not but hear the obscenities spat from their lips, as more and more inmates caught on that a tour-group was being led past the cells, a phenomenon that must have been familiar to them, and maddening.

Not all the inmates behaved like enraged beasts. The Intern would realize later. Probably less than one-half. Less than one-third. But these others, who held back, or simply stared at the swift-passing procession of frightened civilians, went unremarked.

Savage animals. What would they do, if they could get at us.

At the females, particularly.

God let me get through it. Just a little farther!

It was a cruel lesson. The Lieutenant wanted them to know: the value of prisons, cell-bars. The value of incarceration, punishment.

Putting human beings against human beings. Rousing human beings to a fever-pitch of resentment, fury. Terror.

Particularly, there was sex-hatred here. The women were made to feel how precarious their well-being was, how dependent they were upon the protection of other men, against these beast-men.

It was a crude, cruel and simplistic ruse. The Intern understood, intellectually. Yet the Intern was deeply shaken, and would not soon forget.

(Wondering: where was the Investigator? Was he thinking these same things? Or, being a man, was he less shaken, less terrified? Probably he'd positioned himself at the very rear of the line, just in front of

the Lieutenant. Here were the most vulnerable positions, for every inmate in the first-tier of the cell block would be aroused and alerted by
the time the Investigator walked past his cell; every inmate was prepared, if he wanted to lunge against the bars, and grab at the civilian.)

(The Intern would learn that the Investigator, far from being
frightened of the march, had not walked fast passing the cells, but
had actually lingered, in front of certain cells, in which there were
men who weren't so frantic and furious; older men, in several cases,
who'd greeted him as he'd greeted them, cordially. *H'lo! How's it going.*
The Investigator was one to exude calm. Very likely, the Investigator
was taking pictures of the cell block, from start to finish. In the noise
and commotion, no one would have noticed. No one among the COs
would so much have glanced at the white-haired gentleman when
so many of the inmates were so wrought-up, so furious with sexual
longing and rage, they were throwing themselves against the bars of
their cells, thrusting their arms through, stretching out their fingers
as if they wanted to grasp, grip, shake and throttle, tear into pieces.)

How utterly silent the tour-group civilians were, on their horrible
forced march! Holding their breaths, waiting for the ordeal to end.

It was a protracted ordeal: the Lieutenant forced them to march
all the way around the cell block, back to where they'd begun. The
march could not have lasted more than a few minutes but felt like
much longer.

The Intern, eyes lowered. The Intern, breathing through her
mouth. The Intern, thinking of Zeno's Paradox: infinity within the
finite.

For each step is but a fraction of the total distance. The total distance is somewhere beyond experience.

In Zeno's Paradox you never reach your goal.

In Zeno's Paradox you are in a state of perpetual *yearning*.

"WELL, FRIENDS! Now you know—the *feel* of a maximum-security
prison."

In the glowering-white March sun they staggered with exhaustion.

Even the Investigator was looking fatigued. Even the Lieutenant, glimpsed in an unguarded moment.

"Time *inside* is not equivalent to time *outside*. When a CO comes home to his family after just one day, or night—he's been away a time they can't measure."

The Lieutenant chuckled, grimly.

In gratitude that they could breathe again, the visitors drew deep breaths filling their lungs. The Intern averted a wave of vertigo, shutting her eyes and biting her lower lip.

Yet she was tough, resilient. The Investigator would be impressed with his girl-assistant who hadn't panicked as several of the other young women had panicked, begging to be excluded from the march.

Though crudely treated by the Lieutenant, who'd subjected them not only to a physical ordeal but to a considerable humiliation, the individuals of the tour-group did not seem to resent him. The Intern took note.

Now that they'd left the dreaded Cell Block C they were saying, marveling—what a good idea it is, how worth tax-money, you could not have civilization without it, prisons, punishment, guards with guns to protect you.

"In this direction, my friends, if you've caught your breaths— Death Row."

The Lieutenant led them briskly along one of the coarse-graveled paths. The execution chamber attached to Death Row was the last of the stops of the prison tour.

Another half-hour, maybe. Then freedom!

The college girls were clutching at one another, breathless and laughing. The experience of the cell block had left them dazed, shaken and giddy. One of the girls had been crying and another had comforted her and another was saying *O God! Was that—was that horrible . . .*

Nightmare . . .

. . . never forget.

But they were out of Cell Block C now. Laughing and gasping for breath like one who has been part-strangled, released and then part-strangled and then released and now grateful simply to breathe, to be alive.

Cynically the Intern thought: they would recall the experience, in the shared giddiness of girls who'd come through a crisis together, as a particular sort of sexual frisson.

In the wake of the Lieutenant they were walking. In the direction of a particularly ugly cinder block building at the farther edge of a compound of buildings beyond which there was open, scrubby land and in the near distance the high electrified fence, the guard-tower stations.

"Don't worry, my friends—we don't visit Death Row. We will visit the execution chamber but not 'Death Row'—you will not come face-to-face with the most *evil*." The Lieutenant paused as if choosing his words with care though they were surely familiar words many times recited at this point in the tour.

One of the visitors asked why wasn't Death Row part of the tour.

"Because the warden has forbidden it, that's why. Because it has happened in the past that 'foes of the death penalty' agitators have managed to get included in the tour, and raised a ruckus in the cell block." The Lieutenant shook his head, in disgust.

"Thing is, like I'd said before—by the time a man has been on Death Row for a while, he's settled-in. He's lost that evil edge, you might say. Just gotten older. Sicker. One of our 'condemned men,' he'd had a colon obstruction, what it turned out to be, poor bastid had lost like one hundred pounds couldn't eat, and his gut all twisted and cancerous—he's still alive, but ain't nothing like the man he'd been back in 1987 when he committed the deeds that brought him to Orion. And there's others like that, all mellow in their old age. Whereas the inmates in Cell Block C, most of them are new-recruits and the real threats—they'd tear out your throats if they could reach you, and not give a damn. There's *evil* in that place—half the men there, or almost, could be on Death Row, you saw what they'd done to be sent to Orion."

The Lieutenant was speaking thoughtfully. A brooding look to his brow.

"See, there's 'lenient' judges and juries—ever more, every year. Folks on the outside have no idea how *evil* flourishes in times of 'leniency'—they think, if they do good, 'good' is gonna get done back to them. But it ain't that way, friends. This tour of Orion should teach you that, at least."

The flush-faced man who'd spoken so vehemently earlier in the tour had been visibly shaken by the march around Cell Block C. He was saying, now, incensed, "'Bleeding-heart liberals'—that's the problem. All they can think to cure crime is raising taxes! A man doesn't want to be punished, like on Death Row, he don't have to commit the crime to get himself punished."

There was a vague murmur of agreement among the men.

The Intern saw the Lieutenant's pebbly eyes moving over them, half-consciously counting. For the Lieutenant was responsible for *fifteen*.

They'd passed the Death Row building. Cinder block with small barred windows like half-shut eyes. By itself isolated within the prison the Death Row facility. Though it wasn't likely, you imagined that the condemned were looking out.

From what they'd seen of the cell blocks, what appeared to be windows from the outside were just apertures in the walls, opening onto walkways or corridors. None of the cells had windows. The dining room walls had been windowless, and the work-spaces where the men had made furniture and license plates were windowless. The hot blinding Florida sun, in summer raising temperatures in such places to as high as 120 degrees, yet did not penetrate most of the prison.

The Investigator planned to interview former prisoners, if he could. The Investigator had learned that the corrections officers' union was one of the strongest in the country, and in the state of Florida; drugs and even weapons smuggled into prison came mostly by way of COs, who were protected by their powerful union.

"Folks, you are privileged: this part of the facility, the execution chamber, is off-limits for mostly everybody. Few people come down this way. Only the death-squad teams, the 'condemned' and the witnesses, and our tours. Might be surprised to learn, this area is restricted from most COs."

The Lieutenant spoke proudly. The Intern was staring ahead, at a stone wall, a door set in a stone wall. Not a door like others in the prison they'd seen but an ancient-looking door.

A damp chill wind lifted from the weedy ground that was strewn with rubble like fragments of cinder block. The Intern shuddered.

The Lieutenant waited until everyone had caught up. Standing in a semi-circle around the door sunk in the wall, that looked as if it would lead down into the earth.

In a jocular voice the Lieutenant was telling his visitors about "Old Sparky"—"Which you will not see today, folks, 'cause Old Sparky ain't on our premises but at Raiburn. Folks think that Old Sparky is at Orion, but no—that's a misunderstanding. We got our own 'lectric chair but it ain't famous like Old Sparky and don't get used anymore, the condemned man is offered his choice of lethal injection or 'lectricution nowadays and he always chooses lethal injection, poor bastid thinking it's an easier way to go, than 'lectricution. Now, either way can be complicated. They had to retire Old Sparky he was throwing off sparks and fire half the time not working right, smoke coming out of a man's head and any fat man, he'd be fried and frazzled and the fat melting off him like a roast-pig, that's caused some witnesses to puke, and faint. Our 'lectric chair, last time it was used, a few years ago now, after the first jolt there's sparks and fire erupting from the 'lectrodes on the man's legs—it burst right from the strap and caught on fire. And smoke and sparks under the hood, on the head. We're talking real fire—flames—half a foot high—out of the man's head. 'Human error' it is attributed to. Damn smoke filled the chamber, even the death-squad guys were sick. So they called in two doctors—I guess they were 'docs'— maybe like hospital attendants—an actual doctor holds himself off from executions like he's too good for it. So these two came in, and tried to find a heartbeat. And the condemned man's lawyer, one of these civil-liberties-union lawyers, just a young kid—he's like sick to his stomach too. He's like *begging* the warden to stop. But no execution is ever stopped—you keep going ahead. So the death-squad pulls the switch again, and there's more God-damned sparks and smoke. And the docs check the man again, and he's still got some kinda heartbeat. So finally a third jolt was administered. Fourteen minutes had transpired. The poor bastid in the chair is charred and smoldering like a big roast, nobody could come near him for a long time, they said. The rest of us, even the next-of-kin of the victim, that had wanted to sit close as they could, was out of there fast as the door was opened."

There was silence among the tour-group. Had the Lieutenant meant to be—amusing? Informative? His ghastly monologue had an air of being much-recited, like a Shakespearean soliloquy in a void.

The Intern had been staring at the Lieutenant, repelled. She had not dared to glance at the Investigator who, she supposed, had recorded the Lieutenant's words and had taken pictures of him.

Visitors asked few questions. Not even the red-faced man had seemed to enjoy the Lieutenant's account though he roused himself to say now, in a faltering voice, "A man don't have to commit the crime, to get himself 'condemned.' Some of us believe in free will."

"All of us believe in free will, sir! We are not animals, and we are not machines. We are *made in God's image*." The Lieutenant spoke emphatically.

A subtle look came into the Lieutenant's face. "This one time I was present at a 'lectricution, here at Orion, had to be a fat man weighed three hundred sixty-five pounds, squeezed in that chair. And every damn thing that could go wrong, like with Old Sparky, went wrong. And he ain't even unconscious but howling-like. And the hood over his head kind of crooked. And the death-squad is wondering what to do, the warden, all of us—then we see there's blood coming out of the head, and soaking through the hood, and it's forming the shape of a cross. See?—a sign that God was approving the execution, no matter the damn glitches."

The Intern couldn't resist glancing at the Investigator. Blood in the shape of a cross! A vindication of capital punishment! But the Investigator only just frowned and ignored the Intern.

"Who can open this door? Any volunteer?"

The Lieutenant regarded them as an adult might regard a group of captive children.

The Intern wanted to run away somewhere and hide. The Intern was feeling sick to her stomach. But she saw the Investigator make a signal to her, with a gesture of his hand, imperceptible to the others. So she stepped forward, bravely. "Sir, I will."

Struggling then to open the door. Which seemed to be sunk in the earth, and locked. And the Lieutenant leering at her. And the Lieutenant urging her.

"It is not locked, fella. Just keep tryin'."

A final budge, and the door didn't give an inch. The Lieutenant positioned himself in front of it and with a flurry pulled at the handle, out, and up—(the Intern saw, this was the trick: you had to lift the damned door not yet yank at it)—so that the door opened like a gaping mouth.

Reluctantly, the tour-group shuffled inside. Inside, and down. Three stone steps. Already an odor worse than Cell Block C, worse than the dining hall, wafted to their nostrils.

Helplessly the visitors descended into the execution chamber. The Lieutenant stood beside the doorway, ushering them inside. The Intern was the last to enter. He winked at her as if to indicate that, if he didn't keep a sharp eye on her, the little *fella* would slip away.

The execution chamber held an astonishing surprise: the inner chamber appeared to be a *bathosphere.*

An octagon, painted robin's-egg blue. And the windows Plexiglas.

The Investigator asked what was that contraption? Looked like a diving bell—*bathosphere.*

The Lieutenant laughed. He'd been herding the visitors into the windowless space, trying to get them to fan out, to sit in chairs near the front of the room. They were edgy, fluttery as frightened hens. After the trauma of the cell block some of them were close to collapse, the Lieutenant had to gauge how much more they could take. He told the Investigator, "Yessir. This is a 'bathosphere.' Bought at a carny over at Dayton Beach."

You could see, the diving bell/bathosphere had a carny air to it. It was eight-sided, like a deformed circle; like an eye, the most perfect robin's-egg blue, gouged out of its socket.

Robin's-egg blue: the hue of bright childlike hope.

Not all of the visitors seemed familiar or comfortable with the word. "Bathosphere" was explained to them—"Used to be, a deep-sea diving bell, that the prison authority purchased from a private source. It was preferred that the execution chamber be airtight and soundproof."

One of the visitors asked about methods of execution? Was the bathosphere a gas chamber? The Lieutenant said that the state used the 'lectric chair from 1923 to 1999, then came lethal injection; gas, never.

Before 1923, there was hangings. Lots of hangings.

The vehement man whose face wasn't so flushed any longer but rather mottled and splotched, said, with feeble conviction, "What the hell, know what I say?—'Dying is got to be cruel and unusual punishment.'"

"Sir, you are correct. And some of these murderers, you knew what they did to their poor innocent victims some of 'em children, you'd be the first to say 'cruel and unusual'—Amen!"

The Lieutenant spoke decisively. The Lieutenant went to close the door—his captives shuddered.

"Here," he beckoned them forward, "is where the family-of-the-victim sit. These chairs here." He was indicating a row of strangely diminutive straight-back chairs resembling furniture of the Great Depression photographed by Paul Strand. The chairs were side by side with no space between them, in a curve facing the robin's-egg-blue octagon. The Plexiglas windows in the sphere were not large but vertical so that you could sit in the first row and peer into the death-chamber only inches away. The Intern felt a swirl of nausea, contemplating the possibility of seeing another human being put to death at such intimate quarters, strapped to what might have been an operating table.

"Notice these chairs, which are where officials of the state, the warden, the death-warrant officer, could be the arresting officer and the D.A. if they wish, a senator or a governor, can sit. And back here, individuals of the press which, in the old days, would be contested-over."

One of the visitors asked if media was allowed to broadcast an execution? Tape, videotape?

"Absolutely not! The privacy of the condemned is respected."

"And you would not want anyone to see Old Sparky lighting a man up—roasting him like a pig." One of the men chuckled, with sudden heartiness. "I mean, you would not want the world to see. To give arms to the anti-capital-punishment movement."

The Lieutenant drew his hand over the front of the robin's-egg-blue octagon in a kind of caress. He said:

"Our 'lectric chair has been banished, now. Nobody chooses to die that way, and who can blame 'em? Now it's 'lethal injection' that's all the rage. Sometimes it's expedient that two condemned go together—one following the first by like a half hour. If they were accomplices to each other, they might be executed at the same time. And yes, if you're thinking to ask, there've been man-and-woman condemned executed at Orion in the past on the same watch. Any-body remember 'Bags and Briana' from the late 1950s? No?"

No one remembered. Or acknowledged remembering. Even the Investigator, who'd researched Orion, and was of an age to remember the late 1950s, did not respond.

"Kidnapped a little boy, to ransom him from his rich parents in Boca Raton. But they did terrible things to the child. And they killed him anyway, despite the ransom. So, terrible things were done to them." The Lieutenant paused, wiping at his forehead with a folded tissue. "'Course, each of 'em tried to blame the other. Eight minutes for Bags to die. That's pretty-near a record."

The woman professor, partway recovered from Cell Block C, ventured a question. Had many women died in the Florida execution chambers?

"'Many women'? Why, ma'am, no—not compared to the many who deserved to die, but had good luck." The Lieutenant smirked.

"And are there many on Death Row right now?"

"Many? Last count was four. Death Row for them is at Lowell Correctional."

"What sorts of crimes did they commit?"

"Pretty nasty crimes, ma'am. You can look 'em up, if you're curious."

The Lieutenant spoke sneeringly. For some reason, the Lieutenant *was not charmed* by the female sociology professor from Eustis.

How low the ceiling in the execution chamber! How oppressive the windowless walls, that seemed to be straining inward.

The Intern looked for the Investigator. His snowy-white hair and white cotton dress shirt were bright in this shadowy place and the Intern felt a powerful urge to make her way to the Investigator, to take his hand in both her hands, to appeal to him. *Help please help me. I should not be in this place. Something will happen to me here.*

She'd had a premonition, when the Investigator had first invited her to accompany him. She'd known, this was a mistake.

In her old, lost life *back there* she'd made numerous mistakes.

She had paid for these mistakes. (Had she?) But still, you are never fully acquitted of any mistake that involves another, and so the Intern had not been fully acquitted of her mistakes, and her shame of such mistakes.

The only way to erase such error, and such shame, is to erase the self—to "extinguish" the self.

But the Intern did not want *that*.

The Intern did not want to *die*—for then, the Intern would have no further chance of helping others, of giving assistance to individuals like (for instance) the Investigator who seemed to need her, and whom she had come to care for.

The Intern saw the Investigator on the farther side of the room, moving about restlessly. What was he looking at? What was he recording, in his little book? Had he been taking pictures with his mini-camera? She felt a voluptuous yearning, an utterly irrational yearning, for the time when, back in the Investigator's office, he would click on his computer, and array for them to see the miniature photos he'd been taking at Orion. Now, he was scribbling into his little book. Badly she wanted to take his hand—her own hands were chill as ice.

That could never be. The Investigator would throw off the Intern's silly little paw like a snake. The Investigator would be embarrassed, offended. The Investigator would be mortified. All relations between them professional and otherwise would cease at once.

The Lieutenant was passing out photocopies of—what?

Bright-color photos of "Last Suppers."

"First thing to get clear, folks, the condemned's 'Last Supper' can't cost more than forty dollars. That is mandated by law."

Forty dollars! To some visitors, forty dollars for a felon-dinner was *high*.

"Also they can't have alcohol, not any kind. The Death Team delivers the death warrant within thirty days of the execution so that gives the dead man—excuse me: 'condemned man'—time to consult his family, to make arrangements to come visit him, and time to consult his lawyer, if his appeals ain't all run out. And he gets to choose the means of execution, and his Last Supper."

The tour-group stared at the photocopied pictures of "Last Suppers" the Lieutenant had passed out to them.

These were gaudy, glossy photos of plastic food trays. In one, the tray was filled with fried things—potatoes, onion rings, chicken wings. Another contained two boxes of Frosted Flakes. Another, two dozen hot dogs in plain buns with mustard and relish on the side, and several cans of Coke.

Some of the visitors were laughing nervously. Was this meant to be funny? The Intern was shocked, the Lieutenant seemed to be offering these photos to amuse.

"Oh—who could eat at a time like that . . . I never could."

"Oh, so sad!"

"How *could you*! These poor sad people . . ."

"If it was me, I sure wouldn't have Cheez Doodles and Dr Pepper . . ."

A more ambitious supper was lobster roll—(from McDonald's)—and corn on the cob. Another was beefsteak and steak fries and Mountain Dew.

One of the more curious suppers, a platter of greasy donuts and two tall glasses of milk.

Another, a quart of Baskin-Robbins chocolate-ripple ice cream and a single tall glass of milk.

Another, heaped Mexican food—tacos, burritos, tamales, hot green sauce. And a tall glass of Gatorade.

The Lieutenant said, "They begin to eat but never finish. They seem hungry at first then change their minds." A sly look came into the Lieutenant's face as if he was wondering if he should tell his visitors this story, he'd told many times. "This poor bastid Scroggs, such a dimwit he was he told the guard he'd like to save half his pecan pie for 'afterward.' Twenty-nine years old when his appeals ran out, he'd confessed to killing a dozen girls in Fort Myers. Too stupid to try to lie to the police, he just said *yes*—he'd done what they were saying he'd done. Then, he thought they'd let him go!" The Lieutenant laughed, heartily.

There was a moment's pause. No one laughed. No one *smiled*.

The Lieutenant paid no heed. Like a stand-up comedian whose contempt for his audience transcends his resentment and fear of their power over him, the Lieutenant simply moved on to his next bit.

"Now, folks: how'd you choose to die, if you have a choice?"

Again there was silence. The Lieutenant continued:

"Like, in Florida at one time, you had your choice of hanging or 'lectrocution. Now, you have your choice of lethal injection or 'lectrocution. In some states there's 'firing squad'—Utah, I think. In some states there's still gas chamber, but maybe not hanging. Everywhere it's mostly 'lethal injection' which can be a hard way to go, frankly. What'd you choose, you had a choice?"

Most of the visitors chose lethal injection—reluctantly. The others stood silent.

The Lieutenant surprised the Intern by turning to her and asking in a haughty voice what she'd choose. The way a schoolteacher would turn to a student he guessed wasn't paying attention to him.

The Intern said she would not choose.

"Between 'lectrocution and lethal injection? You wouldn't choose?"

"I would not."

"In some state where there was gas chamber, 'lectrocution, hanging, fire squad, lethal injection—you wouldn't choose? Sure you would."

But the Intern was sure she *would not*. She *would not* participate in her own death.

"You, sir? What would you choose?"

The Lieutenant was addressing the Investigator who was the sole person in the tour-group who seemed to have challenged the Lieutenant's authority.

The Investigator shrugged. He, too, would not choose. "I would force the state to choose. I would not participate in my own death."

The Lieutenant said, exasperated, "But you would! If it was a matter of the easiest death—or what you think is the easiest."

The Investigator persisted. "No. I would not participate in my own death because I would not grant to the state that power over me."

"But then, you would be granting to the state the power! What you say doesn't make any damn sense."

The Lieutenant seemed offended, genuinely annoyed with both the Intern and the Investigator. Two such very different individuals, clearly strangers to each other, yet clearly temperamentally akin. You felt that, if the Lieutenant had his way, he'd have sentenced half the visitors in the tour-group to death just to teach them a lesson.

"I suppose you think, sir, that the death penalty is 'barbaric.' That's what you think?"

"Did I say that? I don't believe that I said anything like that—the word *barbaric* never crossed my lips."

"But you think so, sir! Don't you! You are some kind of—leftist-liberal judge—you are not a Florida judge . . ."

"I am not a *judge*, Lieutenant. Not even a retired judge."

"Well, so—a lawyer, then. A professor. You'd let murderers *go*? Rapists, serial killers—child-killers?"

But the Investigator was too canny to be drawn into a heated discussion with the Lieutenant at such a time and in such a place. The Intern guessed, he was eager to take forbidden pictures of the robin's-egg-blue death-chamber and would speak no more to the Lieutenant.

"Well, now—who will volunteer to step inside? Just for a minute, to demonstrate."

The Lieutenant meant the diving bell. The Lieutenant leered at his captives, who shrank from his gaze.

How hateful this was! A nightmare, and there was no way out except to comply with the Lieutenant.

"We require a volunteer. Who?"

The Intern didn't wait for the Investigator to signal her. She said, "I will, sir."

The others stared at her. The Intern saw gratitude in their faces.

The Lieutenant seemed annoyed. "You! Well, fella—have to give you credit, you're a stubborn little guy. But there's other folks here, could help us out . . ."

"I will do it, sir. To spare anyone else."

In a daze the Intern approached the robin's-egg-blue octagon. Her head was ringed with headache-pain and her stomach churned with nausea. At least she was so small, she had no difficulty stepping through the doorway and into the interior; she had no difficulty straightening to her full height. (The ceiling inside the bathosphere, that seemed oppressively low, was in fact, at its apex, at least seven feet high: an adult man could stand comfortably in such quarters, for a while at least.)

The Lieutenant was glaring at the Intern. Yet, the Lieutenant was pleased with the Intern: the way the Intern had seemed to be obeying *him*.

The Lieutenant leaned inside the doorway, gruffly instructing the Intern to climb up onto the table and lie down on her back.

The Intern complied. The ugly bathosphere ceiling was close above her head and so she shut her eyes. The Lieutenant's voice continued, with restrained excitement.

"There'd be the Death Team, if this was an execution. They'd be strappin' the little fella in, he wouldn't have gone inside by himself."

The Lieutenant spoke with regret, this wasn't an actual execution, or even any kind of demonstration. But it was all the tour could offer.

"We never had any 'Old Sparky' like I said—our 'lectric chair is in storage. Lethal injection, there's nothing much to *see*."

Yet the Lieutenant continued in a zestful manner to describe botched lethal injections he had witnessed over the years: "Like, your veins are all wizened from shooting heroin, they've got to stick you all over—arms, legs, inside-thighs—feet, haunches—underneath the jaw—foot. Poor bastids like a pincushion some of 'em, squeaking *No no no more! God help me I am sorry.*" The Lieutenant paused, for effect. "And sometimes the chemicals are botched, the solutions ain't right, or what they call in the right 'proportion'—so the stuff that comes into the condemned man's veins is fiery-hot—like acid—and he's screaming, inside the head-hood. Even with a rag or a sponge in his mouth, he's screaming and you can hear him. No 'merciful death'—it ain't what they deserve. So don't waste pity."

The Lieutenant's listeners shuddered. The Lieutenant was an impresario at the mast of a careening amusement-park ride—roller coaster, demon-twister. You could not escape the hellish ride until the Lieutenant released you.

Visitors asked questions—the Intern couldn't hear. A roaring had begun in her ears, a pounding of blood like a distant surf.

The Intern was fingering the leather straps. Fortunately the Lieutenant hadn't asked her to place the straps over her arms and legs.

She understood that an IV line, dripping toxins into a vein, would be inserted in one of her arms, or in the back of her hand.

At a little distance the Lieutenant was speaking. In his bragging bullying way, that had an undercurrent of excitement.

The Intern began to remember—something.

The Intern began to remember—how she'd lain curled upon herself. Not on a table and not on her back but on the ground crawling, and her face bloodied, her nose and mouth bloodied, dirt in her eyes.

Don't want you get away you disgust me.

"Thing is, a death warrant is served these days it don't mean what you'd think. There's all these appeals—'writs'—'briefs'—'arguments'— drags on for years. Any man—or woman!—gets to Death Row, let me tell you 'innocence' ain't no likely factor in what got him here. Might be he's 'innocent' of the crime for which he will be executed but no way he is *innocent*—or her. That is a statistical fact."

There was a pause. The Intern shut her eyes harder and strained to see and to hear.

She was very frightened now. A sensation as of death was upon her, a numbness in her feet, her legs—rising . . . A numbness in her fingers, and in her face. Her tongue he'd ripped out.

So she could not speak. Would not ever speak.

. . . can't talk? Maybe she's deaf too.

Face looks broke. Lemme wash that blood away.

Whoever done it he'll come back. They always do.

"Our last execution was in February. Like, a month ago. There's been an execution—this 'Richard Karpe' in the news—that's been postponed two, three times. Jesus! Nobody thinks this is any damn good for all involved like the victim's kin nor even the condemned man himself jerked around like a damn puppet. A condemned man comes to terms with his life, he's ready to die. You can ask them on Death Row, most of 'em will tell you. Most of them is solid Christian-religion, by that time. They will tell you. 'Let's get on with it,' they will say. This last one, Pop Krunk. Have to tell you, I kind of got to like Pop Krunk—and Pop Krunk liked *me*. He was seventy-six when he died. He'd been in Orion since 1987. Before that, Raiford. He'd done time for robbery, aggravated assault. He was an old-timey kind of character with long hair, long beard—like in the Everglades, you'd find. Sent to Death Row after he beat to death somebody resisted him in a robbery, also he had warrants on other probable homicides in Tampa, that caught up with him. Pop would say he was 'conned' into it—confessing—then tried to 'recant' like they do—but the judge shut that out, fast. Right-away there's some team of young lawyers trying to get Pop's sentence overturned, and a new trial—Christ knows why! You can always have a new trial, there's never gonna be any trial that's 'beyond a shadow of a doubt' whether somebody's lawyer falls asleep in court or shows up sick or drunk—that's how it is. So last month they're arguing for another reprieve, trying to argue the governor into commuting his sentence, Pop Krunk himself never bellyached he was afraid to die or treated unjustly, least not to *me*. His Last Supper was a good one: Big Mac with French fries, fried onion rings, chocolate milk shake. Asked if I would keep him company and I said *yes* but the sad thing was, old Pop started eating pretty hungry then kind of slowed down, and never got to the halfway point even, laying down the Big Mac saying shit, he ain't hungry no more.

"Would you like the milk shake? Pop says. So I says OK, thanks!

"Did I say Pop Krunk was in a wheelchair? Started out just on crutches, his legs and hips was shot with arthritis, he wasn't malingering but in pain you could see, his face all creased with pain, so he had this wheelchair from the infirmary, he spent most of his time in, in his cell. The death warrant's delivered, once it is then the clock starts ticking, you know—only a call from the governor can defer it. But this time, there wasn't gonna be any call. This time, Pop's luck run out. He knew this. Like he could foresee certain weather—a hurricane, for instance. His bones just ached all the more, in that kind of weather. So he could foresee, no call from the damn governor. When the chaplain and us came to get him, Pop didn't look nothing much like himself. Which is sobering to see. You come to expect a certain—you expect certain behavior from people you know. Drops of sweat were running down Pop Krunk's face. He'd shut his eyes tight, his mouth, trying not to breathe. Trying to choke himself, suffocate himself, cut off his breathing. But he could not, the instinct to breathe is too powerful to resist. So next, poor bastid tries to hang back. In his wheelchair. He was panting, and sweating, and praying. We wheeled him into the chamber here, down a little ramp by the steps. But the wheelchair doesn't fit into the diving bell, so he had to be hoisted to his feet and walked. I was one of the guards assigned to walk with him. Poor Pop Krunk shaking like I never seen him before. I'm saying to him—'Pop! You can do it. Hell man, you're gonna be OK.' There's the victims' next-of-kin in the front chairs, some of 'em oldern Pop himself. Jesus they all been waiting a damn long time for this. And the warden is here, and prison commissioner, and some journalists. Pop was balking, scared. The wheelchair had to be surrendered. He caught on the edge of the doorway into the diving bell, his fingers had to be pried off. The chaplain said, 'Don't disappoint us, Pop. Not now. We expect more of you, Pop. There's the relatives of the victims right here, looking for justice. You give 'em what they deserve, Pop.' And Pop saw, this was only just. Right-away sat up straight as he could in that chair, they were strapping him in. All the witnesses were surprised. Pop Krunk said, with a sudden smile, 'Hey! This is a beautiful day to die.'

"Saying so, was the signal. We lowered and secured the black hood over his head."

He will hurt you again. He will murder you.

You can't go back. Not ever.

. . . will protect you. I swear.

The Intern had ceased listening to the Lieutenant's voice. The Intern was feeling that her heart had been slowed and stopped and was being revived now again and she did not know where the strength would come from, to return her life to her.

Men had died on this table, on which she lay. In the robin's-egg-blue diving bell, men had died hideous deaths. Those others, who'd

preceded her, the old man—Pop Krunk—had died strapped in here.
They'd stabbed needles into his skinny old-man arms and drained
poison into him and he'd slumped and ceased breathing and the witnesses could see nothing further except that the black hood over the
head had slumped, and was no longer the head of a live man.

In desperation the Intern managed to sit up. Heavy air pressed
against her: she was feeling weak. She stumbled to the door of the
diving bell and past the surprise-faced Lieutenant and the other visitors to the door of the execution chamber which the Intern shoved
open, in an impudent outburst of strength.

There were upraised voices behind her. Abruptly now, the tour
would end.

The Intern had stumbled outside, and had fallen. But the Intern
was breathing normally. The Intern had not fainted. The Intern's
knees had been scarred, years ago. The old scars had not been lacerated. For the Intern wore corduroy trousers, to protect her legs. The
Intern lay where she'd fallen on a patch of scrubby ground outside
the execution chamber at the farther end of the bleak cinder block
facade of Death Row. She was summoning strength, to stand. The
Lieutenant called after her in reprimand. The Lieutenant called after
her, annoyed. And the Lieutenant was frightened, for a civilian fallen
on his tour, a civilian casualty, was not a good thing. This was not a
good thing for the Lieutenant, and for the Orion tour. The Lieutenant exited the execution chamber to approach the Intern who was
trying to rise now, on her knees. Was her face bleeding? Was her
nose dripping blood? The Intern wiped at her face in chagrin, shame.
The tour-group visitors were peering at her, some of them. From the
doorway of the execution chamber they were peering at her. They
were not clear what had happened. What had happened? In the diving bell, the Intern had obediently lain on the table in compliance
with the Lieutenant's command but then, suddenly, she'd jumped
down from the table, and escaped. You could see that the Lieutenant
was not accustomed to being disobeyed.

The Intern had panicked, and begun to faint. That must have been why she'd stumbled outside. And now the white-haired gentlemanly Investigator pushed past the others, to come to her.

Help her to her feet. She was on her knees shivering with cold.

Belatedly realizing, he'd wanted her to take pictures inside the diving bell! Of course.

Why she'd been outfitted with the Sony watch. Was that why?

Her brain was working fitfully. Her brain had been deprived of oxygen, toxins in her bloodstream and her brain had begun to die.

But that was why he'd given her the watch of course. Why he'd wanted her to accompany him to this terrible place. And she had not thought of it, at all. She had thought of other things but she had not thought of that.

Nor did she think of it now. All that—even *him*—was swept away, in the enormity of the moment.

Saying, "This is a beautiful day to die."

TEN

The Betrayal

Temple Park, Florida, March 2012

S HE COULD NOT bring herself to say.
To utter the words. Could not.

" . . . have to be leaving you. I'm so sorry."

He did not reply. He might have been shocked.

He might have been *incensed*. She could not look at him!

Saying, stammering, "—think that I have to go back to where I—
I've . . ."

She was feeling faint. That ringing in her ears, that is the pressure
of heightened blood.

" . . . I've been gone from. I've been 'missing.'"

THE INVESTIGATOR TURNED from her. Abruptly, the Investigator
walked out of the room.

She heard a door shutting, hard. Another door, slammed. She
pressed her hands against her ears.

This had not ever happened before, between them. The Investigator and his Intern: their relations had always been wholly professional, impersonal.

He had not noticed her watching him. (Had he?)

He had not noticed her smiling at him, behind his back. (Had he?)

The Investigator's pale-blue gaze, moving over her. It had not been a tender gaze, it had not been an affectionate gaze, and yet—seeing the Investigator looking at her, his quizzical smile, his bemused and beguiled smile, she'd felt a stirring of hope, and yearning; she'd felt a stirring of something she had long believed she'd quenched, out of self-disgust and shame.

"McSwain! Come here, I need your advice."

Or, he would call: "McSwain! Here."

It was the Investigator's pretense that he was, like many of his generation, computer-illiterate. He could not navigate a computer as the Intern could. (In fact, this was not true. The Investigator was reasonably skilled at the computer, at least the computer programs he knew. The Intern's method was random, hit-or-miss, a patience that is the consequence of a desperate need not to become hysterical. The Intern exuded *calm* as a principle.)

"McSwain!"—sometimes the call was pleading, a *cri de coeur*. Yet the Investigator was being funny, too.

Asking her to open a jar for him. A tall hefty bottle of his favorite juice—pomegranate. Why?

"Your fingers are stronger than mine, obviously, McSwain. You're young, you can *grip*."

Anything requiring fine-print-reading. Anything requiring the use of a remote control, a "menu"—"Never learned to use a 'menu.' Just do it for me, McSwain."

But now. There was no humor, no playfulness between them now.

For she was trying not to shatter into pieces. Carrying herself with extreme care, caution. In the diving bell that had been painted a bizarre robin's-egg blue she had been made to realize how close she'd come to annihilation, extinction.

Death had been precipitated, in that place. Death had not come haphazardly or by a "natural" sequence of events—death had been bidden, death had been *executed*.

Sick with guilt. Gut-sick, guilt.

This evening at the Investigator's glass-walled house on the Rio Vista Canal. This evening after their exhausting tour of the Orion prison, from which they hadn't returned until late afternoon.

The Investigator had had to drive the SUV most of the way. The Intern had felt so weak, light-headed. The Intern had felt so *emptied out*.

The first time she'd broken like this, in at least a year.

The first time, as the Intern.

Pieces like shattered glass. Slipped from her fingers, broken.

You scream, but it's too late. Once *shattered*—too late.

She tried to tell him at first, it was nothing. It was nothing, and she was fine, and she was—well, she was disgusted, as he was, at the Lieutenant's revelations, and the tour—the tour through that terrible prison!—and she was anxious, and she was . . .

Terrified, she was. Her life like water rushing in a drain, circling a drain, then in an instant gone.

HE'D STOPPED AT a mini-mall at South Bay.

He'd sent her into the liquor store. As the Intern, this was her usual task: store purchases. While the Investigator remained in the vehicle peering through his little notebook, taking notes.

Then, he came inside, too.

Tall white-haired gentlemanly Investigator who did resemble a retired judge, in a TV episode.

And she the young woman who resembled a boy, boy's clothing, boy's hair razor-cut at the nape of her neck, corduroys, flannel shirt, hiking boots. Drifting along the aisles pushing a shopping cart beneath the bright fluorescent lights, uncertain why she was there.

In convex mirrors like mad distorting eyes positioned to glare along each aisle of dark-glittering bottles her figure moved stealthily, hesitantly—might've been (in the sharp gaze of the proprietor who'd been shoplifted, held-up how many times in the past decade) an ashy-faced junkie/hooker looking like a kid of twelve, not to be trusted. In the convex mirrors her distorted face, scarcely recognizable.

Why here, what was her mission here. But where was *here*.

"McSwain."

Blindly she turned. The name came to her—*Zeno.*

She was trying to remain upright. All her strength went into this—the effort of remaining upright. At the execution chamber, she'd had to stumble outside, into the fresh air, or what had struck her with the force of fresh damp air. Yet she'd fallen, to her knees. She'd lost the strength of her young body, she'd wakened to discover herself lying on the ground. Voices were uplifted, she'd violated the protocol of the tour-group by fainting.

Not vomiting. She had not been gut-sick, as she'd feared she would be.

In the wine-beer-liquor store. Somewhere on the North New River Canal headed south, to Fort Lauderdale.

Her lips were cold, numb. Her face was bloodless. The Investigator who was a gentleman in his early seventies was not one to take alarm, easily. His public manner was poise, cool, aloof, in control. His public manner was courteous. Yet now staring at the Intern, frowning.

But you are my young Intern! You are younger and healthier than I and you are to outlive me, I've hired you for that reason, to take care of me. McSwain!

She'd managed to select the whiskey the Investigator had requested: Johnnie Walker Black.

She'd managed to drop into the shopping cart a six-pack of seltzer water which the Investigator favored, and which the Intern often drank at their impromptu meals together.

The Investigator took the shopping cart from her faltering fingers. Pushed the cart to the front of the store, to the cashier now frankly staring at them—this ill-matched couple—had to be, what?—father, grandfather—young guy, or maybe girl. The cashier rang up the charges with quick-darting fingers, long painted-plastic fingernails it was a miracle to observe.

"McSwain. Go back out. I'll take these."

"No. I can help you, sir."

"I said *go on*."

Their accents weren't Florida. Nowhere near.

SO EXHAUSTED! The Investigator glanced over at her, in the passenger's seat.

Not ever had the Intern been so—*helpless*.

Worriedly the Investigator wondered: Maybe we should take you to an ER.

Maybe you need a shot of cortisone. Maybe you've had an allergic reaction to the execution chamber.

Driving south on Route 27, back to Fort Lauderdale. All the signs, gigantic billboards, drawing travelers south, to Fort Lauderdale and the Atlantic Ocean.

Female bodies horizontal on white sands, in tiny bikinis. Female bodies with luminous golden-glowing skin.

Weakly the Intern protested: No.

No ER, no medical examination. The Intern was fine, she insisted.

The Intern had a fear of being examined. The Intern had a fear of being *found out*.

SHE WAS HALF-CONSCIOUS. She was comforting herself, felt an almost voluptuous thrill, the prospect of—seated close beside the Investigator, at his large desktop computer, as the Investigator displayed on the screen the many mini-photos he'd taken surreptitiously at Orion. As they peered at the images, tried to identity the images, and the Investigator would play the tapes he'd recorded, or had tried to record—(for such surreptitious taping, in miniature, was not a flawless operation)—and the Intern would take notes, the Intern would number and name and eventually print out the photos, and file. And there was a comfort in this, the Intern wished badly to think.

We are collaborators. In a project of social justice.

We will work together from now on.

For he knows he can trust *me*.

THAT NIGHT AT 10:40 P.M. It seemed clear, the Intern would stay the night at the Investigator's rented house where there was a room for her, a narrow bed, a bureau of drawers and a private bathroom.

Where she'd stayed in the past, from time to time.

Stammering she had to—in the morning—would have to . . .

She had no choice now but . . .

. . . had to return home.

(*Home!* This had not been a word in her vocabulary, the Investigator had ever heard. No more than *home* had been a word in his vocabulary, the Intern had ever heard.)

(For hadn't she assured him, hadn't she insisted, she had no parents living, no family—or the remnants of a family, from whom she was estranged? No *home*. And no memory of *home*.)

Her employer was astonished. He was stunned. He was not a man—(you could see this)—accustomed to being surprised but rather—(of this, he was proud)—a man who surprised and upset others.

Saying, was she ill?

What was she saying?—*home* . . .

It was so, Sabbath McSwain wasn't looking good. Eyes stark in their sockets with too much seeing.

He was saying, No shame in being sick. Or weak.

We are all weak at times, McSwain.

Tenderly he spoke. Or tried to.

He did not want a personal relationship with his assistant. It was something of a joke, to call her "Intern"—she knew.

He did not want an emotional relationship nor did he want—this was clear, this had not ever been an issue—any sort of sexual relationship.

She knew. She would not have wished to upset him.

He said, "Fuck. I took you to that God-damn place, and it has made you sick."

She hoped he would not blame himself. She'd have preferred, he blame *her*.

He'd opened the bottle of Johnnie Walker. Rarely the Investigator drank and only at such times, as the Intern had observed, when he believed he'd completed a difficult or arduous assignment, or had failed to complete a difficult or arduous assignment; when he wanted to "celebrate"—(inviting the Intern to join him, please). Now splashing whiskey into a glass and drinking and still he could not believe any of this, what the Intern was telling him, and trying to tell him.

"Something happened to you in the 'execution chamber.' In the 'diving bell.' God damn, I shouldn't have sent you inside."

"You didn't, sir. I volunteered."

"Fuck 'sir.' Call me—"

The Investigator paused. For there was no name he could offer to his employee.

"—call me 'asshole.' For making you sick."

"But you didn't. I volunteered."

"Yes, but I signaled you to volunteer. Both times."

Silence fell between them. The Intern feared to shut her eyes, she might lapse into unconsciousness, extinction.

Hearing herself say, faltering: "Just that I—love you. I think I love you. Sir."

The Investigator laughed. A flush rose into his face as if the Intern had slapped him.

"But you are fifty years younger than I am. Christ, you are a *girl*."

"I am not a 'girl.' I don't think that I was ever a 'girl.' I was—I am—some sort of freak. But I have the strength to love you, because you don't want love from me."

The Investigator laughed again. He could not believe any of this.

Another several inches of precious whiskey. He drank and still—could not believe.

A speeding vehicle, headed for disaster, and no one to clutch at the wheel.

Silence between them. But an agitated silence not the companionable silence of the past eight months.

When she'd thought *If this could continue. Not forever—there is no forever.*

Observing the Investigator—(for whom she had no name, in fact: he was supremely *he, him*)—in another part of the large office at the Institute, or at his computer in the home-office, whistling through his teeth, cheery and absorbed in his work, listening to crystalline notes of early-Mozart like raindrops—thinking secretly, subversively *If this could continue it is all that I could want.*

All she'd hoped was to help the Investigator assemble the new *SHAME!* exposé. The Investigator had planned eighteen months of traveling and research. The Intern had been surprised to discover that, despite his best-selling books, the Investigator didn't really seem to know what he was going to write until he began to write it: like groping in the dark, he'd said. Yet, he had faith, after the other groping-starts, that he would assemble the manuscript, and it would repay the effort.

He believed that the strongest passages would be eyewitness accounts of executions. He hoped—(was this unreasonable? The Investigator had contacts in law schools)—to be granted a pass, to actually witness an execution in one of his target states—Florida, Texas, Louisiana, etc. If he was lucky—(but this was terrible to speculate!)—he would witness one of the numerous "botched executions" that occur routinely, and are rarely reported. In this way, in *SHAME!* and in the media he would bear witness to the inhumanity of the death penalty; he would lobby in Congress, maybe. Certainly the strongest passages in the book would be eyewitness accounts of "botched executions"—in the ordinary vernacular speech of Americans like the tour-guide Lieutenant.

He'd become dependent upon the Intern, these past eight months.

Not on *her,* he'd have been quick to explain. But on her as his assistant.

Now, abruptly and unbelievably, unconscionably, their association seemed to be ending.

She was saying—oh but what was she saying?

He was saying—Betrayal.

Furious with her now. In an instant his surprise, his concern, his sympathy, his embarrassment at her faltering words—now fury.

"You'd given me your word. You would help me in this project. I told you—about eighteen months. I've trained you, and I've invested time in you, and now you're saying you need to leave—to go 'home'—which means that you'd lied to me, when I interviewed you. You lied to me and you've betrayed me."

"I—I will try to come back. I don't know when, I . . ."

" 'Come back'! If you leave now, you will not 'come back.' "

"But I—I would hope to see you again, Dr. Hinton . . ."

(Though "Hinton" wasn't his name. What his name *was,* the Intern had not been told.)

Stiffly he said, "There is no need for you to 'see me again,' Mc-Swain."

"But when—if— After—"

"I can't wait for you to return. From wherever you think you're going—'home.' Where is it, upstate New York?"

The Investigator spoke sneeringly, his voice hoarse. The Intern had never seen the Investigator so agitated.

"I will call you. I will try to . . ."

"You gave me your word. You betrayed me. I could never trust you again, McSwain."

The Intern tried to think of a way to reply. The Intern was weak with shame, self-disgust.

The Intern did think, she had betrayed the Investigator.

Betrayal—that was the correct word.

She had *betrayed.* Numerous others, she'd *betrayed.*

"I will interview for another assistant. I will run ads. I'm sure that I can find a replacement. I will stress 'computer skills' this time. But I will not contact Chantelle Rios again."

The Investigator spoke bitterly. It was clear, the Investigator was badly hurt.

The Intern wanted to clutch at him but dared not. The Intern knew that this man fifty years her elder would stare at her in disgust, throw off her fingers as you'd throw off a snake brushing against your arm.

The Intern felt again the sensation of breakage, from within. Her personality was falling apart. She'd cobbled together a self, out of fragments, she'd glued and pasted and tacked and taped, and this self had managed to prevail for quite a long time. But now, after the airlessness of the execution chamber, after the death sentence she understood was her own, she was falling apart.

In fact stumbling out of the Investigator's rented house. She would not be staying the night of course. She would never return. The Investigator was waiting for her to depart, the Investigator would slam the door behind her and lock it.

On the stairs the Intern lost her balance. The Intern would have struck her head against a railing except she managed to block the fall, just barely.

"Fuck. God-damn *fuck*."

In disgust the Investigator hauled her up the stairs. Into a chair.

The Investigator's breath smelled of whiskey.

Fury-fumes. Disgust.

The Investigator held the Intern in the chair, so that she didn't slump, sink, fall.

The Investigator held the Intern in his arms. The Intern was stupidly weeping.

The Intern was saying she had to leave. She had to return—*home*.

Years she'd been gone. How many years she wasn't sure.

She'd done something wrong, *back there*. She'd made a mistake.

Or rather, something had happened to her, that had been a mistake.

And so, she had to return. She would have to beg forgiveness.

The Investigator couldn't make sense of much of this. The Investigator listened, with a pained expression.

This day, March 11, 2012, had begun a very long time ago. The Investigator was seventy-five years old and as he liked to complain to the Intern, not so young as he'd once been.

The Investigator had no choice, he had to comfort the Intern who grasped his hands, and kissed his hands. In a paroxysm of foolishness the Intern who had never betrayed the slightest emotion for eight months was now crying. Warm tears fell on the Investigator's hands. The Intern was filling her lungs with oxygen like one in danger of suffocating, for so little of the oxygen she inhaled was making its way to her brain. He said, All right—take this.

From the middle finger of his right hand he removed the silver star-ring. The Intern had never dared to ask him what this ring was, what this ring might commemorate. Now, the Investigator tugged it from his finger, and slipped it over hers.

Of course, the star-ring was much too large for the Intern's slender finger.

The Investigator sent her away. For it was time, the Intern must leave.

The Investigator said, You have my number. If you need me to come to you, call me. But otherwise, if you need me, come to me. Until then.

The Intern went away scattering tears on the pavement. The Intern went away uncertain if she'd heard these words of the Investigator or if she'd imagined them or would imagine them that very night in her bed, in her exhausted delirious sleep bearing her back to the Nautauga Preserve, to the lost debased girl stumbling through the Preserve in terror of extinction.

Went away from the Investigator's house on the Rio Vista Canal turning the beautiful silver-star ring on the middle finger of her right hand, loose on the finger, round and round.

ELEVEN

The Rescue

July 2005–October 2009

H E'D SAID *Don't want you get away you disgust me.*

FOR A LONG time then unable to speak.

Mute as if her vocal cords had been cut. As if handfuls of dirt had been shoved into her mouth, and into her throat.

Her face ground into the dirt. *Ugly ugly ugly girl you don't deserve to live.*

DIED WHEN he'd shoved her from him.

Died when he'd shoved her away like trash.

Like a wounded animal crawling through underbrush. The shame of such injury, physical mortification. The wounded animal wants only to hide, to expire. Dying, dissolution must be solitary.

They—the Mayfields—had owned a dog, when the girls had been young children. Beautiful speckled-chestnut setter, Rob Roy his name, he'd been twelve years old when he began to disappear from the household, at first for only a few mysterious hours, then longer, at last overnight, his lustrous brown eyes so suddenly fading, his attention turning from them as if averted, drawn elsewhere.

They'd called and called *Rob Roy! Rob Roy! Good boy Rob Roy come home!* But Rob Roy had not come home and they'd found him at last, the girls shrieking with grief, Zeno and Arlette heartbroken, the valiant Rob Roy had crawled away to die in the dense underbrush beyond the Episcopalian churchyard of what a veterinarian friend had later guessed might have been cancer and ever afterward Zeno had only to say quietly *Like Rob Roy . . .* for intimates of the family to know that he meant *dignity, courage, selflessness, a wish to spare others, a great dog's heart.*

THAT WAS THE MOTIVE, the disgraced girl could not have named.

Such shame, such mortification. Not to be named.

On her lacerated hands and knees crawling. Rocks, sharp-edged pebbles strewn at the narrow shore. In pitch-dark, beneath a befouled sky. And he'd called after her furious, frightened—*Cressida! Where are you! Come back here—God damn come back here! I'm sorry—*

Or maybe he'd called after her, and she had not heard.

Or maybe he'd called after her, and his words had lacked the strength to reach her blown back into his face by fierce hot wind-gusts out of the sulfurous summer sky.

For he, too—*Iraq War vet, wounded, Purple Heart, multiple disabilities, neuropsychological deficits*—had been dazed, stunned; he'd been drinking, despite having taken psychoactive medications though he knew, should have known, had been warned that he should not drink even lightly while taking these medications and particularly, he should not be driving any vehicle; his words had been slurred, the vision in his good eye blotched, he hadn't the strength to act as he'd have acted ordinarily—climbing out of the Jeep and pursuing the mortified girl, the bloody-faced girl, young-girl sister of his fiancée.

Pursuing her, and bringing her back. Daring to lift her, carry her back to the Jeep.

Instead, she'd escaped him. He could not see where she'd gone, after she'd thrown herself from the Jeep.

A faint moon high overhead. Obscured by rain-heavy clouds.

The rushing sound of the Nautauga River. Frothy-white current, rapids in the shallower water.

Farther out, the river was about fifteen feet deep. The drop-off was sudden, treacherous.

NO SWIMMING signs grown weatherworn with the years were posted at intervals.

She'd intended to crawl into the river and the river would bear her body away, and no one would know how she'd been rejected, cast-away.

Stop this! Get away from me! Don't mean this—you don't want . . .

Pushing her from him blindly as a shocked boy might—a fastidious boy—brother, cousin—whom she'd dared to touch in a way *wrong, distasteful* to him.

Instinctively he'd reacted. This was *wrong.*

Though he'd been drinking for several hours, and was no prude.

Brett Kincaid: a guy you didn't mess with.

Sure he'd been a nice guy—before. But now, after his fiancée dumped him, her family treated him like shit 'cause he's shot-up and not pretty to look at—now, Kincaid isn't a guy you messed with.

Still, Brett had driven the young-sister home, that was the intention. That, witnesses would report.

Not that they'd gotten *home*—that hadn't happened.

Still, he'd meant to. Brett wasn't so drunk he didn't know what he was doing or who this girl was, the younger Mayfield sister wasn't the kind of girl he'd choose to become involved with sexually, for sure not the kind he could take for granted knew what sex meant. There were women, and there were *girls*—now he wasn't a kid any longer he wasn't so interested in *girls* any longer. After Iraq especially. *Girls* he turned from quickly, fighting a sensation of sick-dread.

And maybe—(these were ugly rumors, suggested with smirks and sneers by Brett's old high school friends)—Corporal Kincaid was impotent since the war. Maybe where the poor bastard's penis had been there was a gnarled stub of flesh, barely adequate to hold a catheter.

They'd misunderstood each other. Possibly that was it.

She—the girl—the younger Mayfield sister—had been drinking, too. A single beer, an immediate sensation of recklessness, audacity, laughter—*Brett. Look at me for once. Know what we are?—soul mates. Now you're disfigured like me.*

He'd been shocked by this remark. He'd been deeply wounded, insulted. But seeing the girl was alone, and had to be his responsibility since he was the one who knew her family, he'd tried to ignore the insult. Thinking *She is just a kid. What the fuck does she know!*

It was clear, Cressida Mayfield wasn't accustomed to drinking. And the din of the Roebuck Inn—loud voices, laughter, music—was jarring to her.

In the parking lot, a deafening noise of motorcycles. Adirondacks Hells Angels.

A solitary girl at the Roebuck, Saturday night—a terrible blunder.

Stupid, heedless. And how to turn back, she had no idea.

And then, why not *take a chance.*

She was in love with her sister's fiancé. She should not have been ashamed, to be in love with him.

And the more she thought of it, of the fact of her love for Brett Kincaid, the more confident she was, despite her rapidly beating heart that signaled alarm, that it was *the right, the moral thing to do*—to tell Brett.

Her sister had given him up—(hadn't she?)—so there was no question that Cressida was hoping to appropriate Juliet's fiancé. Was it so terrible, so unnatural, nineteen-year-old Cressida who had not yet had a lover, had not yet so much as kissed another person with passion, nor been kissed with passion, should feel so powerful a yearning for Brett Kincaid; that she should want him to look at her in the way he looked at Juliet; that she should want to touch him, to caress him, the serrated scars on his neck and the underside of his jaw, scar-welts, sinewy-snake-welts she'd had a glimpse of, on his back. That he limped, that the vision in one of his eyes had been destroyed, that he winced with pain like currents of electricity darting through his body yet managed to laugh—to try to laugh; that he would not complain, or denigrate the U.S. military as some had urged him; that he was the individual he'd once been, now trapped within the disfigured body of the *wounded vet,* and you could see in his eyes the shock, misery, and resignation of his condition—all these factors made Cressida love Brett Kincaid the more.

Months now and yet what seemed to her much of her life in recent years adrift in a dream. *Now it is my turn. Why should it not be my turn?*

She was convinced, she loved Brett Kincaid more than her sister had loved him, or was capable of loving him.

Convinced *He must know this!*

That evening at Marcy Meyer's house. That evening she'd come close to fainting seeing herself at the table with the others—with the *females*—Marcy who was her high school friend, Marcy's mother, and Marcy's grandmother—the food they'd eaten, the kitchen-smells, the familiar wallpaper, scented pink toilet paper in the guest bathroom adjacent to the dining room and the adults' well-intentioned blundering questions *And how is St. Lawrence University, Cressida? Did you enjoy your professors?*

This life she found herself living—a *half-life.* At Canton, in early-morning solitary hikes along the St. Lawrence River she'd been happy, at unpredictable times—only when she'd forgotten her particular life; the (arbitrary, accidental) circumstances that boxed her in, like a trapped animal.

She'd been in love with Brett Kincaid, even then. Before returning at the end of the spring term.

Before seeing him again, so altered.

Himself and yet—*altered.*

So very difficult to comprehend—(she could imagine herself making this argument, in a public forum)—*how if you feel very strongly, if you believe very strongly, with no doubt, that what you feel and believe is not true.*

In "History of Science" at St. Lawrence their professor had lectured on *hyper-selectionism.* This was an evolutionary theory at odds with Darwin's theory of evolution through the randomness of natural selection.

Darwin's rival Alfred Russel Wallace had not finally believed in *natural selection*—this was too radical a belief, for the era. Wallace had believed that the brain of *Homo sapiens* is "overdesigned" and can't be the consequence of random accidents—*A superior intelligence must have guided the development of man in a definite direction.*

In recent years, *hyper-selectionism* had been resurrected in conservative-American religious quarters as *intelligent design.*

Cressida knew, it was Darwin whom every intellectual and every scientist revered, and not Wallace. Cressida knew, it was very likely the randomness of life, and not the "design" of life, that triumphed.

Yet, her feeling for Brett Kincaid was so powerful, and so *particular*—it felt to her as if "overdesigned."

Her secret, she had not told anyone. Of course, Cressida Mayfield wasn't one to confide in anyone.

With Marcy Meyer she'd fabricated a shrewd-canny-cool Cressida-self who hadn't given a damn for boys, and now didn't give a damn for young men; a sarcastic girl who joked—(cruelly, unconscionably)—about those few boys who'd seemed to "like" her in high school. (Nothing so provoking of hoots of laughter as a stammered invitation Cressida had received from a boy in her advanced math class—a "fat slow slug" of a boy—to attend a school dance; or, invitations from girls perceived as even less popular than Cressida and Marcy, to have dinner at their houses, attend birthday parties, sleepovers.) Never would Cressida have confessed to Marcy how she felt about Brett Kincaid. Never hide her face in her hands, and weep—*Oh God! I want to die, I love him so much.*

(Cressida liked it that, however inarticulately, shyly, and meekly—Marcy Meyer adored *her.* She did not scorn Marcy Meyer outwardly but could not take Marcy altogether seriously, as a consequence. Dismissing her closest friend to her parents—*Oh just Marcy! If nothing better comes up and I guess nothing better will, I'll be seeing Marcy tonight.*)

Thrilled then, in her mean little charcoal-lump of a heart, to be deceiving Marcy. Who'd expected Cressida to stay after dinner, after cleanup in the kitchen—(with which Cressida helped, of course how could Cressida fail to help however bored by this time with the Meyer household)—and watch a DVD. But Cressida had said she couldn't stay late, she was planning to get up early to run/hike and to work on a new set of ink drawings, seeing the disappointment in her friend's face—"I'll give you a call. Maybe we can do something next week."

Thrilled to think she was going out to Wolf's Head Lake. She, Cressida Mayfield!

Marcy had tried to insist, of course she wanted to drive Cressida home—"It's Saturday night. Lots of people are out. You know— bikers, from out of town. I'll drive you."

"No thanks! I want to walk."

"But, Cressie . . ."

Fuck Cressie! I am not your fucking Cressie don't think it.

Suddenly irritable she'd repeated no thanks, she wanted to walk.

As if to say *Want to be alone. Have had enough of your bland banal boring conversation for one night.*

Zeno had teased Cressida about making her (girl) friends cry. Since middle school Zeno had teased Cressida without seeming to realize, or to acknowledge, what it might mean if what he were teasing his daughter about were true.

Any girl has a crush on me, I will crush beneath my boots!

Don't whine and blink at me, I'm not going to feel sorry for you.

And don't call me "Cressie"—not so anyone can hear.

She'd said good night to Marcy and the others. Thanked them for a "wonderful dinner—as usual" and strode out the front walk as if propelled.

At last, free!

At last, she could breathe!

All evening she'd been thinking of Corporal Brett Kincaid. All day, all the previous night. Rehearsing how she would speak to him, and in what sort of voice.

Rehearsing what she'd say, hitching a ride out to Wolf's Head Lake.

For it wasn't so very unusual, if you didn't have a car, or a ride.

At least, this was what Cressida had gathered. Easy to get a ride out, and a ride back, on a weekend night in summer.

Aged nineteen. Cressida Mayfield had not ever been at Wolf's Head Lake at night.

Long she'd resented girls who'd been taken there, to the lakes, boating on the lakes and drinking parties, dancing at the lakeside taverns, Fourth of July fireworks. Miles away, back in Carthage, they'd seen how the sky at Wolf's Head Lake had smoldered and brightened on the night of July Fourth and the sounds of detonations were like whiplashes in the flesh.

But though she'd resented these girls to whom boys and men were attracted, she would not have wished to be one of them. Cressida Mayfield was too vain and too proud of the Mayfield name to wish to trade places with anyone.

The smart one. And the one she'd come to resent most was *the pretty one.*

Still, Cressida wouldn't have wished to trade places with Juliet. What she wanted was that she might remain herself, yet be admired, loved, adored as her sister was.

In the Roebuck, she sighted him. In actual life the injured corporal was not what you anticipated but another person with a raw-looking face, truculent and intimidating.

All that she'd rehearsed—*Brett! Hello! Can I join you*—melted from her.

She was frightened. She was confused. The noisy tavern had no charm. Rude-jostling men, a smell of men's bodies—she'd made a mistake to come here.

Yet, there was Brett Kincaid. Blindly she made her way to him through the crowd that barely yielded to her, indifferent to her, or inhospitable.

Not a good-looking girl. Who asked you to come here. Who gives a fuck about you.

Seeing, not wanting to see, the look of surprise, chagrin and disapproval in the corporal's face.

Even this face that was scarred, and stitched. Even this face with but one good eye in a ruin of a socket.

And his friends were there. His hateful friends.

Somehow it happened, she was sitting with Brett. Maybe he'd taken pity on her, or felt responsible for her—tugging at her wrist, embarrassed, saying sit here, Cressida. OK, Cressida.

Want a beer, Cressida?

Her head was ringing. It was very difficult to hear, in this clamorous place.

To speak, you had to shout. Had to lean to your companion, to shout in his ear.

She'd never anticipated this! Such noise, confusion . . .

Juliet who never complained of her fiancé had complained of these high school friends of Brett's, who "took advantage" of him—who "weren't worthy" of him. How Cressida feared them, disliked them—couldn't recall their names, out of repugnance—as they stared at her in genuine surprise. And then, their leering smiles.

Jesus! Juliet's sister—what's-her-name.

Some weird name—Cassie? Cressie?

And soon she'd swallowed several mouthfuls of beer sharp and sour and vile-tasting and yet—how delicious it tasted, how thrilling, in this place with Corporal Brett Kincaid.

And no one knew where she was. No one *at home.*

Yet the Roebuck Inn was so loud, you couldn't hear your own voice. To be heard by another you had to lean close to him, raise your voice, half-shouting, hoarse in his ear.

In her dream of Brett Kincaid, it had not been like this. In her dream Brett Kincaid and Cressida Mayfield had been together in a place of solitude and beauty and they had not needed to say much to each other.

In silence, they'd understood each other.

For it was so—obviously. They were *soul mates.*

Brett would understand. Brett had always known. Juliet had been a distraction to him, a detour. But now.

But now, Cressida heard her voice weakly faltering, plunging: "Brett? Maybe I could help you? The way Juliet did? Drive you to the hospital?—'rehab'? Please? I'm serious. I want to help. Or if you needed—I don't know—some kind of medical help—blood transfusion, kidney—bone marrow transplant"—these bizarre words tumbling from Cressida's mouth though she'd never considered such remarks before—"or if you plan on going to college, somebody was saying maybe Plattsburgh?—I could drive you there, I mean like to visit the campus, or to register—it isn't so far from St. Lawrence where I—I'm—" (In his disfigured face an expression of shock, and of insult beyond shock so she'd wanted to plead *Why don't you help me? Why won't you smile at me? You know me—Cressida.*)

Later, she was making her way—unsteady on her feet, swaying—to the women's room.

She was sick in the women's room. Or maybe—almost sick.

Splattering with water the front of the little striped-white cotton sweater, with tiny pearl buttons, that had once belonged to Juliet.

Then later. Wishing that his friends—*Rod, Stump, Jimmy*—would go away.

Telling Brett she was OK, she was fine. He didn't have to worry about her getting home.

And Brett told her they were leaving now. He was driving her home.

In the parking lot. Amid a deafening din of motorcycles.

Men's voices, shouts and raw ribald laughter.

Telling him she didn't need him, thank you. As he was escorting her to the Jeep Wrangler.

Telling him no. God damn she didn't want his charity.

Don't be ridiculous, he said.

She would go with—someone else. Get a ride back to Carthage with someone else.

No, he said. You will not.

It wasn't a quarrel. Yet possibly the two were observed by wit-nesses in the parking lot of the Roebuck Inn, sometime past mid-night.

Corporal Kincaid in black T-shirt, khakis speaking earnestly with the younger Mayfield sister. Helping her up into the cab of his Jeep. The girl had seemed just slightly resistant. Her knees were weak, she'd seemed to lose balance and so had to clutch at his arm to keep from falling.

Her voice was slurred as she tried to explain to him—exactly what she could not have said.

DON'T WANT YOU *get away you disgust me.*

These words he'd uttered. These terrible words, she would never forget.

She would think *Like napalm. Sticking to flesh.*

In the Preserve. Somehow this had happened.

Along the unpaved road north of the river. High overhead a faint, fading moon.

Somehow, they'd come here. It was clear that Brett had driven them here of his own volition.

Things they had to talk about, in private. The broken engage-ment, and Juliet.

And yet she'd said again—she'd pleaded—how *alike they were—soul mates.* And how rare this was in life, and how precious.

He'd seemed to understand. He'd seemed to be listening to her.

Then, he'd recoiled.

No. This is crazy. Get away.

Hadn't meant to hurt her. In surprise and revulsion pushing her from him.

And she struck at him as a child might strike.

Striking at an adult in all confidence that the blow won't be re-turned. But Brett pushed her away angrily, irritably—struck her head against the windshield, bloodying her nose.

So quickly this happened! So quickly, and irrevocably.

Calm-seeming and then in an instant out of control. For he wasn't well—this wasn't the corporal's *right mind*.

Knew better, Christ he had to know better. Mixing alcohol with his meds.

Drinking, and psychoactive drugs, and driving a vehicle—the Jeep Wrangler, Brett Kincaid was no longer licensed to drive.

He knew this. And he knew, the girl had to be protected, driven home—safely home.

Though they'd expelled him from their family yet the Mayfields were his family, still. For he had no other family.

Except, the weird sensations in his brain were making him crazy. Hallucinatory faces darting and dissolving. Had to defend himself—(but where was his rifle?)—since they would kill him otherwise.

Loyalty. Duty. Respect.

Service. Honor. Integrity.

Personal Courage.

She was one of them, a menacing shape. Or—the one he'd hurt badly, smashed and bloodied her face.

Yet—it had not been *him*.

Corporal Kincaid hadn't been one of the guys. Except if they lied, to incriminate him.

Out of spite, and hatred of him.

It was puzzling to him, why this girl—why so furious at him. Spiteful and crazy and her nails clawing his face.

He'd had to protect himself. He'd gripped her skinny shoulders, and shoved her.

But now, she was free of him. She'd squirmed free of him. The little cotton sweater, one of the sleeves ripped and a little pearl button torn off.

She'd fallen onto the ground clumsy and desperate. She was crying, she was screaming at him. *Hate hate hate you I hate you* as a child would scream not knowing what she said.

Did she believe that he would hurt her? Kill her? Or, did she believe that he detested her so much, he wished he could be rid of her forever; and now she'd thrown herself out of the cab of the Jeep and onto the rocky ground and her hands and knees were bleeding.

He was calling to her. He was leaning out the opened door of the Jeep calling to her. Now frightened, repentant. In his confusion thinking that the Jeep had been in motion and that the girl had thrown herself out of the speeding vehicle to injure herself and to spite him who could not love her as she wished to be loved.

Calling to her, Cressida! Come back!

But she was gone. He saw only the underbrush, the glittering river. Trying to follow her. Meant to follow her. His bad leg clumsy as a wooden leg and his head pounding with pain and what strength he had drained from him leaving him helpless.

Wracked with pain, and shame.

Inside his brain a coin-sized hole opened. And then it opened farther like a well fascinating to see for it was the antithesis of *visible*—it was no-color, purely black.

Sucked the corporal inside.

> → ←

She saw: in the river her body rushed downstream. Her clothes were torn from her.

Naked female body fish-pale turning in the frothy current amid sharp-glistening rocks.

Never the one loved. Never the one adored.

Better, then. Better to be carried away in the river like trash, and gone.

AND SO THE SURPRISE of waking, being wakened. Not in the riverbed but in a roadside ditch where she'd stumbled out of the Preserve on the ruins of an old asphalt road.

Mosquitoes whining in her face, through the long night. Bites, swellings on all the surfaces of her body.

Her limbs were knotted together. Her mouth and her nose had been bloodied. Her face looked as if it had been ground into the dirt. The tall woman crouched over her astonished. Who did this to you?

She could not speak. Her eyes were part-shut. She was trembling convulsively. She was very cold. The long-limbed woman touched her, hesitantly.

The swollen mouth, grotesque. The bloodied nose.

Can't talk? Hey.

Maybe take her to—where? ER?

Like hell. Like fuckin hell no fuckin ER.

Looks like they dumped her. Like out of a car . . .

Face looks broke. Lemme wash that blood away.

Should call 911?

Fuckin sheriff like fuckin hell! Deliverin her to the enemy!

Well—if she's hurt bad . . . If she needs like an X-ray—could be her skull is fractured?

Like hell I'm gonna deliver this girl to the hands of the enemy! No fuckin way.

Seems like she can't talk? Maybe she is deaf, too.

A plastic water-bottle held to her mouth. But most of the water ran down her chin, she couldn't swallow.

Try to drink, see? Could be you are *de-hy-drate-ed.*

And so she'd tried. But another time most of the lukewarm water ran down her chin.

In a voice of cold quavering fury saying to her where she lay curled upon herself in the wet grasses, Whoever hurt you like this will hurt you again. I know those fuckers. I know their kind. You can't go back. You can't *press charges—bear witness—*against them. I've seen other girls like you. Fuckin sheriff says get a fuckin *injunction*—nobody gives a fuck what happens to you. He will hurt you again, he will murder you. Don't be afraid, girl—I will protect you.

The long-limbed woman spoke vehemently. The other woman, whom she was never to see, made no reply but deferred to her companion who was leaning over Cressida now, grunting as she wrapped shivering Cressida in her arms.

Smelling of something minty, astringent—toothpaste, chewing gum.

IN THIS WAY, she was rescued.

Borne out of the Nautauga Preserve and out of Carthage and all of Beechum County though it would be a long time before so coherent a thought would fuse itself together in her hurt brain *I have been rescued, by a miracle.*

Like one who has been suffocated, strangled, the oxygen in her brain about to be extinguished except a straw is thrust into her mouth, or into her nostrils, allowing her to breathe; and no more astonishing miracle than that fact—*to breathe.*

And beyond this, all was blurred and uncertain as those mists lifting in the foothills of the Adirondacks at dawn.

Rescued. And never go back.

SHE'D BEEN UNABLE TO SPEAK. For a long time mute.

Her head had been injured. Slammed against something hard and unyielding.

And she was too sick, gut-sick. Too shamed.

For now the effort of even simple speech was beyond her like swimming across a vast dark rushing river.

On the Interstate headed south. In the 1999 Dodge pickup painted what the long-limbed sandy-haired woman called *oh-ber-jene*— "*eggplant*"-*color*—which the woman thought was a beautiful grave spiritual color.

She wasn't able to eat—swallow—solid food. Something had tightened and twisted in her stomach. Tenderly the woman fed her liquid fruit-drinks, through a straw. Chocolate milk, banana-strawberry smoothies.

Vow to Christ I will make you healthy again. I will bring you back to life again. No one will hurt you again, girl.

Haley McSwain. She was thirty-two years old. She'd been a sergeant in the New York State National Guard. Haley was from Mountain Forge, New York—in the northern Adirondacks. She'd been called up for Iraq but had not seen active combat. In that terrible place she'd come to loathe as she'd come to loathe her fellow soldiers—(not "sister"-soldiers: "fellow")—she'd been discharged with a disability. A chronic cold, bronchitis untreated and then a virulent strain of T.B. she'd been misdiagnosed, hadn't been able to see a doctor for weeks. Her superiors had been indifferent to her suffering. She'd been brought up not to complain and not to show weakness but came to learn that was a mistake even among family let alone strangers. Yet, she hadn't been treated so badly by the military as others, who'd died of infections. A friend had died of a raging fever. And it was said to her—you let this happen to yourself, you have only yourself to blame. Haley McSwain. Her sister Sabbath had died aged seventeen, when Haley had been deployed in Iraq. It was the tragedy of Haley's life. Died in a car-crash their drunk stepfather at the wheel and a head-on collision on the state highway at Keene. Photos of Sabbath, her birth certificate and Social Security card Haley kept with her, cherished always, for it was believed by Haley that this was a way of keeping Sabbath alive and not to be forgotten; and it was believed by Haley that one day she would re-encounter her sister in the form of another. She would never lose faith.

These she would give to the badly beaten girl they'd found at the roadside by the Nautauga Preserve.

Early-morning Sunday which is the time for miracles.

It is Sabbath acquiring life again. This is all I ask, that Sabbath will live again somehow.

The girl resembled Sabbath. So Haley was convinced.

Like Sabbath, the girl had large liquidy-brown eyes. Like Sabbath, she was small-boned, and had dark curly hair.

Sabbath had been a beautiful girl, Haley believed. This poor beaten-girl with swollen mouth, nose and bruised eyes was far from beautiful but Haley had no doubt, her soul would shine forth radiant and new once she was borne to a new life far from her tormentors.

HALEY WAS DRIVING to see her friend Drina. Last heard of Drina she was living in Miami.

Quit her job in Mountain Forge where she'd been a driver for Valley Oil fuckin dead-end job she thought it and near as she could figure out she took home less wages than the male drivers.

Drina had been stationed in Iraq too. They'd hooked up there but lost contact when Haley shipped home sick.

Three-four years Haley was in love with Drina and liked to say she was *patient* and *faithful* as they come.

"Like, you see pictures of dogs, they're lying by the graves of their masters? Don't ever *give up loving*? I'm like that, see. I can be patient. I can wait for years, for Drina. We do email, that's our connection. If she don't answer me no big deal, I just keep writing. And Drina will answer. She's with someone else right now, but that won't last. Her feeling for that person will burn out. I know this. I have faith. Her feeling for this person will not *endure* in the way that my feeling for Drina will *endure*."

Haley McSwain was not one to interrogate another. She was not one to puzzle over mysteries.

Enough to know, her beloved Sabbath had been returned to her.

How grateful Cressida was! *Cressida Mayfield* had become hateful to her, repugnant. How much more beautiful, *Sabbath McSwain*.

And it did seem, this encounter was fated. Though she had been born in April, and Sabbath had been born in August, yet both had been born in 1986.

In Haley's long arms. Gathered in a blanket in Haley's arms, deeply asleep as she'd rarely slept in her old life for her hurtful brain was always rattling and chattering and careening like a berserk roller coaster that had flown off its tracks and capsized and crashed and now all that was finished, she wept for joy.

Understood that the beaten-girl who'd become Sabbath had no people who cared for her. Understood that no one would miss her except to worry she might contact the Beechum County sheriff as another beaten-girl might've done, but she had not. For she'd *fled the evil place of her destruction.*

Not once but every evening on the drive south to Miami, Haley had bathed the beaten-girl when she'd rented a motel room for the night. (Otherwise most nights, they camped out in the pickup. If at a campsite, there was water available but not hot water.) Tenderly washed the beaten-girl's face with stinging soap and water and applied Bacitracin and bandages. Sergeant McSwain had been attached to a medical unit in both her Iraq deployments and had much admiration for doctors and nurses if but hostility and detestation for her fellow-soldiers and superiors.

In a man's flannel shirt, bib-overalls. In a Valley Oil cap pulled down low over her short-cut sand-colored hair. In work-boots despite the summer heat for she distrusted any other sort of footwear—"Like if you have to run, suddenly. Run for your fuckin life. You'd naturally take to the woods, and there's rock-hills in the woods, and you can break your fuckin ankle if you don't have the right footwear. So best to be prepared. One fuckin good thing you learn in the military."

Driving south on I-95 in the rattly Dodge pickup. Painted the precious hue of *aubergine* and on each of the doors a hand-painted butterfly with rainbow wings and in the back, beneath a waterproof tarpaulin, suitcases, tote bags, shopping bags and boxes of Haley McSwain's *earthly possessions.*

Drina didn't know she was coming to Miami, exactly. Thought she'd keep the probable date of her arrival a secret.

Haley McSwain listened to country-and-western music on her satellite radio. Told that Sabbath McSwain had been crazy for Johnny Cash—"Hurt," "I Walk the Line," "Ring of Fire"—the new Sabbath McSwain came to cherish these songs too.

Haley and Sabbath singing together in the cab of the Dodge pickup.

Haley sang in a raw-girl voice, Sabbath almost inaudibly. But it was thrilling to sing!

Drinking from a can of beer positioned between her knees as she drives Haley says, "Know what, hon? Humankind creates their own laws and morals. There was a Jesus Christ but he was 'human'—see? If you're a little ahead of the crowd you see how the laws and morals can be shifted. One time, a person would die for a belief—like, for God, or for his country—but now, almost nobody would."

Though Haley McSwain had seemed, to her young companion, to be bitterly contemptuous of the U.S. military, yet Haley seemed now to be arguing that the trouble with the U.S. was that nobody gave a good God-damn for their country and would not sacrifice for it. "Comes back to same old thing—in the U.S., nobody will die for a belief."

Saying of Timothy McVeigh the man went too far, but—"He had the soldier's ideal. He was a patriot in some damn army hadn't yet been formed."

Haley's companion listened to Haley's hoarse-grinding voice. It wasn't just that Haley's hair was sand-colored, and her skin was coarse-textured like fine sand, it was also the case that Haley's voice sounded like sandpaper rubbed against sandpaper.

Sabbath wasn't going to protest. Though it was puzzling to her, to hear her friend Haley defend Timothy McVeigh she knew to be a *domestic terrorist* who'd killed innocent children in a bombing in Oklahoma City.

Haley said excitedly, "Now I know what you're thinkin, hon. But the point is, not that McVeigh killed innocent people and children, he called it 'collateral damage'—that didn't go down so well with folks. But in the U.S. military, it's a principle of war. It's a strategy. McVeigh was a *patriot*. I'd have been a sister or brother or cousin of his, I'd have tried to help him with his mission—I'd have cautioned him to be damn careful not to kill any innocent folks. Because there are those that are God-damn guilty, that are traitors to their own government. It might've been done, with a different federal building or even that particular building, some different time. He did not intend to kill anyone really, I think—it was a warning."

Haley paused. Haley was breathing hard.

"McVeigh was a good soldier, even so. A good soldier dies for his beliefs."

IN JACKSONVILLE, the air turned spit-hot.

Air-conditioning in the motel didn't lower the temperature much. A bad headache settled over Haley's young companion like a vise gripping her head tight.

She was *Sabbath McSwain* by this time. But, in Jacksonville, it was the last time she would recall *Cressida Mayfield*.

Obviously, Haley was correct. Who you'd been did not matter much of a damn. Only who you would be.

This last chance to try to comprehend. Seeing a swath of water-stained newspapers, headlines. Or a glimpse on TV news, faces of strangers, Iraq War footage, Afghanistan war footage and how small it was, where she'd come from and who she'd been, and quickly forgotten.

Like in a rearview mirror. What you see is rapidly shrinking.

There were girls in the TV news—lost girls, runaway girls. Murdered girls.

Photos of mostly white girls with long straight blond hair. But sometimes, dark-skinned girls, women.

Missing. Gone missing. Last seen.

Have you seen.

Please call . . .

Reward!

Grimly Haley said standing flat-footed in front of the TV drinking beer, Poor damn girls didn't escape in time. Nobody to help *them*.

In the pickup, Haley had her weapons of protection: a tire iron kept beneath the driver's seat, a Swiss Army knife kept in a glove compartment, a hammer, a screwdriver.

Saying, Had me a nice little firearm until last week, a thirty-eight-caliber Smith & Wesson revolver. But not a permit for it, and for sure, not for carrying across state lines.

No reason that made sense, a Florida state trooper stopped Haley's pickup just south of Jacksonville the next evening. Pulled up close behind the Dodge with the rainbow-butterflies though other vehicles were speeding past and sounded his God damn little siren like a smirk you could not ignore.

Officer what is wrong? Haley asked swallowing hard for you could see the fright in Haley McSwain's face, she had learned not to trust any uniformed man, not ever.

Routine check, ma'am. Looks like your right rear light might be broken.

This was a surprise, and a suspicion. For Haley was scrupulous in her care of the pickup and had checked it out thoroughly before the long drive south.

Driver's license? Vehicle registration? Hand over ma'am please.

Mean little smirk, *ma'am please.*

Shone his long-handled flashlight into the glove compartment as if something suspicious surely had to be tangled inside there, he'd come along in his state-trooper cruiser just at the right time to expose.

H'lo what's this?—taking out the Swiss Army knife. What're you planning to do with this, ma'am?

Ain't against the law to own a knife, Officer.

What's this?—sneering at a plastic container, remains of a tofu-curry salad from a day or two before.

Officer I hope you are not harassing me because I am a woman, Haley said quietly.

And the officer said not so quietly, Ma'am, both of you step out of your vehicle hands on your heads.

Haley and Sabbath climbed down out of the pickup. Standing in front of the pickup positioned on the shoulder of the highway, their hands on their heads.

What is your relationship to each other, the state trooper asked. Shining his flash rudely into Haley McSwain's face, and into Sabbath McSwain's face.

Haley protested, She's my sister, Officer. Younger sister.

Sabbath McSwain's ID was presented. Not the birth certificate but a Mountain Forge High School laminated-plastic card expired since June 2003 so you could see the dark-curly hair, the dark eyes and a pale skin that might've been Haley's new young companion, in shadowy light.

The Florida state trooper was more suspicious of Haley McSwain's ID he had to check a second time—driver's license, credit cards.

What's all this stuff in the back? You movin to Florida?

No sir.

What's all this stuff, then?

Just my things.

All these boxes?

My things like—clothes, CDs.

The state trooper shone his flash into the rear of the pickup for a few minutes muttering to himself.

OK, girls. Where're you goin so fast?

We wasn't going *fast*, Officer. Not like other drivers on the Interstate, see?—out on the highway, enormous trucks rushing by, trailer-trucks whipping along at seventy miles an hour, minimum.

You was going over the speed limit, I clocked you.

Plus, you were *weaving*. Why I noticed the taillight.

Of all driving charges *weaving* is impossible to prove, and impossible to prove you weren't doing.

Slow and easy Haley drew in her breath so you couldn't tell how she was trembling with rage, indignation.

Haley was wearing a man's T-shirt, sleeves cut off at the shoulders. And Haley's shoulders were hard-muscled. On her long legs, worn and tattered jeans, and on her size-twelve feet, hiking boots.

Officer, why're you detaining us? We did not break any law! Seems like, you are harassing us. I was a sergeant in the New York State National Guard, Officer. I was deployed to Iraq February 2003 to July 2004.

State trooper interrupted it don't matter any God-damn who's been in the National Guard or in the U.S. military, he's asking them a question *right now*.

So Sabbath said quick and eager, Sir, we're going to visit a good friend in Miami. We're looking to get there tomorrow if nothing goes wrong.

Yeh? Who's this "friend"?

Her name is Drina . . .

Girlfriend eh? You goin to visit a *girlfriend?*

And so like this. The officer had more questions to ask of them like dragging a fine-tooth comb through their snarly hair and laughing at them but Haley McSwain had quieted, some.

It was good that Sabbath had spoken up, Haley would say later.

It was what her sister would have done, in her place. Haley was certain.

Finally, the state trooper let them go. Fifteen minutes harassing them at the side of the road and traffic rushing past at seventy miles an hour. Sneering and frowning saying OK girls, lettin you girls off with a warning, see. Get that taillight looked-to and drive at the speed limit, see? And watch that *weaving.*

In the cab of the pickup then as the cruiser pulled away Sabbath glanced sidelong at Haley shocked to see that her companion was hiding her face in her hands and it seemed to Sabbath that her lips were moving and just-audible was a whisper *Oh Christ fuckin Christ have mercy.*

SO NEXT DAY stopping outside Fort Pierce at a 7-Eleven. And Haley is high-strung and edgy and still talking about how Sabbath saved them from a ticket, or worse, the night before. But talking fast and excitable so Sabbath has a premonition that something is wrong, or might soon become wrong. And in the 7-Eleven there's a man smirking at Haley, trying to talk with Haley, following Haley outside to the pickup where Sabbath is waiting. And somehow it happens, when Haley opens the driver's door he's crowded close behind her, and leaning inside so she can't close the door; and he's calling them *girls* like the state trooper called them *girls* the night before; and without a word Haley reaches beneath the driver's seat for the tire iron she keeps there, swings it and strikes the man on his shoulder, not hard enough to break the bone but when he falls screaming she swings again this time striking him on his knee with a resounding *crack!* and he's on the pavement like a puppet whose strings have been cut and Haley has slammed shut the door, turned the key in the ignition and backed the pickup around and out of the 7-Eleven parking lot like a Nascar racer.

Laughing deep in her throat. You see the look in that fucker's face?

Seconds later, they're back on I-75 South. Signs for WEST PALM BEACH, FORT LAUDERDALE, MIAMI.

Eighteen months then Sabbath McSwain lived with Haley McSwain and a shifting company of (mostly women) friends in rented bunga- lows, mobile homes, and apartments in the Miami area. And follow- ing this, several years in Hollywood, Fort Lauderdale, Miami (again), and North Miami Beach. As the women in Haley's life were ever- shifting so too the places in which they lived and the jobs at which they worked—in Miami for instance Haley drove a FedEx delivery van, and Sabbath worked in a succession of fast-food restaurants; in Hollywood, Haley was a security guard at a shopping mall, and Sabbath worked in a pizzeria at the mall; in Fort Lauderdale and North Miami Beach, Haley worked for UPS, driving a van and as a dispatcher, and Sabbath worked at whatever employment she could find—always, Sabbath's employment was temporary, until Haley an- nounced to her they were moving.

Gettin restless, eh? Me, too!

It had turned out to be, as Haley had surmised, that her friend- from-the-army Drina Perrino was involved with another person. But it had not turned out, initially, that Drina was likely to switch her feelings to Haley McSwain, as Haley had believed.

This other person—*Opa Han.*

So many times over a duration of years Sabbath would hear the name *Opa Han* yet just once had she caught a glimpse of this person as she and Haley crouched together in the cab of the Dodge pickup in a drizzling rain outside the bungalow in which Drina and Opa lived in North Miami Beach—a female figure of no striking distinction except her hair was jet-black, straight to her shoulders, and her shoulders were wide, and sloping. *Opa Han, Drina Perrino.*

Only "just friends" but Haley and Drina saw each other frequently and Sabbath was often in their company, as Haley's *kid sister livin with me for a while*. Drina Perrino had been a surprise to Sabbath for Haley had spoken of her obsessively as a *beautiful radiant blessed* individual but in fact Drina was short-tempered and peevish, with plucked eyebrows, a dissatisfied little beet-colored mouth, glittery piercings and studs in her ears, left nostril, and right eyebrow; a round little heavyset woman with thick arms, thick legs, sizable breasts and hips, and a girlish moon-face; "not an ounce of fat" (as Haley marveled) but defiantly firm-fleshed, like a rubber doll. Drina dressed flamboyantly in tight-fitting clothes that outlined her breasts, hips, and belly; her hair was alternately dyed and bleached—chestnut-red, platinum-blond. She rubbed rouge on her cheeks for a bright, febrile look; she made up her "Egyptian eyes" (as Haley described them) with inky-black mascara and green eye shadow; she wore cascades of flashy, cheap jewelry, and high-heeled shoes. Drina was several years older than Haley McSwain but looked younger than Haley whose plain earnest coarse-grained face was coming to be crisscrossed with worry lines ("worry over you-know-who" as Haley joked); though she did not resemble a soldier now, she'd once been a private first-class in the U.S. Army from Hazard, West Virginia. In some earlier life, Drina had been married, and divorced; as Haley McSwain waited patiently for Drina to tire of Opa Han, and turn to her, so it was hinted—(Haley herself joked about this, but Sabbath could not think it a laughing matter)—that Drina's ex-husband, still a resident of Hazard, entertained a hope of Drina returning to him, too.

Drina exuded an air of glamour, set beside Haley's sobriety. She'd trained to work as a beautician in the upscale specialties "cosmetol-ogy" and "electrolysis" but her employment was sporadic in Miami and South Beach. It seemed—(so Haley surmised, but was too proud to inquire)—that Opa Han, a forty-year-old radiologist at Miami-Dade County Hospital, was supporting Drina much of the time.

Somethin I could do just as well, Haley said. Or better.

She'd give me a chance, I would show her.

Sabbath worried: Haley would do something reckless, dangerous to impress Drina Perrino. To get the attention of a person like Drina you couldn't be just *you*.

Like one evening, Haley turned up with a heavy urn filled with red roses, for Drina.

Wouldn't say but Sabbath had the strong suspicion that Haley had appropriated the urn and the roses from a cemetery or riskier yet, a funeral home.

So excited, had to climb into the pickup and drive a half hour through congested traffic to get to Drina's place in North Miami Beach and even then, Drina was slow to come to the door, stared and blinked at Haley looming over her—(Haley was at least eight inches taller than Drina)—as if almost she'd never seen Haley before; took the urn and roses from her with a muttered "Thanks!" and a brush of her beet-colored lips against Haley's cheek but didn't invite Haley inside. (Of course, Opa Han was there. They'd seen Opa Han's shiny little red Volkswagen Beetle at the curb.)

Next week is Drina's birthday, Haley explained. I want to be the first one givin her a present.

Sabbath disliked Drina for how Drina treated Haley. But Sabbath felt a little thrill of excitement at the prospect of seeing Drina, as oth-ers did. Drina was a kind of *ferment*.

For one thing, Sabbath never knew what sort of mood Drina would be in. First time they'd seen each other, and Haley so anxious for them to like each other, Drina had been aloof and sarcastic as if she'd been jealous of Haley's "sister"; but other times, Drina treated Sabbath as if she was in fact Haley's younger sister, and so "family."

What made Drina an edgy person was, Drina was always passing judgment.

Maybe it was a beautician kind of eye—not content with what *is* but how it could be *different, improved.*

Sabbath overheard murmured exchanges—Drina's petulant voice *Why's she always with you? Why's she so clingy? Don't she have anybody except her big sister to hang with?* and Haley protesting *Sabbath is all my family, right now. That has survived.*

Drina wasn't the only woman-friend in Haley's life, though Drina was *the* woman-friend in Haley's life. Other women—Lisha, Luce, Jen-Jen, Zanne, "M"—figured in Haley's emotions less excruciatingly, yet still Haley felt obliged to lend them money, or invite them to stay with her; less frequently, in difficulties with her own landlord, Haley was invited to move in with one of them. (Of course, Sabbath moved with her. Haley was her "protector" as she'd promised.) At first Sabbath made no effort to remember the women's names though the women themselves were quite distinct; by degrees, she came to know them, as they came to know her—*Sabbath McSwain. Haley's younger sister who had some kind of accident—or medical condition—like brain damage not visible to the eye.*

(Sabbath wondered was this true? She knew—she had a suspicion—that in others' eyes she *wasn't quite right.* Long ago she'd been diagnosed as [maybe] "autistic"—or somewhere on the "autism spectrum." Not shyness but resistance to looking at another's face, meeting another's eyes. Not hearing impaired but just *not hearing* which is a way of *not caring.*)

Except when Haley went away for a day or two—or more—a week, ten days—in the thrall of a new person who might/might not be introduced to Sabbath eventually—she and Sabbath were always together. Never would Sabbath forget her gratitude to the woman who'd rescued her, nursed her, brought her back to life.

It was a matter of food. "Nurturing."

Haley was determined to bring Sabbath's weight "more back to normal" and so Haley was in charge of meals, and saw to it that her young companion ate everything placed before her.

Proteins, carbohydrates, fats, calcium. The more intransigent greens, kale and chard.

And at least one bowl of ice cream a day. If Sabbath's stomach reacted queasily to the high-sugar content of ice cream or to a memory of what once *ice cream* might have meant to her as a child Haley said sternly this is *medicine*.

Haley loved ice cream. A dozen flavors were Haley's favorites. So they ate together, before bed.

Separate beds in which they slept, had always slept and would always sleep. Except on nights when Sabbath could not sleep her limbs twisted in nightmares and her brain racing berserk and self-hurting like a vehicle plummeting into a concrete wall when Haley would wrap her in a blanket and hold her in her lanky hard-muscled arms murmuring *Hey it's all right. It's gonna be OK. Whoever it was, they are far away now. Never gonna hurt Sabbath no more now. OK?*

In the months they lived together or shared a common household with others Haley was always bringing home "strays"—cats, dogs, even a pair of part-bald African gray parrots abandoned beside a pile of trash at a curb. Bedraggled and limping, eyes swollen shut, scars, oozing sores, eczema, fits of trembling. Haley McSwain was the one, everyone joked about Haley McSwain the Good Samaritan but Haley took such responsibilities seriously. To Haley there were no actual accidents or coincidences in life and so it meant something that a lost or abandoned creature crossed her path, for this seemed to mean that the creature had been set in motion to cross Haley McSwain's path at a certain predetermined point of time. Jesus Christ was a human man, but a man who stood on his toes to stretch and reach higher. Least we can do.

Haley didn't trust the ordinary scales in her possession and so she took Sabbath every two weeks to the Miami Cancer Center to have her weighed and examined by a friend who was a "tech" at the Center: this friend, a young Filipino woman named Luce, took Sabbath's temperature and blood pressure and administered antibiotics if it looked as if Sabbath had some sort of infection—for Sabbath was susceptible to sore throats and respiratory ailments. Luce hoped to return to nursing school to become a fully-licensed nurse and in the meantime took pleasure in helping her dear friend Haley who was known for her generosity, kindness, and Christian heart.

In the Center cafeteria Luce and Haley fussed over Sabbath, urging her to eat. For often, Sabbath had little appetite. Though smiling, trying to smile to please her friends. Yet distracted, as if what remained of her battered mind were *elsewhere.*

Your sister has had some kind of—trauma? That's it?

We think so. Some bastid she'd got mixed up with, made a mistake with, like young girls will do—he beat the shit out of her. Like, she has amnesia we think.

Is it known did he—rape her? Or—is it not-known?

They think prob'ly he did. Yeh.

But she don't remember.

She don't remember.

Could be a blessing, huh?

That's what we think.

She does seem like a nice girl. Like—some younger version of you.

Not no young version of me. No. Sabbath is Sabbath—her own self.

Haley's laughter was a comfort, when you'd forgotten what laughter could be.

IN THE COMFORT of what *is now,* she'd ceased thinking of *what had been back then.* Or what *was to come.*

Had not given any thought at all—(how strange this would seem to her, in retrospect)—to what would happen to her, to her and Haley McSwain, when Drina *burnt out* on Opa Han and *fell back deep in love* with Haley.

So then abruptly it happened. All that Haley had confidently predicted years before.

One day Haley was telling her in a solemn voice that Drina and Opa Han are *having issues.*

Another day telling her in the same solemn voice that Drina and Opa Han are *splitting.*

It was a time, a complicated time, when Sabbath hadn't really known what was happening in her friend's life. When it might have been evident, to another, more perceptive person, that Haley McSwain was drifting from her, attaching herself more firmly to another.

Forgetting to cajole Sabbath into eating, for instance.

Forgetting to buy their favorite shared ice cream—blueberry ripple.

Staying away overnight, so Sabbath slept, or failed to sleep, alone.

It was a time when Drina was having medical issues. It was not a happy time in Drina's life but it was a time when Haley McSwain was present, and devoted in a way that others were not.

Unknown to Sabbath, Haley had driven Drina to a doctor's office and later to an outpatient clinic for something ugly-sounding—colonoscopy and biopsy. And the consequence of this was that Drina had to have emergency surgery at that very same Cancer Center to which Haley took Sabbath.

And the consequence of this was that Haley was away for several days—and nights; and when she saw Sabbath again, she was wearing the identical T-shirt and khakis and her sand-colored hair was matted, her eyes were bloodshot and her skin grainy and gray but she was smiling and her voice lifted and lilted like a feather in the breeze.

For it seemed, the emergency surgery of which Sabbath had not known until this moment had turned out to be "very successful—they hope." And it seemed, Drina now adored Haley, and was so very grateful to her, she and Haley would be living together from now on, through the ordeal of Drina's post-surgical treatment which would involve both radiation and chemotherapy.

Though she'd heard this news, Sabbath could not comprehend it.

Where would Haley be living? Not with *her?*

Now with regret Haley was saying that Drina needed to be *the only person* in Haley's life. Drina could not bear sharing Haley with even her younger sister Sabbath—"That just isn't Drina's way, see.

She's not a family-type person. She has never learned to *share*. She is in love, or not-in-love; and if she's in-love, she wants that person all to herself every minute."

Haley smiled dazedly. Haley shook her head, she could not believe the happiness of her news.

Bravely then Sabbath said she was happy for her—for Haley. She said she was happy for Drina, too—and hoped that Drina would regain her full health.

(Though thinking meanly *She still might die! Then Haley would come back to me.*)

(And then thinking frightened *If something happens to me! Haley would have no room in her heart for me.*)

At this time in the fall of 2009 Haley and Sabbath were living in Fort Lauderdale where Haley was a security guard at one of the sleazy-swanky resort hotels on the beach and Sabbath was working at a photocopy store and taking "Intro to Economics" as a night-school course at Broward Community College. And they were living in a communal-type household with several other women ranging in age from twenty-one to sixty-one of whom one was a language instructor at Broward Community College and another was an assistant administrator there. Haley and Sabbath had two rooms at the top of the house: one strewn with Haley's clothes and possessions and dominated by a part-collapsed double bed with a brass headboard, and the other, the smaller room, sparely furnished with a cot-sized bed, a child's knotty-pine bureau, books, notebooks and papers in neat stacks and taped to the walls charcoal drawings of girls and women—(predominantly Haley and other residents of the house)—deftly executed in a minimalist style.

Sabbath had overheard Haley saying to other residents in the household that it was a new discovery to her, and she was impressed and proud—her *kid sister* was *some kind of artistic talent*—nobody in the family had ever guessed!

Bravely Sabbath faced the loss of her friend though Haley insisted that she would see Sabbath as often as she could, email her and talk to her on the phone as if "almost nothing" had happened.

Haley promised too that she would send money to Sabbath when she could—maybe not as often as she wished.

Drina was sensitive about that kind of *sharing* too.

Also, Drina would not be working for who knew how long— weeks? Months? And so Drina would have no income, as Drina had no medical/hospital insurance.

She would be paying for Drina's medical expenses, what she could. And what she could not, she would *beg, borrow or steal*.

To this, Sabbath could think of no reply. A shivering sensation had begun deep inside.

So! Haley rubbed her hands together. The dazed elation in her face.

Sabbath managed to say, she was very happy for Haley.

Haley said, Oh shit Sabbath, I'm happy for me too. For now.

Haley wrapped Sabbath in her long, tight-muscled arms. For a long time the women held each other not daring to step away, open their eyes, breathe.

MOVED OUT OF THE HOUSE in which she and Haley had lived— disappeared with no farewell to her housemates except on a folded sheet of paper the terse message *I am leaving now. Thank you & good-bye. Sincerely, Sabbath McSwain* and a half-dozen neatly-smoothed twenty-dollar bills which by her calculation was just slightly above her share of the rent for the remainder of that month.

The women had been Haley's friends, not hers. She could not believe that they would miss her, as they would miss Haley.

Sabbath took with her only what she could carry. What she was obliged to leave behind she erased from her memory as you'd wash down a wall—quick, crude, effective.

She moved then to Temple Park. She knew no one in Temple Park. In an area of Fort Lauderdale near the ocean Haley was living with Drina in a new place they'd rented together.

Emails she received from Haley each day, or nearly.

Hope you are well! We are doing pretty well here.

Maybe come for supper sometime. Or we could meet somewhere.

But such meetings were rare. Sabbath didn't have a car and it was a distance for Haley to drive after one of her long workdays, for soon Haley was supplementing her full-time employment at the resort hotel with part-time work as a security guard at a shopping center.

In a rotting Victorian house near the University of Florida campus Sabbath rented a single room. The majority of the other residents were students—foreign-born graduate students. Like a wraith she passed among them unobserved. That her skin was *white* and her national identity presumably *Caucasian-American* made her less and not more visible in their eyes.

An infinite number of discrete steps in a finite amount of time.

It was Zeno's Paradox, restated: you were confronted with infinity within finitude. Naturally, your brain would shatter to pieces..

Yet, she persevered. Though Haley had abandoned her, yet she persevered. Though others had thrust her from them as unloved, despised, disgusting yet she persevered and even, by chance, became acquainted with new friends, of a kind: by chance, she was living just across the street from a university residence called International House where she could eat inexpensive "ethnic" meals at long communal tables at which it wasn't so very unusual to be sitting alone, with just a book for company, or a sketch-pad. She became acquainted with a circle of women associated with Females Without Borders of whom one, Chantelle Rios, would become one of her closer friends.

"Girl, you always *alone.* Why's that?"

"I guess"—Sabbath laughed, awkwardly—"I don't know."

"Well, I know."

"Yes? You do?"

" 'Cause you got a look in your face like the way some kinda nasty lizard looks—iguana, I'm thinking of. Mean ugly thing sayin *Leave me alone. Don't fuck with me.*"

Sabbath laughed, embarrassed. Yet it was not so surprising to her, that another might so interpret her expression.

Chantelle Rios was a clinical psychology post-doc in her early thirties. She wore her shiny-black hair in braids and her clothing, outside the Psych Department, was bright-hued; at Females Without Borders, and to make Sabbath McSwain smile, though she had an advanced degree from the University of Florida at Gainesville, she affected the sexy-insinuating style of an Hispanic rapper.

Like Haley McSwain, Chantelle Rios was involved with another person—(whom Sabbath was never to meet). But, like Haley, Chantelle seemed to want to take up Sabbath McSwain as a cause.

"You don't have any family, girl? At all? Is that possible?"

Yes. It was possible.

"Everyone you know is—dead? Y'know, li'l dude—that don't hardly seem likely."

Sabbath sat inert, silent. She could not think how to speak: how to defend herself.

For by this time it did seem to her, *back there* had vanished.

Her memory had been so washed-away, as with a crude hosing, all that remained were swaths of "familiar" scenes—a room that had once been *her room,* a view of a residential street seen from a window in this room she could not recall was called *Cumberland Avenue.* If she shut her eyes tight she could see a house—a large, sprawling house with many staircases—(too many staircases not to be a dream, or a drawing by M. C. Escher)—and harried stick-figures on the staircases rushing up and down oblivious of one another: the foot of one sharing a step with the foot of another who is upside-down. (If you turned the house-drawing upside-down, ingeniously it would be revealed as the same drawing; whether this-side-up, or its reversal, the drawing of the house of many staircases is only one drawing.)

No idea what any of this meant. Why the fuck did it haunt *her.*

Why her instinct to hide her face in shame.

"Know what, Sabbath? I'd like to get you in our lab. We're working with volunteers but we can pay you a few dollars an hour. It's an experiment in 'induced amnesia'—pretty damn interesting."

Sabbath shook her head mutely, *no*.

For it was hopeless to speak. To try to explain.

Like stammering in a foreign language in which you know only a few words but not how to connect them.

There are fairy tales in which one sister is the good beautiful sister—one sister is blessed. And another sister is damned.

I am that sister. The damned sister. Yet, I am still alive—a mistake not yet corrected.

TWELVE

The Guilty One

March 2012

H E'D SAID TO HER *You betrayed me.*

Those words ringing in her ears. In her brain. *Betrayed. You have betrayed.*

Like harsh-glaring sunshine on a beach littered with storm debris, the dead and desiccated bodies of creatures once living. This sunshine was blinding to her, terrible.

For she was beginning now to see the devastation of her life—that she herself had precipitated.

For perhaps it had been a mistake, to have fled. To have erased her life *back there.*

She'd allowed herself to believe what her rescuer had wished her to believe—that whoever had hurt her, would hurt her again.

That whoever belonged to her past would not miss her. Did not love her and would not claim her.

Had she been sick? For so long?

Turning the silver star-ring around on her finger, and around.

SHE CALLED. Tried to call.

The old number so long-ago memorized: her own.

But a recording clicked on: *The number you have called has been disconnected.*

PANIC GRIPPED HER: the Mayfields no longer lived in the house on Cumberland Avenue.

One of her parents had died? It would be Zeno.

And then, her mother had moved from the house. And Juliet—of course by now, Juliet would have moved from the house.

Juliet would be—how old? Twenty-nine.

How strange it was to her, that the house on Cumberland Avenue had existed in some way unknown to her, all this time.

Her father Zeno, her mother Arlette. Her sister Juliet.

In ways unknown to her, they'd outlived her.

Six years, eight months.

And *he*—Brett Kincaid.

In those years she'd scarcely given them a thought. She'd become Sabbath McSwain and all of her energy had gone into the effort of maintaining this imposture as a one-legged person with a single crutch must concentrate upon her ability to move, not easily, not gracefully, nor even without pain, but simply to move in a clumsy simulacrum of "walking."

Sabbath McSwain was of little value in the vast world yet of inestimable value to Haley McSwain. It is required that we must be fiercely beloved by one individual in order to exist: for Sabbath, Haley was that individual.

And so, she'd lost the capacity to recall the Mayfield faces. And the face of the corporal.

A part of her brain had seemed to shut down. Much of her memory had become like a paralyzed limb, attached to the body but estranged, useless.

Since having entered the execution chamber at Orion, she was beginning to see differently. She was beginning to wonder if her behavior had been a primitive sort of revenge for their failure to love her.

Her family, and Brett Kincaid.

How otherwise could she have erased them from her memory!

She would have liked to explain to the Investigator. She would have liked to ask his advice: What, now, should she do?

He would know. He would give an immediate answer.

Yet how could she confess to him, or to anyone—in all those years she'd made no attempt to contact her family?

Never called, never tried to call.

She'd never sought information about them, online. She'd never typed into any computer the names *Zeno Mayfield. Arlette Mayfield. Juliet Mayfield. Corporal Brett Kincaid.*

Still less, she'd never typed into any computer the name *Cressida Catherine Mayfield.*

THE INVESTIGATOR had named her: *betrayer.*

She'd wronged him! Never would he forgive her, nor would he trust her again.

Turning the ring on her finger, round and round.

"SABBATH MCSWAIN."

These precious documents she gathered: the birth certificate, the Social Security card, the laminated Mountain Forge High School card long outdated, and the Florida driver's license.

Mailed in an envelope to Haley McSwain at the new address.

Dearest Haley—

I am saying good-bye to you now. I will not see you again.

I will pray for you & Drina—that she will be well, & you will be happy together as you deserve.

I know you would not look for me and it is a good thing if you do not. I am going back to my home—it is time.

I should not have left as I did. This is what I think now.

I may be mistaken. I will return there, to see.

Still I owe my life to you. I am so grateful to you.

Sincerely & with Love—
Your Sister Who Was Sabbath

STRING SHE FOUND to wrap around the inside of the silver star-ring
the Investigator had given her, that it would fit her finger less loosely.

It was her fear, the ring would slip from her finger and be lost.

SHE'D FLED. Like a kicked and terrified dog she'd fled. Like a dog
she'd wished only to hide, and lick her wounds. Her shame that was
a kind of wound. It did not occur to her, it had not once occurred to
her, that others might have been injured as well.

"But they didn't love me. Did they?"

IT WAS RIGHT, that they should be punished. If they had thought her
dead, all these years.

She had not been beautiful in their eyes. She had not been loved.

The smart one. She smiled, a ghastly struck smile—so she had hurt
them, she hoped!

Then, a moment later, the recoil came over her, the revulsion—
Betrayer! You have betrayed those who loved you.

"HELLO? Is this—Juliet?"

"Yes. This is Juliet. Who is this?"

The voice was both friendly and guarded. She would not have recognized the voice perhaps except knowing it was Juliet, she gripped
the little phone tight against her ear and for a moment could not
speak.

"Hello? Who's this?"

"Juliet, this is Cressida."

Silence. You could guess, a shocked silence.

"What do you mean—'Cressida'?"

"It's Cressida. Your sister."

This was mistaken, what she was doing. She was speaking too
bluntly, and yet in a weak guilty voice. Juliet said sharply:

"My sister is not living. This is not—this is not funny . . ."

Abruptly the line went dead.

Not living. Strange that Juliet hadn't said *My sister is dead.*

Cressida called the number again. This time, there was no answer.

It had not been easy for Cressida to acquire her sister's cell phone number. The old way of landlines was passing—there was no national directorial assistance any longer.

She'd acquired the cell phone number from the mother of a girl-friend of Juliet's who lived on Caledonia Street, Carthage. Mrs. Hempel had been happy to look up Juliet Mayfield's number for her, in an address book. She had not recognized Cressida Mayfield's voice.

Cressida had told Mrs. Hempel that she was an old high school friend of Juliet's who had lost touch with her. Mrs. Hempel hadn't questioned the name Cressida provided, which was the name of an actual girl who'd gone to Carthage High at that time.

This matrix of old, lost names. A vast spiderweb of associations long forgotten and now resurrected for a desperate whim.

She'd said, "Thanks for Juliet's number, Mrs. Hempel," and Mrs. Hempel said, "Of course! No problem. But Juliet doesn't live in Carthage any longer, you know." And she'd said, "She doesn't? Where does she live now?" and Mrs. Hempel said, "Well, I think—I think she lives in Albany. Her husband has something to do with—I think it's a state government position," and she'd said, "Oh. Juliet is married. I—I didn't know," and Mrs. Hempel said, lowering her voice as if they might be overheard, "Well, you know—after that terrible thing that happened to her sister . . ." and Cressida listened in silence, gripping the phone, scarcely daring to breathe, "Juliet had some sort of breakdown. Because it had been her fiancé, you know—who'd killed her sister. He'd drowned her in the Nautauga River, people thought—but the body was never recovered. And Juliet moved out of Carthage and never has moved back but Carly sees her sometimes in Albany, and they keep in touch, by email and phone. And I think Juliet is well, now—I think she has a child, or two children—that's what Carly has said."

All this information, volunteered to a stranger. Cressida thanked
Mrs. Hempel and said good-bye.

Killed her sister.

Drowned her in the Nautauga River.

Body never recovered.

IT SHOULD NOT have surprised her that, in Carthage, she was believed to be dead.

Missing for so many years, presumed dead.

And maybe it was better that way? As she'd always thought, with
that part of her mind in which *back there* remained prominent.

Better to have vanished. That she would cause no one any further
grief.

But there was the matter of the corporal, who'd been with her
at the time of her vanishing. And there was the matter of Cressida
Mayfield's family, she realized now must continue to miss her as one
lost to them, and her body never recovered.

ZENO HAD SPOKEN OF an ancient Greek philosopher whose teaching
was *It is better never to have been born.*

How they'd laughed! Rob Roy had barked in delight, frisking
about their legs and with his long swishing setter-tail coming dan-
gerously close to knocking over glasses and bottles.

She'd asked who had said this and Zeno had screwed up his
quizzical-Daddy face and said it was (maybe) Sophocles, and it was
(maybe) Socrates. And it was (certainly) Schopenhauer—centuries
later.

Better never to have been born.

But how then would you know?

They'd thought the philosopher was silly—had to be an *old grouch.*

A typical weekend evening at the Mayfield house on Cumberland
Avenue. When the girls were young, which meant that Zeno had been
active in politics at the time, perhaps even mayor of Carthage. Frequently they'd had visitors, dinner guests and houseguests, friends,

neighbors, Zeno's Democratic party friends, friends of Arlette's—companionably crowded at the long table in the dining room covered with a beautiful Irish linen tablecloth.

Candlestick holders, and bright-colored candles. Flames reflected dancing in the darkened windowpanes.

The consensus was, this cranky old philosopher had obviously never (A) been in love (B) held a baby in his arms (C) inhaled the smell of fresh-mown grass (D) sipped Champagne (E) won an election.

In the gaiety of the moment all had laughed. Zeno's friends had lifted their glasses to him in a toast—one toast of many. So perhaps it had been an evening to celebrate Zeno's election to the office of mayor of Carthage. And Rob Roy had trotted about the room, licking fingers as they stroked his sleek handsome head. And Cressida who'd been a child at the time hadn't laughed with the others for the fear of *never having been born* had pierced her heart, so young.

A FOURTH TIME, and a fifth she called Juliet's number.

Then leaving a message, in a careful voice.

Juliet it is me—Cressida . . .

I am calling from Florida . . .

I will be coming home—back home—if people would want me . . .

I am well. I am not ill or—hurt in any way. I have not been incarcerated or hospitalized . . .

I have a job here in Temple Park. Or, I had a job . . .

I am living alone. I am alone but I am—I am not . . .

I am not *a sick person.*

Her voice broke. She began to sob. She had no control over the tears that spilled from her eyes hot, stinging and blinding.

I did not think that any of you would miss me—much.

I did not think that any of you loved me much . . .

I was very frightened, I think. I am frightened now.

I wonder if you can forgive me . . .

She was sobbing now. She could not catch her breath, now.

The cell phone that had been given to her by the Investigator slipped from her fingers, fell to the pavement and shattered into a dozen pieces of plastic.

THE TRIP NORTH would not be an easy one, by bus.

The trip north she did not wish to be easy, or quick—it would require all the days she would spend on the bus, to prepare herself for Carthage.

(She might have flown, or taken a train. Which would have required her traveling as *Sabbath McSwain.*)

(Her own identification, as Cressida Mayfield, had been lost long ago.)

Air-conditioning in late March when the bus disembarked from Fort Lauderdale. In a seat near the rear of the bus she huddled hoping to remain alone, avoiding the eyes of fellow passengers who shuffled past. Her few belongings were in the rack overhead, books, notebooks and papers on the seat beside her.

It was March 16: five days since the visit to Orion.

Five days since, in the execution chamber, she'd known that she must return to Carthage.

She had not tried to acquire her parents' phone numbers. She might have called her mother's sister Katie Hewett, assuming that Katie was still living in Carthage, and had a landline; but she could not force herself to call her aunt, who would recognize her voice immediately.

The prospect of seeing her family again filled her with an almost unbearable apprehension—dread, shame, yet also anticipation, hope.

Forgive me. I thought you didn't . . .

. . . was sure you didn't . . .

. . . love me.

She forgot, Zeno might have died. This awful thought came to her frequently but seemed then to fade almost at once.

She did not think that Arlette would have died.

(Oh but what if Arlette had died! In a panic she recalled how her mother had been plagued with false-positive mammograms, cysts in her breasts that turned out to be "benign." And once, Arlette had had a "benign" tumor, not small, removed from her large intestine. And Cressida had practically shut her bedroom door in Juliet's frightened face, when Juliet had wanted to talk about Mommy, and Cressida had not wanted to talk about Mommy. *Go away leave me alone! I don't want to talk about it OK!)*

So Juliet was married! And had a child, or two children.

The pretty one had prevailed. She, too, had left Carthage—the debris-littered landscape.

Had some sort of breakdown. Her fiancé—killed her sister.

Drowned in the Nautauga River but the body never recovered.

It was a (plain) sister's revenge against her (beautiful) sister. Yet, Cressida had not ever thought of it in this way.

Like one who has been circling a devastated site seeing now the gaping wounds, ravaged and gouged earth, broken trees and exposed roots from another perspective she was beginning to realize: a catastrophe is not one individual—a single "victim."

She had not given thought to the corporal, much. That he had shoved her from him, with such disgust for her—it had been a kind of murder.

A murder, and over.

Who she'd been, in his eyes—finished, gone.

She had not thought that he—the corporal: Brett Kincaid—might have had to account for her, after that episode.

That others might have believed he might have murdered her, too.

And if the corporal had murdered her, the younger sister of his (ex)-fiancé, he must have been punished for this murder?

She'd had to be very sick, mentally ill, these years as *Sabbath Mc-Swain*, not to have realized this.

Not to have realized, and not to have cared.

From Drina had come a ghastly yet in its way comical tale told to her by her then-lover Opa Han of a sixty-year-old woman who'd come to the Miami-Dade County Hospital radiology department for

X-rays with an enormously distended belly, so large the poor woman had to walk with a cane, for at least a year the woman had suffered this disability with the vague explanation that she'd thought she "might be pregnant"—and so, "it would come out by itself"—finally convinced by relatives to see a doctor who'd diagnosed a fibroid tumor that must be removed as soon as possible.

They'd laughed at this story, shaking their heads. But there was nothing funny about it. Rather, a horror story.

How we don't "know" what is self-evident to others.

Don't "see" what is before our eyes.

Or if the eyes "see," the brain doesn't interpret.

If she'd thought of Brett Kincaid it was to acknowledge all power to him—the power of rejection, the power of superior physical strength, the (male) power of (female) annihilation. She could not have thought of Brett Kincaid as in any way by her *hurt*.

"Is he alive? Is he—in prison?"

Her battered laptop wasn't functioning any longer. She had no access to the Internet. Though on this unexpectedly comfortable, modern, aggressively air-conditioned bus there were electrical outlets at each seat and so she might have dared to type into her computer the name *Brett Kincaid* to see what it might call up.

YOU KNOW *he must have been punished.*

His life wrecked—after that night.

Know but don't know. Did not wish to know.

"Dead to me—all of them."

Waking from a headache-ridden sleep on the bus headed north, crossing the state line into Georgia.

So cold from the relentless air-conditioning, she'd wrapped herself in all of the clothing she'd brought with her, huddled low in the seat, hiding her eyes, shivering, alone.

➵ ➴

To know the Good is to wish to do Good.

To be in ignorance of the Good is to be less than fully human.

Ninth grade, she'd been reading Plato. Her father's hefty water-stained college text *Collected Dialogues of Plato Including The Republic, Laws, Symposium.*

Riveting to her as a girl of fourteen to discover her father's earnest schoolboy underlinings and annotations in this book, as in other college texts identified as the property of *Mayfield, Z.* on their inside covers.

Beside a passage in the *Meno* was written the query, in red ink: *Socrates serious?* The *Meno* was a dialogue between Socrates and a young man named Meno about virtue, and whether one knowingly can desire evil; it employs a slave boy's seeming knowledge of elementary geometry though the boy had never been educated, to make the point that the "spontaneous recovery" of knowledge is recollection.

The lesson of the *Meno* is that we already know what the Good is. All inquiry and all learning is but recollection.

At mealtimes, when Zeno was home, and in his affable-argumentative mood and not distracted by thoughts of the day's political/professional strife, Cressida liked nothing more than to engage him in animated conversation of a kind that, not so much deliberately as incidentally, though perhaps with an undercurrent of the deliberate, excluded Arlette and Juliet who claimed not to enjoy *arguing.*

Especially, *arguing at mealtimes.*

"Any kind of halfway serious, intelligent conversation you call 'arguing,'" Cressida objected. "Which is why 'family' life is so *boring*."

At fourteen Cressida was very young. Not just she looked younger than her age but in most respects she was younger—immature, childish.

Being intelligent as she was, and quick-witted, her father described her as "wielding a whip."

"Take care with your whip, my dear daughter. It can lash back into your own face, you know."

Cressida knew. At school, she had few friends. Scornfully she'd have said she wanted few friends.

Certain of her teachers seemed to like her. But only cautiously, guardedly.

For no teacher ever knew when Cressida Mayfield might turn on him or her. In the classroom, with an audience, she could be sharp-tongued, sarcastic. Many a friendly teacher had been stung by Cressida, having hoped to co-opt the girl's unpredictable nature.

"Daddy! If 'to know the Good' is 'to wish to do Good' "—so Cressida challenged her father, at the outset of dinner—"why is there so much evil in the world? And stupidity?"

Briskly Zeno rubbed his hands over his face. You could see that Zeno was shaping the Daddy-face, essentially a benign, bemused, and yet not complacent face, out of the Zeno Mayfield–face that was his public identity in Carthage, New York.

"You've been reading—Plato? Socrates? Sounds like Socrates."

"Yes. But why is Socrates so important?"

"Because—before Socrates philosophers thought of many of the things Socrates thought of, but not so thoroughly and systematically; and not with such personal involvement. Socrates chose to die rather than repudiate his beliefs or even go into exile. He lived and died for philosophy."

Zeno spoke enthusiastically. Socrates had a long life, a public life in the *agora;* he'd challenged the conventional pieties of the day; he'd been impetuous, outspoken, unwise, reckless. He'd taken on the role of the *eiron,* the one who knows only that he knows nothing: thus knows more than all of Athens.

Cressida could see by the particular way in which her father spoke, his usually sardonic voice quavering with a kind of suppressed tenderness, that Zeno Mayfield thought highly of Socrates. Sharply she objected: "If Socrates was so special, why was he arrested and sentenced to death?" and Zeno said, with a wink to his listeners, "Thus with us all! The more special, the more despised. Where is my hemlock?"—

groping for his glass of foam-topped beer, to make his little audience laugh.

"Socrates didn't even write the *Dialogues*. Plato did. How do we know that Plato didn't make everything up, including Socrates?"

And so while their food grew cold, Zeno lectured on Socrates—the "heritage of Socrates"—the political situation of Socrates' time, the so-called Golden Age after the victory of Athens and Sparta against the common enemy, the Persians; and before the slow, terrible, irrevocable decline and collapse of Athens in the Peloponnesian War, with the former ally Sparta. "Imagine our Vietnam War tragedy multiplied many times. That was the Peloponnesian War. Not only did Athens lose, in a military sense, but in a moral sense—defeated utterly. And in this, a man of independent spirit like Socrates, a man who believed in a singular, invisible 'Good'—'God'—was perceived as a rebel."

It was thrilling to Cressida, to hear her father speak in this way.

She'd heard Zeno Mayfield speak in public: he was a politician, and very gifted as an orator, with a sense of humor, a (slightly feigned) air of personal modesty, even reticence. But such remarks, uttered at mealtimes, in the privacy of their home, they were for no purpose other than the moment. The way Daddy spoke to *her*.

Arlette and Juliet looked on, of course. Both listened, and both asked questions, sometimes. But Daddy was addressing Cressida for it was Cressida's intelligence that was most like his own, and that most engaged him.

"The terrible irony is that the 'Golden Age' of Athens was based upon military victories, originally. The flowering of philosophy, art, and culture was out of the dung-heap of war, acquisitions of Greek city-states, exploitation of conquered people. The quasi-democracy of Athens was for only a privileged few. And at the height of Athens's splendor, already the civilization was in decline, for their leader Pericles, like our bellicose American presidents, was pushing for conquests, ever more conquests, with disastrous results. There is a parallel between the death of Socrates and the death of Athens—as there always is, between the exemplary spiritual leader of an era, and the era itself."

Cressida wondered at this. Cressida was struck by this.

"Why didn't Socrates go into exile? I hated it, when he just—when he just stayed in jail, and drank poison."

Cressida had read the *Phaedo,* with Zeno's numerous annotations and exclamations.

Zeno said, "Exile was equivalent to death to the Athenians. Exile wasn't the way it would be perceived today, as a kind of pastoral escape."

Cressida persisted: "I *hated it* that he died. I think I *hated him*—for being so stubborn."

Startled then that her family laughed at her, spontaneously— Zeno, Arlette, Juliet.

But why, why was this funny? Was *she* funny?

Stubborn?

Cressida didn't quite get it. And she didn't laugh.

SHE'D THOUGHT, each day she would do something Good.

Deliberately, consciously—without telling anyone, she would embody the Good.

Not as Juliet was "good"—as a Christian. She, Cressida, would emulate the Good as the ancient Greeks had taught.

Soon then, the opportunity came: volunteers were requested for the newly founded Math Literacy Squad, to tutor inner-city middle school students who were having trouble with math.

Only ninth-grade A-students at Church Street Middle School were invited to volunteer. Cressida liked this—being singled out for an elite venture.

Overcoming her shyness to sign up for the Squad with her home-room teacher who looked at her, Cressida thought, with some surprise. "Why, Cressida! Good."

So rare it was for Cressida Mayfield to volunteer for anything.

Still rarer, for Cressida Mayfield to consent to be on a *team.*

Taken then by school bus on a Friday afternoon with ten other ninth grade volunteers and brought to downtown Carthage, into the South River Street section and to dingy-looking Booker T. Washington Middle School. The Squad leader was a high school senior named Mitch Kazteb who'd passed out to the volunteers several photocopied pages of the first day's lesson plan and instructed them to "just help, any way you can"—since the students were "mathematically illiterate" and any small improvement would be "great."

On the bus, Cressida sat with a girl from her algebra class named Rhonda. The two would cling together at Booker T. Washington, nervous and excited. Rhonda wasn't a close friend but a nice girl, one of the nicer girls in ninth grade, who didn't avoid Cressida Mayfield for her fierce, frowning looks and sarcastic remarks.

Everyone on the Math Squad was given a shiny yellow smiley-face button to wear: MATH LITERACY SQUAD.

The surprise was, almost immediately Cressida liked "tutoring."

She liked her young students—the majority were girls, between the ages of ten and twelve—who looked to her for help so openly. Even the boys were somber and serious-seeming.

The math problems were really just simple arithmetic. Adding long columns of numbers, subtracting, multiplying, dividing— patiently the Math Squad tutors from Church Street Middle School went through the steps of instruction, using sheets of yellow paper, with the backup of pocket calculators to "double-check" answers. Rapidly Cressida sketched out little cartoon-narratives to illustrate the math problems—her fingers flew, gripping a pencil, surprising her as much as her observers.

It had not occurred to her, how easy "fractions" were to understand, if you drew, for instance, a pumpkin, and divided it into sections. At least, the more elementary sort of fractions.

Seated at opposite ends of a small table, pupils between them, Cressida and Rhonda worked together companionably. It was a surprise to both girls, tutoring was *fun*.

Nine students, all dark-skinned, of whom six were girls, three boys. The boys were more restless than the girls, but laughed more readily at Cressida's lighthearted little jokes. All of the students seemed serious—hopeful. Cressida was touched by their reaction when they were told that, at the conclusion of a problem, their answer was "correct."

Close-up, the young students fascinated Cressida. They were just enough younger than she was to be physically smaller, and unmistakably childlike. (Though the largest of the boys, whose name was Kellard [?], was Cressida's height.) Their skin colors were so *various*. Gradations of dark: smoky-dark, cocoa-dark, buttery-dark, eggplant-dark, dark-dark. Their hair, their eyes, their facial characteristics— fascinating to Cressida who had always seemed by instinct to recoil from her own kind, and to avoid eye-contact with them, as if fearing invasion.

It was a revelation to Cressida, tutoring her pupils for ninety minutes with scarcely a break, that working with others, in such a setting, could be so easy, and so pleasurable. *Teaching*—a way of life?

Zeno had always said that he wished he'd gone into teaching instead of law.

Except of course in the law, Zeno continued, you had a chance to direct public policy. Coming of age in the aftermath of the great revolutionary decade in twentieth-century American history—the 1960s—Zeno understood that if you wanted to lead reform, you had to take direct action; the life of a teacher is indirect.

Yet, the Math Squad seemed to Cressida an encounter with the Good. She'd liked working with Rhonda who was a quiet good-natured girl and while smart at math, not quite so smart, or so quick, as Cressida, so that Cressida was made to feel good about herself; she liked it that the young pupils clearly admired her, and were eager to learn from her. And even the other Math Squad students—her classmates at Church Street—who ordinarily would have annoyed her with their chatter and laughter on the bus, seemed likeable to her.

And Mitch Kazteb, more than just likeable.

"So, honey, how'd it go this afternoon? 'Tutoring' math?"

Cressida told Zeno she'd liked it very much.

At dinner, Cressida wore her shiny yellow smiley-face button. It was a joke—yet not exactly a joke.

As she told her family about the Math Squad session at Booker T. Washington she saw her parents exchange a glance, one of those enigmatic glances parents exchange at such times, in the presence of their children, and had to smile—she knew that, over the years, she'd been the daughter about whom it had been said that she had difficulty "relating" to others.

She supposed that they'd been concerned for her, surprised that she'd volunteered for a program of the sort Juliet was always volunteering for, and Zeno, in his mayoral role, was always trying to promote under the rubric *community outreach*.

The following Friday, the second session went well also. Though two volunteer-tutors from Church Street School were absent, and probably wouldn't return; and the older boys in the program, including the boys at Cressida and Rhonda's table, seemed to become more quickly restless after concentrating on a few problems, and were more easily discouraged than the girls. Yet, Cressida was able to win them over, she believed, with her clever cartoon drawings and her light, droll sense of humor, and praised them when they did something—(in fact, anything)—"correctly."

It was mildly discouraging to the tutors, that the majority of their inner-city pupils seemed not to have retained the modest math-skills they'd learned the previous week. Mitch Kazteb said that was to be expected—"Math Squad just keeps plugging away, and helping whoever wants to be helped, and anything that's an improvement is good. Got it?"

Cressida pointed out, Mitch was wearing his shiny yellow smiley-face button upside down.

Again Cressida was surprised at how relaxed she was, as a tutor; how well she got along with the other tutors, and particularly with Rhonda; several of the pupils she'd come to like very much, and was quite fascinated by them—their large, quick-darting eyes, dark-

brown like her own; their way of smiling, shyly at first, then laughing, as if permission to laugh had to be granted by their tutors. And
she'd memorized all their names, which were, to Cressida, exotic
names—

*Opal, Shirlena, Vander, Marletta, Junius, Satin, Vesta, Ronette, Kel-
lard.*

How different this experience was from Cressida's relations with
her classmates at Church Street Middle School—in fact, with her
classmates since kindergarten. As a child Cressida Mayfield had
learned to move among her peers with a pose of indifference; if they
didn't see her, she didn't see *them.*

Again at Friday-evening dinner Cressida spoke warmly of the
Math Squad session. This time there were dinner guests, old friends
of her parents, who plied her with questions; this was a couple who'd
known Zeno and Arlette before their daughters were born, and had
not always felt quite comfortable in Cressida's company. Clearly now,
the Masseys were impressed with *the smart one!*

Then, the third Friday. Which was to be Cressida's final Friday.

Abruptly the romance ended—as entering the school room with
her fellow tutors Cressida saw at a little distance one of her boy-
pupils nudging another boy, saw their covert but derisive expres-
sions cast in her direction, and heard, unmistakably—*You got the
homely one has you?*

Though she'd been listening to something Rhonda was saying
yet Cressida heard this remark, shot like an arrow to her heart, and
would have stopped dead in her tracks except the momentum of the
situation carried her on, and forward—of course, she was too proud
to acknowledge that she'd heard the childish insult, or that she'd
been wounded by it.

In the next instant both boys had turned away, Kellard had ducked
his head (guiltily?) giggling and slip-slid into his chair at their table
with a clatter. With a guileless expression the boy would greet his
white girl-tutors as if nothing were wrong.

Cressida's head pounded with shame, mortification. She was reasonably certain that Rhonda hadn't heard the boy's remark but she had a sick, sinking sensation that Mitch Kazteb had heard.

(He hadn't so much as glanced at her, since they'd entered the room. Of course, he was embarrassed for her. The lighthearted repartee between them would die, irrevocably.)

And so, the third and final session at Booker T. Washington. Bravely if resentfully Cressida managed to get through it.

Only just glancing at Kellard, and at the others. For it seemed to her now obvious, they all disliked her. A spiteful voice pounded in her head.

Hate hate hate you. God damn hate you. You are homely—ugly—too.

Poor Rhonda must have noticed that her friend Cressida was far less involved in the lesson this week than in previous weeks. Cressida Mayfield who had a reputation for being moody and unpredictable now participated only minimally, without enthusiasm; she allowed Rhonda to do most of the talking; she, who'd entertained their pupils with her deftly drawn cartoons, didn't joke or draw a single cartoon this week.

The pupils, too, sensed that something was wrong. Kellard sat a little apart from the others, shifting in his seat, frowning and gnawing at his fingers, aware that Cressida ignored him, and did not praise him once.

On the bus back to their neighborhood in a northern, hilly section of Carthage, Rhonda asked Cressida if something was wrong and Cressida shook her head *no*.

Rhonda remarked disapprovingly that two or three more tutors had dropped out that week. Rhonda seemed about to express a hope that Cressida wouldn't be one of these, the following week, but Cressida, slumped in her seat, staring gloomily out the window, said nothing.

How unfair it was! She knew, Kellard had liked her—as she had liked him. Yet, he hadn't been able to resist saying what he'd said—and now she despised him, and could not bring herself to look at him.

And the other pupils—she knew, of course they were innocent. The little girls particularly, whom she'd liked so much. But now—it was over. Nothing could bring her back to Booker T. Washington School ever again.

That evening, at dinner, Cressida was sullen-faced. With some hesitation her parents asked her how the afternoon had gone and Cressida said, with a bright, blithe smile of indifference, "It was OK. But I'm not going back next week."

"Not going back? Why?"

"Because it's a waste of time. The students don't really 'learn' anything—they memorize. And then they forget."

"But—you enjoyed tutoring so much . . ."

Cressida shrugged. For her, the subject was closed.

"You thought you might like to be a teacher, you'd said . . ."

And Juliet protested, "But, Cressie! You and Rhonda were having such fun, you'd said. Maybe you should give it one more try?"

Cressida shook her head, *no*. No more delusions!

She'd tossed her Math Literacy Squad smiley-button into the trash.

HOMELY ONE. With the passage of time she would come to believe the boy had said *Ugly*.

Thinking it was just as well, she'd learned beforehand how stupid and cruel young students could be. Before she'd made some idiotic, idealistic mistake.

And discovering, too, how shallow she was, herself—how easily wounded, defeated. Like a drawing by M. C. Escher that is all surfaces, dazzling and clever, ingenious, lacking depth and heart.

ON THE BUS moving north. The last time she'd glanced out the window the terrain was rural, hilly. They'd left Florida behind—and Georgia—and were now in South Carolina, unless already it was North Carolina.

In a paralysis of dread she was being borne north.

Thinking *Maybe they have forgotten me, truly. Maybe I was correct all along.*

And thinking *Maybe the bus will capsize. Maybe—in "flaming wreckage on I-95."*

In her seat she'd slept huddled. No one had asked to sit with her.

How badly she missed the Investigator! Even the man's disgust with her, his sharp disappointment with her, she missed.

Yet he was correct: she'd betrayed his trust, she was of no possible future use to him. And she was fifty years younger than the man which made any relationship apart from a professional relationship ridiculous.

Still, she hadn't lost the ring. Turning it around her finger, and around.

If they will forgive me, I can return to him. If he will have me.

She'd been sleeping in her clothes for what seemed like a long time. A nasty dream of Booker T. Washington School—though the labyrinthine building in her dream hadn't resembled the actual building, much.

The dark-skinned children hiding from her. Laughing at her, and rushing at her. *Ugly ugly ugly girl! Why don't you die.*

She'd behaved badly there, too. She'd known even at the time.

Mitch Kazteb had tried to convince her. They were all discouraged with tutoring, sure some of the kids were God-damned little brats, he'd been insulted too, more than once. But you kept going, Mitch said, just kept slogging forward, and it turned out OK—or better than OK.

He'd called Cressida, when she'd failed to return for the fourth week.

A boy calling Cressida Mayfield! A senior boy, who spoke to her as if he liked her, or liked something about her.

She'd been attracted to *him*—but only at first. Only when things had gone well.

Feelings like cobwebs. Nothing durable about them. Her feelings, at least.

And Rhonda had called her, saying she missed her. Begging her to return, try again.

Cressida had been deeply moved, that Rhonda and Mitch had called her. How could she possibly confess to them *I can't risk it again, I am too easily hurt.*

Thinking of these blunders of adolescence she'd begun coughing in the chilly bus-air. Other passengers had complained to the driver about the gusty air that was much too cold, now that they'd left south Florida.

Her throat was beginning to feel raw and scraped. Her skin, hypersensitive as if she were becoming ill.

A fear of being sick in so public a place, and so far from anything like home.

SHE WAS *the smart one.*

God damn she knew it: *the smart one.*

Slamming out of the house on Cumberland Avenue by a rear door.

Not caring if anyone inside saw, or heard, her leave.

Not caring if she ever came back.

Inside her was a clockwork mechanism wound tight, tight, and ever tighter—tickticticking close to bursting.

"Hate you all. Wish you were all—"

But she could not quite utter the word *dead.*

For of course she didn't mean it—*dead.*

Why so angry, why her heart beating so hard. Why the hot-beating pulses in her head. Why this wish, so lately powerful in her, as, in another girl her age, a wish to be touched, to be kissed, to be made-love-to, to *vanish*?

For as long as she could remember, Cressida was uncomfortable with being looked-at, assessed in the eyes of others. But lately the sensation was growing stronger.

Since the trouble at school with her geometry teacher Mr. Rickard who'd said such stupid cruel unforgiveable things to her after she'd taken him into her confidence and shown him her portfolio of drawings—"Hate *him.* Wish he was *dead.*"

Fear/revulsion—being observed by others.

Usually it was strangers from whom she wanted to shrink, make herself small and *disappear*.

But often it was people who knew her name—or worse yet knew her as the younger Mayfield daughter—*the ***** one*.

Sometimes, her own family.

Slamming out of the house so she wouldn't *scream*.

In khaki shorts, long-sleeved T-shirt, sneakers. Loose-fitting boy-clothes, that disguised her (boy)-figure. And her hair that needed washing, brushed back carelessly behind her ears.

She was angry. But mostly, she was ashamed.

What she'd done to hurt Juliet! Ashamed.

It was a Saturday in April. A week or so after Cressida's fifteenth birthday.

Confined inside the house practicing piano. Compulsively and without joy at the piano in the living room, in a corner of the room in which natural light rarely fell and so even at midday she had to have a lamp burning, and this too she resented. The previous afternoon she'd had her weekly piano lesson that had been a disappointment to her as—(she knew)—to her instructor Mr. Goellner; she was determined to play the Beethoven sonata smoothly, rapidly, and without errors, to surprise Mr. Goellner the following Friday, and to refute the man's (probable) estimate of her musical skill; yet despite her ferocious concentration, and her willingness to repeat, repeat, repeat those passages of sparkling arpeggios, she kept making mistakes—striking wrong notes, losing the beat—blundering, slip-sliding, disgusting. For this was the Sonata no. 23—the great *Appassionata*. It was wounding to Cressida's pride that she would never play this sonata except as a mediocre girl-pianist in Carthage might play it, though each time she struggled through it—if Zeno or Arlette were anywhere within earshot—her effort was rewarded with a wild outburst of applause.

"Cressie! *Terrific.*"

Her parents meant well of course. Her parents made a show of *loving her*.

Yet she knew: their love for her was a kind of pity, like love for a crippled child, or a child dying of leukemia.

Slammed out of the house. No need to tell anyone where she was going.

Vaguely she recalled she'd promised to do something with her mother, or with her mother and Juliet—sometime that afternoon.

No one observed her bicycling out the long driveway to the street. As always when she climbed onto her bicycle Cressida took pleasure in moving so swiftly, and with so little effort.

Her legs were strong, hard-muscled. It was her chest, her shoulders, her upper body that were weak, and thin; her collarbones that showed through her skin the hue of watery milk.

At Cumberland Avenue she turned east, bicycling to the Episcopal church at the end of the block, and the beautiful old cemetery.

The cemetery was one of Cressida's *places*. Since she'd been a child needing to slip away from her family, and hide.

Always in the cemetery she visited the old, familiar grave markers. By heart she knew the "historic" names on gravestones so very old and smooth-worn, the letters and numerals were scarcely legible.

There were *Mayfelds* in the oldest part of the cemetery, dating to the 1790s. But Zeno was convinced these were not ancestors of his since his great-grandfather Zenobah Mayfield had emigrated from northern England in the 1890s, as a young child; also, no Mayfield had ever attended the Episcopal church, so far as Zeno knew.

Cressida's hot-beating brain slowed a bit, in the cemetery. For it was peaceful here, a secret sort of place.

She hadn't been drawing so much, lately. Since that idiot Rickard had insulted her.

These are impressive, but—why repeat what Escher did so well?

Her mistake had been to trust her geometry teacher. Because he seemed to like her, often praised her in class and smiled at her; and laughed at her ironic remarks, murmured out of the corner of her mouth.

Because he was one of the few teachers she'd ever had, she'd thought, capable of appreciating her.

And maybe, she'd thought, he had *liked her.*

Now, that had ended. Now, she hated him.

And now, she hated geometry. She would fail to hand in homework assignments through the remaining weeks of the term, she would miss classes. Slumping in her seat staring out the window indifferent to Mr. Rickard clicking chalk against the board and asking questions which the brighter students would volunteer to answer but not Cressida Mayfield, any longer—not ever.

Curious it seemed to Cressida, in the cemetery: death was so general, and so unexceptional—death was everywhere.

And yet, death in actual life was terrible, unspeakable. Nothing mattered more than individual, unique deaths.

She found herself staring at an awful sight—a large green insect, a grasshopper, trapped and thrashing in a gigantic spiderweb, in which the carcasses of other insects were visible. How ugly! This was the sort of "biological" imagery you were spared, in the cerebral and paradoxical art of M. C. Escher.

Cressida took up a stick and smashed the spiderweb, in disgust. Where the grasshopper ended up, broken against a grave marker, still trapped in the remnants of the spiderweb, or liberated, she didn't know.

Their mother's mother, who'd wanted her granddaughters to call her *Grand'mère Helene,* had died just before Christmas. Cressida had had nightmares after her death and could not now look at older, white-haired women without feeling a stab of loss. Yet, she hadn't been able to love *Grand'mère Helene* as Juliet had loved her, and felt sick with guilt afterward; she hadn't been able to cry, as Juliet and Arlette had cried, but, at the funeral, had gnawed at her knuckles in resentment that she had to be where she was, so confined. But *Grand'mère Helene* hadn't been buried in the Episcopal cemetery.

Cressida could not bear to think of the circumstances of her grandmother's death. She could not bear to think of the (future) death of her parents—Zeno, Arlette. Her brain just stopped like a garbage disposal into which a spoon has fallen. (When sulky Cressida helped clean up after mealtimes, often it happened that spoons, forks and knives slipped into the whirring blades of the garbage disposal, which wrecked them.)

She thought *It's so far off, it will never happen. Don't be silly!*

Amid the familiar, old part of the cemetery she stood on a gravel path. She liked the newer parts of the cemetery less, though they were on higher ground, beneath tall chestnut trees at the edge of the churchyard.

Newer meant the likelihood of seeing a surname she might recognize.

Now she spied a funeral party in the newer section, in dressy clothes.

They appeared to be strangers, which was a relief.

Hesitantly she followed the gravel path. She did not want to turn around abruptly to avoid the mourners, but she did not want to attract their attention, either.

Feeling ill-at-ease in khaki shorts, baggy T-shirt in the churchyard. Yet there was the thrill of believing herself unknown and unnamed, unrecognized.

Someday, she would go out into the world: anonymous.

But then, as if to mock her, one of the women mourners looked pointedly at her, and nodded to her.

Lifting a gloved hand, and not quite a smile.

Of course, the woman was known to Cressida: Mrs. Carlsen.

Ginny Carlsen, Patrick Carlsen's wife. Mr. Carlsen was a business associate of Zeno Mayfield.

The Mayfields and the Carlsens were friendly acquaintances. Though the Carlsens were older than the Mayfields. Very likely, it was an older parent who'd died and whose coffin was being lowered into the earth.

How like a netted animal she felt, for a moment breathless as several other mourners looked over at her, lifted their hands in greeting.

Who is it?—the Mayfield girl. The younger one . . .

Soon then she left the cemetery, pushing her bicycle roughly along the gravel paths. Though the sky was darkening with rain clouds yet she didn't return home but descended Cumberland Avenue in a series of hills. Much of the residential neighborhood was still undeveloped, vacant lots and woodland between properties of several acres. She knew the names of the families who lived in most of these houses but her mind had gone blank. She was feeling strangely light-headed, mildly anxious, as if she'd narrowly escaped—something.

Several of the hills were steep, glacier-hills. She had to get off her bicycle to walk it downhill. A voice like nettles in her brain—*Arlette! I saw your daughter the other day—we were at the cemetery. What a strange wild-looking girl alone and not with friends on a Saturday afternoon.*

There was a phobia—*autophobia*—which meant a terror of being alone. And *isolophobia*—a terror of solitude, which came to the same thing.

Such peculiar phobias, she'd discovered: *spectrophobia* (a terror of seeing yourself in a mirror), *ornithphobia* (a terror of birds). And there was *zoophobia* (a terror of animals), and *anthrophobia* (a terror of people).

More common phobias, with which most people could identify, were *claustrophobia, agoraphobia, acrophobia* (a terror of heights).

Her heart was beating quickly, like a trapped bird's wings. It was a kind of claustrophobia, conjoined with anthrophobia—her fear of other people, trapping her with their eyes, making a claim upon her.

Zeno had joked the other evening about the common and yet "utterly bizarre" phobia—*triskaidekaphobia*—a terror of the numeral thirteen.

Zeno liked to boast that he was without superstition as he was without any "supernatural" benefactor but most other people, including even Cressida herself, in a weak mood, were fearful of *something*.

A fear of the unknown: what was that called?

Worse yet: a fear of the *known*.

Cressida laughed, this was all so absurd.

Her brain was tangled and snarled like loose thread in a carpet, sucked into the spinning, wooden wheels of the vacuum cleaner.

Oh Cressida!—have you messed up the vacuum cleaner again?

One after another household task, Cressida was excused from.

It wasn't her fault—truly! Until finally, Arlette assigned her to tasks that didn't require close concentration but allowed her to day-dream freely without disastrous results, like folding towels out of the dryer and carrying them to the upstairs closet.

Cressida climbed back on her bicycle, though the hill was still fairly steep. She'd gone out without a safety helmet: her parents would scold, if they knew.

Careless about hurting herself. Since she'd been a toddler, often she bumped into things, bruised and cut her legs. The thought came to her of a need to punish herself, for her bad behavior with Juliet, and Juliet's friend Carly Hempel.

Shame! Shame on you Cressida Mayfield.

Your punishment is: splattered brains.

Yet a better escape would be simply to vanish.

For, if she disappeared, just never returned from this bicycle ride, who would miss her?

She'd heard them—her family—talking and laughing together, their words muffled, at a little distance, many times. When abruptly she'd gone upstairs to her room and shut the door to be alone—with her books, with her "art"—knowing that her parents and her sister were baffled by her rudeness; yet knowing that soon, within minutes, they would cease to miss her, they would forget about her, Zeno, Arlette, Juliet—relaxed and happy together.

They'd become accustomed to Cressida's behavior, within the family. Relatives and friends understood. Allowances were made for Cressida. You wouldn't expect Cressida to answer with a smile when she was greeted, or make eye contact with most people; you wouldn't expect Cressida to jump up, with others, to offer to prepare a meal, drag picnic tables and benches into the backyard, set a table or clear a table.

You'd hardly expect Cressida to sit still for long enough to eat—to try to eat—a meal; you'd hardly expect her to linger after a meal, as others did, not out of obligation but because they wanted to, because they enjoyed one another's company, and took pleasure and not pain in the presence of others.

Needing desperately to get away, and be alone. And when alone, her thoughts turning against her like maddened hornets.

Recklessly she'd bicycled downhill, into the city of Carthage. Her nostrils pinched at a smell of chemical waste, organic rot and smoldering rubber borne by the wind in this old, semi-deserted part of the city bordering the Black Snake River, that had once been an area of small factories, mills, and active warehouses. Now what remained were scattered businesses looking as if they were on the brink of bankruptcy, or beyond—gas stations, fast-food restaurants, taverns, pawnshops, bail-bondsmen, NO WAIT CHECK CASHING OUR SPECIALTY.

How like Cressida Mayfield, they would say, to have made her way, downhill, steeply downhill, unthinking and stubbornly, *here.*

She'd made a mistake, maybe—she wouldn't be able to bicycle back up those hills but would have to walk her bike, much of the time.

But she wouldn't call home to ask for someone—(it would be Mom of course)—to come in the station wagon and rescue her.

Big deal if they missed her at home—if she missed whatever it was she'd miss, by not being home.

Cressida honey where were you for so long?—we were worried about you!

Did you tell me you were going for a bike ride? Did you even say good-bye?

We looked in your room, honey—we called you—I even called Marcy Meyer thinking maybe . . .

On Waterman Street there was traffic: trucks, delivery vans, rust-flecked vehicles careening along with conspicuously less concern for the well-being of a lone girl bicyclist than in the residential hills of north Carthage. Yet Cressida liked it here: this mild sensation of risk, danger, alarm as traffic passed close beside her and her bicycle jolted over railroad tracks, quick and unexpected, so that she nearly lost control of the handlebars. (She wasn't the only bicyclist on Waterman Street: some distance ahead were several boys, lanky teenagers, who hadn't noticed her. Maybe one of them was Kellard.)

(Cressida wouldn't easily forget Kellard. Foolish to say so, but the boy had broken her heart.)

(Certainly she knew: it was all so petty! It was utterly trivial, forgettable. But she would not forget.)

The sharp chemical odor was becoming stronger, as Cressida made her way along Waterman Street. She was passing, on her right, a derelict railroad yard and in this yard, stretching along the river, sprawling for a quarter-mile, were abandoned box cars, a scrap heap of metal debris, piles of sinister-looking grayish gravel, or powder—a smell of nitrogen? And something sulfurous beneath.

She passed Fisher Avenue—(Booker T. Washington Middle School was a block or two away)—and now, at 200 Waterman, the beige-brick facade of Home Front Alliance—a community-service organization which operated a soup kitchen and a "store" in which impoverished, homeless individuals and entire families—("clients," as Zeno carefully called them)—were invited to shop once a month, moving along the aisles as in a grocery or a discount store, filling up a designated number of carts: one for each adult, plus another for "family." Zeno Mayfield had helped to initiate Home Front Alliance when he'd been mayor of Carthage and on the city board; he was still involved in the administration of the organization, lobbying for funds, hosting fund-raiser evenings. Of course, the Mayfield family had been involved in a number of the programs at Home Front Alliance; particularly, Arlette and Juliet continued to participate in the soup kitchen and in the store—Cressida wasn't sure how often, for Cressida had little interest in such things.

Though, initially, she'd allowed herself to be talked into coming with her family to a Home Front Alliance activity—some sort of fund-raiser involving volunteers, community organizers, church-related members, and "clients." She'd helped ladle baked ziti, covered in a molten crust of mozzarella cheese, onto paper plates, at a buffet; she'd even helped, in a trance of misery and boredom, with the massive cleanup that followed. (Noting that Zeno, MC of the evening, avoided the kitchen as if it were a place of contagion.) Then she'd slipped away to wait for her parents in their car, relieved that so many volunteers had turned out, predominantly white, educated, well-to-do women acquaintances of her parents.

Cressida teased her social-activist parents by paraphrasing a remark of W. H. Auden—"We're here on earth to help other people. But what the other people are here for, nobody knows."

Still, despite her lack of interest in Home Front, and her heartbreak over Math Literacy, Cressida hoped to do Good. She would think of the Good as a high mountain to be climbed. But a distant mountain, not in the southern Adirondacks.

Pedaling past Home Front she saw a line of people straggling into the entrance to the soup kitchen. The majority were men, probably homeless. Cressida bicycled quickly past.

Was she ashamed of herself, or—defiant? Guilty-feeling or contemptuous?

Don't care about any of you, any more than you care about me.

Why should I?

I am the ugly one.

What she'd done to Juliet's cashmere sweater, the beautiful heather-colored cardigan *Grand'mère Helene* had given Juliet for a birthday two years ago—she did feel ashamed of this.

With a nail scissors, cutting just a few crucial threads in the sweater, on the inside. Shivering with elation, for who would know?

Other times, Cressida erased phone messages for Juliet, if they were recorded on the family phone.

Other times, Cressida appropriated items of Juliet's—including Juliet's new, shiny little cell phone that had been a gift from their parents—and tossed them away.

Oh damn! I'm losing every—damn—thing I own, I could just cry.

And Cressie the younger sister said teasing, with her particular tormenting smile *Poor Julie! Maybe you caught chemo-brain from
Grandma.*

(A truly nasty remark, which Juliet deflected with a startled little
laugh.)

(Which, if their mother had overheard, would have been shocking
to her.)

So frequently sick with spite, jealousy, envy of her popular-pretty
sister whom all adored, *and whom Cressida herself adored,* Cressida
found herself entering Juliet's bedroom in stealth to sit at Juliet's
computer. Juliet rarely turned off her computer or quit email and so
there was no difficulty getting into Juliet's computer to delete email
including new messages in her in-box from friends; Cressida read her
sister's correspondence with her numerous girlfriends and her boyfriend Elliot Keller—(and other boys as well, which had to be a secret
from Elliot)—deleting at will, with childish satisfaction. Why should
her sister have so many friends, even these shallow, silly friends,
while Cressida had so few friends?—it was unjust. Particularly, Cressida resented the letters that ended with *Love*—for she herself rarely
received emails from classmates, only just one or two girls, and in all
of these there were no *Love*s.

A few times, Cressida employed her limited-but-lethal computer
skills to muck up Juliet's files.

With the result that poor Juliet came pleading to *her—Oh Cressie!
Can you help me? I'm so stupid—I must have done something wrong—
clicked something wrong—you won't believe it, all of my "desktop" is gone!*

So Cressida took pity on her older sister. *OK, hey I guess I'm the
"smart one." I'll try.*

Now at the intersection of Waterman and Ventor in a derelict
neighborhood of warehouses fronting on the river Cressida became
aware of a delivery van uncomfortably close beside her, in the street;
though she was bicycling as close to the curb as possible, still the van
seemed to be pressing inward, to frighten her; the driver had slowed
his speed to keep pace with her, unmistakably. For, after the traffic

light turned green, the delivery van didn't surge forward and leave her behind but lingered, just slightly behind her.

Was a radio turned up high, in the van? Or—was that the driver's voice Cressida was hearing, a soft low mock-caressing voice, words she couldn't decipher?

Words she didn't wish to decipher.

Cressida was so frightened, she turned the bike's handlebars sharply, and was nearly thrown from the bike as it hurtled over a curb onto a vacant lot covered in cracked and crumbling concrete, an abandoned gas station property. Scattered across the pavement were shards of broken glass, scrap metal and trash, tough little weeds poking through cracks like sinister fingers. The van driver had braked his vehicle to call after Cressida more distinctly. *Hey-you li'l cunt— where're ya goin so fuckin fast li'l cunt know what?—somebody's gonna tear up ya sweet li'l ass.*

Halfway Cressida had been thinking, pedaling her bicycle along Waterman, that she'd be attracting the attention of men—and of boys—and that they might be "interested" in her; as, bicycling on Cumberland Avenue, or in the vicinity of Convent Street School, she aroused the "interest" of no one. And now—a rude rebuke of her fantasy.

Maybe the man was joking. Or maybe, threatening.

In any case it was hardly flattering, this attention from a man—it was an insult, obscene and hateful.

He could see that Cressida was young. He could see that Cressida was very frightened. Trying to ignore him but increasingly nervous and self-conscious as boldly he turned his vehicle into the lot, jolting over the curb and careening through trash, leering at her through the windshield. She had a confused impression of a youngish man with a low, furrowed forehead, unshaven jaws, mocking smile—and in a panic she lost her balance, pitched forward from the bicycle and fell, hard.

On the broken and oil-stained pavement she lay sobbing, shuddering. She knew she'd cut her knee, she hoped she had not sprained or broken any bones. Her head had struck something hard. The bicycle handlebars were beneath her, jabbing her ribs. She heard a man's voice—another man?—and saw another driver braking his vehicle to a stop, on Waterman Street. A young man threw open his door, climbed out and ran toward her even as the van driver wheeled his vehicle around, in a semi-circle, to escape.

The young man called after the van driver, raising his fist.

To Cressida he said, in a disgusted voice, "I saw that! Jesus."

The young man was no one Cressida knew, or could recall. She had an impression of fair brown hair, stark-staring eyes, an expression of utter revulsion mitigated with concern for the fallen Cressida, whom he helped to her feet, gripping her hand and half-lifting her. Then he picked up her bicycle, checked the wheels by spinning them, and corrected a misalignment in the back wheel.

"You all right?"—he peered at her sidelong.

Cressida rubbed at her knee, which was bleeding through a film of dust and dirt. Her head rang, her eyes spilled tears. She tried to laugh, saying yes, she was all right.

At the curb the young man's car motor idled. He'd rushed to help Cressida leaving the keys in the ignition.

"What was he, trying to run you over? Or just scaring you? Asshole. Should've got his license plate number."

Cressida was too embarrassed to reply. Inanely she was smiling, trying to laugh. But what was funny?

The palms of her hands too were scraped. Tiny rivulets of blood oozing through. And her ribs felt as if they'd been cracked.

"Y'know, I think my mother works for your father—he's Zeno Mayfield, right? The mayor? My mother works at City Hall. Your dad is a great guy."

Cressida stood tentatively, wincing. She couldn't meet the assessing gaze of the young man, who was smiling at her.

Twenty-two or -three years old, Cressida guessed. But she had no idea who he was.

Shyly she murmured yes, Zeno Mayfield was her father.

"My mother is Ethel Kincaid. Tell your dad hello from me—Brett."

Brett Kincaid took from his pocket a tissue which he unfolded to check if it was clean; this tissue he gave to Cressida, to soak up the blood running from her knee.

Down the calf of her left leg and into her sock, onto her foot in a grimy sneaker the blood-rivulet ran. So like menstrual blood, Cressida's face flamed.

"Might be, I should drive you home? Put the bicycle in the trunk? You don't look like you're in a condition to bicycle much more."

But Cressida insisted, no she was all right.

Brett Kincaid didn't argue with her. But examined the bicycle another time, gripped the handlebars and moved it swiftly back and forth, determining that the wheels seemed in workable order now, and the hand-brakes hadn't been damaged.

Then doubtfully he said: "Still maybe I better drive you home. Yeah, I'm thinking I better."

Cressida weakly protested. Cressida's heart was pounding in a ridiculous way. She saw that Brett Kincaid was regarding her with a look of concern as if he were a brother, not a stranger.

"No trouble. I'm on my way home anyway. Where d'you live? Up around Cumberland?"

Brett Kincaid carried the bicycle to his car and placed it carefully in the trunk, lowering the trunk door without shutting it; wordless Cressida limped after him and slid into the passenger's seat of the car—(she had only a vague impression of Brett Kincaid's car, for she knew little of automobiles and could never recognize a brand, still less recognize its age and/or special features)—and so Brett drove her home into the hills of North Carthage almost exactly reversing her reckless bicycle-ride into the city, as if he had some idea of where she lived. At the sprawling Colonial on Cumberland Drive, to which Cressida had directed him, Brett parked his car saying in a matter-of-fact voice in which there was not a vestige of envy or irony, "Real nice house you guys live in. This is a great neighborhood. I've met your dad a few times—maybe he'd remember me—

like from *J-C-C* softball?—he'd come out for a few games at Solstice Park."

J-C-C softball. Cressida had no idea what this was.

Junior Chamber of Commerce? Zeno was always involved in what he called community sports. Some of it was community-action for the children of poor people but maybe not all.

Cressida's cheeks were still burning. She muttered something like *Thanks!*

She would note: Brett Kincaid had parked on the street, and not in the driveway; and not directly in front of the Mayfields' house but a little to the side so that, if someone inside the house were to glance out, he or she wouldn't see Brett's car, or Brett lifting the bicycle out of the trunk for Cressida to take from him, with a muttered *Thank you.*

She would note: he hadn't asked her name.

Hadn't wanted to embarrass her further, or just hadn't thought of it.

Nor had Cressida looked at him, met his gaze. Or smiled at him, as he'd been smiling at her.

The phobia against looking at another person. For then, the other will look at you.

Quickly then Cressida walked the bicycle up the long driveway to the garage. Limping just perceptibly, for her knee throbbed with pain.

Yet her heart continued to beat, with excitement.

The thrill of—she wasn't sure—being *alive.*

And if she never saw Brett Kincaid again, and if next time he saw her he didn't remember her, that would not alter this profound experience in Cressida's life in the slightest.

SEVERAL YEARS LATER when Juliet brought Corporal Brett Kincaid home to meet her family, it did seem—(unless Cressida imagined it)—that Brett remembered her.

Smiled at her, shook her hand, happily.

A knowing smile, an intimate smile, and yet a smile that assured

Cressida that he would never embarrass her by bringing up their shared memory.

We have a secret between us. We always will.

→ ←

Now crossing the state line from Virginia and into Maryland and soon, New Jersey; immediately beyond New Jersey, New York City where in a clamorous bus terminal Cressida would disembark and take another Greyhound bus, north on I-87 to Albany.

Grungy in her slept-in clothes, her unwashed hair. It was possible to wash, if not bathe, on a bus trip of several days but you had to make the effort at rest-stops—Cressida hadn't the energy to make the effort.

At last the air-conditioning throughout the bus had turned to warm air but it came too late, Cressida had become ill: her throat was sore, her skin hurt when touched even lightly by clothing, helplessly she'd been coughing, spitting up a nasty greeny phlegm into wadded tissues and, when these ran out, into strips of toilet paper from the lavatory. With a pang of loss Cressida recalled Haley McSwain leaning over her, forehead creased, asking was she all right?—she'd been coughing. Or, drawing her cool stubby fingers across Cressida's forehead asking did she have a fever?—she felt "clammy-hot."

At the Cancer Center Haley's friend Luce had examined her— "Sabbath"—Haley's younger sister of whom she took such good care, like a frantic mother. Now she was so very alone, on this Greyhound bus plunging through a landscape increasingly sere and wintry, it was a shock to Cressida to recall that for seven years she'd been "loved"— "protected"; that she'd even, in her ignorance, taken for granted the curious fact that the little Filipino tech who was a total stranger to her helped oversee her welfare at Haley's request, providing her even with sample-cards of antibiotics, free meds that, in a drugstore, would have cost hundreds of dollars, and weren't available in any case without a prescription.

Oh God! She missed Haley.

She missed the Investigator, yet more.

And her parents, and Julie. And Brett Kincaid—as he'd been, in his early twenties, before he'd been injured, made monstrous and lost to them.

Still maybe I better drive you home.

Yeah, I'm thinking I better.

Never thinking *I love him*. For Cressida had not that capacity, for either the emotion or its articulation.

But rather thinking *With him in the world somewhere, I can be happy.*

It seemed to her not so very surprising, that Juliet would bring Brett Kincaid home. That Brett Kincaid would *marry into the Mayfield family*—this was good!

In this way Cressida and Brett would become related. It was thrilling to Cressida to think she would be acquiring a brother, at last.

She'd had enough of just herself and her sister. How boring it seemed to her, she'd actually brought up the subject to her startled parents, that they'd stopped at *just daughters*.

"Most parts of the world, everyone wants sons. Like China, and now India, where the 'live births' of girls is plummeting. But you, you stopped with just girls. Why?"

It was a preposterous remark to make to one's parents. Yet in all innocence Cressida spoke, for truly she wanted to know.

Arlette said, awkwardly, "Why, honey—that's a—a kind of a private matter, you know?—between your father and me. I'm not sure how to answer it."

Zeno said, "Are you asking, Cressie, why we stopped with 'just girls'? Or are you asking why we stopped at all?"

Cressida wasn't sure of the distinction here. Zeno fired such queries at her the way that he'd shot Ping-Pong balls at her in those years when they'd played Ping-Pong in the basement; when she'd begun to shoot the little balls back at Zeno, and to win a game now and then, Zeno had been less avid to play.

"We 'stopped' because we realized we were very happy, as we were. We were *perfect*—as we were." Zeno smiled slyly so you knew he was about to say something clever. "If we'd had another baby, it might have been a daughter. And another—a daughter. These things happen. There isn't any necessary probability that the next child would be a son, or the next. And who needs a son? I've been spared little Oedipus eyeing me out of the shadows. My two darling daughters are the answers to all my prayers."

YET SOMETIMES she was lonely. And sometimes, embittered.

Though Brett Kincaid was in the world, somewhere—"deployed" in Iraq—how could this be a solace to Cressida?

At St. Lawrence University she was so very unhappy. Far more unhappy than she'd been living at home, and attending Carthage High School where she knew everyone, or consoled herself that she knew everyone—their (shallow) depths, their (unsurprising) particularities.

In savage repudiation of their ordinariness she'd drawn her contemporaries as stunted stick-figures climbing stairs, to infinity. Her drawings were her revenge even as her drawings were a consolation. For she could look at these curious works of art—with a cold, objective eye—and see that they were strikingly rendered, unsettling and "profound" in a way that little else in her life could be.

But that was high school, in Carthage. And now she was away at college, in the small city of Canton, New York. At a university that hadn't been one of her first choices but which, with her erratic grades, she'd had to settle for.

Almost now, Cressida regretted her impulsive behavior, so frequent in high school. Her angry hurt feelings against a teacher—Mr. Rickard was but one example—that resulted in her failing to hand in crucial assignments, failing to study for a final exam, sabotaging

her own efforts. It was not uncommon for Cressida to ruin an A average in such ways and so instead of graduating as valedictorian of the
Carthage High School Class of '04 she'd managed to graduate with a
grade point average lower than that of her sister Juliet, who'd graduated in the class of 2000.

And so—was *the smart one* really so *smart,* after all?

Of course Cressida hadn't been admitted to her first-choice
universities—Cornell, Syracuse, Middlebury, Wesleyan. She hadn't
received offers of scholarships even to second-tier schools. She'd been
humbled, disgraced. Her pretensions to being superior had been rebuked. Obscurely she felt that in punishing herself she was punishing
her parents and anyone else who'd predicted academic success for
her—for how bitterly she resented such facile predictions!

*Cressida is really so very—original. Her mind isn't like any other child's
mind we've ever encountered. If only Cressida were less unpredictable—
more cooperative in the matter of her own good.*

Her parents had pleaded with her since tenth grade, and the upset
with Mr. Rickard, which had nearly resulted in Cressida failing geometry, that she was sabotaging her own career with such impulsive
behavior—but of course, Cressida hadn't listened.

Like running the sharp points of a nail scissors against her skin.
Against the tantalizing pale-blue veins on the inside of her wrist. Or
brushing her fingers against the gas-flame on the stove. *Pain? What
is pain? A shadow in the brain, to be conquered.*

Even teachers who admired Cressida Mayfield had been obliged,
surely, to write qualified letters of recommendation for her. They
could not in all conscience write the sort of glowing letters they
wrote for their best students.

Your own worst enemy, Cressida. Why?

But Zeno had a new idea: if Cressida excelled in her freshman
year at St. Lawrence, she could transfer to another university for the
following year. "'There are second acts in American lives'—if you
seize them."

Still pressure put upon her! Sometimes Cressida felt it as an (invisible) vise tightening around her skull, squeezing her brain out of shape.

At St. Lawrence, she should have excelled. She knew, there was no reason for her not to excel. And at first, she worked in the way of a good, diligent student—the kind of girl-student whom professors reward with high grades; then, the old, self-sabotaging impulse set in, her wish to disobey, resist. Like a bratty child she resented *being assigned* anything—that was the crucial problem. A subject she might have zealously researched on her own became boring to her, when it was *assigned*. Like a leash around her neck.

And it was strange, discomforting, to be away from Carthage, where everyone knew her as the younger Mayfield daughter; she hadn't quite realized how her father's reputation defined and protected her, as water heavily saturated in salt buoys up the least skilled of swimmers, unwittingly. Even as she'd scorned her father's political "reputation"— her family's social "stature"—so she'd taken these for granted, all of her life. And now she was in Canton, New York, not so very far from Carthage, but far enough that no one knew the Mayfield name; or, having heard of it, was much impressed. And now she wasn't living in her parents' house, that had long sheltered and confined her, there was no one to notice, still less to care, if she skipped meals, skipped classes. If she rushed outside in freezing weather carelessly dressed and couldn't be bothered to return to her residence to dress more sensibly.

No one to call chidingly to her *Cressie honey! Of course you're going to wear boots today, yes?*

Or *Come in here and sit down, Cressie. You are not leaving this house without eating breakfast!*

She found it distressing to accept that Brett Kincaid had enlisted in the U.S. Army—the young man who'd been so kind to her, and had made such a powerful impression upon her; with the declaration of war against Iraq, in March 2003, Private First Class Kincaid had been among the first American servicemen shipped to Iraq, to an area called Salah ad Din—she'd tried to locate on maps. Brett Kincaid, her (secret) friend!

Her sister's fiancé and beloved of all the Mayfields including even Zeno who was edgy and funny and awkward in the young man's presence never seeming to know the appropriate tone in which to address him—handsome in his dress uniform as an heraldic figure in an ancient frieze. Always Cressida would recall how Brett had gripped her hands in farewell, how he'd smiled at everyone who'd come to see him off at the airport in a way they were never to see him smile again. For hadn't Brett said, his father had "served" in the Gulf: though he hadn't seen (Sergeant) Graham Kincaid in years yet he seemed to believe that his father would know about his enlisting, and be proud.

Cressida was shocked that Juliet's fiancé would behave so—*ordinarily.* Since the terrorist bombings of 9/11 the media had been filled with propaganda speeches by politicians, news of "weapons of mass destruction" hidden in Iraq, the horrific dictatorship of Saddam Hussein who'd seemed to be mocking his American enemies, daring them to declare war and invade. On TV Cressida had seen newsreel footage of President George W. Bush declaring to his American viewers that the terrorist enemy that had struck the Twin Towers on September 11, 2001, was part of a vast fundamentalist-Muslim army determined to destroy our *American way of life;* gazing into the TV camera as if he were addressing very slow-witted and credulous individuals, the President said, deadpan: "They want to come into your home and kill you and your family."

A pause. And then a slow studied repeat of the same words with the President's gaze fixed upon the vast invisible TV audience.

"Is that guy serious? What does he take us for, total idiots?"—so Zeno had raged, ranted.

But it had soon become evident that it wasn't just the bellicose conservative-Christian-Republican U.S. government that was campaigning for war in the aftermath of 9/11, but moderate and even liberal politicians in the Democratic party. Soon Zeno was predicting that "patriotic fever leads inevitably in one direction—to war."

Cressida felt such distress, she had difficulty breathing.

Not contempt for the political propaganda fanned on all sides like deliberately set fires but fear—of what the new military invasion would lead to, beyond estimation.

And how petty their lives seemed now, "civilian" lives. In particular, her life as an undergraduate at St. Lawrence University in the small town of Canton, New York. *Why have I come here! This is such a mistake.*

IT CAME TO her then: the wars were monstrous, and made monsters of those who waged them.

The Iraq War, the Afghanistan War.

In time, civilians too would become monstrous, for this is the nature of war.

Even before Brett Kincaid had returned from Iraq disfigured and broken, Cressida had believed this.

That first year at St. Lawrence University she'd spent much of her time alone. Walking along the great wide rushing river—the St. Lawrence River. Alone with books, alone with her work. And in the near distance like cascading water the buzz and thrum of others' voices, laughter.

She'd become deeply immersed in one of her courses—"Romantics & Revolutionaries." It was like Cressida to focus on a single area of study to the neglect of others as it was like her to admire one of her instructors above the others, in this case a professor named Eddinger who lectured in a rapid voice that dazzled and intimidated even as he paced about at the front of the lecture hall like a raptor preparing to strike. He was a short slight-bodied man of her father's approximate age. His face was weatherworn, ugly. Yet a face of such *intense ugliness,* Cressida was captivated.

And captivated too by Eddinger's impassioned readings of excerpts from Mary Wollstonecraft's *A Vindication of the Rights of Women* and William Wordsworth's *Prelude;* poems from William Blake's *Songs of Innocence & Experience* that entered her imagination powerfully. Cressida had never before read Mary Shelley's *Frankenstein; or, The*

Modern Prometheus, and chose to write her term paper for the course on this curious prose-parable that was so very different in both tone and substance from the myriad manifestations of "Frankenstein" in the popular imagination.

Soon, *Frankenstein* entered Cressida's dreams. Not content with composing a conventional paper of about twenty-five pages Cressida felt obliged to present her material in an experimental form: a collage of texts by Mary Shelley and other "revolutionary" thinkers (Friedrich Nietzsche, Oscar Wilde, Sigmund Freud, Franz Kafka), illustrations of Dr. Frankenstein and his monster (including original drawings by Cressida herself), and a "deconstructed" argument about *Frankenstein* (by Cressida Mayfield). The more Cressida worked on the project, the more driven she was to work on it further; as she'd become obsessed with M. C. Escher in high school, so she became obsessed with the *Frankenstein project* in the spring term of her freshman year at St. Lawrence University. As usual in such circumstances she neglected her other courses; her awareness of her residence-hall suite mates was so slight, often she couldn't recall their names, or their faces. *Am I rude?—so sorry!* But Cressida wasn't sorry, and she never apologized.

Weeks passed. The May 1 deadline for term papers in "Romantics & Revolutionaries" passed. Vaguely Cressida was aware of the deadline yet with a part of her mind she seemed to have thought of herself as exempt from it since, unlike Professor Eddinger's other students, she wasn't involved in writing a mere term paper for a university course but in presenting the ultimate interpretation of *Frankenstein* in all its forms.

Yet each time Cressida believed the *Frankenstein project* was finished, she discovered yet another theme that had to be explored. And then it seemed to her necessary that the various texts, including her own "argument," should be presented in appropriate fonts, and in some cases written by hand (by Cressida herself, in imitation of the original writers' handwriting); it seemed necessary that the entire project be presented on double, oversized pages, with hand-bound covers; for in the Age of the Computer, what is more appropriate to an evocation of Mary Shelley's (singular, fated) monster than a one-of-a-kind project that could not be replicated? Brilliantly, or so she believed, Cressida presented "Cressida Mayfield's" term-paper argument in the distinctive font of a typewriter, to set it apart from computer-fonts. And then, she discovered H. G. Wells's *The Island of Dr. Moreau,* and felt obliged to consider it in her project, since Dr. Moreau was a debased type of Dr. Frankenstein; she felt obliged to include a deliberately crude comic strip to dramatize her thesis that mankind is destined to create monsters that, once created, turn against their creators. And she was inspired, very late one night, to include a dialogue between two individuals on the subject of the federal government's "crusade against terror": one of them a young soldier in the U.S. Army and the other an older man, a veteran of World War II. (These were, respectively, Brett Kincaid and Zeno Mayfield though of course Cressida's father had never served in the military.) Girls in her residence hall were curious about Cressida's project, which involved original and striking drawings, except—"Isn't this too long? Aren't you working too hard? When is the deadline?"

Cressida shrugged. Deadline?

How petty it seemed to her, how *school-girlish,* to worry about a deadline. When Professor Eddinger received her project, he would make an exception of her, she was certain.

A first draft of the completed project was fifty-two (thick, double) pages long; the fourth, final draft was seventy-six pages. Not a term paper but an outsized book measuring fourteen inches by six inches, with a beautiful hand-designed cover into which was set an original drawing (by Cressida Mayfield) of Frankenstein's monster as an uncannily human-looking figure in a military uniform.

At last, near the end of the spring term, Cressida brought to Professor Eddinger's departmental office a large box containing the *Frankenstein project,* leaving it with a (disapproving) secretary who promised to place it on the professor's desk. She thought *He will summon me! He will call me to come see him.*

She was sure of this. She'd seen how, through the semester, Eddinger had often glanced in her direction, even when she hadn't raised her hand to answer one of his provocative questions. *He is aware of me. He knows me.* Cressida had not missed a single class in "Romantics & Revolutionaries" nor had her grades in the course been lower than A.

And so, she wasn't surprised when Eddinger sent her a terse but friendly email asking her to please come see him.

She wasn't surprised when she entered his office, to see that he'd spread out the *Frankenstein project* on a table, and that he clearly admired it.

Standing beside Professor Eddinger, Cressida saw that he was a wiry-trim little man, just slightly taller than she was, with legs that appeared foreshortened, like a dwarf's; though in no way was his body misshapen. He wore a checked shirt with short boxy sleeves to the elbow and trousers of some plain fabric, no necktie and on his feet, surprisingly, sandals with black socks which he had not worn during the semester, at least not while lecturing in their class. His hair was thin, a gray-buttery color; his face was fine-creased like something that has been left out in the sun. And his eyes were startling-bright, fixed upon her.

"Miss Mayfield! This is extraordinary work. I have never received anything remotely like it in thirty-six years of university teaching, here at St. Lawrence and previously at Williams."

Cressida was stricken with shyness. Though she'd imagined words like these yet now she could not respond.

"Decoding *Frankenstein* as a cultural and 'biological' phenomenon is a wonderfully original approach, Miss Mayfield. And I feel quite the same way that you do, about our current wars—the 'crusade against terror.' Is it possible that you are just a—freshman?"

Cressida nodded, *yes.*

"It's amazing, bold work. It must have required weeks of effort. I'm particularly struck by these brilliant line-drawings of the 'monster' as a boy-soldier who becomes a 'military strategist'—his metamorphosis is entirely convincing. In fact I'm flattered, Miss Mayfield, you've handed in more than we would expect at this university for a senior honors thesis, and the assignment was just a term paper, to count for approximately forty percent of your grade in my course."

Was she expected to speak? Cressida could not think of anything to say.

"The problem is, Miss Mayfield, which you must have considered— this 'term paper' is twelve days late. Even if I'd extended the deadline for you, that would have been over a weekend at the most—let's say that you've handed it in nine days late."

To this, Cressida had no excuse.

She'd rushed to Professor Eddinger's office in tossed-on clothes— denim jacket, jeans. Her hair was a mad scribble about her small pale girl's face. Vaguely she'd thought the day would be chilly and overcast with fog but now at near-noon it was brightly sunny, and warm. She could not think what to say to Professor Eddinger who spoke to her so reasonably, and with regret.

"You see, Miss Mayfield, in the most elementary sense it isn't 'fair'—it isn't 'just'—to make an exception for a single student, while others struggle to get their work in on time."

Cressida stood stunned. Cressida did not dare lift her eyes to the professor's bright alert eyes, that were fixed upon her in a way she wished to perceive as kindly, and not assessing.

"That no one else in the class could possibly have accomplished this in the same period of time is beside the point, you see. I'd given a deadline—many times. And you chose to ignore it."

Ignore. Cressida tried to comprehend *ignore.*

"Can you explain why this is so late? Apart from its length, and its excellence, I mean."

Cressida stood very still trying to think. A flutter of thoughts in her head, like frantic butterflies. A terrible impulse came to her, to seize the *Frankenstein project* in her arms, to take it back from Professor Eddinger and run from his office—except, where?

The river. To the river. You must throw yourself into the river.

"I hope you were not 'experimenting' with me? Testing me, to see if I would accept this late paper, despite the deadline?"

Numbly Cressida shook her head, *no.*

In slow drowning waves the knowledge washed over Cressida, her professor did not think that she was so special after all.

He didn't know her father Zeno. Was that it!

To the river! You are so ridiculous, so ugly.

Ugly should not be allowed to live.

When Cressida couldn't seem to reply, Professor Eddinger continued, now in a rapid, vexed voice: "Miss Mayfield, there is no question but that your work is good. I mean—very good. I mean—brilliant. I found myself utterly enchanted by this 'project' even though, initially, I'd been reluctant even to examine it, because you handed it in so late, and without any attempt of an excuse—a medical excuse, for instance." Eddinger paused, as if giving Cressida an opportunity to claim—what? (Dyslexia, autism? Schizophrenia, bipolar disorder, paranoia? Stupidity?) "Unlike some gifted students I've had in the past, you don't work swiftly and carelessly—or, if you work swiftly, you take exceptional care, and revise. And expand. This is the way of the 'creative artist'—to revise, expand. But there really isn't time for that sort of perfectionism in a university semester. And 'Romantics & Revolutionaries' is an undergraduate, three-hundred-level course. I would not criticize you for spending too much time on this project but only for refusing to acknowledge the restrictions others were obliged to acknowledge. Obviously this is an A-plus project, if it were to be graded at all." On a sheet of paper, Eddinger scrawled, in red Magic Marker ink, A+, as if he were speaking now to a kindergarten student. "You see, this is the 'grade' if there were a grade. But the project is nine days late, and I have made my requirements as clear as possible, and cannot and will not alter them for anyone. I realize that this is petty, Miss Mayfield—but it is necessary, for pettiness can be a virtue, at times. Because the project is late, it must be penalized. Not the project, which is A plus as we have seen, but its lateness—

that grade is D." With an irritable flourish, Eddinger scrawled D.

Was he intending to suggest the childishness of grades? The pettiness? Yet Cressida stood stunned, uncomprehending.

In truth, she'd forgotten that she would be *graded*. In her long hours immersed in the project, particularly in the numerous line-drawings she'd done out of which she'd selected just a fraction to include in the project, she had forgotten that she would be *handing in* the work to a professor, to be assessed and judged.

"I—I don't know what I . . . I don't . . . I guess, I . . ."

Like a brain-damaged person Cressida stammered. These words were thick and ungainly in her mouth like big clots of uncooked dough and her mouth was suddenly dry of saliva, she could not swallow.

"Unless," Eddinger persisted, "—there is some sort of 'disability' you might claim? A health issue, medical excuse . . ."

Cressida shook her head, *no*.

Vehemently Cressida shook her head, *no*.

She felt a wave of disgust wash over her. Self-disgust like a bad taste in the mouth.

For there was a *familiarity* about this situation, it was not new or original. *Déjà vu* was the term, always accompanied by a sensation of disgust, nausea.

In high school too Cressida Mayfield had surprised, shocked, disconcerted, disappointed and annoyed her teachers, she'd heard their voices of regret tinged with vexation, frustration; she heard her parents' voices—*Oh Cressida! Oh honey—again?*

And Zeno, registering disgust as well as dismay. *God damn, Cressie! Not again.*

Blindly Cressida turned, and ran out of Professor Eddinger's office. She heard him call after her but paid no heed.

Run run run you are so stupid, so ugly. Get to the river before it's too late and they stop you.

→ ←

At the river, south of Canton.

On the riverbank walking swiftly. Away from the small town, and from the university she'd come to despise.

For it was a death sentence, unmistakably.

If she did not lack courage.

Better to have never been born. This is the most ancient wisdom.

As far as her legs could carry her. Though she'd been exhausted from sleepless nights working on the *Frankenstein project* yet now she was suffused with a strange radiant throbbing energy and she was whispering and muttering to herself as in a language newly discovered and known only to her.

How she hated the university, and all who dwelled there! Misshapen creatures ascending and descending stairs and many of the stairs upside-down and none took notice for the damned souls in Hell have no eyes with which to see their own ludicrous fates.

(The university that despised *her.*)

(The university that had rejected *her.*)

(But Cressida could not ever admit this! How to explain to her parents?)

(In all of the biological world it is only the *human world* in which parents are stricken by the shame of their offspring. Not in any species other than *Homo sapiens* is this possible.)

Better just to die, to put an end to her life. It would be a mercy certainly to spare poor Zeno saying another time with forced Daddy-bravado *But still, Cressie—you can try . . . Maybe transfer in your junior year to Cornell . . .*

And Arlette would want to hug her, to console her. And Cressida in a paroxysm of self-loathing *did not want to be consoled.*

As far as her (now faltering) legs would carry her. Whispering and muttering and laughing to herself. The professor had not liked her. Always you believe that those whom you adore will adore you. Not in any species other than *Homo sapiens* is this possible—this delusion! The professor had seemed to be inviting his most brilliant student to *claim a disability*—or did he think she was crazy?

"The fact is: I am the sanest person I know."

Sadly Cressida laughed. *That* was a depressing fact.

Running out of the professor's office like a little cornered rat that has managed to escape her corner. The look in the man's face—in his eyes. He'd been frightened of her!

God damn she wished now she'd taken the *Frankenstein project* away with her but she'd have had to step around the stunned professor to approach the table and might've come close to touching him and the professor might've recoiled from Cressida or might have attempted to restrain her and—

Better to forget. Erase from her mind.

Trembling at the thought of stepping so close to him. Risking the man's touch.

As it was, his eyes had caught at hers. She would not soon forget *that.*

Because the project is late it must be penalized.

Better for you to die. Never to have been born.

Her other university courses she'd neglected for weeks in order to work on the project for Eddinger who'd rejected her anyway. And now exams in a few days for which she wasn't prepared. And an exam in Eddinger's course, she could not possibly take.

Could not possibly see the man again.

He had rejected *her.*

And now she hated *him.*

Thinking how she deserved to be annihilated, obliterated. Erased. All so *petty.*

And what a clean death it would be, to throw herself into this rapidly-rushing river so much wider and deeper than the Black Snake River of Beechum County. Swept downstream, vanished. No one would know where she'd gone.

No one would miss her. Not for hours.

Except the riverbank was choked with underbrush and debris from recent storms. Thorns catching at her clothing, her hands.

The St. Lawrence had flooded its banks a few weeks before. Small bridges over local creeks had been washed away. She was desperate to find a bridge, for she would have to throw herself from a bridge in order to drown most effectively.

The nearest bridge was back in Canton. But traffic flowed over this bridge in a continuous stream.

There stood Brett Kincaid at a little distance, on the riverbank.

Cressida don't, that is a mistake.

Wanting to hide her face in shame so that Brett Kincaid would not see.

I am your secret friend Cressida. You can't hurt yourself, you would be hurting me.

Was this true? Cressida wanted to think it was true.

Now she was more than two miles from Canton in the country-side she was beginning to feel better.

Beginning to feel relieved, less exhausted.

It was so, she wanted to "die"—she wanted to "disappear"—but she did not want to *be dead.*

Dead was dull flat black-matte. *Dead* was an empty hive.

If *dead* she would never see Brett Kincaid again.

Her brother he would be, her brother-in-law—her *secret friend.*

She would not ever see her parents again, and Juliet—whom she loved.

"If they love me I guess I love them."

She had no existence, in herself. From earliest childhood she had believed this. Rather she was a reflecting surface, reflecting others' perception of her, and love of her.

So strangely her heart was beating, she could not catch her breath.

This happened to Cressida sometimes when she was very excited, anxious. When she was very happy.

Her narrow rib cage rising and falling and quavering with the quick pulse of her heart.

Heedless if anyone might be observing her she lay down on the weedy riverbank, amid thorns and spiky grasses. This was not a comfortable place in which to lie but when Cressida's heart beat quickly she had learned to lie down flat on her back and lift her arms above her head and slowly inhale/exhale and to repeat this several times and often then the rapid heartbeat would slow to normal. She'd never told anyone about this infirmity, if that was what it was.

Heart palpitations. Racing to keep pace with her thoughts.

She had hiked several miles from Canton. Now her legs were tired, with a pleasurable ache. In the May sunshine lying on her back in the spongy grass she fell into a doze. She fell into a dream of home—of the creaky porch-swing on the side deck of the house on Cumberland Avenue in which suddenly she was lying, wrapped in Daddy's disreputable old red-plaid camping blanket from L.L. Bean, that Mom was always trying to throw away and Daddy was always retrieving from the trash. She smiled, remembering: that scratchy old blanket, that gave such comfort on chilly nights! Yet still she was lying in the sun—the sun beat against her eyelids. *Cressida? Cressida.* Not twenty feet away the young soldier regarded her with concerned eyes. He alone knew her heart, he alone cared for her. He was leaning on crutches—this was a new development. She could only just make out his face which was cruelly scarred.

"MISS?"—it was a male voice, more annoyed than concerned, waking her from her stuporous sleep; a man, a young soldier, in U.S. Army fatigues, wanting to sit in the seat beside her and so would she move her things? "Thanks!"

In New York City in the massive Port Authority bus terminal she transferred to a bus bound for Watertown in upstate New York. Here she saw many young soldiers in fatigues, in small groups in the cavernous waiting room and queuing in bus lines and among these soldiers were young women. By this time she was very sick.

Head wracked in pain. Each thought was a shard of glass sharp and wounding.

Skin burning and sensitive to the touch as if the outermost layer had been peeled off and she was dazed and exhausted from a dozen trips to the lavatory her insides emptying out in rushes of scalding diarrhea. She could not keep food down but gagged helplessly. Even water, she could not tolerate.

Coming home. If anyone will know me.

Forgive me.

PART III

❧ ☙

The Return

THIRTEEN

The Long Wall

April 2012

*D*RIVING THE LONG WALL.
    Sixty-foot-high wall with no (visible) end.

So suddenly the wall looms close beside you—you failed to see the beginning of the wall and can't see the end.

The wall is of finite substance: concrete. But its circumference is infinite.

You are outside the wall, driving the long wall. Inside, the wall encircles.

Though the (exterior) wall can be measured the (interior) wall cannot be measured.

The color of old, soiled bones. The long wall.

In the distance you'd seen the long wall but had not recognized it for never before had you seen anything like the long wall sixty feet high bordering a state highway.

Inside, hidden from civilian eyes, the Clinton Correctional Facility for Men at Dannemora, New York.

Until suddenly the long wall looms beside your vehicle so high you can't see its height nor can you see the guards' watch-towers at intervals at the top of the long wall.

The long wall, that looms just a few feet to the right of your vehicle. The long wall that swallows up most of the view from the windshield of your vehicle.

How many miles on Route 375! How many hours through the careening countryside, glacier-hills of the Adirondacks in the coldest most northern edge of New York State.

The long wall, of the hue of old bones. Bordering the small town of Dannemora.

To the right of Route 375 North, the long wall stretching to infinity.

To the left of Route 375 North, the bleak storefronts of Dannemora.

Driving the long wall where at the (gated) entrance you will be permitted inside. Where somewhere inside the long wall he is waiting for you.

Into the small bleak town of Dannemora outside the long wall as the banks of the Styx border that bleak river. Into and through Dannemora which is a deserted town at this hour of the morning and yet, the long wall continues.

FOURTEEN

The Church of the Good Thief

March 2012

HE WAS A TRUSTEE. He was *trusted*.

In the mental unit and in the adjoining hospice he was an orderly, for it was his role to establish and maintain *order*.

Though not a (baptized) Catholic yet he was Father Kranach's closest and most trusted assistant in all matters of the upkeep of the Church of the Good Thief and at counseling sessions in which the chaplain participated; and an editor of the prison newspaper which appeared on alternate Mondays.

He'd been a corporal in the U.S. Army. Wounded in the U.S. Army in the war in Iraq and somehow, this was known and respected in the prison among both inmates and guards.

Though long-ago discharged. Sent back home wounded and broken and less than a man yet through prayer strengthened and reclaimed to himself as a man trapped to the waist in quicksand might haul himself out of his imminent death by the frantic actions of his hands, hands and arms, pulling himself up by a rope to save his life so the corporal had managed to restore some measure of his manhood and the dignity of his manhood and some measure of his ruined soul.

Prayer to others beside Jesus Christ for instance to Saint Dismas who was the Good Thief, he'd learned to pray as you might speak to one of your own kind, a lost brother.

Of the two malefactors crucified beside Jesus on Calvary hill it was Saint Dismas who was the "Good Thief" of legend. For it was Saint Dismas who had rebuked the other thief who'd taunted Jesus if ye be King of the Jews, save thyself and us, with the fierce words, *Dost not thou fear God, seeing thou art in the same condemnation? And we indeed justly; for we receive the due reward of our deeds: but this man hath done nothing amiss.* And he said unto Jesus, *Lord remember me when thou comest into thy kingdom.*

And in his last agony yet Jesus said unto him, *Verily I say unto thee, Today shalt thou be with me in paradise.*

Many times the corporal had read these words in the Bible, given to him by the Catholic priest Father Kranach. Many times reading the book of Luke which was one of the shorter books of the New Testament, filled with wonders as with horror and revulsion.

For Jesus did despair. There was no doubt, Jesus did despair as a man would despair in his place.

And it was about the sixth hour, and there was a darkness over all the earth until the ninth hour. And the sun was darkened, and the veil of the temple was rent. And when Jesus had cried with a loud voice, he said, Father, into thy hands I commend my spirit: and having said thus, he gave up the ghost.

Holding the Bible at an awkward angle in front of his face. His single "good" eye. Near-transparent fine-printed pages lifted to a wan fluorescent light in his cell shared with another inmate.

Gave up the ghost. These words so struck him.

Gave up the ghost. He had wished this but God had not taken from him his life that was damned, and worse than damned—of no more worth than trash, feces dried and flaking on a nearby wall not hosed-down in years.

In his former life in his former religion which was the Protestant religion the corporal had not known of the Good Thief for he had known little of the existence of saints and the influence of saints upon humankind. And still in this new radically altered life—(he did not wish to think this was the *afterlife*)—he was slow to believe in the authority of the Holy Roman Catholic Church and in the rituals and prayers of that Church though his closest friend was Father Fred Kranach who had counseled the corporal in his hour of need seeing in the corporal's ruined-boy's-face the innocence and purity of his heart and the remorse for all he had done to injure others.

It was Father Kranach who'd explained to the corporal that the Church had not canonized the Good Thief but the common belief was, Jesus had himself canonized the Good Thief in his agony on the cross.

Nor was the name "Dismas" to be found in the Scripture but only in common legend.

Meaning that Saint Dismas is outside the Church. An outlaw and a loser yet blessed of God.

And so it is, Father Kranach said, no one prays to Saint Dismas who is not an outlaw and a loser.

The corporal said, But your church is named for him, Father—the Church of the Good Thief!—for this seemed to the corporal very strange, and wonderful. And Father Kranach said, That is the wisdom of the Church. Saint Dismas is a rogue saint recognized as the only way to God for men like the most desperate inmates of Clinton Correctional, those who have committed unspeakable and unforgiveable acts and who are as far from God as the inhabitants of a cave are far from sunlight. Those men who would be ashamed to approach Jesus, for the evil in their hearts, yet are able to approach Saint Dismas for all that they know of him through legend.

But he isn't a real saint?—in the Catholic Church?—the corporal seemed anxious to know; and Father Kranach said, If Dismas is a "real" saint or not is irrelevant, Brett. For all that matters is that men come to God through him, and find Jesus through him, who would otherwise be lost. That is enough *sainthood*.

WERE YOU COERCED into confessing he'd been asked repeatedly and always he said no, I was not.

Of his own free will he had confessed to the terrible crimes he'd committed even those he could not recall clearly through the mist of memory and when trying to recall, it was like trying to hear a small still voice amid a crazed clanking and clattering of heavy machinery.

There is something hurt in my brain the corporal told them. In a hoarse and numbed voice answering their questions for seven hours and his gray-ghost-figure and faltering words videotaped through the long night. Hoping he would be granted mercy, a death by firing squad which was a soldier's proper death standing at attention in some remnant of pride despite the black hood over his head.

Informed then, such an execution would be only in Nevada.

He would sit on Death Row at Dannemora, they told him. For it was rare any prisoners were executed in New York State in recent memory.

And this was stunning to him, and a cause of dismay.

For he had pleaded guilty. To all charges, to any charges brought against him he had pleaded guilty for there was no yearning in the corporal greater than a yearning for expiation, and for annihilation.

Such a death then would be instantaneous and he could not but believe, his soul too would be annihilated.

Give up the ghost—he had wished for this release!

Yet somehow it happened despite his intentions, the corporal was not allowed to enter a plea of *guilty* to first-degree homicide after all.

The question was, where was the girl's body? Without the girl's body could the corporal be charged with *murder*? For the corporal's confession was of no more intrinsic legal worth than the corporal's denial of the crime would have been, in the absence of witnesses to the crime and "substantial" physical evidence.

So the corporal's lawyer argued.

Yet, the prosecutor denied this vehemently.

The prosecutor argued that there is legal precedent for such charges. Verdicts of *guilty* have many times been brought against defendants in cases in which the bodies of the victims have not been found, having been hidden or destroyed by the defendants; and in this case, there was the defendant's confession, the corroboration of several witnesses having seen the defendant with the missing girl earlier in the evening, and enough physical evidence to proceed to trial.

He'd led them to Sandhill Point in the Nautauga Preserve. Desperate to reveal to them the girl's broken body. He'd told them of the shallow grave in which they had laid her—in which he had laid her—covered her with dirt and leaves, with their hands—the butts of their rifles—then it seemed to him this was a mistake for there had been no grave in this rocky soil but he'd staggered carrying her body that was still warm, limp and heavy for one so small he carried to the river to be swept away and lost where the Black Snake emptied into Lake Ontario miles away to the west. By this time exhausted and staggering and sick in his gut, terribly sick having to lean on a deputy's arm and his wrists cuffed at his waist in front of his body yet still he was having difficulty keeping his balance. And the disgust for him in their faces, he could not bear to see. And worse yet the irritation, the impatience, as in a game among the more deft and skilled players there pass glances of derision aimed at those less deft and skilled, and these scarcely disguised from the objects of derision. And he was made to think *I am not a man now. I am something less than a man.* Some of the deputies had known Brett Kincaid as a quarterback on the Carthage High School varsity team two years running and one of those years a championship year in the Adirondack District, not so very long ago. And now to see Brett Kincaid in this state and to hear his shamed words was very hard for these men who'd known Graham Kincaid also.

Afterward too weak to stand he was taken to the Carthage hospital ER to be given IV fluids for "severe dehydration" and kept in the hospital overnight before being released to the Carthage jail still weak and uncertain on his feet and kept in isolation and under twenty-four-hour suicide watch it was believed *for his own protection.*

At all times under suicide-watch until finally he gave up all hope—for the present.

And then in the Beechum County Courthouse where he was taken in shackles. Here the large, first-floor courtroom was strangely crowded and the mood was agitated, excited. For there were strong feelings in this place—a strong bias against the corporal who had killed the nineteen-year-old girl and dumped her body in the river and a strong bias in favor of the corporal who was a wounded war-veteran believed to have possibly confessed to a crime he had not committed in order to shield certain of his friends, and suffering from "neurological impairment."

After months of deliberation there was to be no trial. In this, the citizens of Carthage were disappointed.

No trial, and no jury. For there was no protestation of innocence on the part of the defendant.

Judge Nathan Brede was presiding. In his late fifties Brede was the highest-ranked judge in Beechum County, a former prosecutor.

Impervious and unblinking Brede was a stranger to the corporal gazing down at the young man scarred and part-blind in the wreckage of his life.

And how do you plead, Mr. Kincaid?

Your Honor, my client pleads guilty to one count of voluntary manslaughter as charged and one count of illegal disposal of a body as charged.

Do you so plead, Mr. Kincaid?

Your Honor, my client so pleads.

Mr. Kincaid, do you understand the terms of this guilty plea? Do you understand the consequences?

In the courtroom there was quiet as the corporal seemed to summon himself from some distance, to lift his eyes to the calm-assessing eyes of Judge Brede.

As in a near-inaudible voice the corporal murmured *Yes Your Honor.*

You are pleading guilty to one count of voluntary manslaughter as charged and one count of illegal disposal of a body as charged?

Yes Your Honor.

Yes? Did you say yes, Mr. Kincaid?

Yes Your Honor.

Yet it was not so clear to him. All that he knew clearly was the word *guilty.*

And the sentence pronounced by the judge—*fifteen to twenty years.*

Fifteen to twenty years! He had been waiting to hear the death sentence.

Stunned and speechless standing shackled and waiting—and yet, the court had been adjourned with a strike of the judge's gavel.

So abruptly, the sentencing was over.

So abruptly, the corporal's fate had been determined.

Not to die but—to live?

Without a backward glance the judge had exited the courtroom. If Nathan Brede had been a former associate, still more a friendly acquaintance of Zeno Mayfield, he had not glanced in Mayfield's direction, where the father of the victim was sitting in the second row of seats; nor was his attention drawn to the bizarre keening of the defendant's mother Ethel Kincaid who could not have reacted more extravagantly if the judge had sentenced her son to death.

At the front of the courtroom the corporal remained stunned and slow-blinking for he'd believed that he had confessed to the murder—murders—hadn't the police officers predicted he would sit on Death Row for the remainder of his life? Yet, the charge seemed to have been reduced to *voluntary manslaughter.*

As if the corporal had not been of sufficient sound mind and body, to have committed a true murder.

And his lawyer confiding in him, in an undertone almost gloating, and repellent to the corporal, he'd be eligible for parole in just seven years.

Good behavior! Out in seven years, man.

He shrank from the man. This was not the original lawyer who had volunteered to represent Brett Kincaid but another, younger.

They knew they couldn't win shit. Not without the body. They knew they were fucked. Man, seven years! Did you luck out.

Yet, the corporal had been sentenced. The corporal would be re-moved from the courtroom under restraint.

Shackled at his wrists and legs. Like a wild animal he'd been shackled to be brought into the courtroom to be seated at a table at the front of the room beneath the judge's high bench where he might be observed by all in the courtroom, in pity and disgust.

For in the jail, the corporal had behaved unpredictably. The COs had deemed him a security-risk to himself as to others.

For it seemed that a sudden fury flared up in the corporal, at un-predictable times. As he could not control seizures of his upper body or paralyzing rushes of pain in his legs so he could not control these outbreaks of temper that ran their course within minutes, or seconds leaving onlookers frightened of him.

In the front row of seats his mother Ethel Kincaid continued weep-ing. Wailing loudly and bitterly like a TV female shameless in emo-tion to no purpose other than to make others uncomfortable and to rouse in them an acute wish to escape her company. For it seemed clear to Mrs. Kincaid that her son's enemies in Carthage had cam-paigned against him, and had won; and in his physical state, a sen-tence of fifteen to twenty years at Dannemora was a death sentence, for he would never be released in his lifetime.

Bailiffs held back the distraught Mrs. Kincaid, who wanted to rush to her son to embrace him. As the corporal himself shrank from the excited woman and could not bring himself to face her.

Exiting the courtroom stiff-walked by bailiffs gripping each of his arms above the elbow. The awkward shackle-shuffle through a door-way at the rear which no one except courthouse employees and law enforcement officers could use as Mrs. Kincaid cried after them—*Murderers! Murderers of my poor soldier-son!*—and then to a corridor and another door outside which a van with barred back windows was waiting to transport Brett Kincaid immediately to the Clinton Correctional Facility at Dannemora, New York, to begin his indeter-minate sentence *fifteen to twenty years.*

AT DANNEMORA, at the Canadian border—"Little Siberia."

For much of the first year, in isolation.

For it was believed by the warden of the facility, K.O. Heike, that the corporal's crime was such, the publicity had been such, some of the inmates would have the impression that Brett Kincaid had raped and murdered a child, and his life in the general population would be at risk.

BUT WHAT RELIEF THEN, in that *other world*.

Now he'd *crossed over*. Now he was imprisoned like a beast, and surrounded by beasts. And in the eyes of the COs—the guards—there was no ambiguity, he was not the corporal but only just a young-white-Caucasian-inmate B. Kincaid with *medical disabilities* who'd been designated *security-risk* at the time of his transfer.

The terms of his incarceration were so much a part of his official identity, it was as if *fifteen to twenty years* had been tattooed on his forehead.

Manslaughter, voluntary. Fifteen to twenty years.

As soon as a man was incarcerated at Dannemora, he would think of how much time he must "do" before being released. How much time before he might apply for parole.

Except if his sentence was life-without-parole. Except if his sentence was death.

Often, the corporal forgot, and thought—*Am I on Death Row?*

For in even his lucid moments the corporal did not truly believe that he would ever be freed from the isolation unit, from a confinement of a few discolored walls, floors and ceilings, and bars, let alone from Dannemora—(of which he had but the vaguest impression having seen the astonishing long sixty-foot-high concrete wall of the color of old, soiled bones when he'd been first brought to the facility in shackles to begin his sentence as prescribed by law); he did not truly believe that time was continuing to pass like a stream bearing him along as in his younger, former life but rather, time had become a molten substance very sluggishly moving and it was against this movement, against the current and not with it, he had to struggle just to stay afloat and keep from drowning.

This effort, this exertion—most days, it required all of his strength.

Except for a shifting team of volunteer-lawyers, most of them newly graduated from upstate law schools—Albany, Cornell, Buffalo—he had few visitors.

He had few callers.

And sometimes, if a call came for B. Kincaid, he refused to speak to the caller.

His throat closed up, as if a fist had been shoved down it.

The *Kincaid case* as it was called had generated controversy in legal circles, in upstate New York. But this controversy did not involve the corporal who refused to give thought to what his life had become as a *case*.

God did not think of a man as a *case*. For a *case* is to be *solved*—and a man cannot be *solved*.

Still it was known to him, for he'd received letters on the subject from numerous parties, that in Beechum County where the search for the *missing girl* had prevailed for months there remained outrage in some quarters that Brett Kincaid's sentence was so "light" and that he would be eligible for parole in so few years; and there remained outrage in other quarters, that Brett Kincaid had been incarcerated at all, and in the notorious maximum-security prison at Dannemora, for the prevailing belief in these quarters was that the wounded Iraq War veteran was not the man responsible for the disappearance of Cressida Mayfield; or, if he was the man, he hadn't been legally responsible for his actions and if he'd been institutionalized at all, he should have been sent to a psychiatric hospital for treatment.

Defense funds had been established, to "bring justice" to Brett Kincaid. Who these individuals were, calling for funds on the Internet, what connection they had with one another or with Corporal Kincaid or any of the volunteer-lawyers officially attached to his case the corporal had no idea. Father Kranach was concerned, none of these strangers was accountable for money sent to them in Brett Kincaid's name but Brett Kincaid himself seemed scarcely to care.

Saying to the priest, "Anywhere I am is Death Row. And where I am, I belong."

ILLUMINATION ROUNDS—*white phosphorus*—*streaming onto the enemy.*

Deafening roar of attack helicopters, he woke cringing and whimpering in his sleep and the interior of his mouth and lungs coated with sand.

Both his legs were gone. Yet, the pain remained.

His hands, his arms to the elbow. Blown off, and the stark white bone shining through the blood bright as ridiculous false blood of a child's TV horror film.

Screaming he'd heard his name, one of his friends screaming his name he was hearing this now but could not see where.

Fuck they deserved some fucking fun, the guys said. If you survived and had not been blown up or shrapnel in your guts or heads you deserved some fucking fun shooting at civilians like rats freaking in terror, cutting off a finger, an ear, a teeny dick, nipples—making a pouch of civilian-Iraq faces sewn together like to keep snuff in, or meds.

See it's like some warrior-custom, Muksie was saying. Pouches made of enemy-faces and actual scalps to wear on your head but prob'ly you'd had to cure the damn things—like "taxidermy"—so they wouldn't rot and stink on your head.

THOSE WHO TELEPHONED Brett Kincaid in Clinton Correctional Facility were few. And all were female, from Carthage.

Of these the most persistent was Brett's mother Ethel Kincaid. For Ethel in her shrewdness had found a way to make calls to her incarcerated son at taxpayers' expense through a county family-services "emergency" fund.

As Ethel in her shrewdness and something very like a subversive sense of humor had found a way to keep alive her son's case in the Carthage press and TV news by announcing "fresh clues"—"new witnesses"—"exculpatory evidence"—at regular intervals, calling such local-media figures as Evvie Estes of WCTG-TV and Hal Roche of the *Carthage Post-Journal* and when they failed to respond to her phone messages approaching them on the street, stalking them to their very homes secure in the knowledge that probably, certainly, no one in Carthage would dare to summon the police to arrest her, Ethel Kincaid the grieving mother of the wrongly persecuted, wrongly convicted and incarcerated Iraq War hero Corporal Brett Kincaid.

Since the late summer of 2005 virtually every lawyer in Beechum County including those long retired and elderly had been contacted by Mrs. Kincaid to aid in the campaign to free her son and had learned to avoid the grieving mother.

Even individuals convinced that Corporal Kincaid was unjustly convicted and willing to contribute money to his "defense fund" had learned to avoid the grieving mother.

It had happened more than once that Ethel Kincaid had approached Cressida Mayfield's parents in public places, individually— Arlette she'd approached on the front walk of the battered women's shelter in the suburban village of Mount Olive at which Arlette had become a frequent volunteer following her daughter's disappearance, with a demand that Arlette "make full disclosure" of the whereabouts of her daughter; Zeno she'd approached in a Carthage restaurant in which Zeno was seated with friends, denouncing him as a "class-warfare enemy" whose daughter had "run off" and was alive somewhere in an "illegal conspiracy" to keep her innocent son in prison.

At a performance of Euripides' *Medea* staged at Carthage Community College in the spring of 2008 the startled audience had at first thought it was a continuation of the play, performed in "modern dress," when, after the lights came up, a middle-aged woman with a ravaged-girl's face leapt into the aisle to declaim in a loud voice that here she was a "true loving mother"—"not a crazy monster-mother like Medea"—but did anybody "give a damn about" *her*?

Only after some minutes did it become clear, to a portion of the audience at least, that the thin, excitable woman with eyes like the glittering steel balls of a pinball machine was in fact Ethel Kincaid the mother of Corporal Brett Kincaid who'd confessed to the murder of Cressida Mayfield in the fall of 2005.

The shrewdest maneuver Ethel Kincaid had yet attempted was to sue for public funds as a victim of 9/11.

Too God damn bad she hadn't thought of this until nine years after 9/11—four years after Brett was incarcerated—so it was hard to get people to take her lawsuit seriously arguing that she, Ethel Kincaid, was a victim of the terrorist attack if indirectly, as her only son Brett had been sent to Iraq to fight El Kwada—that is, the Muslim terrorists—and in that terrible place he'd been wounded in combat and sent home "disabled" and "defective" and as a result of this was "incarcerated" in a maximum-security prison in a Godforsaken corner of the state, hundreds of miles away virtually in Canada. None of this was her fault as the damaged lives of family members of individuals killed in the World Trade Center or in the hijacked airplanes were not their fault but the result of the terrorist attack from which the U.S. government had not protected its citizens. Ethel had written to the President in the White House as to other, more local politicians and not one of them had responded; and now she was picketing Beechum County family services believing that she deserved an upgrade on her payments and should not have to prove "paupership" but be allowed to own a car, at least.

In her state of nerves since July 2005, Ethel had retired from clerical work. She had not yet sought out employment, knowing there was a bias in Carthage against her.

She did collect unemployment. But that was a laugh, living at the "paupership line."

Far away in Dannemora, New York, Brett knew of these remarkable episodes in his mother's life through Ethel's boasting of them over the phone.

Steeling himself to listen. And sometimes, as her voice rang in his ears like struck glass, he did not listen.

"Never guess what your crazy old mother was doing just this week!"—so Ethel would exclaim as soon as Brett came on the line.

Saying, when Brett failed to respond as a normal son would respond, "Somebody has got to keep your case alive, God damn it! And that somebody has got to be your mother since nobody else gives a shit."

Ethel yearned to visit Brett at the prison but couldn't make the long trip by bus, her health had been ruined since that terrible summer of 2005—a bus trip would kill her. There was an offer from a cable-channel talk show to tell her son's side of the story if Mrs. Kincaid would allow the TV crew to drive her by "limousine" to Dannemora and accompany her to the prison gate and afterward be interviewed by the host *frankly and candidly* on the subject of visiting her only son in prison and such invitations Ethel considered seriously—wistfully—but Brett flatly refused.

"The world needs to be educated to your side of the story, Brett. So you will be granted a new trial or your sentence commuted by the governor."

And when Brett still failed to respond, saying in a wounded voice, "All the world believes you are *guilty*, Brett. Your enemies never gave you a chance and some you'd thought were your friends turned out to be your enemies and you have to do something about it."

The corporal seemed to be summoning himself from a long distance but then could manage only a shrug of a murmur his mother could barely hear: "Why?"

AND ANOTHER CALLER from Carthage was Arlette Mayfield.

Juliet's mother! Mrs. Mayfield! The corporal could not bear to hear the woman's voice and refused to come to the phone.

Out of cowardice, shame. Could not come to the phone.

And so, Arlette wrote to Brett Kincaid in the Clinton Correctional Facility, Dannemora, New York. He'd had to steel himself to open the handwritten letter for his instinct was to quickly dispose of it.

Dear Brett,

I am sorry you will not speak with me. But I will try again—of course.

I would like so much to hear your voice, Brett. I would like to see your face. I think of you so often—I pray for you. I think the bond between us is very deep though you and my daughter Juliet were not married yet it had seemed at times—(forgive me, this is strange to say, I know)—that you were my son-in-law. And of the Mayfield family.

There is so much between us, Brett, we must speak of before it is too late.

We were in the courtroom at the sentencing and it was then I felt so strongly, that you were of my family. Though I could not acknowledge it at that time. My heart was broken, I think—the loss of Cressida, that was also a loss of you.

I would not ask you about Cressida, Brett. So many others have asked you Why? Why do such a thing *but I would not ask you. If I came to visit there I would only just request to sit with you for a while in quietness and we would discover what God wishes from us. (I know it is forgiveness on my side but there may be more than this.)*

No one knows that I am writing to you, Brett. Not my dear Juliet nor my husband Zeno who would not understand for these years have been hard on him, without faith in God to guide him. My husband is a public man as they say—he is not so easy in his own soul.

And even Juliet, who is a Christian, as you know, has not had an easy time, so I would not tell Juliet, at least not at this time.

You are in my prayers, Brett. There is so much more that must pass between us!

In Jesus's name
Arlette Mayfield

This letter was dated July 9, 2008. The third anniversary of *that night.*

Several times Mrs. Mayfield wrote to Brett and each time he did not reply but kept the letter neatly folded in the Bible Father Kranach had given him; then, for what reason he could not have said, impulsively he did reply to Mrs. Mayfield's letter of November 11, 2008, writing on lined notebook paper with a stub of a pencil *Dear Mrs Mayfeld thak you. I have read your letters many times & but I don't think it is a good idea right now. Sincerly, Brett Kincaid.*

SCREAMING. *Like some sort animal torn apart by hyenas.*
Screaming screaming! But worse, when the screaming ceased.

AT THE START of his incarceration it had been his thought—(it was both a hope and a fear)—that—maybe—Juliet might call him, or write to him. For it was astonishing, that so many individuals kept in phone contact with prisoners in the facility, presumably women who were wives, mothers, girlfriends, sisters; no inmate so unattractive, so truculent or debased, so much a *loser,* there wasn't at least one female willing to remain attached to him in some mysterious way.

It was true, the corporal had received letters from women in Carthage and elsewhere, a number of these from young women who'd known him as long ago as high school, even middle school—but he hadn't answered any of these letters nor even in most cases finished reading them. And more often now, a letter with a return address not known to him was quickly disposed of for he had no wish to enter into the fantastical musings of another regarding himself.

For the female entranced by the prisoner, particularly a prisoner who has been convicted of killing another female, filled the corporal with disgust.

You don't know me Brett Kincaid. But I believe that I know you.
Hello! In a dream you bade me write to you Brett Kincaid. And
so—

Such letters on pastel-colored stationery exuded a sickish fragrance. You were meant to luridly imagine, the writer had pressed these pages against her breasts powdered in talcum.

But Juliet Mayfield had not written. And in truth, Brett had not expected her to write to him.

What he'd done! Not only Cressida but Juliet had been destroyed, he saw that now.

Yet still, in a weak moment he fantasized that Juliet might wish to contact him. If only to state that she would not ever see him again, and had not forgiven him.

They'd been so very close at one time.

He had loved her so much. So deeply.

Strange to think of it now, as one whose limbs have become gangrenous might strain to recall a time of health, what it could have been like—*then*.

He'd sent her away, finally. Fearful of hurting her. It had been the wisest decision.

In confused dreams she did come to him. Though it wasn't always evident if the female figure was Juliet Mayfield.

Her features blurred as in a film that has begun to disintegrate.

Her terrible screams. Such screams, the girl could not have drawn breath between them.

Before he'd left for Iraq for the second tour, he'd had a premonition.

The first tour, blindly he had not—he'd believed that he was a U.S. soldier on a mission of justice. He'd believed that God would protect him—everyone in his platoon had believed this, without question.

But the second time he'd known. He'd given to Juliet the sealed envelope *Only open this if you never see me again.*

Juliet had stared at him frightened. For she too had taken for granted that he would return exactly as he'd left her; whether by the grace of the Christian God or by the U.S. forces' superior firepower, American soldiers were protected.

He'd been in a state of extreme emotion when he'd written that letter. Yet now, a few years later, he could not recall what he'd written.

He supposed that Juliet might have opened and read it. And, after he'd confessed to killing her sister, thrown it away.

Couldn't remember a single email of the many—hundreds?—he'd sent to Juliet and to others from Iraq. Pictures he'd sent. A dizzying succession of emails and each so immediate, so urgent and breathless typed hurriedly in those brief minutes of relative privacy snatched from the buzzing oblivion of the soldier's life.

They'd been proud of him. For a while, damned proud.

He'd wanted to think that his father Sergeant Graham Kincaid had been proud, too.

No matter the elder Kincaid had said of the Gulf War it was a shit-hole and everything to do with the war, the U.S. military, and "patriotism" was for asshole-suckers.

He'd taken a dim view too of *folks back home*—asking their damn questions like they had a right.

Still, Brett had to think his dad would be proud of him—if just his father *knew*.

Before the injuries, that is. Just Corporal Brett Kincaid in his dress uniform standing so straight and tall and looking so good, you had to smile.

Makes you feel good to be proud of the young corporal who'd been a good sweet decent kid, a great athlete at the high school, before 9/11 and the U.S. Army.

Purple Heart—that was the medal everybody knew.

Iraq War Campaign medal which was just a shitty medal everybody got who was sent to Iraq and didn't seriously fuck up like get killed or jailed by the military police.

The Infantry Combat Badge was a good one. Bravery under fire, soldierly courage and skill. Not bad for the corporal with half his brain shot to shit.

Highest medals were the Silver Star and the Medal of Honor he had not been awarded of course nor had anyone he knew, or would ever know. He'd explained this but somehow writing the "human interest" feature about Corporal Brett Kincaid focusing on his "return home" and his "rehab" and "upcoming marriage"—(at the time, he and Juliet Mayfield had been engaged)—the giddy female journalist had included in the last line of her piece for the Carthage paper some-thing called *Gold Medal for Valor.*

Juliet had tried to placate him. He'd been disgusted, furious.

Like it's all a joke, fucking joke he'd said furious and Juliet had stared at him as if she'd never seen him before and he'd said like toss-ing a match into something already smoldering, Fucking cunt make a joke of me she'd better stay out of my way.

FLARING UP, like a match tossed into gasoline.

First time anyone saw him in a rage—cell mate, fellow inmates, COs who'd come to trust and to like him—was astonished, disbe-lieving.

Kincaid? Him?

Yeh shit he lost it. Man!

First eighteen months at Dannemora he'd been OK. As near-normal as he would ever be "disabled" and "defective" and on a drug-regimen like the HIV inmates whose meds were mandated by the New York State Department of Health. (How many of these inmate-patients in the facility, some of them visibly sick, gaunt and dying in the infirmary, the corporal would discover when he became an orderly in his second year at Dannemora.) Initially he'd been kept in isolation and on suicide watch which necessitated twenty-four-hour fluorescent lighting in his cell, he'd had to learn to sleep with his face hidden in his hands like some kind of wounded nocturnal creature. In isolation and kept separate from one another the majority of in-mates were criminally insane sex-maniac-murderers and criminally insane sex-maniac-child-murderers and among these Brett Kincaid was the youngest and most "cooperative" inmate. *Crossing-over* into this place which was a clear and visible manifestation of Hell in which his punishment was assured was placating to him, who did not now feel the obligation to punish himself.

Soon he would realize that the prison was a place of madness. A malaise like a great toxic cloud had settled upon the weatherworn buildings of the Clinton Correctional Facility at Dannemora contained within the long encircling sixty-foot-high concrete wall and this was a malaise breathed-in by all without exception.

He would learn, from Father Kranach, that Dannemora had formerly been the site of a nineteenth-century mental asylum, the largest in New York State.

How many had died on this site, and their bodies buried in a forgotten graveyard somewhere outside the prison walls.

Madness like spores blown out of the rich dark soil, into the grayish air.

Much of the time, he did not speak. He did not speak aloud. Though like ceaseless thunder thoughts raged inside his head. He could handle such thoughts like rotting inside but not outside so that you gave off an actual stink and attracted attention. He did not wish to attract attention. Very still he could hold himself, in wariness and in readiness, as if his legs had been shot off; as if he was just a torso, a trunk of a man, a body—*corpse*. Worst times when he panicked having to check his fingers and his toes—(removing his shoes, socks)—to see that those jokers Shaver or Muksie hadn't clipped off trophies with the trauma scissors meaning the corporal might've lost fingers or toes; or earlobes, or his dick and balls.

Took his meds as prescribed. These too were mandated by the New York State Department of Health, with which the officials of the correctional facility had to comply.

Prescribed for chronic pain, muscle spasms, "rushing thoughts"— shortness of breath, diarrhea/constipation—these were powerful drugs of the category called *psychoactive*.

There were others in the facility so "disabled" and "defective"—an army of the walking wounded.

He was liked and trusted by the COs. White kid, Iraq War vet, sulky-quiet but "cooperative."

Not often, the corporal was taken to see a doctor.

A medic took his "vitals"—blood pressure, heartbeat, weight, height. Peered into his eyes with a bright blinding light, inspected the interior of his mouth.

His mother would bitterly complain, he wasn't receiving the kind of medical attention, *neurology-CAT-scan treatment and rehab,* his condition required. His mother would file lawsuits against the New York State Department of Corrections and the Clinton Correctional Facility at Dannemora, her wounded-veteran son was being discriminated against by officials in collusion with their enemies.

What'd he need of *rehab,* he could exercise by himself in his cell. In the yard, he could exercise. After eighteen months transferred out of isolation and into another part of the prison population where he was allowed hours out of his cell, and he was OK.

How're you feeling, son?

OK.

Taking your meds, son?

Yessir.

You sure, you are taking your meds?

Yessir.

Not throwin em in the toilet, son?

Nossir.

Not sellin em, eh? Not?

Nossir. Not.

FLARING UP, like a match dropped into gasoline.

It was Muksie solid-bodied as a wrestler, grown older, heavier and his bullet-head cocked to one side as in the deafening din of the dining hall he'd flashed what appeared to be a weapon fashioned out of a toothbrush harassing one of the younger inmates. And Kincaid was on him quick and silent as a pit bull and like a pit bull impossible to pull off striking and pummeling the bullet-headed inmate until both men were struggling on the floor and guards rushed shouting to pull them apart.

Shrieking, shouts and screams like females being killed. Chairs were overturned, plates and trays thrown to the floor. Fights broke out among inmates in the large space like a sequence of small explosions rising to a single deafening roar.

Last the corporal knew, the alarm was blaring.

Dragged away from Private Muksie he'd have murdered if he hadn't been stopped.

Struck by guards' billy clubs he lost consciousness.

Wasn't self-defense but an aggressive attack to protect another inmate as witnesses would testify but still, Kincaid had violated the prison rules. Just to disobey an officer's command was a violation of the prison rules. To resist officers, try to shove them away, strike them—violations of the prison rules. On Brett Kincaid's otherwise unblemished prison record was a notation of *assault, refusal to obey officers, instigation of riot.*

The man he'd mistaken for Private Muksie had been hospitalized in the prison infirmary. The younger man Muksie had been harassing had escaped with only lacerations and bruises.

Kincaid drew "administrative punishment" of eight weeks in solitary confinement.

Warden Heike's gravel voice thickened and deepened with outrage was amplified through the prison in lockdown for twenty-four hours.

Zero tolerance for infractions of Clinton Correctional rules. Zero tolerance for fighting, threatening and intimidating, possession of weapons, insubordination and resistance of officers' orders.

Sentenced to solitary confinement naked. Hoofed-creatures like horses pounded through his sleep and these sharp heavy hooves striking close beside his head he could not turn, he was so exhausted.

In solitary he was the torso, the stump. No purpose now in struggle and so he ceased.

His medications had ceased. Only vaguely did he miss his medications as you might miss a badly rotted little finger after it has dropped off and is no longer yours to fret over.

Eight weeks in solitary. *Cruel and unusual punishment* Zeno Mayfield would charge if Zeno Mayfield were on Brett Kincaid's side and not now his enemy.

In solitary you have no appetite. You lose weight steadily—Brett

Kincaid lost twelve pounds. Medications he took if they were brought to him but most meds he forgot since they were not brought to him in his new quarters. *Man, you on some kinda diet? Or, whadajacallit— chemotherapy? You real sick, man? God damn!*

Once a day for an hour removed for exercise in a segregated part of the Yard, every other day removed for a (lukewarm) shower so his skin crawled with festering microbes invisible to the naked eye. Yet the corporal submitted to his punishment without resistance as without apology or remorse for the corporal could not see how he had erred. The instinct to help the harassed inmate, a stranger to him, young kid looking scarcely twenty, had come so strong.

Saying, to Father Kranach who came to visit him concerned and alarmed *Fuck I would do it again.*

First he could after solitary was go to the Church of the Good Thief where he knelt, prayed.

Like a hungry man, feasting.

It was not God and it was not Jesus Christ but Saint Dismas to whom he prayed.

Help me, I have sinned. It did not seem a request of madness wishing to save his soul in the twilit interior of the Church of the Good Thief where he knelt hiding his contorted face.

Only enter my soul and my soul shall be healed.

HE WAS SINCERE. Desperately he wanted to be *good.*

Yet a second time fifteen months later, the *flaring-up* overcame him.

This time in the mental unit where B. Kincaid was an orderly under the supervision of a light-skinned black CO named Foyle—(for there was a shortage in the facility of men like Brett Kincaid who gave evidence of being intelligent, responsible, reasonable)—he'd attacked a guard who'd been harassing an inmate—(the inmate a soft fat slug of a man with albino eyes, pasty skin, white eyelashes)— poking at him with his billy club and Kincaid told him to stop, Kincaid spoke sharply to him telling him to stop but the guard ignored him laughing and so Kincaid strode to him and this time too without speaking he seized the billy club out of the guard's hand and brought it down hard over his head fracturing the skull.

So swiftly! The corporal heard the *crack*.

This time the warden intervened, directly. The corporal had assaulted a corrections officer and would be charged with a felony—*assault and battery, aggravated.*

There would be formal charges, brought by the Clinton County district attorney. There would be more than simply administrative punishment, months in solitary confinement: seven-to-ten years added to the corporal's sentence.

God damn he didn't give a damn!—didn't give a *fuck*.

Recklessly he waived his right to an attorney as he would waive his constitutional right to a trial. Not repentant for he didn't see that there had been any other course of action possible for him.

Fucker who'd hit him, tried to break up the scuffle, and his CO-friends, dealt drugs in the facility. The corporal knew.

Drugs were everywhere in the facility. No way in but through guards but the guards' union was so strong, their connection with downstate drug smugglers so established, Brett could not see how the situation would ever change.

(The CO he'd assaulted had been dismissed from the facility for excessive force, drug dealing. But that did not mitigate the corporal's sentence.)

Shitty to think how you were but the sum total of brain cells inside your skull. No mystery why people went crazy like rabid beasts sometimes just wanting to bite and tear with their teeth—there was a wild elation in this.

Fucked up like he was, he wouldn't have to face a parole board for a long time at least.

Remorse? For what?

His sentence was so long now, he couldn't envision its ending. If he maxed-out, without parole. And maybe he'd accumulate yet more administrative-punishments to set his release time back, back, back.

Twenty-seven years old when he'd been incarcerated and so

now—(but what month was this? what year?)—thirty-one, or –two.

The girl he'd murdered would remain always a girl. Yet the other, the one he'd loved so much, and had almost married, would remain a girl too, a beautiful young woman for he would never see her again.

She'd died to him too.

All of the Mayfields—died to him.

Or was it instead that the Mayfields lived, and the corporal had died?

(Secret) meaning of the Purple Heart.

(Yet the shameful fact was, Brett had coveted a Purple Heart. In his fantasies of serving overseas, impressing his absent-drunk-daddy and his sweetly naïve fiancée and all of Carthage gaping at him in his army dress uniform like Tom Cruise he'd considered the Purple Heart as the most likely medal he might be awarded; and if so, the trick would be to be *wounded* but not to *die*.)

Ten days into solitary his brain was sluggish and functioned like his mother's decades-old Mixmaster set to *liquefy* but the blades barely turning and the contraption rattling, vibrating and listing to one side.

Ten days more, a watery gruel leaked from his raw-burning anus and what (tepid, sickening) water he managed to drink, he vomited back up again in a spume of the hue of watery urine.

Father Kranach came to see him in his delirium. Father Kranach pleaded with the warden to have Kincaid hospitalized in the infirmary but the angry warden paid no heed. *Won't be the first to precipitate his own demise and won't be the last.*

Waking a week later and where was he after all?—strapped to a metal bed in the infirmary stinking of human feces, vomit and disinfectant strong as lye.

Flies crawling the windows. Out of caulking cracks and out of zigzag cracks in the ceiling.

What he'd thought in his dream was an old-time (World War I?) dirigible floating high above his head was in fact a bag of IV fluids dripping into a vein in the crook of his right elbow.

And that pinch in his penis, not an incandescent wire shunted up into his gut but a catheter draining toxic liquid out of his gut into a bag beneath the bed.

A medic was telling him *Seems like you was pretty sick, man. Your temperature was a hundred and three degrees F with a nasty blood infection and just the medication alone it's damn strong it can kill you. If you don't remember this last week that ain't such a bad thing.*

CAN'T GUARANTEE YOUR SAFETY, *Corporal. Take precautions.*

IN THE CHURCH of the Good Thief he prayed.

On his knees prayed. In the quickened beat-beat-beat of his heart prayed.

In the alcove to the church the astonishing figure of the crucified Saint Dismas. The perfect male body naked except for a cloth about his loins and how realistic the torso, the thighs and calves, the head and the face contorted in agony as it is passing into something else— peace, a kind of joy.

And he was struck by the perfect male body—not disabled, not "defective" but perfect and yet, rigid in death.

He thought *The body is crucified on the cross of the world. There is no escape from the crucifixion as there is no escape from the body.*

He had not ever thought of the male body as beautiful, still less *perfect*. Yet now, contemplating the sculpted figure of the legendary Good Thief, the figure's muscled shoulders and arms slung around the horizontal bars of a thick wooden plank, he felt such intense pity, sorrow—he felt that something was breaking inside him, that was not for him but for another, who stood outside all that he, Brett Kincaid, could know.

In the church services he'd visited in prison there was much of Jesus in your heart and if you would accept Jesus as your savior but Father Kranach did not speak of Jesus but of Saint Dismas.

Patron saint of thieves, losers.

He will intervene for you. If you ask.

The Church of the Good Thief had become his place of solace. His place of comfort. Ever more now, he'd spent so much time in solitary and had felt his soul like a small landslide.

The Church of the Good Thief was not a chapel or even a small church but a good-sized church that could hold as many as two hundred people built inside the sixty-foot-high concrete wall circling itself like a snake swallowing its tail. The church was comprised of rock that looked as if it had been hewn by pickax out of a nearby mountain.

The Church of the Good Thief had been constructed by Dannemora inmates in the late 1930s and early 1940s. The materials were secondhand from abandoned houses, barns, local buildings. Some materials were donated. The Appalachian red oak made into pews, said to have been a gift from the notorious Lucky Luciano, a former inmate at Dannemora.

There were numerous carvings, stained glass windows bearing the faces of saints that had been modeled by Dannemora inmates.

In a Protestant church, at least in those churches Brett Kincaid had visited, he'd never felt this *inwardness*.

He'd never felt his soul stirred. The deep root of his being, impossible to name.

In the churches of his past, including the Carthage church to which he'd gone with Juliet, the focus was *outward*. Smiling faces of others, singing together the familiar hymns, prayers in unison. Gripping hands. But in the Church of the Good Thief he came to understand the stillness and secrecy of the elusive god.

For it was the *inwardness* of God for which he yearned not the communion with others.

In this *inwardness* he came to understand that his maimed body was in its way a perfect body. As his maimed soul was in its way perfect. For this was the fate God had provided for Corporal Kincaid. No other fate would have allowed Corporal Kincaid to continue to live.

He'd tried to speak of this to Father Kranach in the priest's small office at the rear of the church. Through the single horizontal, just slightly sinking window of the office you could see a broad swath of gardens tended by inmates at the rear of their cell blocks—you could not see, from Father Kranach's office, the sixty-foot-high concrete wall without end.

Father Kranach had become his friend. His only friend.

The priest was of no age Brett could determine: not young but not old, nor even middle-aged. He was short and broad-shouldered with spidery limbs and a nervous habit of stroking his hair—flat straw-hair combed across the hump of his head.

Always his greeting was a brisk handshake. *How are you, Brett?*

And he was sincere, he sincerely wanted to know.

Seven days a week at the prison the Catholic priest Father Fred Kranach was on call. Unlike the Protestant chaplain who came only when required for services and counseling and then it seemed, judging by his edgy smiles, reluctantly.

Why a Catholic priest is single and celibate. For a wife, children distract a man and drain his energies from his calling.

Why a Catholic priest when he is a good priest *is* an incarnation of Jesus Christ: the single one who is for all, who has died for all, who will dwell in the hearts of all if but beckoned.

The corporal had never known any Catholic priest in the past. He had not once stepped inside a Roman Catholic church though at the foot of Potsdam Street was old dour-red-brick St. Mary's, the oldest Catholic church in Beechum County, past which he'd often bicycled as a boy.

Strange that Father Kranach didn't seem to care that Brett Kincaid was not a Catholic.

Father Kranach did not question the corporal about his wartime experiences nor did he allude to the corporal's disabilities. Only obliquely did he allude to the fact that Brett had "served" in the Iraq War at a young age. More vehemently he spoke of the war—the wars—against terror: the *crusade* that would never end.

Like wishing to eradicate evil. But evil will never end.

In the prison Brett Kincaid rarely looked another inmate in the face. It is wisest not to make eye contact. Yet lifting his eyes to the priest almost shyly, in yearning seeing that Father Kranach was smiling at him seeing *him*.

Happy in knowing a secret. Like one who has died and has returned to help others.

He had thought it was a curse, the wreck of his body. Yet now he understood, God had allowed this wreck of a body to prevail, and to endure.

In other, earlier wars fought by American soldiers, such severe wounds would have meant death.

Feeling in the Church of the Good Thief not happiness but a cessation of grief, pain.

Cessation of guilt.

These were temporary and not permanent. Yet, his spirits were lifted.

For Father Kranach had explained to him, at his bequest, the principles of the Catholic confession.

Father Kranach instructed him in an abbreviated act of contrition *O God I am heartily sorry for all my sins. Only enter my soul and my soul shall be healed.*

In the fourth year of his incarceration, she came to see him.

Many times she'd requested permission from him to visit and always he'd told her no, not a good idea. Often he didn't reply to her letters at all.

Yet of course, Arlette Mayfield did not give up. She was a Christian woman for whom pride was a sort of shining cloth, expensive silk for instance, the value of which lies in trampling on it and allowing others to trample freely on it.

Until finally Brett said *yes*.

Though he didn't want to see Arlette Mayfield, did not ever want to see any of the Mayfields, or anyone from his life *back there,* yet he gave in, he wrote back to Mrs. Mayfield saying *yes.*

And immediately Arlette replied to him, saying she would drive to Dannemora the following Friday, stay overnight in a motel and arrive at the prison when visitors' hours began at 8 A.M.

For Arlette would be driving alone, it seemed. A lengthy drive following narrow circuitous routes through the foothills of the Adirondacks.

This was a relief. He could not bear to ever see Zeno Mayfield again.

Juliet's parents. So very close to having been his parents, too.

PROCEDURE WAS: visitors arrived at the front entrance of the prison, passed through security checkpoints, signed in and the prisoner whom they wished to visit was notified, and escorted to the visitors' room; no visitors were allowed into the visitors' room except by escort, after the prisoner had been brought there.

When the call came for him, his first instinct was to say *no.*

Steeling himself for seeing her after so many years. And the strangeness of having a visitor who knew him not as the *Kincaid case* but as Brett.

For Ethel had not made the trip—every month her health was *worsening,* such a damn long bus ride would *kill her.*

The visitors' room was a large bright-lit clamorous and inhospitable space. All of the inmates were men and most of the visitors were women.

Here and there in the large, open space were children, some very young. Brett felt the sharpness of his loss as he'd never quite felt it before—not only of his life as a man, a husband, but his potential life as a father, a man with a family.

All that, he'd thrown away.

Brett saw a tall thin woman with silvery-brown hair being led in his direction by a guard. She was smiling at him—was this Arlette Mayfield? He felt a faint shock—the faded woman, the bright smile.

There are the parents of your friends who are *old,* and there are
the parents of your friends who are *young*—in the Mayfields' case,
both Arlette and Zeno had been *young, youthful.* In jeans and pullover
shirts, returning from a "run around the cemetery" in waterstained
jogging shoes, Arlette Mayfield had seemed more like an older sister
of Juliet's than her mother.

"Brett! Hello . . ."

Her eyes were larger than he recalled, in her thin face. Her hair was
feathery-thin wisps. Her smiling mouth looked bracketed by pain.

Brett stammered a greeting. Thinking *This is a mistake, I can't do
this.*

But somehow, Arlette Mayfield was seated across from him, at a
table. Between them was a Plexiglas barrier. Through a grated opening in the barrier they could speak to each other; or rather, Arlette
could speak to Brett who was shocked and stunned into silence.

Visits with prisoners were limited to a half hour. The corporal
recalled from training that in a dangerous situation in which the
immediate future is unpredictable you must slow time down by an
act of will, you must separate and "own" each second, otherwise you
will be seized and swept away.

It was not possible, what was happening now. That he was facing
this woman whom he had avoided, for years. That she was speaking
to him warmly and with emotion yet not at all reproachfully, even
with respect—(he would recall this afterward, astonished: *respect*)—
and he was able to respond if only crudely, awkwardly—*yes, no, I
think so, maybe . . .*

He guessed that she'd been ill. Juliet's mother.

The thin, wispy-graying hair—female relatives of his had looked
like this—had to be cancer, chemotherapy and the hair growing back
but not as it had been.

He could not ask her. He could not ask her a single question about
herself.

You can call me Mom—soon!

She'd joked with him. Part of the joke was, Arlette Mayfield was so very young, funny and playful as a girl, quicker to joke than Juliet in fact.

Calling Mrs. Mayfield *Mom.* Brett had laughed.

His own mother was no *Mom.* That was part of the joke.

But he had to acknowledge: Arlette was not *Mom.*

Never his mother-in-law. Rather, the mother of the girl he'd murdered.

(Strange: he rarely recalled that girl's name. An eccentric name, he'd never heard the name before, possibly he'd resented her for this, for such "special" qualities, her air of knowing herself "special" in the very presence of her older sister whom everyone adored as they did not adore *her.* And what right had she, this plain, fierce sister, making a claim upon *him!*)

(Though they'd been friends, initially. There'd been an understanding between them. A secret, he'd helped her when she'd had a bicycle accident on Waterman Street by the river. Just a girl at the time—so young.)

Feelings rushed through him leaving him sick, stunned.

As if it weren't enough that he had killed the girl, and thrown her body into the river to destroy the evidence of his crime. Not enough, but that he must hate her also.

Arlette leaned forward. On this wintry-autumn day she was wearing a cable-knit sweater-coat of the hue of burnt leaves. Her wrist bones were knobby, too thin. Brett had a sudden sensation of such terrible loss, he felt faint.

"Brett? It isn't so bad—is it?"

Arlette was smiling. A wistful sort of joke.

Seeing the mother of the girl you'd murdered—it isn't so very bad is it? How brave you are!

"I think it must be something very simple—God wants us to be together, like this. No other purpose than to be together."

Arlette spoke softly, matter-of-factly. It was difficult to hear her amid the noise of the visitors' room.

The corporal had not often been in the visitors' room for during the years of his incarceration the lawyers who'd come to see him had met with him in small, private rooms without the presence of guards.

The Kincaid case. Manslaughter conviction on the basis of confession, circumstantial evidence. Victim's body never found.

"It had come to me after—you'd been taken away . . . That we were still a family and it didn't matter if something had happened to make a rupture in our family. It came to me as long ago as then but I—I didn't understand at the time. I was—wasn't—so strong, then."

Arlette spoke slowly. Lifting her right hand to press the palm against the Plexiglas barrier in a gesture of appeal.

A small hand, thin fingers. With a pang Brett saw that there were no rings on Arlette's fingers.

"If Jesus is with us, He is with us all. Those who are living and those who are—not living."

Voices lifted in another part of the visitors' room. At once a guard stepped forward speaking sharply *Quiet there! Stay seated.*

Brett steeled himself for louder shouts, for an earsplitting alarm.

Here was a place of hallucinations. Myriad anonymous dreams mixed together crudely, jeeringly.

Lifting his hand he placed it shyly against Arlette's hand on the other side of the barrier: a larger hand, a man's hand, the fingernails blunt and stubbed.

"*She* is with us. She is happier now, knowing we love her."

In this way wordless and obscurely comforted they remained together until a bell rang rudely awakening them and signaling the termination of the visit.

EVERY SEVERAL MONTHS Arlette returned.

She stayed overnight in a motel in Dannemora, visited the prison early and drove back to Carthage alone.

Rarely did she speak of Zeno, or of Juliet. Rarely even of Carthage.

Their visits together were primarily silence. Seeing them in the visiting area you might have thought they were mother and son bound by a singular grief.

The silence between them was deeply comforting to Brett, in retrospect. Like a medication so powerful it can't be absorbed into the bloodstream at once but must be released slowly over a period of hours, days.

Now he ceased hating himself, so virulently.

Now he thought *I have a friend. Two friends.*

He thought *If I am a shit that is not all that I am. I am—something more.*

Inside the sixty-foot-high encircling wall the corporal's damaged reputation gradually healed. By default Kincaid was a favorite of the COs who saw in him a person like themselves: his personality, his intelligence, integrity, *sanity.*

He volunteered to help teach literacy classes in the facility. Again as an orderly in the prison infirmary, and in the mental unit of the hospice. Though he wasn't a Catholic and didn't take communion at mass yet he was Father Kranach's most diligent assistant in the maintenance of the Church of the Good Thief: sweeping, mopping, polishing the Appalachian red oak pews, repairing broken steps, washing the stained glass windows and keeping clean the sculpted figure of Saint Dismas crucified.

Enter my soul and my soul shall be healed.

He began to assist Father Kranach at the priest's group-therapy sessions that met several times a week in the church. (Father Fred Kranach, the most popular therapist/counselor in the prison, had a degree in clinical psychology from Notre Dame, in addition to his seminary degree.) He passed out materials, he helped Father Kranach counsel the men. It was thrilling to him when others looked at him with gratitude and not with suspicion; that he could encourage others if not himself.

Father Kranach spoke of a "career" for Brett Kincaid, in social work, counseling, when he was released.

Released! The term seemed strange to him, mocking. If he served his full sentence he wouldn't be released until sometime in 2027; he'd be forty-six years old.

IN THE SIXTH YEAR of his incarceration in mid-March 2012 there came a summons for the corporal.

Father Kranach had been dispatched to bring Brett Kincaid to the warden's office.

"I think this is good news, Brett. I believe it is. You must prepare yourself."

There was a strange agitation in the priest's face. Brett had not ever seen his friend so—*intense.*

Good news. It would not be his mother, then—his mother's death.

In Warden Heike's office he was told several times to sit down.

Never in the warden's office were inmates invited to sit down.

FIFTEEN

The Father

March 2012

HE KNEW: she was alive.

He knew: if he persevered, if he did not despair, he would find her.

She was his younger child. She was the difficult child. She was the one to break his heart.

THIS WAS HIS SICKNESS, he must keep hidden close to his heart like a poker hand so wonderful, its cards are ablaze and blinding.

SIX YEARS, EIGHT MONTHS. And this day, March 27.

A call from Juliet on his cell—*Daddy? Call me back when you can.*

Didn't say *Daddy it's urgent.* For that wasn't Juliet's way, to stir apprehension. Yet he sensed it, *urgent.*

Fumbling to call his daughter back.

SHE, THE ELDER DAUGHTER, poor Juliet had been driven away from Carthage. Could not bear to revisit Carthage. Even to recall Carthage, too painful for her.

Moved away, married. A man older than she was by nearly twenty years.

See, Daddy! I have grown up, I am an adult. I am not your little girl any longer and would not fall in love with a silly soldier-boy to break our hearts.

SO HE'D LOST his other daughter, too. As if the corporal had murdered both daughters.

Juliet was the "surviving" sister: a tabloid heroine, or hapless fool, whose younger sister had been "brutally murdered" by her "war hero" fiancé.

Weeks, months. The coverage had been relentless.

Juliet had to quit her teaching job which she'd loved. Her volunteer work at Home Front she'd loved. Graduate school for an advanced degree in public education she'd postponed, indefinitely.

At first, she'd stayed at friends' houses avoiding the family house since reporters and TV crews awaited her on Cumberland Avenue like predator birds. Forbidden by law to trespass on private property the news-media people were spread across the front of the Mayfields' front lawn on the public sidewalk and in the public street; if you wanted to turn into the Mayfields' driveway, you had to plead with them to let you through amid a barrage of camera-flashes.

Finally, Juliet had moved away from Carthage to live somewhere "anonymously"—even her parents weren't always sure where she was living.

None of the Mayfields had guessed at the toxic after-life of a violent crime. The shimmering-sick phosphorescence of scandal accrued to a name: *Mayfield.*

The mild notoriety Zeno Mayfield had known as a controversial mayor of Carthage faded to nothing, beside this virulent and protracted attention.

It was illogical, since *Mayfields* were the victims. The murderer was *Kincaid.*

Somehow it was the *sister-sister rivalry,* so-perceived, or misperceived, that had excited the media interest. A lurid rivalry for the love of Corporal Kincaid, the two Mayfield sisters *bitter enemies.*

In blogs, it was suggested that Juliet, the fiancée, was pregnant: that she'd had a miscarriage, or an abortion; or, depending upon the blog, she'd had Corporal Kincaid's (premature, doomed) baby.

His younger daughter he'd been powerless to save. And now the older.

Beautiful Juliet Mayfield hounded and harried like the Unicorn of medieval Christian legend. Obsessively Zeno was moved to think of this peculiar and incongruous image: the elegant white Unicorn memorialized in the fifteenth-century French tapestries, the cruel and barbarous hunters, the imprisonment, the bright blood of innocence.

In the Cloisters Museum in New York City he and Arlette had been fascinated by the tapestries even as they'd been repelled by them. A fastidious sadism in such beauty, the apotheosis of Christian martyrdom.

And yet, in the final tapestry—the Unicorn is miraculously restored to life, though imprisoned like any barnyard creature in a small pen.

A WOMAN HAD COME into his life to drink with him.

A woman not one of his *women.* Not one who'd known him.

His old, lost Zeno-self. She hadn't known.

Though probably she'd *known of.* Everyone in Carthage seemed to *know of* Zeno Mayfield.

Like an old Roman general, he was. A Roman of antiquity. He'd fought many wars against the Goths and lost his numerous sons in the effort of decades and now he'd survived into another era in which only his name was "known"—except not why, and whether with merit.

Her name was Genevieve. A classy name and she was a classy woman or had been, not long ago: with wide-set hazel eyes, a soft mouth that looked as if it had been bruised, thick brunette hair to her shoulders. She'd lost a husband, an eighteen-year-old son: the one to divorce, the other to drugs. She'd had to sell at a loss her house in the Cumberland section of Carthage and lived now, coincidentally, though in such accounts there are really no coincidences, in the Cedar Hill condominium complex in which, since the dissolution of his marriage, Zeno Mayfield also lived, in squalid bachelor quarters in a two-bedroom apartment on the seventh, penthouse floor.

Genevieve had come into Zeno Mayfield's life after Arlette had departed. Just to make that clear.

"Please tell people, Zeno. Tell them the chronology."

"Why? Why does it matter?"

"Because of course it matters."

"But—why? At our age?"

"All the more at our age."

Genevieve knew that all of Zeno's friends who'd been Arlette's friends would resent her. For Arlette Mayfield was a woman whom other women liked very much and would have liked to protect from harm.

Especially, since the loss of her daughter.

Since the so very *public* loss of her daughter.

Zeno was amused by Genevieve's sense of propriety. Though he was touched by the woman, too—so badly she wanted things to be correct, proper between them.

Though she was forty-seven years old and a divorced woman and by her own account she'd had "relationships" with men since her divorce.

They were eager and clumsy in intimacy like actors—middle-aged, yet inexperienced actors—playing roles for which they were unprepared. Scripts they hadn't memorized nor come close to understanding. So long married and accustomed to a woman living with him without particularly *seeing* him, Zeno was chagrined to realize that this new woman would *see* his dissolute physical self in a way that had to be unsparing; on his part, he was inclined to view her, in the affable confusion of bedclothes and nightwear, with gallant part-shut eyes.

In fact Genevieve had known Arlette first, before she'd met Zeno. She'd been a volunteer at the Carthage H.E.L.P. Center Wig Boutique which was patronized predominately by women needing hair replacement in the aftermath of chemotherapy; she'd consulted with Arlette on the matter of customizing some sort of wig, synthetic or human hair, or a blend of the two, following the loss of Arlette's hair during six months of post-surgery breast cancer treatment.

(Arlette's breast cancer had been diagnosed relatively early, at Stage II. Zeno had been more terrified than Arlette, it had seemed. As, with months of grueling chemotherapy, and radiation to follow, Arlette had grown ever more thin, ethereal-thin, "radiant" and "spiritual" as Zeno had grown more distracted and slovenly and his drinking had veered as it's said in AA circles *out of control*.)

Unlike Arlette whose idea of reckless shopping was to spend beyond twenty-five dollars at Second Time 'Round Consignments, Genevieve dressed with care, and style; where Arlette wore much-laundered jeans, patchy pullovers and nylon parkas, Genevieve wore designer jeans, cashmere pullovers and chic faux-fur coats; Genevieve spent more money on shoes and boots in a season than Arlette had spent through the entirety of her marriage with Zeno.

In his more casual way Zeno too had been a careful dresser, when active in public life. He'd known the value of a boldly colored necktie. He'd known the value of stylish but not extravagant clothes, which Arlette had helped him choose—the politician should inspire confidence, not envy or resentment. It had been a stubborn fetish of Zeno's, ridiculed by his family of pragmatic-minded females, that he refused to wear a hat and often an overcoat in even the arctic winter of upstate New York.

Now semi-retired, demi-semi-alive, whatever this condition of anxious ennui was, Zeno wore his familiar old clothes, tweed jackets, sweaters out at the elbow, torn jeans, remnants of J. Press suits that had come to fit his sagging body like a glove, without much attentiveness or interest; he'd stopped wearing neckties entirely, and rarely the crisply-laundered white cotton dress shirt that had been the mayor's signature. His old habit of showering every morning, shampooing his thick-graying-frazzled hair, he retained out of a sense that, if he missed even one morning, it would be the beginning of the fabled *end*.

Initially he'd been flattered by Genevieve's gifts. Touched and grateful, this attractive woman should think of *him*. Then by quick degrees it had come to seem that the gifts she gave him which were nearly always clothes—Italian designer shirts, cashmere sweaters, leather belts, gloves—were a rebuke to his taste, or his absence of taste. And Genevieve made presents to him of her small Fauve-floral oil paintings and ceramics, which she positioned in strategic places in his apartment, to "enliven" the atmosphere.

Also she brought him fancy wine—wines. Genevieve was an adventuress in wine—New Zealand, Moroccan, Brazilian, among the more dependable Italian, French, and Californian. Their pleasure in each other's company had much to do with wine as well as whiskey, gin, vodka, brandy, and distinctive sorts of beer and ale, of which Zeno was the adventurer.

Gallantry wasn't required when you were affably/happily drunk but came quite naturally.

As high-pitched girlish laughter, spontaneous-sounding and utterly delighted laughter came quite naturally to Genevieve in this state.

"It's good to laugh again, Zeno. Thank you for that."

And he hadn't known what to say. He'd been struck dumb.

For it was a script they hadn't memorized, yet. A clumsy hopeful script, in the making.

Examining Genevieve's little square-cut paintings, not one of which was larger than eight by eight inches and all of which exuded a lush, sensuous, giddily exuberant life, Zeno thought *How different from Cressida*.

Meaning *How different from Cressida's art*.

Zeno had shown Genevieve some of his daughter's ink drawings. He'd been surprised to see how large they were, and how complex in execution; how *particular* the vision of the artist, and *difficult of access.*

The paintings of Genevieve and her women-artist friends, whose work Zeno saw frequently at gallery exhibits in Carthage, to which Genevieve took him, lay almost exclusively on the surface like gaily colored lilies in a pond; Cressida's finicky, fussy art was a matter of depths.

You were instinctively drawn to the boldly colored art, that celebrated life. Yet it was the other more complex art, that provoked and disturbed, that captivated your attention.

"How strange, for a girl! How—unusual . . ."

Zeno winced inwardly hearing this inane remark. He could imagine Cressida's reaction.

"And you say she was—how old? Still in high school?"

Zeno said he thought so, yes.

In fact, the drawing of vertiginously interconnected bridges, a fantasy of M. C. Escher superimposed upon the distinctive six bridges of Carthage, New York, had probably been done when Cressida was younger, since there were traces of color in the bridges' "shadows."

Genevieve had no idea of the Escher influence, and Zeno had no interest in telling her.

As it turned out, Genevieve remembered seeing the exhibit of a selection of Cressida Mayfield's drawings in the Carthage Public Library in January 2006. This exhibit had been arranged by Arlette and the head of the library and had been greeted with much local acclaim focusing upon the "tragic loss" of the young artist at the age of nineteen.

Genevieve hadn't known the Mayfield family and had not spoken to them about it but years later, after she'd met Zeno, and he'd showed her some of Cressida's work, she remembered vividly—"Those drawings made a strong impression on me. I thought, what an unusual *girl*. And I thought, it must have been a challenge to be her parent."

"That's so." Zeno paused. "I mean—it was so."

Zeno had been flattered by the local response to Cressida's work but subtly repelled by it as well. He could imagine his daughter's sardonic reaction—*Where were all these "fans" when I was alive?*

In the Carthage newspaper, two full pages were devoted to the exhibit. Headlines were exuberant.

STUNNING EXHIBIT TRACES GROWTH
OF UNUSUAL ARTISTIC TALENT
"A Posthumous Gift"

Rare family photos of the young *artiste* Cressida Mayfield in a smiling mood, or at least not actively scowling, accompanied the library exhibit which, in an expanded version, reopened some months later in the Carnegie House, a former mansion donated to the municipality for community-service and non-profit activities.

Zeno thought it ironic that the stark, minimalist, Escher-inspired drawings, created out of what ferocious despondency of lonely and embittered adolescence, had become the means, *posthumous,* for his daughter's local fame. Virtually everyone in Carthage—all ages, including her adolescent contemporaries—now knew the name *Cressida Mayfield* who'd been both the (alleged) victim of (alleged) rape-murder as well as the heralded *artiste.*

"Jesus! Cressida would be mortified." Zeno shook his head like a beast that has been prodded with a dull instrument that might soon turn sharp.

Arlette took offense. Arlette had become sensitive, since July 2005, of what she defined as cynical, scurrilous, irreverent, *negative-reinforcing* language.

"You don't know how Cressida would feel. You have no idea how Cressida would feel. There was a side of our daughter, we saw it when she volunteered for the math program, that wanted to connect with others—with the community. Cressida wasn't a negative person, she was—complex."

Zeno had come to note how the very word *negative* seemed often to be a concern of Arlette's. How any suggestion that Cressida might have reacted to the maelstrom of attention focused upon her, since July 2005, scarcely abating since the confession of Corporal Kincaid in October of that year, with anything like Cressida's usual skepticism, drew a sharp, unflattering crease between Arlette's eyebrows. As if the mother Arlette, not the father Zeno, had become the missing daughter's interpreter: the missing daughter's surrogate.

He'd heard, after a death in the family there will be a seismic realignment among survivors. The old connections have been ruptured, new connections must be established, but how?—the absent party remains both absent and tantalizingly, teasingly present.

In their focus upon the missing daughter, Zeno knew that he and Arlette were now neglecting their surviving daughter. So long, Juliet had been the center of their parental attention, to Cressida's disadvantage; now, all that had changed. And Juliet too had been wounded, irrevocably.

(Juliet's way of coping with the loss of her sister was to say very little about it. Her way of coping with the loss of her fiancé was to say nothing about it.)

(Juliet's way of coping with the wreckage of her Carthage-life was to depart from it—moving finally to Albany where she would enter the graduate school of public education at the State University at Albany and earn a master's degree in English education; she would acquire a teaching position at the prestigious private Hedley Academy in suburban Albany and almost simultaneously a new fiancé whom her left-behind Carthage parents would scarcely know before the wedding.)

In the wake of Cressida's disappearance from their lives Arlette undertook to commemorate their daughter in ways that were touching to Zeno initially, then discomforting; finally, disturbing. He sensed that Arlette was able to accept that their daughter was *deceased* in a way that somehow he could not; despite every effort of his rational being, every application of what might be called common sense, in some part of his brain Zeno still held out a measure of—skepticism? *Hope?*

From undergraduate days he recalled the brainteaser-conundrum *Schrödinger's cat.*

A thought experiment of the 1930s. A paradox in which the (en-boxed) cat is simultaneously alive/dead until one opens the box to see for oneself if the cat is alive/dead.

Zeno couldn't recall if the observer, the one who opens the box, also controls the cat's fate. Maybe opening the box precipitates the cat's death? Zeno remembered something vague about radiation, poison pellets . . . No one considered that the thought experiment was "cruel to animals" for no one at the time, apart from a few eccentric antivivisectionists, gave a damn for the suffering and deaths of experimental animals; certainly, no one seemed to give a damn about Schrödinger's famous cat.

Sleepless for years he lived, relived those early hours of the Search.

Those early hours of almost unbearable intensity, excitement—hope . . .

The search party in the Preserve. The professionalism of many of the searchers who knew how to look for hikers lost in the Adirondacks.

We'll find her, Mr. Mayfield. If Cressida is here—we'll find her.

And he'd believed. Wanted to believe.

The final exertion of his life as a physical being, a *man.*

For despite his zealousness he'd failed. Despite his Eagle Scout skills he'd failed to find his daughter.

Failed more fundamentally—(though no one would have condemned him except himself)—as a fellow searcher in the wilderness Preserve for pain had felled him early on, after only a few hours. (Well, maybe it had been eight hours?) Zeno Mayfield who'd prided himself on his hiking skills, insisted upon Adirondack weekend retreats for his mayoral staff and associates, now forced to acknowledge how out of condition he was, how inadequate. Now years later unless he drank himself into oblivion he was prone to the cheerless habit of wounding himself anew recalling the particular humiliation of collapsing in a paroxysm of pain, sinking to his knees as a younger man came bounding to his rescue.

Mr. Mayfield! Zeno! I got you.

WON'T TELL GENEVIEVE this background. Pathetic etiology.

Let her discover for herself that Zeno Mayfield isn't any longer what he'd been rumored to be in certain quarters of Carthage (in fact erroneously—he'd loved it): *sexy, sexual, irresistible to women and a lover of women.*

PARENTS OF MISSING GIRL, *19.*

Grieving Parents of Murdered Girl, 19.

Arlette had dealt with their daughter's disappearance in a way no one could have anticipated. She'd made of mourning a kind of celebration, relentlessly public. Soon after Corporal Kincaid had confessed, was convicted and incarcerated at Dannemora and it had seemed that the search for the *missing girl* had come to an end she'd helped organize the exhibit in the Carthage Public Library and she'd been active in local fund-raisers for battered women's shelters; she'd been a guest on an afternoon talk show, on a CBS-TV affiliate in Watertown; she'd arranged for other art exhibits in local galleries and at Home Front Alliance; she'd donated one of Cressida's larger drawings for the annual Home Front auction, where it had brought in a considerable price—two thousand dollars. (Zeno had been furious, Arlette had given away their daughter's *Descending and Ascending* without consulting him. And she'd been shocked at his anger.) She'd made donations to the Math Literacy Squad with such enthusiastic public commentary, you'd have thought that Cressida had had a brilliantly successful experience with the volunteer program and not, as her family knew, a disappointing one.

More ambitiously, with the help of sympathetic women-friends Arlette established a hiking trail and "memorial garden" in Friendship Park, that ran along a bluff above the Black River for several miles, in commemoration of their lost daughter; a beautifully crafted cedar bench overlooked the river, with a little brass plaque—CRESSIDA MAYFIELD *1986–2005*—which Zeno so resented, he'd shouted at Arlette that it was perverse, it was wrong, it was obscene: "Can't we just have her name? Why do we need those dates? Why does everything have to be dated, finalized?"

Another time Arlette was stung by her husband's anger. She had expected Zeno to be deeply moved, as she was, and others had been; she said, in a hurt, puzzled voice, "I don't know, Zeno. Why? You're the intellectual in the family. *Why* do things come to an end?"

It might have been at the reception that inaugurated the memorial in Friendship Park, in a gazebo above the river, or in another, similar reception in Carnegie House, that Zeno had conspicuously too much to drink, where previously he'd only just had too much to drink; his drinking was beginning to be noted by others, outside his family and close friends. For Zeno was unhappy, and it wasn't in Zeno Mayfield's nature to be unhappy alone. He was a public man ill suited to the discretions of private life. Yet in the midst of the chattering crowd he felt ungainly, exposed. He'd always taken refuge in social life, in the peculiar thrill of a social event, in which Zeno Mayfield was one of those who shone with an indomitable luster, yet now he felt out of place. Lines from Shakespeare's *King Lear* were running through his mind, the despairing words of the elderly Lear to his murdered daughter Cordelia whom he'd stupidly misjudged and wronged—"'Why should a dog, a horse, a rat have life / and thou no breath at all?'"

This was the profound question, to which there was no answer.

He drank too much wine, out of small plastic cups. You are supposed to sip white wine sparingly, while conversing with others who are sipping wine; you are not supposed to *drink* the wine as Zeno *drank* the wine, in thirsty gulps. You are not supposed to wipe your mouth with the back of your hand.

And then Zeno's crude fingers misjudged the strength of the plastic cup, squeezed too hard and cracked it and white wine splattered onto his clothes.

"Fuck."

"Oh Daddy." Juliet was staring at him in dismay.

She'd been about to dab at him with a paper napkin but now hesitated, the fierce look in Zeno's face.

Soon it would be said *Poor Zeno. The drinking is getting out of hand, even Zeno can't hide it.*

And soon it would be said *Poor Arlette! How long can she endure it?*

HE LOVED HER. His little family, he'd loved.

Hadn't had a son, who'd have challenged him in ways other than the ways in which his daughters had challenged him. And so maybe, Zeno had to concede, he was incomplete, immature: he'd always been the adored husband, adored Daddy.

But he'd loved them, to desperation. Each of his daughters had seemed to him a miraculous birth. And his wife Arlette he'd come to love ever more deeply.

Yet, he'd come also to resent her, after Cressida's disappearance.

After the acknowledgment of *death,* and the need to *memorialize, celebrate.*

At first they'd mourned together. They'd even been drinking together.

Then by degrees it had seemed that Arlette was detaching herself from him. Like one in a comforting embrace that had turned smothering.

Bitterly he'd resented her, what he saw as her Christian *acceptance* of their loss. While in a part of Zeno's brain, it may have been his most primitive brain, he continued to believe that their daughter might be alive simply because they had no proof of her death.

In his confused and anarchic dreams, Cressida was certainly alive.

Not his daughter as he remembered her but as a wrathful though silent female figure, a daughter out of mythology. The alcohol-fueled dreams were mixed with alcohol-fueled memories of the Nautauga Preserve and the nightmare search that had come to nothing. And yet at the time it had seemed to the deluded father quite natural, the daughter had not been found. *Of course. She is nowhere near. She has vanished. But she is alive.*

Folly to think this way. Not-healthy, morbid and neurotic.

Yet after a few bottles of beer, a few glasses of wine, whiskey-and-ice, it became the natural, the logical, the inevitable and even the *commonsensical* thing to think.

Vanished. But still alive.

Zeno wanted to rage: no one understood who didn't drink. Drinking makes all of history present-tense. The past is lost, the future is inaccessible, all that is, is now.

He'd smiled, such solace! Pouring another drink.

"IT'S AGAINST NATURE to stop time. To try to stop time. You used to say—the fallacy in Plato is that he believed you could 'stop' time—that nothing that changes can be good. But change is our lives, Zeno—God would not wish us to remain unchanged. It is part of God's plan that our daughter should vanish from our lives."

In such ways Arlette began to speak. Not while drinking with Zeno but in the aftermath of drinking with Zeno.

Zeno listened in astonishment. As if another individual, a stranger to him, stood in Arlette's place.

His wife! *His* wife.

"What Brett did—he hadn't meant to do. It was brave of him to confess such a terrible thing. He can't bring Cressida back but our anger at him can't bring her back, either." Arlette paused, choosing her words with care as if knowing how each would stick in Zeno, irremediably.

Then, plunging head-on: "He's sick—he's a victim, too. Both their young lives—destroyed. We must try to forgive him."

Arlette's brave voice cracked just perceptibly with *forgive.*

Zeno muttered something inaudible.

"Zeno, what? What are you saying?"

"I said fuck that! Fuck 'forgive.'"

He'd blundered out of the room. A wounded bear on its hind

legs baited and blinded beyond endurance, desperate to escape but where to escape?—in his own household, where the woman with whom he shared the house naturally followed him through all the rooms and if he locked a door, locked himself inside a bathroom for instance, she had every right to rattle the doorknob alarmed and anxious and straining to keep her voice level in the way of a responsible wife-mother.

"You are only wounding yourself, Zeno. We have to forgive. Cressida is beyond harm now."

IT WASN'T CLEAR that Arlette was moving away. As it was painfully clear, Juliet had moved away.

Was it Zeno's fault? That the tightrope-walk of sobriety, each day, unfailingly each day, the dull-ghastly horror of sobriety, the *banality* of sobriety, was too much for him?

That, descending a flight of stairs, there began to be times when he gripped—*grasped*—the railing to keep from pitching forward headfirst? Or that, seeing awkward smiles before him, at a dinner party for instance, he'd have to laugh, embarrassed, and confess— "What was I saying? Sorry."

It had long been a custom in the Mayfield family that, in any vehicle in which Zeno Mayfield was riding, Zeno Mayfield was the designated driver. (With the exception of those periods of time when his daughters were taking driver's education and had driver's permits.)

Now it began to be the custom that Zeno drove to a social event at which there was alcohol, and Arlette drove them back; then, it began to be a custom that Arlette drove both to the event and back home.

Then, it began to be a custom that Arlette declined such invitations. With or without consulting Zeno.

Social drinker.

Not so bad as a solitary drinker!

(Of course, Zeno was a solitary drinker, too. But no one knew.)

(No one knew? Not likely.)

It began to be a—kind of a—floating weirdness: a gaping emptiness beyond Zeno's foot shy-groping on a flight of stairs *down*.

As if, if all of his senses weren't sharp-alert, he'd lose consciousness, lose balance and *down-fall*.

Saying to Arlette, as if their argument had been smoldering underground like those subterranean fuel-fields in a blistered Pennsylvania landscape smoldering for decades, "If you forgive him, you are insulting those of us who love her. You are insulting *her*."

He was shaking. Such resentment he felt for this mild-mannered woman his wife, such sudden hatred, a shock to Zeno as to her.

"Zeno, no. Forgiveness is an individual choice. If you chose to hate Brett Kincaid rather than forgive him—I mean 'forgive' him in some way—that is your prerogative. You can't know what our daughter would have wanted. By now, she might have forgiven Brett herself."

It was a brave tremulous speech. Guessing how close her husband was to grasping her shoulders and shake-shake-shaking her, in husbandly indignation.

"That's bullshit, Arlette. Kincaid hurt her, and then he drowned her. Her tossed our daughter away like garbage."

"You don't know that. You don't know how much of his confession was 'true.' His memory has been damaged. We've discussed this."

Discussed. This was an understatement.

As the father of the victim Zeno had been astonished—you might say outraged, furious—that observers assumed a right to have opinions on the case; assumed a right to comment, some of them in print, that Corporal Brett Kincaid hadn't been of sufficiently sound mind to understand the criminal charges against him and to participate in his defense; still more, hadn't been of sufficiently sound mind to have committed any crime. And whether the charge brought by the prosecutor after negotiating with the defense attorney should have been second-degree murder, or manslaughter.

Others believed that Kincaid had committed a vicious brutal murder and that the prosecutor was being overly lenient in allowing him to plead guilty to reduced charges of manslaughter.

Some might have wished for Kincaid to be sentenced to death. But Zeno was not one of these.

For Zeno didn't believe in the death penalty. Even for the vicious brutal murderer of his daughter.

As to the matter of Kincaid being capable of participating in his own defense and knowing "right from wrong"—Beechum County sheriff's deputies had testified that Kincaid had lied to them when he'd been first apprehended and brought to headquarters; he'd made an effort to "cover up his crime"—"to mislead." This is a principle in criminal law, that a perpetrator who tries to cover up his crime has understood that he has committed a crime: one who seeks to "mislead" understands that he has a reason for doing so.

In Nathan Brede's courtroom, Brett Kincaid had not spoken in his own behalf. His expression of "remorse" like his plea of guilty had been communicated by his attorney while the shackled corporal stood mute and staring into space like a dangerous beast brought to bay, and now but a piteous sight.

Zeno had no doubt, Kincaid was guilty. No doubt, Kincaid should be sentenced to prison for a long time.

Voluntary manslaughter was a weak indictment. *Fifteen to twenty years* meant eligibility for parole in seven years. Zeno knew this, and Zeno was sickened by the knowledge. But Zeno knew not to object publicly: he would not rant for TV cameras like a tormented bear on his hind legs. He would not provide an entertaining spectacle for the insatiable news media.

Yet, as a lawyer, Zeno knew: there remained the prevailing question of the corporal's confession through seven hours of police interrogation, with no lawyer present. (No lawyer because Kincaid had refused a lawyer.) How authentic was this confession? How could its details be corroborated? Had it been coerced? Had there been others who'd participated in an assault upon the victim that had begun at the lake? In the parking lot of the Roebuck Inn?—or had the assault taken place entirely in the Nautauga Preserve, with Brett Kincaid the sole assailant? Zeno had been allowed to view much of the origi-

nal interview with Kincaid through a TV monitor, at the Beechum
County Sheriff's Department, and he'd been allowed to examine the
videotapes not all of which were entirely coherent, audible. This experience he would later describe in semi-drunken *noir*-humor as an
experience not unlike seeing his guts dragged out of him, twisted,
stabbed and burnt as he observed, if such exquisite torture could be
protracted for seven hours and the victim still reasonably conscious.

Yes. Zeno could see that the young man who'd confessed to mur-
dering his daughter was sincerely repentant. You could see that Kincaid was repelled by his own physical being like a rabid creature
about to tear at itself with its teeth. But this did not make Corporal
Kincaid less guilty in Zeno's eyes. It did not make Zeno hate him less,
or feel in any way inclined to *forgive*.

It had been rumored that Corporal Brett Kincaid had provided
information against certain of his fellow platoon-comrades, in Iraq;
that he'd participated in an army investigation into atrocities committed by U.S. soldiers against Iraqi citizens; that some or all of his
injuries might have been the result of his providing testimony, and
that he'd had to be hurriedly dispatched out of his platoon, out of
Iraq, to prevent his being killed. None of these rumors was ever sub-
stantiated and when Zeno Mayfield tried to discover what had happened, both directly and by way of what Zeno wanted to think was a
high-ranking personal contact at the Department of Veteran Affairs
in Washington, D.C., he'd been informed that there was no such investigation on record: no charges had been filed against anyone in
Corporal Kincaid's platoon.

Meaning—what? That the U.S. Army had buried the investigation, or that there'd never been an investigation? That Corporal Kincaid had been injured by the Iraqi enemy, or by his own comrades?
Or both?

AFTER THE INITIAL INTERVIEWS when it had seemed that Cressida
was merely *missing*, and that their public appeals might be of help in
finding her, the Mayfields never gave another.

After Evvie Estes contacted them one too many times Zeno told her bluntly *No more. We're done with entertaining.*

FELT NO DESIRE for his wife, or any woman.

His only desire was for—(he knew: an insipid fantasy)—the restoration of all he'd lost though at the time of his losing it, in July 2005, he'd had but a vague awareness of its vast unfathomable worth; and of his own worth, mirrored in it.

Consoling himself, these solitary evenings when Arlette was "out"—(carefully she'd explained where she was, which volunteer organization, or which women-friends)—with a smudged tumbler of whiskey and *The Personal Memoirs of Ulysses S. Grant.*

Belatedly he would realize: even Arlette's sickness had been an estrangement between them. An occasion for estrangement.

Where once such a personal, physical crisis would have drawn them together more intimately, as in the intense, emotion-rife days preceding and following the births of their daughters years ago, now the discovery that Arlette "had" cancer was like an elbow in the husband's ribs nudging him aside.

So Zeno felt. All the more reason then in his suspended-terror state to have an occasional (surreptitious, at-home) drink. Just one.

Or maybe, one and a half.

(For who would know?)

(Not Arlette in her life ever more tight-scheduled like a cobweb of maniacal precision in which, the husband was given to know, his anxious presence was a detriment and not a blessing.)

For from the first discovery of a tiny lump in Arlette's left breast through a sequence of mammograms, CAT scans, biopsy and surgery—the grueling regimen of chemotherapy, radiation, and medication that stretched on for more than six months in the late summer, fall and winter of 2006 to 2007—it hadn't been her husband in whom she'd confided so much as in her sister and other women-friends who'd rallied to her like dolphins in a treacherous sea rallying to one of their own stricken kind.

Zeno was sick with fury anew, at Kincaid. Who'd killed his daughter, and was now killing his wife.

It could not be a coincidence, Zeno thought. That his wife, Cressida's mother, should be diagnosed with cancer approximately a year after Cressida's disappearance.

(Zeno had reason to believe that others, close to Arlette, like her sister Katie Hewitt, thought so, too; but were too tactful to mention it to either of the Mayfields.)

The tiny lump "the size of a persimmon seed"—(so Arlette persisted in describing it in the vocabulary of a children's storybook)—seemed to Zeno the way in which the destructive element that had snatched away his daughter had found, in his marriage, another way *in*.

He'd wanted to take Arlette to Buffalo, to the Roswell Park Cancer Institute. He'd wanted her to be in the care of the very best breast cancer doctors upstate. But Arlette had demurred, wanting to remain close to home. She'd conferred with her women-friends, she'd made a decision to continue with local doctors—surgeon, interventional radiologist, oncologist. "Buffalo is more than two hundred miles away. It would just complicate things. Please, let me handle this in a way that isn't distressful to me."

"But you're my wife! I want the very best for you."

Only reluctantly had Arlette told Zeno her alarming news when he'd questioned her about a "surgical procedure" she was scheduled to have at the Carthage Hospital—Arlette's euphemism for "biopsy."

If she'd wept, if she'd broken down to weep in anyone's arms, it had not been in her husband's arms.

"Weren't you going to tell me? When were you going to tell me?"

"I didn't want to worry you, Zeno. You've been so—you have a tendency to be so—"

"To be so *concerned?* About my *family?*"

"Please don't be angry with me, Zeno. You're so often—"

"I'm not angry! I'm surprised, and I'm upset, and I'm disappointed, but—I am not angry."

Seeing that it was all Arlette could do, to keep from stepping back from him.

He knew, in recent months he'd lost his old, Zeno-equanimity. He knew, he was frightening his wife away even as he meant to beckon her to him.

"I didn't see any reason to worry you prematurely, Zeno. If the cyst turned out to be benign, as often they do . . ."

"Of course you should have told me! That's ridiculous, and insulting."

"I—I didn't mean to be insulting . . ."

"You know how news spreads in Carthage. What would people say if they knew that Zeno Mayfield's wife had had a biopsy at the hospital and he hadn't even known?"

Zeno heard *Zeno Mayfield's wife. My wife.*

Zeno knew, this was not the right thing to say. Not to his wife who'd been so bravely trying to hide her anxiety from him; not to Arlette who loved him, and wanted to protect him. Yet he couldn't seem to stop himself, his hurt was so deep.

"I want to take you to Buffalo, Arlette. We'll make an appointment, we'll drive there—tomorrow. I'll call my doctor-friend Artie Bender, in Buffalo, he can get us an appointment with the very best breast-cancer specialist at Roswell."

"Zeno, no! I can't."

"What do you mean, you can't?"

"I have a surgeon, and an oncologist. I—I like them both very much. I trust them. I've been talking to people, women-friends, who recommend them, and who've gone to them. And Katie likes them, too. You know how critical Katie is . . ."

"Fuck Katie! Katie isn't your husband, I am."

Your husband. I am.

In his head these crude words echoed. Yet he could not stop himself, he must argue with the woman, try to impose his will upon her for *nothing but the very best for Zeno's wife.*

"You're excluding me from your life, Arlette. In other ways, too—I hate it."

"I—I don't mean to."

It was so, Arlette had begun attending church services more frequently. Community-service meetings, fund-raisers for local causes, evenings away from home when Zeno had only the vaguest idea where she was and what she was doing and with whom.

Arlette, where the hell were you? Why are you getting home so late?

Zeno, I told you. I explained, but you weren't listening.

Then you should tell me again. I will listen.

It was so, Arlette had begun attending church more frequently, alone.

For Juliet had moved away. And Zeno never went to church.

(Though he'd have joined Arlette at the Congregationalist church if she'd asked him. He'd wanted her to think so.)

And it was so, Arlette was beginning to say things that disturbed Zeno, the supreme rationalist.

"Sometimes I feel, Zeno—something is trying to tell me something. I try to 'read' it—but can't. As in a dream, you can't read."

"What do you mean, 'in a dream, you can't read'?"

"If you dream of holding a book or a newspaper, and trying to read the words, you can't. Your eyes just don't focus."

"Who says this?"

"Nobody says it!" Arlette laughed, with something of her old, fond exasperation. "I think it must be a common experience."

Zeno was skeptical. He'd email a professor-friend of his at Cornell whose specialty was cognitive psychology, to ask for an expert opinion.

"Next time you dream, Zeno, see if you can make yourself 'read.' Look at a paper or a book. You'll see that the letters are all blurred."

Zeno laughed, this seemed to him so fanciful. Not that it might not be true but that his dear wife Arlette, who knew little of psychology, still less of the human brain, should think so.

AND YET: Zeno was himself becoming ever more irrational, superstitious. In the particular way of a defiantly rational, ego-centered male of late middle age, confronted with a crumbling, collapsing facade beyond the reach of his will to mend. As a local politician Zeno Mayfield had been *the man to see, to get things done;* mostly, his presence had been a beneficent one, and even political adversaries had liked him, as a man; but now, years out of office and losing interest in maintaining his old Carthage contacts, he had nothing to occupy his time, his seething churning thoughts like tires spinning in mud, that *mattered.*

He'd have made his wife's cancer a campaign, if only!

Saying to Juliet *Why didn't your mother let me help her? Didn't she know that I loved—love—her?*

And Juliet replied *Yes Daddy, Mom knows. But this is her new life, now.*

THEY COULDN'T BEAR to sell the house.

The beautiful old sprawling Colonial on Cumberland Avenue on a three-acre lot dense with tall oak and cedar trees, in the high, hilly neighborhood close by the Episcopal cemetery—*they could not.*

Though Arlette had moved out. And Zeno could not bear to live alone in so large a house like a beetle—(he said)—rattling inside a beetle-trap.

For two weeks, Arlette had visited with Juliet in Averill Park, ostensibly to help out with the children. And when she'd returned she moved out, for it was a time of renewal, she said.

Not a time to resume the old.

She told Zeno of her plans. She told Zeno of plans already in place. His wife who'd rarely made any major decision of her own for nearly three decades, explaining to him now what she'd done, and what she would be doing, of her own volition and singly.

Zeno protested he'd had no idea. Had not guessed. Though of

course he'd known, must have guessed—those weeks and months of subtle and then not-so-subtle estrangement in the house on Cumberland Avenue.

Weeks, months of drinking. Solitary, and with others.

Late-afternoon naps from which he woke sodden and dazed at 8 P.M. not knowing if it was dusk or dawn; if he was alone in the house or if Arlette patiently awaited him downstairs with a meal he couldn't bring himself to eat.

Ever more frequently, Arlette wasn't awaiting.

Excluding me from your life it's like my life hemorrhaging from me how can you when I love you.

Too proud to protest and certainly too proud to beg the woman to stay with him.

Getting high he called it. Never *getting drunk.*

"High" had a hippie-innocence to it. "Drunk" had no innocence.

Yet he was stone-cold sober or nearly, when Arlette came to him to explain.

Taking his hands, his big-bear paw-hands, in hers. To explain.

She was moving eight miles away to Mount Olive, she said. She would be sharing a house with a woman attorney named Alisandra Raoul who was a co-director of a battered women's shelter there and she would be working at the shelter more or less full-time.

Zeno had been hearing about this—*shelter.* Hadn't been paying enough attention it seemed.

But—"'Alisandra Raoul'? Who?"

"Zeno, I've told you. I've spoken of Alisandra many times."

"No, I don't think so. I've never heard the name before, you know how good I am at remembering names."

Still, they would not sell the house. Juliet had begged them not to sell it and if Cressida were alive—(*if Cressida were alive* was Zeno's mangled logic)—she'd have begged them, too.

Neither could have quite explained: the marriage could be reclaimed at any time but the house, once sold, would not be reclaimed but would pass into the hands of strangers.

Neither could have quite explained: if their missing daughter were to return home, yes improbably, yes of course impossibly, still what a further shock for the daughter, to discover strangers living in her family home.

In the front lawn a Realtor's sign, bright brash yellow-and-black FOR RENT/LEASE. After the first windstorm the sign was left slanted just slightly askew.

Arlette had gone to live in Mount Olive and heartless and distracted by her new, busy and so-fascinating life did not return to Cumberland Avenue. Zeno living in a condominium in downtown Carthage in a riverfront area newly gentrified, now prime real estate, drove often to the house to check it, seeing such vigilance as a husband's duty.

Heartbreak: the smell of an abandoned house.

Unmistakable: the smell of an abandoned house.

Untenanted, the house still had electricity, gas, water. Those services had not been discontinued. Most of the furniture remained in the rooms intact. Even a television set, in what had been the basement family room, remained intact.

Yet when the real estate woman called Zeno with "good news"— offers from clients if the monthly rental price could be reduced just slightly—Zeno was adamant *No.*

And if the real estate woman called Mrs. Mayfield to reason with her, Arlette would say with an apologetic little laugh *Oh no! The real estate is Zeno's territory, I would never interfere.*

In this way, the house on Cumberland Avenue remained untenanted.

IN HILLY MOUNT OLIVE Arlette lived in an older residential neighborhood of large old Victorian houses renovated and refashioned as office buildings for young lawyers, architects, dentists; gift shops, herbal-medicine shops, Beechum County Ecological Engineers. The battered-women's shelter WomanSpaceInc. which held thirty-five beds was housed in a large red-brick building that had been a girls'

Catholic school, set back in a grassy lot behind a wrought-iron fence.

At night, the property was lit with bright lights and monitored by surveillance cameras with alarms connected to the Mount Olive Police Department. When the battered-women's shelter had first been established in Mount Olive volunteers had been rudely treated by neighbors and disdained by local law enforcement authorities; but since a changeover in the police department, the small police force was now supportive of WomanSpaceInc. in their aim to "reduce domestic violence"—"reduce violence in the world by beginning at home." (It did not fail to help that a lieutenant in the Mount Olive P.D. was the brother of one of the founders and that the formerly all-male P.D. now had a female police officer.)

Posters designed by local woman artists called for volunteers and donations—VIOLENCE BEGINS IN THE HOME. TAKE CARE. Arlette had appropriated one of Cressida's early, pre-Escher pen-and-ink drawings, in which childlike figures played together with animals in a floating oasis of green, as the background artwork for a Woman Space poster.

Zeno who'd often been offended by Arlette's appropriation of their daughter's art was touched by this. The charming drawing had belonged to a time in Cressida's life when she'd been less inward and difficult, happier.

On lonely afternoons Zeno drove to Mount Olive as if sensing that Arlette might be thinking of him. Calling him to her.

He knew where she lived: 18 Cross Patch Lane.

Cross Patch Lane! An address out of a children's storybook.

And the old rebuilt shingle board house painted bright green with a tidy little front lawn and coral-colored front walk on a cul-de-sac lane of similar houses rebuilt and painted magenta, peacock-blue, cream—Zeno would cruise slowly past knowing that Arlette wouldn't be home, nor would her house-mate Alisandra be home, not during the day, for the women were at the battered-women's shelter, the women were working, only Zeno Mayfield was cast adrift.

He might have taught a course at Beechum Community College, he'd taught in the past—"American Originals: Tom Paine to Woody Guthrie." He might have spent time at Home Front Alliance where adult-male volunteers were particularly needed. There was much he could do but not much he wanted to do.

He drove past WomanSpaceInc. Here were warning signs PRIVATE PROPERTY DO NOT TRESPASS. A six-foot wrought iron fence and behind it the austere red-brick building converted into a dormitory for desperate women and their children. When he'd been mayor of Carthage he'd learned a good deal about domestic violence and he'd done what he could to provide aid for women who'd had to flee their domestic arrangements. Some of them were terribly beaten, in terror of their lives. Yet, it was a frequent irony, the battered women changed their minds and refused to press charges against their men.

Maybe times had changed. Maybe in Mount Olive, at Woman SpaceInc., the desperate women were more resolute. Their rescuers, like Arlette Mayfield, would be their protectors.

Once at WomanSpaceInc. he saw Arlette walking with two other women, to a vehicle parked in the driveway. It was a bright windy day: Arlette had tied a scarf around her new hair, that gave her a blithe girlish look though she was very thin still, and did look like a woman in recovery. He'd wanted to call her attention to him, waving out a window, tapping his horn—but no, better not. The property of WomanSpace was off-limit to the male species with the exception of the mailman, delivery men and boys younger than twelve in the company of their mothers. There must be a "safe house" for women where no man can come, Arlette said, as passionately as if she were a woman hunted by men herself.

Though Zeno hadn't attended such meetings, which would have been too painful for him, he knew through intermediaries that Arlette was outspoken in front of audiences telling of how she'd lost her daughter to "male violence"—"male violence exacerbated by alcohol." She didn't, she claimed, blame the young man, an Iraq War veteran, so much as she blamed the "sick, violent, cruel and heartless consumer culture" in which young girls were used as advertising commodities, to sell products. It was a shock to Zeno to realize that if he wanted to, he could not approach WomanSpaceInc.: he wouldn't be allowed inside the fortress-like residence even to speak with his wife.

How many violent men, seeking their fleeing wives, claimed to want only to "speak" with them.

HE SAW ARLETTE for dinner sometimes in Mount Olive. But they did not speak of Cressida now.

They did talk about Arlette's health: for this was good news, on the whole. The chemotherapy seemed to be working, the cancer had not spread.

On her head Arlette wore a human-hair wig, dark-blond, wavy, very like her own hair except that it was thicker and more lustrous than her own hair had been for years. A woman-friend had counseled Arlette to have a wig in readiness for when her hair began to fall out in clumps during chemotherapy—"Having a double mastectomy wasn't as awful as being bald. I know that sounds ridiculous but it happens to be true for lots of women including me."

Zeno winced, hearing this reported to him secondhand. *Double mastectomy* sounded too much like *double testectomy*.

Arlette hadn't had a double mastectomy, or even a single mastectomy. Her *persimmon-seed* had been caught early. And so, Arlette believed herself very lucky, and would not ever complain about the chemical-infusion treatments that left her dazed and exhausted and nauseated. It was a curiosity of Arlette's new life that she never seemed to complain about anything.

"I feel as if we're all passengers on a plane that has entered a patch of 'turbulence'—we should be grateful we haven't crashed yet."

Arlette laughed, almost gaily. Zeno winced.

He was seeing other women now. Or rather, other women were seeing him: calling to invite him to dinner, to accompany them to social gatherings. As nature abhors a vacuum so Zeno Mayfield was wryly discovering that a solitary man is a kind of vacuum, to whom solitary women are irresistibly drawn.

None of his encounters were very real to him. None of the women lingered in his memory. He was still in love with his elusive and unfathomable wife.

The Mount Olive restaurants were likely to be in refashioned wood frame houses, with candlelit tables crowded close together, organic-food menus, no alcohol served. Shrewd Zeno knew to call beforehand to inquire about a liquor license; he knew to bring his own wine.

"Won't you have a little, Arlette? Just a half-glass."

"Thanks, Zeno. But no. I'm on call."

" 'On call'—how?"

"At the shelter. We're terribly understaffed, we're more or less always on call."

Arlette smiled happily. To be always *on call!* Zeno envied her.

Whether he was drinking or not he was beginning to feel that many things were unreal and unnatural. To be having dinner with his wife in the candlelit front room of a stately old Colonial house with a bare plank floor and to know that he would have to go away without his wife, in a separate vehicle, was deeply strange to him like knowing that, when he stood, one of his legs would buckle beneath him.

Life is a dream a little less consistent.

(Who'd said that? Centuries ago? Pascal?)

(Who'd also said When all is equally agitated, nothing appears to be agitated.)

The estranged husband imagines himself re-encountering his wife, courting and winning her a second time. If she'd fallen in love with him once, why not a second time? So Zeno imagined. So Zeno plotted. Daring to brush his fingers across Arlette's slender hand as if accidentally even as he could not fail to see that Arlette was distracted while speaking with him, or rather listening to him; too often, her cell phone rang during their meal.

"I'm so sorry, Zeno! I have to answer."

Where once he'd have been furious, his wife cared so little for him as to answer her cell phone at dinner, the very sort of rude behavior neither Zeno nor Arlette would have allowed in their daughters, now Zeno was touched that Arlette felt the need to apologize. *She still loves me. If I need her, she will come back to me.*

To Juliet he'd pleaded, in frequent phone calls: Why has your mother left our marriage? Why has she moved *out*? He'd never asked Juliet why her mother had ceased loving him for he could not truly believe that this was so.

Embarrassed, Juliet had told Zeno she didn't know.

Often in one or another of the small ethnic restaurants in Mount Olive where they had dinner together Arlette had to leave early with a flutter of apologies and a brush of her lips against Zeno's cheek. Alone then the abandoned husband sat finishing a glass of wine, brooding.

(The temptation was to finish the entire bottle, which he'd brought.)

He'd insisted upon paying the bill of course. He knew that Arlette didn't have much money though she seemed incapable of asking him for money.

If the house on Cumberland Avenue were to be sold, Zeno and Arlette would each receive half of the sale price. But that would make their break irrevocable. The very prospect was unnerving to Zeno.

The estranged husband imagines his wife bound to him by need—a need for money, if nothing more. In her zeal for community volunteer-work Arlette seemed to have little need of her own.

Next time they met for dinner Zeno surprised Arlette by handing her a check.

"Oh Zeno! What is—?"

A check for three thousand dollars made out to *WomanSpaceInc*.

"Oh Zeno. Thank you."

She stood, came to him and hugged him, and kissed his stubbly cheek. Might've been Zeno's imagination, her tears wetted his face.

IN A WEAK-MAUDLIN mood half-drunk descending bumpy Potsdam Street. And there, the Kincaid house or what remained of it—peeling wood frame, set close to the sidewalk, shades pulled at all the windows and a litter of old newspapers and flyers accumulated by the front stoop like ancient bones.

No one lived here now. Ethel Kincaid had departed Carthage.

She'd left the city she so hated, her rented house filled—(so it had been reported in the media)—with trash of all kinds including raw garbage and decaying rodent-carcasses, the woman's final gesture of outrage. No one had been informed where Ethel had gone though there were reports initially that she'd moved to the village of Dannemora to live near her incarcerated son.

This turned out to be unfounded. Ethel Kincaid was not living in Dannemora but with relatives in Tonawanda, a suburb of Buffalo. She had broken off all relations with Carthage. She had even ceased giving angry interviews—or rather, it may have been that the tabloid media had tired of the vet's grieving mother.

Staring at the abandoned and derelict house Zeno recalled the anxious hope with which he'd hurried to the door, on that morning in July 2005.

Already then, his daughter had vanished. His daughter *was no more.*

And yet, as he'd knocked on Ethel Kincaid's door he had not known that melancholy fact. His brain had been in such a tumult of hope, almost now he could envy that old, lost father-Zeno, imagining that, through bravado and belligerence of his own, he might find his missing Cressida.

Asking the astonished Ethel Kincaid to let him into her house. To let him into Brett Kincaid's room. The wild thought like a fragile rope he was pulling to save his life that his daughter might be there, with Brett Kincaid: the most unlikely of lovers.

And Ethel had sent him away jeering.

And Ethel had sent him away with a curse flung at the head of all the Mayfields of the world, those who dwell on Cumberland Avenue and not on steep-shabby Potsdam Street *My son hates all of you.*

The woman had come into his life to drink with him.

To shore him up, to listen to his rants and laugh at his jokes. To love him.

"Zeno? Maybe you could come for dinner sometime? I'd love to make us dinner."

He'd hesitated. What was this? The first stumbling step of his new life? His life-after-Arlette? Or was this the first, stumbling step of a sequence of blunders?

Her name was Genevieve. He hadn't heard the last name clearly.

They'd met at a gathering in Carthage, in January 2012. He'd known her husband—hadn't he?—but couldn't inquire for he failed to recall the husband's name.

He'd smiled. He'd hesitated. He'd had a drink in hand, one of those fragile plastic cups his big fingers were at risk for cracking.

Told her thank you! Gentlemanly regret: *See honey, I'm a burnt-out case. Run for your life.*

Yet, she'd prevailed. Smiling woman waiting for Zeno by the coat room.

No choice but he'd had to invite her across the street for a drink at least. A drink to erase the sour taste of the cheap white wine at the reception.

It was flattering—unless it was disturbing, sad—that, at the reception in Carnegie House, in celebration of the retirement of the director of the Carnegie Arts Foundation, Zeno Mayfield had been one of the centers of conversation, as in the old, lost days. For everyone in Carthage who was likely to be invited to this social event knew Zeno Mayfield: wanted to warm themselves with his good humor, laughter, sagacity and audacity, affability. Possibly Zeno was drinking too much lately, possibly since the departure of his wife from their marriage he was indeed becoming a *burnt-out case,* but amid the cheering din of voices and laughter who could tell? Who could *care?*

"Genevieve—is that your name? To be frank I don't think it's a good idea."

He'd been apologetic, stumbling. He had left his eloquence back at the brightly-lit reception.

She'd looked no more than thirty-five years old. He'd looked older than his age which was—never mind.

"Just dinner? What can be such a risk, a simple dinner? You know we live in the same building, don't you? You're on the penthouse floor, I'm on the fifth."

He'd heard: something had gone terribly wrong in this woman's life. The husband, a teenaged son. He wouldn't inquire. He didn't want to provoke tears. He didn't want to provoke sympathy. Like hemorrhaging it was, this sort of sympathy. He saw that there were several rings on her attractive hands but no wedding band, a danger signal.

Zeno's wedding band had grown into his fatty finger, most likely. A Celtic design, silver. Arlette's fingers had grown too thin, she'd had to remove all her rings.

The smiling woman was saying, "We each have losses. I understand. Yours may be deeper and more tragic than mine, but . . ."

Zeno resisted the impulse to touch her hand. Take her hand. He would not. Instead, lifted his glass.

Better a wineglass than the damned cheap plastic cups.

He saw her lips move. Earnestly she was speaking. Better this dim-lit interior than the over-bright Carnegie House.

"I've 'lost' my son though he's still—he's living. He's twenty-four years old and I haven't seen him in almost two years. I think that people who have similar losses can understand and help each other though I don't mean—I don't mean dwelling upon the past . . . I mean—I think I mean—trying to live *now.*" Suddenly she laughed with unexpected gaiety, lifting her glass to touch Zeno's.

Much better wine in the Mercer Street Lounge, than at the crowded reception across the street.

"Well. I'll drink to that."

"*I'll* drink to that."

They laughed. They drank, and laughed.

What more precious than the opportunity to drink, laugh and drink.

Telling Genevieve how furious he was with his wife for being so God-damned brave and God-damned *good*. God-damned *stoic* about her health making him feel like a quivering asshole, he'd been so scared for her.

But mostly couldn't forgive her for "forgiving" their daughter's murderer.

"Oh! Oh, Zeno."

Arlette had gone to visit him in prison. She had not ever told Zeno about the visits but—he knew. He'd found out.

God damn her, her precious Christian soul. *She had forgiven the unforgiveable, he hated her.*

Now, it was uttered. He'd sworn he would not ever talk in this way with any stranger nor even with well-intentioned relatives urging him to talk in this way yet now, he heard, shocked he heard his voice careening on like a runaway wheel down a steep incline.

And for "forgiving" God—he hated her for that, too.

"God damn fucking *God*."

Spoke so vehemently, customers at other tables glanced in their direction. Genevieve laughed.

A sensible woman would have fled. Genevieve poured more wine into both their glasses and laughed.

And how good it felt, laughed-at instead of cringed-at.

"I've thought that too, Zeno. Many times. *God damn fucking God*."

He told her of the ancient Greeks. Blood-passion. Aeschylus, *Oresteia*. Some spring seemed to have been tripped in his brain like desiccated suet liquefied by heat. He'd always been an eloquent drunk but hadn't had the opportunity lately.

Saying how laws had been invented to stem the primitive passion for revenge but the feeling of outrage, the wish to exact blood-
revenge, is not easily quelled.

Told the woman listening so intently to him, flatteringly-intently,
about a documentary he'd seen on television the previous night, honor
killings in Muslim families in the United States, some of the families
solidly middle-class, even educated. Fathers in police custody weeping
because they'd killed their "disobedient" daughters who'd "defiled"
the family name. The grief in the face of one of the Muslim men, so
like Zeno Mayfield they might have been brothers, though the act had
been insane.

The unbearable fact was, his daughter had been murdered—but
he'd been too weak to take revenge.

Of course: too civilized.

"Officer of the court."

And now, he didn't feel that he had any honor remaining. His soul
had dried up, a husk.

Now it had been years. More than six years. He carried it inside
him like malignant marrow in his bones. In even the semi-dark you
could see the malignancy inside him, luminous, lethal.

The woman had said, "I can risk that."

Phone rang. Caller ID wasn't *Trachtman* which was Genevieve's
name but *Stedman* which was Juliet's married name.

"Daddy? I had an upsetting call today."

What was today? Bleary-eyed seeing it had to be mid-March. On
the calendar above his desk was March with a half-dozen dates feebly
X'd out. But that was last week.

Juliet was telling him of a "young-sounding voice" she'd heard
that morning. A stranger—she thought—calling her claiming to be
Cressida.

Zeno gripped the receiver tighter not certain he'd heard correctly.

"I mean—of course—it has to be a stranger—but"—Juliet paused; Zeno could imagine her quick confused smile—"it didn't—she didn't—sound anything like Cressida at all. I'm sure."

"Honey, wait. Someone called you?"

"She said—I'm not sure what she said. I didn't think for an instant that it was Cressida of course but only some kind of cruel prank. Then, the person called back and left a message and somehow, it got erased."

"The message is erased?"

"I was upset, I guess—somehow, I erased it."

Calmly Zeno asked if Juliet had any record of the phone number.

"On my cell phone, yes. Just the number, not the message. But there's no answer—the number at the other end doesn't seem to exist."

Zeno, seated at his desk, was sitting forward now elbows on the desk and eyes shut in concentration.

"Julie. Why would anyone make such a call, as a prank?"

"Daddy, I don't know! Maybe from the Internet. There's still information online about Cressida. I never look at it, any of it, but I know it's there because people tell me. There's some sort of 'mystery' about Cressida, for some people—where she is. What happened to her body. And people do cruel things for no reason."

Still calmly Zeno said, "This call you received. This caller. Did she say where she was calling from?"

"No." Juliet thought. "Yes. I think—Florida."

Juliet thought again. "She said she was 'coming home.' I *think*."

"She said she was 'coming home'?"

Gripping the receiver so tightly now he feared he would break it.

"I didn't call Mom. I didn't want to upset her. She's made her peace with what happened, I think—it's a way Mom has dealt with losing Cressida. To get her hopes up would be cruel."

"Yes. You're right. I'm grateful that you called me, sweetie, and not your mother. And I'm sure that this is what you say it is—a cruel prank."

Carefully Juliet said: "Brett did confess. And they found the—you know—the sweater."

Zeno didn't reply. So many times they'd spoken these words or similar words it was like entering a tunnel—you could not bear it another time.

Though sometimes, discussing this matter, Juliet would say *My sweater.*

As if she hadn't known what she was saying. *My sweater.*

Zeno said, "This caller—who didn't sound like Cressida—what else did she say?"

"In the message, what I remember of the message, she said she was calling from Florida—some place in Florida, I think. But I couldn't hear clearly. The connection was poor. Or her voice was muffled. She said something strange—'I am not a sick person.' And I think she said—'I did not think that any of you loved me much . . .' "

"And what else, honey? Did she say anything else?"

"No. I don't think so."

"But—what did you say to her?"

"I don't think I said anything. I think—I think I hung up."

In the background, at Juliet's house, was the high-pitched chattering of a child.

Distractedly Zeno asked Juliet about the kids, and about her husband. The very word "kids"—so relaxed, colloquial, ordinary—was a balm to him, in this bizarre moment.

Juliet spoke in her usual animated way about her family. If there were problems in Juliet's new family, if ever there were health or medical issues, it would be a long time before Juliet's bright soothing manner would acknowledge these problems.

Politely too Juliet asked her father about his *woman-friend Gwendolyn.*

Zeno answered briefly, distractedly. Not troubling to correct his daughter.

More animatedly he said, to fill in the stiff stunned silence between them: "A dozen times a day I remind myself—how Goddamned happy I am to have grandchildren."

"Oh, Daddy. Yes! I feel the same way—about my children."

Juliet had married a man very different from Brett Kincaid. He was nineteen years older than Juliet and of another generation. The Mayfield name was unknown to him, with its political resonances in Beechum County. He'd been a lobbyist for the public school teachers' union and he was now a high-ranking official with the New York State Department of Education whose office remained fundamentally unchanged through changes of state government—governor, legislature. He'd published articles in *The Chronicle of Higher Education, The New York Times Education Issue.* He was from an old Albany family, a great-grandfather had been an aide of Governor Thomas Dewey. He'd served in the Peace Corps in Ghana, just out of Williams College. He'd been married before and the marriage had ended in an "amicable" divorce, no children.

The Stedmans had made a fortune in railroads in the 1890s and retained some portion of that fortune into the twenty-first century. Why Zeno resented his middle-aged son-in-law he could not have said for truly he was grateful for David D. Stedman in his daughter's life.

In fact, David Stedman was a man of integrity, dignity. He was taciturn, but kindly. He'd learned to manipulate strangers in the precise way in which Zeno Mayfield had learned to manipulate them, in the snarls of the political machinery of public life. So Zeno respected the man even if he couldn't feel warmth for him.

All that Zeno cared about waking in the middle of the night anxious and clammy-skinned in terror of the future was that David D. Stedman loved his daughter, and wished to protect her.

It seemed crucial too, Stedman had never met Cressida. His sympathy, pity, outrage were abstract and not particularized.

Zeno was thinking what a good thing, his grandchildren would outlive him.

A law of nature, younger generations outlived their elders.

Zeno asked again about the call, since Juliet had fallen silent.

Juliet repeated what she'd said but in a slower less certain voice.

As in a lawyerly interrogation of a benign type Zeno asked, "Was it 'I didn't think that any of you loved me much'—or 'I did not think that any of you loved me much'?

"I think it was—'I did not think . . .'"

"'Did not'—as if avoiding the contraction."

"Whoever it was seemed to be speaking stiffly. Formally. Like someone who didn't know English well, or"—Juliet paused—"someone who doesn't talk much."

"She actually said she was 'coming home'?"

"'If people would want me.'"

"'*Would* want me.' That isn't colloquial English, exactly."

"It's the subjunctive. Or, it's someone who doesn't feel comfortable speaking English."

"Someone who doesn't feel comfortable speaking to you."

"But I don't think she knew *me*. How could she know *me*."

"And how would she have gotten your telephone number, in Averill Park?"

Juliet had no response. In the background, the happy high-pitched chattering continued.

"'Coming home'—well, we'll see!"

Zeno laughed, and hung up the phone.

Scarcely making it into a corner of his study where he collapsed, all 199 pounds, onto a leather sofa.

NOT THAT DAY nor the following day but the following week a call came from a Cumberland Avenue neighbor.

"Zeno? Looks like somebody's lying on your sofa-swing. You know, on your side deck. My wife says he's been there for about an hour."

Zeno asked who it might be. A homeless person?

Though not very likely, a homeless person in the residential Cumberland neighborhood.

Zeno thanked his friend. He'd been planning to drive over to check the house anyway, later that day—"I'll come over now."

VETERANS: THE COUNTRY was filling up with them. In obscure rural areas of Appalachia, in Hispanic communities in the West and the Southwest, in the Great Plains states as in western and upstate New York veterans of the crusade against terror: the barely-walking-wounded, the (visibly, invisibly) maimed, "disabled." Driving along the river and into the city and through the working-class neighborhoods of west Carthage he saw them ever more frequently, young men, old-young men, on crutches, in wheelchairs. Dark-skinned, white-skinned. Casualties of war. Now that the wars in Afghanistan and Iraq were winding down, the veterans would be returned to civilian life, litter on a beach when the great tide has gone out.

As a political person, as a liberal, Zeno Mayfield was sympathetic with their lot. He knew, the federal government could never begin to repay the veterans for all they'd sacrificed in the naivete of their patriotism. Yet, as a father, he felt an unreasonable rage. They'd learned to kill in the wars and they'd brought their killing-appetite home with them and his daughter had been murdered by one of them, a killing machine gone amok.

It was said that no other suspect in the history of the Beechum County Sheriff's Department had given such a long disjointed candid and self-incriminating confession as Brett Kincaid. He'd seemed to be speaking of numerous murders, and not just the murder of Cressida Mayfield.

He'd given the names of his platoon leaders. He'd given the names of his fellow soldiers. He'd had to be reminded that he was no longer a soldier in Iraq but a civilian in Carthage: he'd had to be reminded that the subject was Cressida Mayfield.

On Cumberland Avenue, Zeno saw with a particular pained pleasure his neighbors' houses unchanged. The procession of tall oaks, cedars. He had not been absent from his house for more than a week, of course nothing much would have changed, in the interim. Yet he felt relief, seeing his house and the Realtor's sign at the curb FOR RENT/LEASE.

He parked in the driveway. At first he didn't see the figure on the deck-swing for the afternoon had begun to wane to a premature dusk, then approaching it he saw more clearly a person—male, female?— possibly a child of about twelve?—wrapped in a blanket; the rough soiled old red-plaid blanket from L.L. Bean they'd kept outdoors on the deck-swing. The figure was female: a girl. A small-boned woman. She had dark hair, her face was partly hidden beneath the blanket. She was curled up tightly as if very cold. (It was just thirty-two degrees Fahrenheit: wet snow fell, melting almost immediately.) She was breathing hoarsely. As he drew nearer, he could hear her. She didn't look well. Should he call 911? He drew nearer. At Home Front Alliance she'd have been offered a bed in the women's quarters, a volunteer medic would examine her and maybe prescribe antibiotics.

Zeno stood, a few feet from the sleeping girl wrapped in the soiled blanket. So tightly curled up, her feet were hidden. He had the unreasonable notion that she was barefoot. She was ill, feverish. She would need medical attention. But he would stand there, he thought, until she began to wake sensing his presence. He could not bring himself to wake the sleeping girl for then the spell would end.

SIXTEEN

The Mother

March 2012

S HE'D JUST RETURNED from the shelter. Her long shift at the shelter that should have ended at 6 P.M. but there'd been a difficult admission that day, a psychiatric nurse had had to be summoned as well as an officer from the Mount Olive Police Department since they'd received death threats from an anonymous caller. Past 8 P.M. when she'd returned to the house on Cross Patch Lane and not ten minutes later the doorbell rang.

Anyone at the door at this time of evening, you weren't comfortable opening it. Their lives had been threatened numerous times. They'd been waylaid and harassed by furious husbands, boyfriends and pimps. There were ever younger girls seeking asylum in Woman-Space, Eastern European by birth who spoke little English, illegal immigrants terrified of being deported. But they'd fled their abusers, they'd taken refuge in the Mount Olive shelter and their "employers" had hired aggressive lawyers to counter the girls' claims of sexual abuse and violence with threats of lawsuits.

Alisandra went to answer the door. Arlette heard her friend's voice lift—*Yes?*

On the front stoop were her husband Zeno and her daughter Juliet.

"Oh."

She was utterly stunned. Her first thought was—*They have come to take me forcibly back home.*

She saw their faces. She knew, something had happened to alter their lives profoundly but she could have no idea what it was.

Juliet embraced her, hugging her tight. Zeno touched her shoulder, with his anxious-Zeno smile.

"Mom. Can we come inside? Can you maybe sit down? We have some news."

She was shaking now. In their eyes, a strange elation, excitement or fear.

She was sitting: at the kitchen table. Since the cancer treatments she'd lost weight and had not regained more than a few pounds and often she came near to fainting. And sometimes in secret she did faint, and told no one. And Alisandra was saying to Zeno and to Juliet that she would be upstairs if anyone needed her.

Through a roaring in her ears she heard them telling her that Cressida was alive. Cressida had returned to Carthage, that day. But Cressida was seriously sick, in the Carthage hospital where they could see her in the morning.

Zeno was explaining, he'd discovered Cressida at the house, wrapped in a soiled blanket on the deck-swing. She'd been semi-conscious, delirious with fever. He'd driven her to the ER and she'd been diagnosed with pneumonia.

En route to the hospital he'd called Juliet. He had not wanted to call Arlette just yet.

Later he would explain he'd been in terror that Cressida was dying. He could not bear to call Arlette to summon her to the hospital in such circumstances.

Cressida alive! Arlette could not comprehend what her husband and her daughter were telling her.

She'd been in Florida, it seemed. How long, how she'd been living, what had happened to her in the Preserve—they didn't know.

Zeno had not been able to speak with Cressida, she'd been too sick.

What did she look like?—of course, she was older; and she was very sick. But—obviously—she was their daughter, Zeno said. She was Cressida, unmistakably.

What had happened with Brett Kincaid, in the Preserve—Zeno had no idea. He'd placed hurried calls to the Beechum County prosecutor, and to the New York State Prison Authority, and to the warden at Clinton Correctional Facility for Men in Dannemora where Brett Kincaid was incarcerated.

Zeno would do more, when Cressida was out of danger. For obviously Brett Kincaid was innocent of manslaughter: he'd given police a false confession.

Maybe he'd been coerced by police officers. Or maybe he had truly believed he'd murdered Cressida.

He had hurt her, very likely. But he had not killed her after all and he had not dumped her body into the Black Snake River as he had testified.

Zeno had no time to pursue this, yet. That Brett Kincaid had been unjustly convicted, sentenced to prison—he would deal with that later. The concern now was Cressida in the hospital, in the telemetry unit with a fever of 103.3 degrees F., a breathing tube in her throat, struggling to stay alive.

Arlette was beginning to feel very faint. The news was dazzling as a sudden bright-blindness scalding her brain.

In a wondering voice Zeno was saying he'd known, as soon as he'd seen her.

Cressida? Returned? After seven years? Yet, he'd known.

Yesterday a neighbor had called Zeno. Zeno had driven to the house at once. And there on the side-deck, on the old porch-swing, there was someone lying wrapped in a blanket and her face mostly hidden, a young person, a girl, very small, unmoving; and he'd known at once who it was.

For Juliet had had a mysterious phone call a few days ago—a cruel joke she'd thought—a woman identifying herself as Cressida.

"I tried to return the call—but I couldn't. I told Dad but not you—not yet—I didn't want to upset you."

Zeno was describing to Arlette how Cressida, exhausted and ill, had wrapped herself in the old red-plaid camping blanket from L.L. Bean—"You know, the one you tried to throw out but every time you put it in the trash I retrieved it? That blanket, that we'd left on the swing."

Arlette smiled. "That torn plaid blanket! I thought I'd gotten rid of it."

In the red-plaid blanket Cressida had been transported to the Carthage Hospital ER. Zeno had lifted her in his arms, and carried her to his car, and driven her to the hospital and on his cell phone he'd called 911 to report what he was doing and then he'd called Juliet in Albany to alert her and at once, Juliet was in her SUV driving from Albany to arrive at the hospital by the time Cressida had been diagnosed, and was being moved to the telemetry unit. Juliet had seen her sister in her semi-conscious state and had burst into tears, in a kind of terrified elation, astonishment.

How changed Cressida was! Yet, Juliet would have recognized her anywhere.

She had never believed it could be true, her sister was *alive*.

She'd known, others had speculated, it was (theoretically) possible that Cressida Mayfield was actually alive, and not dead; it was (theoretically) possible that Brett Kincaid had not killed her, as he'd claimed; possibly she'd run away, and was alive somewhere where no one knew her. Such speculations had raged on the Internet for at least a year after Cressida's disappearance but Juliet avoided such postings as she might avoid online pornography. She'd never believed that there could be any truth to them. But now—

"We'll take you to the hospital, to see her, Mom. Come on!"

"Yes. Please."

Arlette was smiling faintly. Lifting her arms to be helped to her feet as Zeno gripped her in his rib-crushing Zeno embrace. Oh! she loved him.

Of course she loved her husband, it had been a mistake to leave him. And she loved Juliet. These people who loved her had come for her, they had tried to spare her a terrible shock, a shock of such extreme happiness it could hardly be borne, and now they were going to drive her to the hospital to see her lost daughter.

Her daughter she'd accepted as lost. Dead, and lost. She'd accepted as taken by God, for what obscure motive she had not questioned as she had not questioned the *persimmon-seed lump* in her left breast, nor any hurt, humiliation, sorrow of her lifetime for in truth in her innermost heart she did believe in the justness of all that existed in the innermost heart of God as humankind resides in God and could not exist without God. All this, she had accepted. And she had cast her husband from her, flailing and despairing in non-belief, she had abandoned her husband whom she loved, for his non-belief had been threatening to her. And now, their daughter was restored. And now, God was revealing to her the most profound mystery: that even the cruel logic of His mercy was beyond human scrutiny, as it was beyond any effort of human comprehension, identification.

She was putting on her coat. She was fumbling to put on her coat.

Rattling his car keys Zeno said in his kindly-pushy voice, he was driving.

SEVENTEEN

The Sister

April 2012

I DON'T FEEL YOUNG NOW. *I think I am old in my heart.*

THE LETTER I'VE kept. The letter of which no one knows I have kept. Treasured.

Love you so Juliet. That is the one true thing that I know.

AND I KNOW: I should forgive her.

They think that I am overwhelmed with joy as they are. They think that I am a true *sister* to her. All of the world thinks—*The Mayfield sisters, reunited.*

But I don't forgive her, I think that I hate her.

The sensation of hatred is raw and new to me, it takes my breath away. How can I forgive her, she has ruined my life and she has ruined Brett Kincaid's life. For seven years she was the cause of my parents' suffering, every hour and every minute of their lives poisoned by her absence.

Her selfishness I despise, the world misinterprets as illness.

Mental illness, psychological distress, "amnesia" . . .

My sister is morally defective. She is not a normal person. She was always *special,* an *artiste.* We others who were not special and not-*artistes* were obliged to make excuses for her, to accommodate her, always to forgive her when she was rude, mean-hearted, selfish.

Your sister is not like other girls Juliet. She will make her own way but with difficulty.

I am not so certain that I am a Christian any longer. In my heart, I have changed.

But I have not allowed anyone to know. For Juliet Mayfield is *the pretty one* of the Mayfield sisters, you don't expect Juliet to become skeptical, a non-believer like her father.

You who are non-believers rely upon us, to confirm your sense of superiority. You need to imagine us as unchanged, unchangeable.

You need to imagine us as ignorant, brain-damaged. You need to imagine us as *children.*

But I am not a child now. I am twenty-nine years old.

Brett Kincaid incarcerated in the Clinton Correctional Facility for Men at Dannemora since April 2006 is thirty-three years old.

Even if his original sentence for *voluntary manslaughter* is commuted, he will still be incarcerated for an indeterminate period of time, for in the prison he'd been involved in "incidents." Even if his sentence is commuted by the governor as Daddy will urge, he has lost seven years of his life he can never reclaim.

Oh Juliet what a miracle! You and your parents—how astonishing it is, Cressida has returned to you. How happy you must all be!

So people proclaim. So the world perceives us.

Yet—what is a *miracle?* That my sister exiled herself from us for seven years and has now returned to us is not in fact a *miracle.*

She has not *returned from the dead.* Not Cressida!

It was deliberate on her part, I think. Her revenge, her spite.

But it is a kind of miracle—my father no longer needs to drink to be happy. And my mother can say in all sincerity *My prayers have been answered. I had never given up hope.*

In newspaper photographs and on TV the Mayfields are smiling of course. Even Cressida.

My public smile is fleeting as a light switched on, off.

The pretty one—switched on, off.

DO YOU LOVE ME, do you forgive me. Her eyes beg.

She knows, her sister does not love her. The old, family-love—the love I felt for Cressida when we were children together—has vanished.

That she had died, she'd been "murdered"—I felt such horror, pity, love for my sister—years ago.

But no longer. I don't forgive her. Even in the hospital at her bedside I'd confessed to God Who understands for He has not given me Jesus's strength to forgive those who have wronged us.

Her recovery from pneumonia has been slow. Illness has ravaged her, she no longer looks like a girl but like an adult woman whom sorrow has struck.

Sorrow, regret. Repentance.

On the long bus ride north as Cressida said she'd been sick. She hadn't guessed it would be so serious. A severe case, both lungs infected. In the Carthage hospital she'd come close to dying and how ironic, how bitterly ironic, how sensationally ironic, the tabloids were gathering like vultures for the kill, if the very girl believed to be dead for seven years had, after her "miracle" return to her family, died in a hospital of pneumonia.

God sees into my heart and knows: I would have prayed for her to die in Florida, before she'd even called me.

Except: my parents have been transformed. And I would not wish to erase that.

Yet, can I speak to her. Can I bear to be in her company.

We would have been reconciled, I think. Brett and me. My fiancé whom I would have married despite his injuries—the change in him, in his soul—for that had been my vow.

In sickness and in health till death do you part.

I'd been strong enough then. I was a young woman—a younger woman—and suffused with the strength of idealism, and first love.

For months, I'd been driving him to the VA hospital. I'd been taking him to rehab. I'd been helping him with his exercises, talking and laughing with him to raise his spirits. Except that my sister intruded in our lives, I would have married Brett Kincaid.

Cressida would say, I spared you! I spared you marriage to a man physically and mentally disabled and I would say in her face, I did not ask to be spared.

SEVEN YEARS I've thought of you as dead. As my sister has been dead.

And now my sister has returned to life so you are returned to life.

You will be released from prison, my father believes. He will do what he can to help you.

I can't see you. I will never see you again.

Never had the courage to see you. My mother has visited you many times and would have told me of you but I stopped her: No!

She'd wanted to take me with her, to see you. But I said No!

Juliet why? Why not? Just once, come with me. Brett would want to see you. He asks after you—your marriage, your children. He is happy for you he says. He is still in love with you he hasn't needed to say.

It would mean so much to Brett, to see you.

(I'D THOUGHT my mother was insane. Her Christian-forgiveness was insane. If Zeno had known how she'd asked me to accompany her to the prison, how she'd entreated me, he would have been appalled, and very angry with her. *Your mother isn't thinking clearly. Your mother has suffered such a profound loss, her judgment has been affected. Don't listen to her!*)

ONCE I PLEDGED to be *your loving wife forever & ever Amen.*

We were not married. We were never married. Yet I pledged to you as you pledged to me as to Jesus our Savior *forever & ever Amen.*

That will never change. Though we will not see each other again.

In my new life I am a happy woman. I am blessed, I have a loving husband and I have beautiful children.

I am strong, I can forgive her. Zeno says forgive her, she is not to be blamed, legally she is not to be blamed: there is no law she violated by remaining away for seven years.

And morally? Is she guilty morally?—I asked Zeno.

And Zeno said carefully, No. She is not guilty morally, or legally.

And why is she not guilty morally, Zeno?—I asked.

It was a question coolly poised. It was not a hot-tempered wrathful question. But Zeno stared at me as if he'd never seen *the pretty one* utter such ugly words.

Your sister has been sick. We don't know what she's gone through. Her health has been damaged. She seems to have lived a desperate life. We can't judge her. We can only rejoice, she has returned to us.

But I can judge her. I do judge her. Harshly.

She has returned to free Brett Kincaid. Years late.

In time, I hope not more than a few months, Brett might be eligible for parole, or his sentence might be commuted.

Zeno spoke thoughtfully stroking his jaws that were now clean-shaven. His hands less shaky, his voice less uncertain since he'd stopped drinking.

I did not tell him *Brett Kincaid was my true love. That will not change though I have changed. I will hate her forever, for ruining my love.*

BRAVELY SHE SAYS, But I want to! I will have to.

She says, I can't hide any longer.

Three days after she was discharged from the hospital my mother and I drive Cressida to Friendship Park.

That is, I drive. My mother is sitting in the passenger seat and in the rear Cressida sits holding herself stiff and her expression distant and acute as if in the anticipation of pain.

In the rearview mirror her face hovers like a lapsed moon.

Her pale skin, her shadowed eyes, her dark curly hair that has thinned with illness—is this my sister? Since her return I'm continually shocked to see her and to see her in such proximity to myself. I thought *She is a person to be pitied and so, why can't I pity her. She has ruined lives but she has not spared herself.*

In the hospital Cressida was slow to recover. She'd been stricken by hospital infections any one of which might have killed her. We were told that she has a damaged liver, and that the damage may be irrevocable; that her white blood count is high, and that she has anemia; there were anomalies in her blood-work initially, that seemed to indicate that Cressida might be HIV-positive, but which had faded with her general recovery.

(HIV-positive! Her family was stunned. Had Cressida become infected somehow?—what could her life have been, for those seven years?)

It's a mildly warm sun-spotted afternoon in late April. Gaudy reflections like broken glass in the Nautauga River, wind-gusts in the softwood trees at the shore that are just coming into bud. In Friendship Park on the steps of the grand old Victorian gazebo there is a young woman in a dazzling-white gown being photographed—that is, a young bride and her bridegroom are being photographed. The bride is wearing a long gown, long sleeves, a veil and a train trailing down the gazebo steps, endearingly foolish. The bride's hair is a pale pearly-blond and braided; her lacy veil ripples from her head in the wind. Staring at this vision I'm not aware that my foot is lightening on the gas pedal until Arlette interrupts my reverie: Oh yes: aren't they beautiful.

It's as if Arlette has more to say. *Oh yes: aren't they brave, to risk so much.*

MY BRIDAL GOWN. So beautiful in design but it was never sewed. So lovely, ivory lace, ivory silk, sheer lace back, pleated bodice and flared skirt never sewed.

My veil, my "train."

(So foolish the bridal train, trailing along the ground, on dirty steps. What possible purpose, beautiful and costly dazzling-white silk so quickly soiled.)

The *bridal design* held us captive. My dear mother, and me.

And so, when I was married to my husband it seemed to me a second marriage.

The first, that had never occurred yet holds me captive. The second, which did occur but does not prevail in my memory.

We were not a "bride" and a "bridegroom"—we did not wear the traditional attire of the wedding couple—nor were we married with any conspicuous celebration. Rather, the marriage was solemnized—(is that the word? It comes to my mind as appropriate)—by an Albany judge, a friend of the Stedman family.

We weren't wearing bride-and-groom attire. For it was midday, a weekday. For the setting was my husband's friend's office lined with law books and journals floor to ceiling. For very few people outside our families were invited to the genial but brisk civil ceremony.

I wore a dusky-cream-colored woolen suit with a pleated skirt which Arlette had acquired for me at a markdown price of eighty-five dollars—a "pre-owned" Versace. (After we'd purchased the suit we discovered a faint stain on the sleeve—but so faint, no one would ever notice, Arlette was sure.) David wore a dark pinstripe suit, white silk shirt and cuff links.

This was my wish. A "small private" wedding. As it came to be David's wish also when he understood more clearly the circumstances of his fiancée's life.

For always I'd dreaded the vigilant "news media" learning of my new life, my marriage and my husband; as I would dread their learning of my children's birth, in time.

Always I dreaded the tabloid media most of all, heartless and pitiless and shrewd with the instincts of predator birds that will gather above their prey hovering in the air beating great black-feathered wings impatient to feed.

Out of nowhere the predator-birds gather. As it's said fruitflies are hatched out of microscopic eggs laid in the very skins and rinds of fruit, that makes it seem as if fruits themselves generate the tiny flies.

Before David there had been other men—not many, but a few—

who'd been drawn to me, I think, for my "tabloid notoriety"—though this wasn't evident until I'd seen them for a while. But David Stedman never asked. If he knew about Cressida, and Corporal Brett Kincaid, which I have to assume he did, he never asked; until one evening I told him.

And he'd taken my hand, and kissed it. David is not an impulsive man and I know that Daddy doesn't feel comfortable in his presence because David doesn't laugh easily at Zeno Mayfield's jokes; but David is a sincere man, a faithful man, who had no need to assure me, as he did that evening, that he would love and protect me from all harm—*I can't undo the past. So we will look to our future together.*

Do I love my husband yes very much, I love my husband and our two young children more than my life!

How then can I hate her, how purely hate my sister, who made my life possible with David and with our children—this is my *future.*

How then can I not forgive this person who'd acted blindly and unknowing of the hurt she afflicted upon others as upon herself.

IN YOUR LETTER which I was not supposed to open unless you did not return from Iraq you'd said the children I would have with another man, a husband, would also be your children.

If you'd died in Iraq. If you'd died of your wounds. If you'd never returned to marry me.

So it sometimes seems, the babies I'd had with David Stedman are in some ways your babies too.

Before you went away for the second time, and were so damaged. Before your soul was damaged. When we were together weeping together that we would be apart for so long and our plans uncertain yet we lay together in such happiness it was a kind of innocence and I thought *If I become pregnant now, we will know that our love is blessed.*

And your words echoed my thoughts, that I had not uttered aloud—*It's like something was decided tonight isn't it. Oh God.*

Together in such happiness as if a pure radiant flame burned about our bed blinding us as it warmed us and protected us from all others.

"THIS IS BEAUTIFUL. What a beautiful day."

We drove to Friendship Park. Cressida's first day in the sun. Eagerly and avidly she was looking about. This was a familiar landscape, we'd been taken to Friendship Park for picnics and outings through our childhood, but now, to Cressida, things seemed to look different. And Arlette was pointing out changes to her—a refurbished band stand, an expanded playground.

Cressida's eyes are newly sensitive to light, she was wearing a pair of my sunglasses. And on her head a colorful scarf, one of Mom's pre-wig scarves, that confers upon the wearer an air of both festivity and convalescence.

We'd told Cressida about the memorial hiking trail named for her. We'd warned her about the bench with the plaque—CRESSIDA MAYFIELD 1986–2005. She stared at the plaque. She ran her fingers over the plaque.

"You did this for me, Mom? It's very beautiful."

"It wasn't just me. Others donated. And Zeno and Juliet helped—of course."

Was this true? I doubt that Zeno was involved, he'd been pained by so much attention focused on our private loss. And I know that I was involved only minimally, for the same reason.

The mother's grieving was public, she'd wanted so badly to preserve her lost daughter in the memories of others; she'd wanted to make of the daughter's disappearance a communal Carthage memory—she'd told us of how other mothers, who'd lost daughters or sons, had embraced her, wept with her.

As if there is a river of grief. And we all must wade into it, and be carried by its current, in time.

"I'm a ghost, I guess. Returning."

Cressida's voice was a hoarse whisper. The pneumonia had left her vocal cords raw.

Arlette said, "The plaque will be removed, soon! The park authority has promised."

"Does everyone hate me here in Carthage? I know that I would hate myself in their place."

"Cressie, no! It isn't like that at all. Everyone understands you've been sick."

Arlette sat on the bench, in a patch of sunshine. She signaled for Cressida and me to join her and so I did, but Cressida remained standing.

Cressida was wearing a pair of lightweight khaki pants, and a pull-over sweater; she was still very thin, and her skin had a sickly pallor, but she was regaining her old energy, in intermittent surges.

On the third finger of her left hand she is wearing a star-shaped ring—a silver ring, I think—not beautiful. The ring is much too large for her thin finger so she has wrapped string around it crudely and it is her habit to nervously turn the ring, round and round her finger turning the ring, unconsciously, maddeningly—I feel a sisterly impatience, wanting to slap lightly at her hand, to stop her.

As when we were young girls together Cressida had the most maddening habits—tapping her foot, wriggling her foot, shifting her weight in her chair at dinner with a loud rude sigh; scratching her scalp, scratching her face, her armpits, God knows where all else, oblivious of others as a little monkey. Did my parents believe "Cressie" was *cute*?

Her sarcasm, her habit of interrupting others—particularly her older sister—did they think this was *charming*? The meanness with which she treated her few girlfriends—the supercilious way in which she spoke of "popular" classmates and many of her teachers—did they think this was *admirable*? The only time in my life I can recall that I shocked my mother was when I'd told her in a weak mood that I was worried about having babies, worried that I carried a family gene of some kind for "autism" or "borderline personality"—whatever it was that defined Cressida, I could not bear to pass on to a child. And Arlette had stared at me in utter incomprehension.

Juliet what on earth are you saying? I don't understand.

Quickly then I dropped the subject. Though I did discuss my concern with David with whom I was engaged at the time. And David said *Juliet please! Our babies will be beautiful and brainy and perfect—have faith.*

Cressida had told me a little of her life in Florida—she'd lived with a woman in a succession of places in several cities and though they'd loved each other they had not been *lovers*.

Shocking to hear this, from my sister. But of course Cressida isn't a child any longer, she's an adult woman of twenty-five. We had not ever discussed sex with each other, any sort of intimate sexual/emotional issues. Cressida's affect had been to scorn such predilections as mere weakness from which she had been exempt.

She'd never been in love, Cressida said. That is, she'd never been *in love with* another person who had loved her in return.

Here, there was a pause. Not a graceful pause. In silence Cressida's eyelids quivered.

Yes I did love him, your fiancé. Of course I loved him and my selfish love precipitated the ruin of our lives.

Carefully Cressida said, she was learning just *to love*. There could be happiness in that, and a secret meaning, *To love* another person and expect nothing in return.

I wanted to scream at her. I wanted to slap at her hand, knock the clumsy ring from her finger.

Quietly in the old sweet-Juliet way I told her that yes, that could be a life. A rich full life—*loving.*

Remembering a stinging rebuke of my sister's years ago, she'd meant to ridicule the others of our family who did volunteer work for community organizations, quoting the poet Auden in some cynical wisecrack about social workers, what's the purpose of *helping people.*

But now, Cressida was speaking sincerely. Now, we must interpret her as sincere.

Loving!

Like one who hasn't been walking unassisted in some time Cressida was making her way along a woodchip trail that ran into the

woods and looped back over a distance of about two miles. Arlette and I sat watching her walk along the path—unsteadily, but
enthusiastically—like a somewhat gawky child—and fumbled to
clutch hands.

Both our hands were chilly. Arlette's fingers are always chilly.

The thought came to me *She will run away again. She will disappear.
This time into the river. That is why she returned to us, to make an ending.*

On the Nautauga River approximately fifty feet below the park
bluff were fleet antic reflections of clouds spinning past high overhead. Though the nights were still cold the days of late April were
balmy, warm. You could feel the subtle pull of the river, like a gravi-
tational pull.

After Brett had left my life, after my beloved Brett had cast me off
like a ridiculous little paper boat, often I stood above the river, leaning against the railing. Thinking *Jesus will not release me, this is cruel.
Why then did Jesus let my fiancé turn against me.*

It was believed in Carthage that it was Juliet Mayfield who had
broken the engagement with Corporal Brett Kincaid. It was believed
that *the pretty Mayfield girl* was a shallow opportunistic bitch who'd
deserved rude remarks, dirty looks, disdain.

Impossible to correct such misinterpretations. For they were covertly murmured, never quite in earshot. Looks of dislike blurred
like reflections in a mirror, at the periphery of vision.

Brett too had sneered at me, at the end. As if his disfigured body
were sneering at me, his scarred face. *Give it up. It's bullshit. Run for
your life. Don't look back.*

On the woodchip trail hikers passed Cressida, walking swiftly on
strong-muscled legs. Perhaps they said hello to her as hikers often
do in such circumstances but they gave no sign of recognizing her.

After a quarter mile Cressida turned back. As if she'd depleted her
energy and must limp back to us and as she approached us suddenly
she burst into tears.

Was she fainting? Sinking to her knees? In astonishment we
watched as my sister knelt impulsively in the grass beside the wood-

chip path. We could hear her hoarse voice—"I am so grateful. So grateful." Like a penitent she lay full-length on the ground with her arms out-flung and her face hidden from us in the pallid grass of early spring and it seemed to me that my sister was kissing the earth in utter gratitude of her life restored to her.

The earth she'd defiled with her bitterness, her hatred. Now, the earth she loved with a frantic passion.

I knew this. Cressida didn't have to explain.

You've been broken. Now, you are mending. We will mend with you. We love you.

ON THE WAY HOME Cressida said, Juliet forgive me?

Calmly I said, There is nothing to forgive.

April 2012

*D*RIVING THE LONG WALL.
    Sixty-foot-high wall with no (visible) end.

I am making the journey alone, to Dannemora. I will be seeing Brett Kincaid alone in the maximum-security prison at Dannemora.

I will see him—Brett—without my mother. Arlette had suggested that we visit him together but I'd said no, that would make it too easy for me.

DRIVING THE MOUNTAIN ROADS. *Narrow twisting hypnotic roads through the Adirondacks.*

My new life. My life restored to me. Always I will cherish the memory of how Brett helped me when I'd fallen from my bicycle on Waterman Street. The way he'd straightened the wheel and the fender, that would have scraped against the tire.

Always cherish the way he drove me home that day. His kindness and tenderness that is his innermost heart.

That other Brett, Corporal Kincaid—he is a stranger.

That other Brett—he too must be loved.

Zeno is confident that Brett will be released from prison within a year.

Zeno is revived and animated in the old Zeno-way on the phone making a stream of calls—to the county prosecutor who handled the case, to the New York State Court of Appeals, to the governor's office, to the Department of Veteran Affairs and the Office of the Pardon Attorney in Washington, D.C.

There is also a veterans' organization—the Wounded Warrior Project.

I will help Zeno, too! I will do all that I can to help Brett.

I pledge to you, Brett! However long it is you are incarcerated here, I will live in Dannemora, and I will be your friend.

I will be your loving friend but I will not expect you to love me in return please understand.

I am not so naïve now. I am an adult woman now.

Arlette has told me—Brett is a changed person. He is not the damaged person we knew nor is he the young Brett whom we'd known but another person like one waking from a painful sleep eager now to be fully awake, and willing to see me.

Arlette had suggested that I write to Brett to ask permission to see him and Brett said yes.

My letter to him was brief. His reply to me was briefer.

Arlette said—you don't have to talk to Brett every minute. Just sit with him, and be still together. Don't make him nervous and he won't make you nervous. If you're in doubt what to say to him just say nothing until the right thing suggests itself.

Like the Quakers—wait for the Inner Light.

I will. I will wait for the Inner Light.

In a diner in the small Adirondack town Mountain Falls a waitress asks me if I am going to Dannemora and I tell her yes I am. She says visitors to the prison are always stopping in Mountain Falls. She says the majority are women—mothers, wives, girlfriends. After a year of incarceration the inmates' visitors drop off and it's mostly only women who continue.

Is it someone special I am visiting, the waitress asks.

I'm not sure how to answer this curious question. I tell her yes, he is someone special. He'd been in the Iraq War and had been seriously injured but not so seriously the State of New York hadn't thought him fit to be incarcerated in a maximum-security prison.

I said, this is my first visit. I will stay overnight in Dannemora and see him in the morning and I'm—I guess I'm—afraid . . .

The waitress says lowering her voice so other customers won't hear Oh hon—everybody's afraid but you get used to it. The first time is the hardest time seeing him in prisoner-clothes but it gets like a routine, see?—I've been there myself, visiting a guy I know.

The waitress tells me about visiting Dannemora. What to expect, going through security. How the vending machines are not reliable. How you have to be polite and courteous and take any shit they give you from the COs who have the right to bar you from coming inside, they can really fuck up your life if you've driven a long distance for the visit.

I'm seated in a booth. Simulated cedar-wood table. A terrible sensation of weakness comes over me, I feel that I could collapse. I am afraid of crying. Breaking down in front of strangers. The waitress sees this and says, Oh honey, you'll be OK. Really, you will. Just take it, like, one breath at a time.

The thing is, don't cry. When you see him, don't. That will not do him any good, or you. A man does not want to see tears because seeing tears is dangerous to him, for a man does not want to cry. So don't.

Along the country highway Route 375 to Dannemora. Many miles, a fatiguing journey. It is reckless of me to be driving so far alone, Zeno didn't approve. Arlette wanted to accompany me. Juliet said nothing—not a word.

My sister is in love with Brett Kincaid still. The young soldier, shining in innocence. She is in love with her memory of Brett Kincaid before he was damaged and so she does not want to see him and feel that love and that yearning awakened in her another time.

I understood that love. I understood, and was bitter in jealousy, and spite. And I killed their love, and can never be truly forgiven.

I must accept it, that I can never be truly forgiven. I would not want Juliet to forgive me. Or Brett.

It is Cressida who should be incarcerated. Cressida, the smart one, inside the long wall like a leper.

The shock of the high long wall close beside the highway and the first sign—CLINTON CORRECTIONAL FACILITY FOR MEN.

The sickening sense of confinement, despair at the Orion prison. The execution chamber, the robin's-egg-blue diving bell containing death.

I remember that sensation of sudden collapse, despair—as if the body's molecules were on the verge of dissolution. The body's proprioception washed away.

I lay upon the death-table. The straps were at my wrists, and my ankles. But I was not strapped down, I was not injected with poison. I did not die.

Arlette warned me—Oh honey a prison is a terrifying place even from the outside.

You will need courage. You will need strength, to hide your distress from him.

I am resolved: I will move to Dannemora to be close to him and I will commute—if I can—to the university at Burlington, Vermont. I will bring books to Brett—if I can—and I will tutor him—if I can . . .

I will be Brett Kincaid's liaison to the world. If he will allow it.

Driving the long wall. And now inside the town limits of Dannemora which is a place to which I will become accustomed in the months ahead.

Long high concrete wall seemingly without end. Like something in a fairy-tale film. The driver's vision on the right is severely restricted by the wall, producing a sensation of claustrophobia, confinement.

Here is the protocol to expect: a CO will call the prisoner, after his visitor has arrived. The visitor does not enter the facility until the prisoner is in the visiting room. Then, at the end of the visit, the prisoner is escorted out, and the visitor leaves. Arlette has said there will be a Plexiglas barrier between you and a small grating for you to speak through but soon, it will come to seem natural.

How soon, I wonder, will it come to seem natural for Brett Kincaid and me?

Driving the long high wall into the village of Dannemora. Driving the long wall.